N.M. THORN

D1516219

THE Burns FIRE

THE FIRE SALAMANDER CHRONICLES • BOOK ONE

THE BURNS FIRE

THE FIRE SALAMANDER CHRONICLES. BOOK 1

N. M. THORN

*To my friend
Jacob.

N. M. Thorn*

Copyright © 2019 by N.M. Thorn. All rights reserved.
nmthornauthor@gmail.com
This is a work of fiction. Any resemblance to actual persons living
or dead, businesses, events, or locales is purely coincidental.
Reproduction in whole or part of this publication without express
written consent is strictly prohibited.
Cover art design by www.originalbookcoverdesigns.com

PROLOGUE

* * *

Approximately 480 B.C.

Somewhere in Ireland

"Nuala, Nuala, wake up," Aodh whispered, tugging at his twin sister's hand, but she wouldn't wake. She was crying and moaning in her sleep, her beautiful golden hair soaked with cold sweat, tears streaming down her tender face. He glanced over his shoulder at the two little boys who were sleeping peacefully in their beds – his two younger brothers, another set of twins, Fiachra and Conn. He didn't want to speak any louder out of fear of waking them up.

Come on, Nuala, wake up already, he thought, shaking her shoulders, almost lifting her off the bed. Finally, her long eyelashes fluttered, and Fionnghuala opened her blue eyes, flooded with tears. Her terrified gaze halted on Aodh's face and she smiled weakly.

"Aodhán..." she whispered, wrapping her arms around his

3

neck, hiding her face in his shoulder. He embraced her, pulling her closer. "Oh, Aodhán, it was horrible." She cried again, her whole tiny body trembling in his arms.

"It was just a nightmare, Nuala," he said, softly stroking her hair and shoulders, trying to calm her down. "It's over now. Do you want to tell me what frightened you so much, my dear sister?"

Fionnghuala shook her head, pulling away from him. "No, brother. I am afraid that if I say it out loud, it will come to pass." She lay down and pulled her blanket up to her chin. Aodh got up, ready to return to his bed. "Aodhán, don't leave. Please stay with me."

No one called him *Aodhán* except Fionnghuala. And he could never say no when she begged him, staring at him with those great blue eyes. Clever and full of life, Fionnghuala was always the mastermind of their mischiefs and pranks, and he already stopped counting how many times she got him in trouble with their father. But there was no other person in his life who he loved more than his beautiful twin sister.

Aodh sighed and climbed on top of her bed, sitting next to her. She turned to her side, pulling her hand through the crook of his elbow and rested her forehead against his arm. "Aodhán, don't leave me... I am scared."

"I shall never leave you," he promised, putting his hand over hers. "Do not be afraid, my fair-shouldered sister. I shall never let anything happen neither to you nor to our little brothers. I swear, I shall protect you with my life."

Fionnghuala sighed and closed her eyes. Aodh watched her for a few minutes, thinking of what could scare his fearless sister so much. When he was sure that she was finally sleeping, he shut his eyes and slowly drifted to sleep, still holding his sister's hand in his.

* * *

THE MORNING TURNED out to be beautiful. As they all gathered for breakfast in the light hall of their father's castle, Aodh watched his sister with concern, but Fionnghuala seemed to already forget about her nightmare. Laughing happily, she rushed toward their father and gave him a tight hug. Lir, the god of the ocean, greeted his children with love, embracing them one at the time. He loved his children and there was nothing he wouldn't do to see them happy.

Aodh didn't notice a dark shadow of fear crossing Fionnghuala's face when their stepmother Aoife walked into the room. Aoife greeted her husband and children with a warm smile and told them that the carriage was ready. She was going to take the children to see their grandfather.

Fionnghuala backed away from her and stepped behind Aodh. She took his hand and squeezed it. "Aodh, I do not want to go. Let's ask Father to cancel this trip."

"Why, Nuala? Do you not wish to see our grandfather?" he asked, searching her colorless face with concern. "Are you not well? You are so pale."

She lowered her eyes and her shoulders hunched. She thought for a moment and then shook her head, like she was trying to get rid of some troublesome thoughts. "You are right, Aodh, I do not know what came over me. I am fine. Let's just get going."

Aodh watched her kissing their father goodbye, not convinced by her words and wondering what that was all about. Their father walked them toward the gates, helping them get into the carriage.

As the carriage took off, Aodh was expecting a long ride, but just a few miles away from their father's castle, Aoife ordered her servants to pull over. She walked out and pulled one of her servants away. Fionnghuala watched their stepmother talking to the old guard and her face got ashen, tears gathering in her eyes. She turned to Aodh and he met her fearful gaze.

"Please, sister," he begged, taking her cold hand in his, "you must tell me what's going on with you? If you don't tell me, I cannot protect you."

Doubt reflected on her face as she silently stared at him with wide open eyes, breathing heavily. "Aodh..." she whispered finally, her voice faltering. "It's the dream I had last night... everything is happening just the way I saw it..."

He had never seen his twin sister so terrified. Aodh felt a cold lump of fear stuck in his throat and he swallowed hard. "Fionnghuala, I am begging you, tell me—," he started to say when the door of the carriage swung open and Aoife peeked inside, smiling sweetly at the children.

"Come on, my little darlings, get out of this stuffy carriage. The sun is shining, and the lake is calm," she said, gesturing toward the Loch Dairbhreach. "It would be a shame, not to enjoy its warm waters. Do you not want to have some fun before we continue our long journey?"

Aodh's younger brothers squealed in delight and rushed out of the carriage. They ran toward the lake, taking their clothes off on their way. But Fionnghuala remained in the carriage, frozen with fear and he decided to stay with her.

"Mother," said Aodh pleadingly, putting his arm around his sister's shoulder, "Fionnghuala is not feeling well. Please allow us to stay in."

Aoife frowned and shook her head. "Don't be silly, Aodh. She will feel better as soon as she steps outside this carriage. Come on, do not make me wait," she ordered coldly, scolding him with her angry gaze.

Aodh threw a quick glance at his sister and slowly climbed out of the carriage. He stopped at the door and extended his hand to Fionnghuala. She gently placed her trembling fingers into his hand and walked out. Slowly, they headed toward the lake, encouraged by their relentless stepmother. They stopped next to the water and undressed. By this time, Fionnghuala started to sob quietly. Aodh glanced at Aoife and shuddered. Flames of anger were burning in her eyes as she glared at them, making sure that they would do as they were told.

He sighed and stepped into the calm water of the lake, where his little brothers were playing, splashing each other, laughing joyfully. Fionnghuala followed him. For whatever reason, Aodh couldn't get rid of the feeling that they were led to the scaffold. They both walked until the water reached their waist and turned around to see what Aoife was doing.

Aoife was standing right next to the lake, a carnivorous smile playing on her face. She bent down and touched the water with her fingers, whispering something. Aodh couldn't hear her words, but he felt a nauseating wave of jealousy and ill wish rushing through him and he shivered like from a cold wind. He stepped forward, spreading his arms wide, shielding his sister and his little brothers from the unknown danger he sensed.

The water around the children rippled, like it was boiling. Fiachra and Conn cried, clinging to Fionnghuala, hugging her waist with their little arms.

"Mother, what are you doing?" yelled Fionnghuala, desperation and fear ringing in her voice. "Why?"

Aoife didn't reply. She was chanting, her voice sounding like a song, getting louder and stronger. And as she continued to chant, wielding her merciless dark magic, a pain like nothing Aodh ever felt before, pierced his body. He cried out, bending forward. Like through a wall, he heard the screams and cries of his siblings. His soul burned with the desire to help them, but there was nothing he could do.

"Mother," he moaned, struggling against the malignant effect of Aoife's spell, "please, Mother. Why are you doing this to us? We loved you… If you want to punish someone, take me, but let my sister and my brothers —"

He couldn't finish his statement, as he began to transform. Large white wings sprang out of his back. His whole body got covered in feathers and his neck was growing longer. Every bone in his body was breaking and every muscle was stretching, plummeting his world into a shapeless mush of sticky torment.

His eyes were tearing from pain and his vision blurred, but he registered a flash of blinding light somewhere behind Aoife's back. He didn't know what it was, but it couldn't be scarier than what he was going through right now. Aoife stopped chanting and spun around. That gave him a moment to breathe as the pain slowly subsided.

He looked down, breathing hard. A large white swan was gazing back at him from the reflection in the water. He yelped in horror and turned his head to see his siblings. In place of his sister and his little brothers, he found three beautiful swans.

"Mother, why did you do this to us?" cried the bigger swan and Aodh recognize Fionnghuala's voice. But now her voice sounded even more beautiful and musical than before.

"Yes, *mother*, why did you do it to your children, who loved you and trusted that you would never hurt them?"

Aodh heard a deep unfamiliar voice and snapped around. A few feet away from the lake, he saw a giant man. His body was emitting such bright white light that he couldn't see his features, but he was positive that he'd never seen this man before.

Aoife stared at the stranger intently. As his reproachful words sunk into her mind, clouded by anger and jealousy, she turned around and looked at the children-swans. Her face changed and for a brief moment, an expression of regret and sadness crossed her features.

She stretched her hand toward the swans and a few tears escaped her eyes. "What have I done?" she whispered, taking a step forward. "I thought they stole the love of my husband from me. He was so different with them, loving them unconditionally, no matter what they said or did..."

"Surely, you can recognize the difference between fatherly love and the love to a woman, Aoife. These innocent children could never steal your husband from you!" boomed the stranger, shaking his head, blazing with the white light. "Reverse your spell, witch, all is not lost yet."

Aoife turned to face the man and Aodh couldn't see her face anymore, but by the way she squared her shoulders and placed her hands on her hips, he knew that the evil in her took over again.

"It is too late," she objected dryly. "I cannot reverse this spell and even if I could, I would not do so. Yet I feel merciful today, I shall leave them their human speech and their beautiful voices."

At her words, the white light around the stranger exploded with a new strength. He growled like a mighty tiger and shifted closer to Aoife. To Aodh, this man looked terrifying, but Aoife didn't seem to care. She crossed her arms over her chest and huffed mockingly. "There is nothing you can do to stop me. You are out of your domain, out of your place. You have no power here. What brought you to this lake in the first place, Hunter?"

The man sighed and bowed his head, his white light dimming just a little. "The pain and the screams of these children's souls," he replied quietly. "Their cries were so loud that I could hear them all the way from the Otherworld... And even though I knew that I have no power here, I had to at least try and help them."

Aoife laughed. "Leave, Hunter, you do not scare me," she huffed. "Leave, before you make it worse for them."

"I am not the one you should be scared of, Aoife," said Hunter with a sigh. "But I want you to know that you will be punished for your evil deed and your punishment will be so terrible that thousands of years from now, people will shudder thinking of your fate."

"You have no future sight, Hunter, and your words do not concern me." She shrugged her shoulders indifferently, ready to leave.

"How long?" the man asked stopping her, his voice hardly above a whisper. "Your curse cannot be eternal. How long must they suffer, Aoife?"

"Nine hundred years," screeched Aoife.

Aodh heard his sister's tearful gasp and loud cries of his brothers. Nine hundred years they will have to live as swans, alone and scared, deprived of love and care of their father and missing everyone they cherished. "Mother, please, punish me for eternity, but let my siblings go," he begged his stepmother hopelessly.

She gaped at him, an uneven arrogant smile curving her lips and shook her head. "You never knew how to keep your mouth shut, Aodh. So, let me improve my curse a little, and you will have nine hundred years to blame yourself for that."

Aodh opened his wings and bent his long neck, bowing to his evil stepmother, silently begging her for mercy.

"Three hundred years, you will spend here, at the Loch Dairbhreach and these will be the easiest part of my curse," she continued frostily, evil dripping from her every word. "The next three hundred years, you will be tormented by the stormy Sruth na Maoile. And for the last three hundred years, you will fly to the Iorras Domhnann. And no one in this world or the Otherworld"— she glanced quickly at the man, whom she called *Hunter* — "can break my curse! Only when the King from the North will marry the Princess from the South will this curse be broken."

After her words, silence enveloped the lake and only the two little swans were weeping softly, clinging to their older sister. Fionnghuala opened up her wings, covering them, trying to console them in their sorrow and dismay.

"Do not shed your tears for nothing, sweet Fionnghuala," seethed the evil witch, gloating over the children's pain and suffering. "You all would do well to thank Lord Hunter. He cannot help you, but because he interrupted my spell, you get to keep your sweet voices."

Aodh raised his eyes and met the blazing gaze of the man without blinking. "I shall not say my thanks to Lord Hunter now," said Aodh, and his voice, loud and clear, was carried far by the light wind over the still waters of the Loch Dairbhreach. "But I shall pray to Lord Hunter every moment of my existence, begging him that one day he will help me get my vengeance. And I swear that I shall not rest in this world or the Otherworld until I have it."

Aoife hooted laughing. "Hunter does not belong here, sweet child, and he is powerless in this domain. He cannot give you what you desire so greatly. Have a nice nine hundred years."

She waved her hand and disappeared into thin air.

But the man extended his arm toward Aodh and nodded to him. Then he waved his hand, opening the door of the blinding light and walked through it, leaving the terrified little swans alone and miserable. And even though he didn't say anything, Aodh knew that he would see this man again. In this world or the Otherworld.

~ ZANE BURNS, A.K.A. GUNZ ~

Modern days, South Florida

*T*he restaurant wasn't anything special, just another tiny hole-in-the-wall located on one of the countless South Florida canals. There was nothing noteworthy about its limited menu either. The only thing special about this place was its relaxed atmosphere. The restaurant had an open porch with three tables on it, facing the canal. But the regulars were never sitting on the porch. They preferred to stay inside, leaving the romantic view to the tourists and lovey-dovey couples.

Gunz discovered this place shortly after he moved to South Florida, and since then he became one of the regulars, visiting the place at least a couple of times a week. He liked the laid-back atmosphere and easy-going crowd. It was a place where he allowed himself to relax and drop his guard. To a degree.

The inside room of the restaurant wasn't big, just a few tables and a bar. A big screen TV was hanging on the wall behind the bar, next to a few shelves with liquor. The air was infused with the smell of alcohol and fried food, and a heavy curtain of cigarette smoke was hanging under the ceiling. The room was relatively dark. Out of six wall lights only three were on, but no one ever asked to turn up the light.

Gunz walked through the room, quickly surveying every corner, and sat down at the bar. Tonight, besides a few regulars, there was no one new. A pretty young woman in her mid-twenties, approached him right away. Here, she was everything – the owner of the restaurant, a bartender, a waitress – all-in-one, cross-functional queen of *Missi's Kitchen*.

"Usual, Mr. Burns?" she asked smiling at him. Her skin, the color of dark chocolate, was smooth like silk and her large gray eyes framed with thick black eyelashes looked unnaturally bright on her face. Her long black hair was braided into countless thin braids and pulled into a ponytail on the back of her head, calling attention to her elegant neck.

"Yes, Missi, thank you," said Gunz.

She put three small shot glasses on the bar table in front of him and filled them with vodka. "I'll be back with your food in a moment," she told him, heading toward the kitchen door.

"Take your time, Missi," muttered Gunz, picking up the first shot glass. "I'm not in any rush tonight." He took a deep breath and downed the vodka without flinching. Placing the empty shot glass on the table, he exhaled and closed his eyes, enjoying the feeling of the harsh burning liquid rushing down his throat.

For a few minutes, he sat quietly staring at the TV. It was set to the local news channel, but he didn't listen to the news, his thoughts far away. Then he sighed and picked up the second shot glass. He gulped the vodka and put the empty glass next to the first one.

"Hard day, Mr. Burns?" asked Missi, placing a plate with a burger and a steaming pile of french-fries in front of him. "You seem to look broodier than usual."

Gunz smirked. He picked up a hot French fry with his fingers and nibbled on it. "You could say so," he said finally. "Just one of those days… This day a couple of years ago, I lost… someone."

"Your friend?" asked Missi, gazing at him with sympathy in her bright eyes.

"Yeah… friend. Vladislav Kirilenko," he replied absentmindedly, taking the next burning-hot fry from his plate. "I lost him to the world of magic. He's never coming back."

"*The World of Magic*," she repeated in disbelief, her eyebrows rising up. "What is that? A fantasy novel? There is no such thing as magic. You're making fun of me, Mr. Burns." She shook her head, a soft smile tugging at her full lips.

Gunz smiled tiredly and picked up the last shot glass, squeezing it in his fist. "Third one for the fallen," he murmured and drank it quickly, returning the empty glass to Missi. "You know, Missi, I've been coming to your restaurant for over a year. Don't you think it's time you stop calling me *Mr. Burns*? I don't think I'm that much older than you. You know that you can call me Zane, or even Gunz, if you prefer to use my nickname."

"I know. I don't like nicknames. You're a man, not a pet," she said lightly, taking away the empty shot glasses and wiping the table top with a white towel. "Zane Burns…" She pronounced his name slowly, like she was sizing it up. "Sounds good, but I prefer to call you Mr. Burns. For some reason, it seems to fit you better."

Gunz felt someone's hand on his elbow and a hardly noticeable wave of magical energy swept through him. He snapped his head to the right and found a fake blond sitting next to him. She was devouring him with her eyes, her lipstick-enhanced lips stretched in a sensual smile. Her hand unceremoniously traveled up his arm, following the shape of his biceps and stopped at his shoulder.

"Yum," she said, gently probing him with her magic. "I'll call you anything you want, hon."

Gunz gave her a frosty once-over, turning his senses up. He had no doubt that she was something other than human. Her fingers softly massaged his shoulder, sending a stronger wave of magical energy through him. For a moment, his mind got clouded with desire and his body responded to her salacious magic with more eagerness than he expected.

Succubus, concluded Gunz, channeling the Fire, burning the poison of her magic out of his body. Her hand traveled down his arm, landing on his inner thigh. He seized her wrist, prying it off his leg and sent some Fire toward his hand. Her skin blistered like from the touch of a hot stove and she yelped in pain.

"Who are you? What are you?" she whimpered, trying to free herself from his smoldering grip, but he didn't let her go.

Gunz glanced around, making sure that no one, including Missy, was watching. "I'm a man who is not looking for company," he growled, sending some fire toward his eyes. The bright flames went up in the depths of his eyes, and she gasped. "Especially not the company of your kind." He released her wrist, observing red spots of burns and blisters on her skin. "Leave this place and forget about its existence. You understand?"

She nodded, fear making her every move jerky, and rushed out of the restaurant, nursing her burnt wrist. Gunz sighed, releasing the Fire and turned back to the bar.

"Hey, Missi," he called and waited a moment as she appeared from the kitchen. "Can I have everything to go, please? And one more before I leave." He pointed at the bottle of Russian vodka that he usually ordered.

She put a shot glass on the bar table and filled it with vodka. "That's unusual," she murmured, her hands quickly packaging the burger and fries into a take-out box. "You never drink more than three shots."

A lopsided smile crossed his face, making a single dimple appear on one of his cheeks. "I know. Usually three shots are my limit, but today I felt like I needed more." He downed the vodka and got up, grabbing the take-out box.

Missi shook her head, checking him with concern. "Do you want me to call you a cab?"

"Thank you, Missi. I'll walk. Take care." He nodded to her and walked out of the restaurant.

* * *

GUNZ WALKED AWAY from the restaurant and turned into a dark alley. He stopped and rubbed his forehead tiredly. *Maybe Missi was right. I didn't need that fourth shot,* he thought smirking. It had been a while since he felt drunk and right now the world around him seemed to be unsteady. Possibly it was a combination of vodka with the residuals of the succubus magic. He surveyed the alley carefully to make sure that no one could see him and once satisfied, he waved his hand unfolding a fire curtain of a portal.

He walked through the fire and ended up in the backyard of his house in Coral Springs. The house wasn't really his. It belonged to his friend, but she was away and wasn't planning to come back any time soon. In the meantime, Gunz had the full use of her house. Dizziness assailed him as he took a step forward. He chuckled and sat down heavily on the steps in front of the backdoor.

He closed his eyes and leaned his back against the door of the house, still feeling a little buzzed. He was about to get up when he felt a soft touch to his leg. Gunz looked down and noticed a small kitten. It couldn't have been more than a month old. The kitten was trying to climb on his lap, its tiny sharp claws catching the hard fabric of his jeans.

"Oh, hello, little buddy. What are you doing here?" said Gunz. He put the take-out box on the steps and gently picked up the kitten, holding it in his hands. The kitten turned on his engine, purring loudly and licked his hand. Gunz laughed, gently stroking the kitten's thick gray fur with his fingers. "You found the wrong man, little buddy. I'm a dog person – give me a giant German Shepherd any day. Well, occasionally, I don't mind dealing with lizards. But cats…"

The kitten ignored his statement and climbed up his shirt, settling on his shoulder. He meowed into his ear and poked his cheek with his wet nose. Gunz petted the kitten leaving him sitting on his shoulder and picked up the take-out box. "Well, you're taking your life in your paws, buddy… but if you're sure that you want to adopt a man like me then let's get going." He unlocked the door and walked into the kitchen.

Inside, Gunz put the kitten on the floor and opened the refrigerator. He poured some milk in a small bowl and placed it in front of him.

"Sorry, little buddy, I don't have any cat food or litter for you"—he quickly glanced at the wall clock that was showing past one in the morning— "and it's too late for shopping. I'll buy everything you need first thing in the morning."

The kitten ignored him, preoccupied with his milk. Gunz squatted next to him and softly stroked his back. The kitten moved closer to his bowl and growled defensively. Gunz laughed, rising. "I think, I'll call you Mishka in honor of my good friend. You sure remind me of him."

He left the kitten in the kitchen and walked to the living room. His body was buzzing with exhaustion of this endless day and the incident with the succubus didn't sit well with him. Missi's restaurant was normally free of supernatural visitors. He was probably the only one. And the succubus' behavior seemed a bit odd too. Until he used his power, she didn't sense a creature of magic in him. Something didn't feel right.

His cell phone rang, making him flinch. He pulled it out and looked at the display. Jim. One o'clock in the morning? That can't be good. He clicked the green button, answering the call.

"Hello, Jim," he said and fell silent for a few seconds, listening to Jim. "You want me to come over now? Can it wait till the morning?"

He lowered the phone down for a moment and sighed, bringing the shouting device back to his ear.

"No, I'm not drunk. Just a little —" Jim interrupted him urgently, obviously not pleased and Gunz fell silent again, listening to his boss. "Yes, sir, I know the consequences of losing control of my power and I assure you, I'm in complete control."

Gunz lowered himself on the couch, rubbing the stubble on his chin tiredly.

"Yes, sir, I know that my job doesn't have weekends and days off," he said, hoping to calm Jim down. "I'm sorry, sir, I needed to unwind a little... I'm not drunk..."

He was working with Agent Andrews for over a year and he never heard him talking like this to him. Something serious was going on.

"Yes, sir, I know what Code Shadow means... I understand the urgency of the situation... No, sir. You don't need to summon me."

Jim didn't have magic and he couldn't use summoning spells, but his partner, Angelique, could. She was a witch and a seer. Gunz hated when they used summoning spells to call him. The persistent pull of the summoning spell on his mind was driving him crazy, giving him a pounding headache afterwards.

"I prefer not to drive right now, so I'll open my portal to your office right away, if you don't mind... Yes, sir, to Angelique's office... I'll see you both in a few minutes."

Gunz hung up the phone and shook his head, biting his lip. Code Shadow. It meant an abnormally high level of supernatural activity, endangering civilian lives. Since he started to work with the secret division of the FBI, dealing with supernatural occurrences, it was the first time that Code Shadow was officially issued.

"Fire Salamander – go," he muttered to himself and waved his hand, opening the fire portal into Angelique's office.

~ ZANE BURNS, A.K.A. GUNZ ~

*G*unz walked out of the portal and nodded at Angelique. She was sitting at her desk, but as soon as she saw him, she closed her laptop and got up, greeting him with a warm smile.

"Vladislav, hi," she said, approaching him and softly touched his shoulder. "Are you okay?"

He sighed and sat down on a chair, stretching his legs. When Gunz moved to South Florida and started to work with the FBI, he changed his name assuming the alias Alexander Burns. His real name was part of his past which he could never go back to and he didn't want any reminders. But Angelique insistently used his former name no matter how many times he asked her not to. Sometimes he thought that she did it just to play on his nerves.

"Not Vladislav, Angelique. That man is gone and he's not coming back. And why wouldn't I be okay?"

"For starters, you look like crap," she said with a light shrug of her shoulders, clothed in a classic, FBI-inspired suit. "And you smell like the world's finest distillery. I think I can get drunk just by standing next to you."

"Enjoy it while you can. How else can you get buzzed for free and without drinking?" he replied, winking at her. "Where is Jim?" The door opened, and Jim walked briskly into the office before Angelique got a chance to say anything. *Ask and you shall receive*, thought Gunz rising and extended his hand to Jim. Jim stopped, giving him a quick once-over and pursed his lips. Ignoring his hand, he headed toward the wall with a city map on it. He pulled a small picture out of his pocket and pinned it to the map, sticking a red pin into the wall with a lot more force than was needed. Then he slammed his hand on the wall next to the map and turned around.

"Fifth case," he growled. His eyes, blazing with aggravation, darted from Angelique's face to Gunz. Gunz met his burning gaze calmly.

"Care to tell me what's going on?" he asked, approaching Jim.

Five small pictures were pinned to the map. Gunz looked at the faces – three women and two men of different ages and races. The pins on the map weren't connected and Gunz assumed that so far neither Angelique nor Jim found any connections between these victims.

"I wish I knew what was going on," snapped Jim. "Five people are dead within five days. Absolutely healthy people. The autopsy reports came back clean – no foul play, no violence. But they can't explain why all these people are dead either. There was absolutely nothing wrong with them medically."

"Jim, why do you think that these cases are supernatural?" asked Gunz, exploring the faces of the victims. "Just because medics can't find a cause of death, it doesn't mean that something supernatural killed these people. Usually monsters leave plenty of signs for medical examiners to discover. There has to be a normal explanation."

Jim sighed, his sigh coming out like a low growl. "You're either too tired or too drunk to think clearly, Gunz," he muttered, throwing the box with pins on Angelique's desk. "The reason this kind of cases are sent to me in the first place is because everyone else already tried everything *normal* and gave up. There is no normal explanation to what's going on. Five unexplainable deaths of seemingly unconnected people in five days. What do yah think?"

"Gunz, I couldn't sense anything about these victims," chimed in Angelique, gently touching his hand. "Nothing at all. It seems like something is veiling these people from my sight. This is another reason why we think that these five cases are somehow connected and of a paranormal nature."

Gunz moved his finger above the map, joining the pins with a thin line of cold blue fire. He stared at the small sparkling circle frowning and then pointed at the center of the circle. "What's here?"

"Nothing special. It's a small plaza with a few shops, a restaurant and a martial arts school," said Jim. "Residential areas all around."

"It's Parkland," said Angelique, adjusting her long thick ponytail and sat down on top of her table. "Safe neighborhood, relatively clean of everything supernatural. But this martial arts school gives me a vibe... I can't say what it is, but I'm sure there is something going on there. Besides that, the supernatural community outside the city limits are behaving strangely active and unusually careless. It seems like they don't care if they expose their existence to humans. Something strange is going on. Strange and dangerous. This is why the Code Shadow was issued."

Gunz waved his hand, extinguishing the blue circle and bit his lip. Angelique was a witch. Her magical abilities weren't anything special, but as a seer she had no equals in United States. It wasn't often that Angelique was talking about vibes. So far, on most of the cases that they worked on together, she had a clear reading on the nature of the crime, predicting with astonishing accuracy what kind of supernatural being they were dealing with. Her words about something veiling her sight made Gunz nervous. That was something to think about.

"I want you to go to this martial arts school and check it out," said Jim, breaking his train of thought. "Don't flash your shiny badge of FBI consultant. Go undercover. Blend in. Take a few Taekwondo lessons or something. I need you to find out what's going on there and if there's anything that may have a connection to these deaths."

"You want me to go to the martial arts school," repeated Gunz, staring at Jim, incredulous. "You want me to go to the place where there are hundreds of humans, mostly little kids. Are you kidding me?"

"Entertaining you is not part of my job description," replied Jim dryly. "I guess you'll have to stop your visits to *Missi's Kitchen* and – oh, the horror – take a vow of sobriety, so you don't endanger all those kids by your *magnificent fiery* presence."

Jim sounded calm and even, but Gunz caught notes of sarcasm in his voice and aggravation expanded in his chest before he could stop it. Together with the aggravation, he felt the Fire slowly rising within him and he closed his eyes for a moment to get in control of his emotions. Right now, he was tired and Jim, being human, was literally playing with fire by provoking him.

"I only go to *Missi's Kitchen* in my off hours. How did you know about that? Have you been following me, Jim?" he asked through clenched teeth, muscle working in his jaw.

"No, I haven't. At least not physically," objected Jim. He cocked his head and stared at Gunz with narrowed eyes. "But I do follow your GPS location. You know, LoJack in your *Mercedes*, or the GPS location of your phone. I want to know where you are at any time, day or night."

"Why, Jim?" asked Gunz. He lowered his eyes, so Jim wouldn't see how deeply his words affected him. "We've been working together for over a year. Have I ever given you a reason not to trust me?"

Jim folded his arms over his chest resentfully. "Trust has nothing to do with anything," he replied coldly. "I'll be honest with you, Gunz. When my goddaughter told me who and what you were and asked me to help you, I had my doubts. But she vouched for you, and I couldn't say no to her. She didn't hide from me how dangerous your natural state and your power could be to humans, and I chose to have you working with me as opposed to against me. The devil you know, so to speak..."

Gunz got up, throwing his hands in the air. "I can't believe it," he whispered, shaking his head.

"What's so hard to believe," exploded Jim, almost shouting. "You are a Fire Salamander. You're scarier and more dangerous to humans than most of the monsters that we're hunting. If a single vampire or a werewolf can kill one human at a time, you can obliterate into ashes hundreds of humans in a split-second, should you lose control of your power. You're like a supernatural weapon of mass destruction. So, yes, I want to know where you are at any time of the day and I want to be sure that an extra shot of vodka won't make you lose control of your power."

"I can't believe it," repeated Gunz. Lost for words, he glanced at Angelique and she averted her eyes under his pained gaze. "All this time, I thought that I was working with my friends. But all you were trying to do was keep me on a leash, to tame a monster..."

"That's enough!" barked Jim, slamming his hand into the map. One of the pictures got torn and fell to the floor, but he ignored it. "I *am* your friend, but I'm also responsible for the safety of this city and when push comes to shove, I'll do whatever needs to be done to protect the people. So right now, I'm here as your boss, not your buddy. Did I make myself clear, Mr. Zane Burns?"

"Yes, sir," replied Gunz, crossing his hands behind his back. He grabbed his left wrist with his right hand and squeezed it, forcing himself to calm down.

"Perfect," growled Jim. "Here is your next assignment. Tomorrow, you'll go to this martial arts school, undercover. Do whatever it is you martial artists do and find out if there is anything supernatural going on in this school or in the area. Is that clear, Zane?"

"Yes, sir."

Gunz knew that when Agent Andrews was using his name instead of his nickname, he wasn't in a joking mood. Even though Gunz was just a consultant and not an official FBI agent, he had to silently comply with all of Jim's commands, no questions asked. A military chain of command. Just like it was when he was in the spetsnaz, Belorussian special forces. Normally, he didn't mind that, knowing that everything Jim was demanding of him was for the protection of the city. But today, he had to work extra hard to keep his true emotions at bay.

"You'll report to me every evening and you will wear this at all times, even at night." Jim threw a watch on the table. "It has a GPS tracker installed. It's not a listening device, so I won't be listening to your conversations, but I'll know where you are at all times."

Gunz took the watch, turning it in his fingers, carefully checking it from every side. "You realize that the first time I need to channel my power for my protection, this watch will go up in flames," he said with a sarcastic lopsided smirk.

"No, it won't," objected Jim, mirroring Gunz's sarcastic smirk. "I asked your favorite Master of Power to make this watch fireproof for you. Enjoy."

"What is this button?" Gunz asked pointing at a small button with a little red stone embedded at the top of it. He put the watch on and locked the bracelet on his wrist.

"Panic button," replied Jim grouchy. "In case you need help."

"Seriously?" said Gunz and burst out laughing. Maybe Jim was right, and he was too drunk, but he couldn't stop laughing for a few seconds. "If I'm in the kind of danger that my power and magic is not enough to save me, do you seriously think that I would summon humans into that mess?"

Jim rolled his eyes, but as much as he was trying to stay serious, an openhearted smile crossed his face. "Well, I wanted to make sure that your stubborn, insubordinate ass is safe. So sue me." He turned to Angelique and waved at her desk. "Angie, give Gunz the files please, so he can get familiar with everything we have on this case so far."

Angelique opened one of the drawers and pulled out a few blue folders with an FBI logo printed on each of them. Gunz took the folders and quickly scanned through the papers inside. The files had everything on the five victims – their backgrounds, autopsy reports, photos of crime scenes and the description of everything that was found there.

"I need more time to review everything," murmured Gunz, without taking his eyes off the page he was holding in his hand. Then he raised his eyes and found both Angelique and Jim staring at him. "Jim, can you call Noah? I want to see the bodies before I go to the martial arts school tomorrow."

"No problem. I'll let him know," said Jim, heading toward the door. "And Gunz, don't forget – I expect your call with a full report tomorrow evening."

"Yes, sir," muttered Gunz, switching his attention back to the folders.

He pulled the photos of the crime scenes out of the folders and lined them up on the desk. Then he got up and leaned over the desk, carefully exploring each photo and comparing them.

Three of the victims died at home, alone, inside a locked house. There were no signs of a forced entry. Two of them were middle-age males. Both healthy and athletic, without any known medical conditions. The third victim was an elderly woman. Even though, she was in her late seventies, she was relatively healthy for her age.

One of the victims passed away at work and there were at least five witnesses stating that the victim suddenly collapsed without displaying any symptoms or signs of distress. The last victim, a teenage girl, died when she was at a shopping mall with her friends. They were sitting at a food court and it happened so fast and so quietly that her girlfriends didn't realize that she was dead until it was time to leave.

There was only one thing in common between these five cases – there was nothing on their bodies or in their surroundings that would suggest why and how these five people died. Gunz sighed and pulled the autopsy reports out of each folder. A soft touch to his shoulder made him flinch and he turned around sharply.

Angelique was standing next to him, her hand resting on his shoulder. She smiled as soon as she noticed that he was looking at her. "Zane," she said, her fingers gently squeezing his shoulder. "Do you want me to stay here with you?"

"No, Angie, thank you. Go home," he replied returning her smile. "It's late..." He glanced at his new watch. "Or early... Just lock your office before you go. I'll open my portal when I'm ready to leave."

"Zane..."

"Mphhh?" he mumbled, his attention back on the paperwork.

"Just be careful out there, okay?"

"Immortal Fire Salamander," he replied without looking at her. "Means – can't die..."

~ TESSA ~

*W*as there a single day since I started to work in this dental office that he wasn't running late? thought Tessa irritably, as she rushed to the computer at the front desk. Today, she started to work at 6:30 AM and it was a long day. She just wanted it to be over, so she could finally leave and go to the dojang. For her, Martial Arts training was always the best way to unwind and relieve the aggravation and stress of the day.

She opened the schedule and quickly scanned through it. Ryan had only one patient left, and it was an easy procedure. But unfortunately, today Tessa had to assist two dentists – Dr. Ryan West and his new associate Dr. Isabelle Davis. Assisting the two dentists at the same time was like being a servant of two masters – *Figaro here, Figaro there.*

Both patients were already sitting in the waiting room. Tessa glanced at the clock on the wall. It was showing 6:10 PM, but she knew that the clock was set ten minutes ahead. So, even though both of her dentists were running late, she was on time. She plastered the brightest smile she could muster on her face and opened the door into the waiting area.

"Mr. Koval?" she said, gesturing at the door. "Please come in."

A tall man in a dark business suit got up, throwing a *Men's Health* magazine on the coffee table carelessly. The magazine slid across the table and fell on the floor, but he didn't care to pick it up. Everything about this man was square. He had a square bulldog jaw, square military-style haircut and wide square shoulders. Even the exorbitant diamond-encrusted watch on his wrist was square.

"First door on your left, sir," said Tessa. She moved aside, allowing Mr. Koval to squeeze his square frame through the doorway. Next to him, Tessa with her height of five feet two and a slim figure, looked like a child. He pushed by her, without giving her as much as a second look and walked into the room.

Tessa followed him inside, picking up a pair of gloves at the door and a patient bib on the counter with a clip already attached to it. She stared at the clip's chain for a moment, wondering if it was long enough to put around the massive set of muscles on Mr. Koval's square neck. Then she approached the patient and placed the bib on his chest.

"Mr. Koval, Dr. Davis will be with you in a moment," she said, looking through the set of tools and materials on the tray to make sure that everything was ready for the procedure. "Can I get you anything in the meantime?"

"Hey, kid, I do not need no small talk from you," he said, and Tessa cringed inwardly at the sound of his voice. "Just shut down the light on your way out and tell your Dr. Sweetheart that I have neither time nor mood to wait for her."

Standing behind the dental chair, Tessa rolled her eyes, happy that he couldn't see her and left the room, flipping the middle finger and the light switch off on her way out. She couldn't stand this man. Rude and disrespectful, with his square Russian accent, he reminded her of one of those Russian mafia types that she saw in the movies. Who knows, maybe he was some kind of a thug. He sure looked the part and behaved like one too.

Tessa let Dr. "Sweetheart" know that her charming patient was ready and zoomed back to the waiting room to invite the last patient. Ms. Kelly was a corporate attorney and she was Dr. West's patient of a few years. Watching her stroll along the hallway, swaying her hips seductively, Tessa wandered if Ms. Kelly truly needed the dental care or was she coming here to flirt with Ryan.

Tessa seated Ms. Kelly in the dental chair and placed the patient bib, covering her chest. Ms. Kelly readjusted her elegantly styled blond hair and moved the bib down as much as the clip allowed her to show off her deep décolleté and the top of her perky breasts-deluxe, perfectly sculpted by an artistic touch of a plastic surgeon.

"Let me get Dr. West for you," said Tessa, ready to leave the room, but Ms. Kelly grabbed the bottom of her scrubs, stopping her.

"Hey, Tessa, how is he today?" she asked in a secretive tone of voice, like she was talking to her BFF.

"Busy," Tessa replied dryly, knowing perfectly well that it wasn't what she was asking about. She carefully unlocked Ms. Kelly's manicured claws off her scrubs and quickly moved away. "Let me get him for you."

As soon as she walked out of the room, she ran into Dr. West. He was already standing next to the door, but his whole demeanor was betraying his internal need to be as far away from this room as possible.

"Do you want me to assist you or Dr. Davis?" asked Tessa before he could say anything.

"You're with me," he whispered urgently, running his fingers through his dark hair, his male-model-worthy face shadowed by dread. "You're not leaving me alone with this patient."

"But why, Dr. West?" asked Tessa, innocently batting her eyelashes at him. "I'm sure Ms. Kelly is not looking for anything other than your undeniably great... um... dental expertise."

Dr. West grunted and narrowed his electric-blue eyes, ready to say something that he would certainly regret later but changed his mind in the last moment. Instead, he grabbed Tessa's shoulders and turned her around, ushering her inside the room.

"Hello Erica," he said as he walked inside, putting on a fresh set of gloves and a mask that Tessa offered him.

"Ryan, darling, how are you today?" Ms. Kelly purred twisting in the dental chair to throw a lustful gaze at him. "It's been so long since I've seen you the last time."

"Not long enough," muttered Tessa under her breath, rolling the dental assistant's chair over and sat down.

"I'm fine, very busy, which is good. So, no complaints," replied Ryan. His eyes tripped over her cleavage and he pulled the bib higher to cover it. Then he grabbed a couple of clean gauzes and placed them on top of the bib. Moving the tray closer, he took the explorer and the mirror and cleared his throat. "Well, let's get started... open please."

Tessa snickered under her mask, noticing that Ryan didn't go for his usual small talk and went straight to the procedure. He readjusted the unit light and moved closer, leaning slightly over Ms. Kelly. Gently, he probed the tooth he was planning to work on, put the tools back in the tray and nodded at Tessa. She had the syringe with the anesthetic ready and gave it to him behind the patient's chair.

As he took the syringe, Tessa noticed Erica's hand sneaking over and landing on Ryan's thigh. With the look of purity and innocence on her face, she gave it a little squeeze and moved her hand higher stopping dangerously close to his crotch. Ryan's eyes widened above the mask and he dropped the syringe, jumping off the chair and staggered back a couple of steps.

Tessa snorted loudly and pressed her gloved hand to her mask over her mouth to stop herself from laughing out loud. Ryan sent a scorching gaze her way, the crimson color of his face clashing with the blue color of his mask.

"New syringe, please, Tessa," he growled, extending his hand but didn't sit down.

Tessa gave him a new syringe, took her gloves off and bent down to pick up the one from the floor. She just reached the floor when the light flickered on and off. But it wasn't a regular power outage. As a matter of fact, it wasn't a power outage at all and Tessa was positive that except for her, no one in the room could see it.

For a moment everything looked like a negative of a photo and then switched back to normal. She felt a chilling presence and a cold wave surged through her body, making the small hairs on her arms stand. She gasped and straightened up, leaving the syringe lying on the floor.

"No, it can't be... I'm not sleeping..." she whispered, panting, fighting the suffocating hold of anxiety.

"Are you okay, Tes —," Ryan started to ask, gazing at her with concern, but he was interrupted by an ear-piercing shriek.

Dr. Davis was screaming at the top of her lungs, her voice filled with undiluted terror. Tessa bolted out of the room, running toward the sound. She rushed through the door of Dr. Davis' room and skidded to a sharp stop. Ryan ran into her, almost knocking her off her feet.

Dr. Davis was standing, her back pressed against the wall. Her face was ashen, her eyes wide with fear. She was pointing at the dental chair with a trembling hand. Mr. Koval was sitting in the chair and he was dead as a doornail. His face was twisted into a grimace of terror. His eyes were wide open, pupils dilated like he was gaping into absolute darkness, and his open mouth looked like a dark square hole.

Ryan quickly appraised the situation and threw his cell phone into Tessa's hands. "Call 911," he ordered and grabbed Mr. Koval's wrist searching for a pulse. Then he lowered the back of the chair, getting ready to start the chest compressions.

Tessa stood motionless, not bothering to make the call. She knew that it was too late. Complete silence surrounded her as she was staring at the negative image of the room again. In the darkness of the negative, the glowing spirit of Mr. Koval looked like a bright lantern. He was standing next to the chair, gaping at his own dead body, his square bulldog jaw slacked.

It wasn't the first time that Tessa saw the spirit of a dead person. It started a while ago, when she just turned sixteen. But normally, she saw the spirits only when she was asleep, and they were always the spirits of people she knew well.

This was the first time that she saw a spirit while wide awake. And there was something disturbingly different about this particular spirit. Usually, the spirits had a soft golden or white glow. The spirit of Mr. Koval was glowing bright red.

"I don't understand... what was that?" mumbled Tessa and shivered, remembering the chilling presence she felt earlier.

"I do not understand either, kid," whispered the spirit of Mr. Koval, weightlessly turning around to face Tessa. "What happened? One moment I was sitting in the chair, admiring Dr. Sweetheart's boobs and the next moment..." His voice trailed away. "All I remember is something cold touching my chest and then a short spike of pain..." The spirit stared down at his glowing red hands.

For a moment Tessa forgot what kind of jerk this man was when he was alive, feeling bad for his current situation. "I'm truly sorry, Mr. Koval," she said, "but I think you are dead. And something tells me that it wasn't your time to die either."

"You damn right, it wasn't my time," muttered the spirit. "I am healthy like a bull, kid. Now, tell me what I need to do to get back into my body."

Tessa shook her head. "You can't. You're dead."

"Dead," parroted the spirit, shocked. "What do you mean – dead?"

"Opposite of alive?" mumbled Tessa.

She approached Mr. Koval and put her hand on his glowing red arm. As soon as her hand came in contact with the spirit, the red glow started to dim down and a second later, the spirit of Mr. Koval was shining with a normal white light.

"Thank you, kid," whispered Mr. Koval. For the first time, Tessa saw this man smiling. His smile was tired and sad, but it was a genuine smile. "Your touch is like magic or something. It's so calming..." He sighed and stilled for a second.

The spirit shone brighter and then dissipated leaving a few bright sparks lingering in the air for a few moments. But as the spirit disappeared, Tessa felt the same cold and menacing presence in the room. A piercing shriek, infused with burning fury rang in her ears. She gasped, pressing her hands to her ears, unable to tolerate the pure evil of this sound. She didn't know what it was, yet she was sure that it was this malignant evil presence that just killed Mr. Koval.

As soon as the spirit was gone, the normal sounds came back flooding the room and her vision flickered back to normal. She inhaled sharply, getting back to reality. Ryan was still performing CPR on the absolutely dead body of Mr. Koval. Dr. Davis was quietly sobbing, standing by the wall.

Ryan threw another look at Tessa and frowned. "Call 911, Tessa. What are you waiting for?"

Mechanically, she punched the numbers on the cell phone, calling the emergency services and brought the phone to her ear. "We have a medical emergency," she said as soon as she heard a voice on the other side. She gave them the address and hung up the phone.

~ TESSA ~

*T*essa ran out of the building and didn't stop until she
reached her car. She pressed the button, opened the
door of her old Honda Civic and dropped into the driver's seat.
She didn't start the car but put her shaking hands on the steering
wheel and sat, silently staring straight into the dimming light of
the evening sky.

She kept thinking about everything that just happened in the
dental office, but no matter how many times she ran through the
events surrounding Mr. Koval's death in her head, she couldn't
find a reasonable explanation. Nothing like this had ever
happened to her, and she kept asking herself questions she had no
answers to.

What was this evil presence she felt in the office? She was sure
that there was something in the room. Something invisible and
malignant.

Why did Mr. Koval die? Like he said it himself – he was
healthy like a bull. There were other people in the office.
Why him?

Why was she able to see the spirit of Mr. Koval? She wasn't
sleeping. It wasn't a dream.

And the most important question of them all, the one she was asking herself since she was sixteen; the question that was always making her feel uneasy. *What am I?*

* * *

IT ALL STARTED when Tessa just turned sixteen. A few days after her birthday, her mother got in a car accident. She passed away a few minutes after the paramedics arrived at the scene. No one could explain what happened that morning on the road. Her mother, a police detective, who was driving since she was sixteen, drove her vehicle into a concrete light post on the side of the road. The car was checked by the police department, but no malfunctions that could cause the accident were found. Medical examiners also didn't find anything out of the ordinary.

A man who witnessed the accident said that he saw a vehicle crossing the intersection and then making a sharp turn to the side, slamming into the post at full speed. He said that there were no other cars on the road, no people or animals. There was nothing that the driver possibly was trying to avoid by running off the road.

All Tessa remembered from that day was her Uncle Justin, her mom's older brother, coming over to her school. She remembered him talking to her in the principal's office, his voice soft and sympathetic, as he delivered the terrible news. She remembered everything spinning as her whole world crashed around her and her uncle's arms supporting her. She kind of remembered him driving her to his house, but after that everything was a blur. Even her memories of the funeral were not clear. A ceremony at their church, a chain of faces, eyes gazing at her with sympathy and understanding, heartfelt words of condolences and encouragement – everything smudged into one nightmarish vision, that couldn't be accepted or processed by her frazzled mind.

The only thing that Tessa remembered clearly was the first night she spent in her uncle's house. She was lying down fully dressed on the queen-size bed of the spacious guest bedroom. She wasn't asking why it happened to her or what would she do now. She wasn't angry with her mom for leaving her or with the powers that be that took her mom away. She was just lying down on the giant empty bed, numb emotionally and exhausted physically, thinking of absolutely nothing.

Her uncle told her that she should get some rest, but she couldn't sleep, silent tears sliding from her wide-open eyes, running down her cheeks into an already soaked pillow. Even as a little child, she was never afraid of the dark, but that night, she left the light on. For the first time in her life, the darkness terrified her. She didn't remember when she finally fell asleep. But she remembered the dream she had that night like it happened yesterday, with the tiniest details.

In her dream, she woke up in her Uncle's guest bedroom. Everything looked exactly like it was in real life. She was alone and the light in the room was still on. She sat up on the bed and at that moment her vision switched from light to dark, like she was looking at an old negative film. In the darkness of the negative, she saw the door into the bedroom open soundlessly and her mother walked inside the room. She looked just like Tessa remembered her, but her whole body was glowing with a soft white light.

She smiled at Tessa and sat down on the edge of the bed next to her. "Tessa, my little darling, I'm so sorry it had to happen like this," she whispered, her voice gentle like the sound of a light wind. She lifted her hand and caressed Tessa's cheek, but Tessa didn't feel her touch.

"Mom, are you really here or am I sleeping?" croaked Tessa, her throat constricted with grief. She was happy to see her mom, but at the same time she felt a light twinge of fear.

"Both. I'm really here, but you're also asleep." Her mom got up and sighed. "Tessa, I don't have a lot of time, darling. I wanted to see you one more time before I..." Her voice trailed away.

"Mom, don't leave me, please," begged Tessa.

"I wish I could stay, my darling. I wish I could protect you from what's coming," said her mom stretching her arm toward Tessa. "I love you, Tessa. You must find out what you—"

Tessa didn't listen; she jumped off the bed and took her mother's hand. As soon as she touched her, the image shone brighter and a moment later, the spirit of her mother vanished from the room.

"Mom, no! Please, don't go! What's coming? What do I need to find out? Don't leave me... Mommy..."

Tessa screamed and woke up, her eyes overflowing with tears. Her vision switched back to normal and she found herself still on the bed, lonely and miserable. The light was on and there was no one in the room.

* * *

AFTER HER MOTHER'S DEATH, Tessa had a few more similar dreams. Every time when someone she knew passed away, their spirits were visiting her in her dreams. She had a few minutes to talk to them, to say goodbye or to comfort them, but as soon as she would touch them, the spirits vanished.

Tessa couldn't explain what it was or why it was happening to her and she was terrified of her dreams. And now, for the first time, she communicated with a spirit while she was awake. She never told anyone about her dreams, but at this moment she had a burning need to speak to someone. She didn't expect that anyone would have an explanation, she just didn't want to deal with all this alone.

"I'll talk to Aidan," she promised to herself, starting the car.

Aidan was Tessa's martial arts instructor, and he was the only person in her life whom she trusted fully, the only person whom she considered her friend. Now, that she made the decision to talk to him, she started to feel a little better. At the same time, her stomach spasmed, reminding her that she didn't eat since breakfast.

She glanced at her cell phone. She had only thirty minutes left before her Taekwondo lesson. That wasn't enough time to go home and eat, so some fast food sounded like a quick and cheap enough solution to take care of the hunger. *Golden Arches it is,* she thought, directing her car from the parking lot toward the nearest McDonald's.

As soon as she pulled out on the street, her car dove into the deranged traffic of the evening rush hour. Not in a rush to join the world of the dead, Tessa had no choice but to forget about the spirits and focus on driving.

As her car crawled along the drive-through line at McDonald's, she snickered, thinking about the look on Aidan's face when he would see the brown McDonald's bag in her hands. She didn't doubt that the treat-your-body-like-the-temple lecture would follow immediately, but right now she couldn't care less.

A few minutes later, she drove into a parking lot of a small plaza. A few mom-and-pop shops, a cozy Italian restaurant and Aidan's martial arts school were still open for business. Usually there was enough place to park, but today every single parking spot was occupied.

Awesome! This day just can't get any worse. Tessa sighed irritably and drove around. There was another small parking lot on the back of the school, but it was always dark, and she didn't like the idea of leaving her car there in the evening. It's not like she had extra money to buy another car if this one got butchered or stolen.

Tessa parked the car in the back and walked out. Surrounded

by a tall fence on two sides and shrubbery on the other side, the parking lot was dark and empty. Stormy clouds covered the sky, wiping out the last weak rays of sunset and throwing long slithering shadows on the cracked asphalt. She threw the sport bag with her uniform and equipment over her shoulder, grabbed the McDonald's bag in her other hand and was ready to lock the car when she noticed a reflection of four dark silhouettes in the car window.

She didn't turn around right away. Staring into the window, she sharpened her senses and listened, her hand remaining on the door handle of the car. It wasn't unusual for people to walk here. It was a convenient shortcut from the plaza to the *Coral Grove* housing development and people used it all the time. However, something didn't feel right about these four. Tessa couldn't explain it. It was something on the level of intuition, but these four people emitted some deadly vibe that set Tessa's nerves on high alert.

Still watching their reflections in the window, she noticed that they stopped a few feet away from her, talking among themselves quietly. For a moment, Tessa considered jumping back into her car and driving away. But she wasn't sure that she had enough time to open the door, put the key into ignition and drive away before these people could reach her. Besides, running away from any danger wasn't her style.

Tessa put her sport bag and the brown paper bag with the food on the asphalt next to her car and slowly turned around. A short distance away, she saw four young men. While there was nothing special about their appearance, the wicked smirks on their faces and their body language were promising trouble.

As soon as they saw Tessa turning around, they stopped talking and leisurely strolled toward her, separating farther apart to surround her. Now Tessa had no doubt of their intentions, but she didn't feel fear. A slow uneven grin spread on her face. She knew exactly what they saw – a small skinny girl, easy prey. She loved when bullies underestimated her and these four were nothing but grown-up oversized bullies.

"Bring it on, assholes," she hissed through her clenched teeth, getting ready to fight her way to the backdoor of the school, praying that Aidan left it unlocked.

The men obviously heard her because they hooted laughing. One of them approached Tessa, towering at least a foot over her. He was dressed in jeans and a shirt that didn't conceal his athletic build. His thick dark hair was shaved closely on the sides, stylishly fading into a dark stubble. He stared down at Tessa, running his cold eyes up and down her body, and flashed his white teeth at her.

"Little girl," he said with a light accent that Tessa couldn't quite place, "how is your math? There are four of us and only one of you. Let's make this experience enjoyable for all of us."

The man put his left hand on Tessa's shoulder and she noticed a colorful tattoo on his arm. A fire-breathing dragon was slithering from under the sleeve of his shirt, wrapping around his arm. Its scaly tail stretched all the way to the knuckles of his hand. But it wasn't the tattoo that caught Tessa's attention. His ring finger was decorated by a gold ring that without a doubt was a wedding band.

"The more the merrier," muttered Tessa, fearlessly meeting the man's dark eyes.

The man's smile got wider and considerably brighter. He turned to his friends and flicked his eyebrow at them. "I think I'm going to like taming this one." His friends replied with a second wave of laughter.

Tessa blinked at the man a few times and cocked her head, studying his face with interest. "What would you prefer?" she asked calmly, taking his hand with her two fingers and throwing it off her shoulder. "A visit to a prosthodontist or to a plastic surgeon?"

"Excuse me?" he coughed out, choking on laughter.

"I hope you have good dental insurance, jackass, because I'm about to rearrange your smile," growled Tessa. She took a few quick steps to the side, giving herself some space to move and then threw her whole body forward, landing a perfect jump punch into the man's teeth.

~ ZANE BURNS, A.K.A. GUNZ ~

*G*unz spent all night going through the files and had no time to get any sleep. From Angelique's office he opened the portal to his house where he took a hot shower, grabbed a quick breakfast and rushed to the medical examiner's office to check out the bodies of the victims. As Jim promised, Noah, the medical examiner, was ready for his visit. He provided Gunz with all the information he needed and left him alone.

As soon as Gunz approached the victims' bodies, he knew that Angelique was right. Just like her, he couldn't sense anything unnatural about them. He headed to the door and locked it to make sure that no one could walk in. Then he connected with his power and examined the bodies again, carefully scanning them with his magical sense. At first, he didn't detect anything out of the ordinary, but when he touched the body of the young girl, he noticed something faint, almost undetectable. It felt like an extremely light residue of magical energy.

He channeled more fire and his arms got engulfed in smoldering orange flames. Careful, not to set anything on fire, he closed his eyes and moved his burning hands over the corps relying only on his Fire Salamander sense. He detected the residual energy of magic right away and this time he had no doubt that it was dark magic. Evil intent and ill-wish that he sensed made his skin crawl.

He checked all five victims and now that he knew what to look for, he found the residual dark energy right away. Jim was right – all five cases were paranormal. And now he knew that all these people were killed by the same supernatural being. However, Gunz had no idea what it was.

From the medical examiner's office, he drove to Parkland. He parked his car at the far end of the plaza, facing the martial arts school. For a while he sat in the car, observing the martial arts school. It was five in the afternoon and children with their parents were going in and out of the school. Nothing special. Gunz frowned, biting his lip. He couldn't sense anything supernatural so far, but possibly he parked too far away.

While sitting in the car, Gunz checked the school's website again. The owner of the school was Master Aidan McGrath who held a few high-ranking black belts in different martial arts styles. He studied Aidan McGrath's photo, wondering how he could achieve all these high-ranking black belts at such a young age. He didn't look a day older than thirty.

Gunz also thought that the name of the school and its logo was a little unusual – *Elements Martial Arts*. Instead of the usual permutation of yin and yang symbol or a kicking man, the logo of this school had stylized image of elements. But instead of four, it had only two elements, water and fire.

According to the schedule that was posted on the website, the kids' lessons were over by about 7 PM. Gunz decided to wait a couple of hours and come back to the school after most of the children were gone. He left his car at the plaza and walked around the residential neighborhoods to see if he could find anything unusual. But just like Angelique said – Parkland was a quiet city with minimal supernatural activity and Gunz didn't meet any non-human residents in the area.

After checking *the Coral Grove,* Gunz walked back to the plaza, approaching it from the back. The evening was rolling in, slowly wiping out the last traces of daylight and the sky got covered in dark clouds. With his heightened Salamander senses, Gunz could feel the approaching rain. The rain wasn't dangerous to him, but he didn't enjoy the feeling. Dwelling in the element of Fire, the touch of cold water to his skin was never pleasant. And the colder the water was, the more painful was its touch.

Following a hardly visible trail in the grass, Gunz walked up to the small dark parking lot in the back of the school and halted. On the opposite site of the parking lot, he saw a group of people. Four men were surrounding a young woman, cutting all her ways out. From where he was standing, the men didn't look like a friendly bunch and the focused moves of the woman were suggesting that she was getting ready to fight.

But it wasn't only the appearance of these men and their behavior that made Gunz take a second look. Even from this distance, he knew that neither of these men were human. They were oozing the dark, sinister energy that Gunz could recognize with his eyes closed. These men were demons. Or better to say, they were possessed by demons.

Contrary to popular beliefs, there were no visual signs of demonic possession. No black eyes, distorted faces or creepy twisting heads. Humans that were possessed by demons looked absolutely normal. A demon could freely walk in the daylight and never be discovered by normal people. But they couldn't hide their supernatural aura. There was nothing that could mask the stench of their ominous energy from a Fire Salamander.

Regular people had a soft white or golden aura that was produced by the energy of their human souls. Some people had magic or elemental powers, then their aura was tinted with the bright colors of the energy of their magic. Once possessed by a demon, the human aura was infected by the demonic energy and the pure glow of the soul was replaced by the darkness of the demonic energy. If the human whose body was possessed was still alive, Gunz could sense the presence of the soul. But in most of the cases, demons were killing the original owner of the body right away.

Stealthily, Gunz made his way around the edge of the parking lot, getting closer to the demons. He still couldn't see the woman clearly, but he was sure that she wasn't one of them. As fast as he was moving, by the time he got close enough, all hell broke loose.

The woman landed a perfect jump punch in the taller man's face, starting the fight. He yelped and fell backward, clasping his hands to his face, blood oozing between his fingers. The other three men attacked her at the same time. She screamed and twirled like a little tornado, punching everywhere her fists and elbows could reach.

With appreciation, Gunz noticed that her punches were well positioned and executed, and even though she was moving incredibly fast, her every move was well calculated. Obviously aware that the high kicks weren't as effective in a close street fight as punches, she wasn't trying to kick.

I guess, Master McGrath is a good teacher, thought Gunz smirking.

Nevertheless, he knew that no matter how well she was trained in martial arts, she stood no chance fighting alone against three men who were a lot taller and heavier than her. Especially, since these men were demons. It was time for him to get involved.

So much for going undercover and laying low, thought Gunz as he crossed the remaining distance between himself and the demons. *Agent Andrews is not going to be pleased.*

By the time he reached the fighters, one of the demons got the woman in a choke hold. She wasn't giving up, struggling in demon's arms to regain her freedom. Gunz sent some fire toward his hands and seized the demon that was holding the woman. He still didn't know if this woman was a pure-blood human and he didn't want to use too much of his power in fear of hurting her.

As Gunz's hand came in contact with the demon's neck, the demon yelped in pain and let go of the woman. She fell on the ground but quickly recovered and jumped up to her feet. Meeting Gunz's eyes for a brief moment, she gave him a curt nod and attacked the closest man on her right. Gunz squeezed the demon's neck, channeling the Fire though him. The demon howled and thrashed violently but couldn't break Gunz's grip. The purifying power of the Fire surged through the demon's body, burning the demonic energy out.

A few seconds later, the demon was gone, but unfortunately the original owner of the body was long dead. Gunz released the man's neck and the corpse hit the ground with a dull thud. *That's no good,* he thought, *how am I going to explain to her that I didn't kill this man.* He threw a quick glance at the woman. She was fighting the other two demons, ignoring him completely. Her lips were split and bleeding, but she looked like she was having fun, her big brown eyes sparkling with the excitement of the fighting.

Gunz turned his back to her and squatted next to the dead body. He placed both his hands on the corps, channeling more fire through it. In a matter of a few seconds, the dead body was gone, replaced by a pile of ashes. Gunz sprang to his feet and rushed back to help the woman deal with the remaining demons.

He halted behind the woman's back and ignited the fire in the bottom of his eyes. "Stop!" he shouted, his voice infused with the power of Fire sounding deeper and stronger than normal. Both demons stopped fighting and stared into his igneous eyes, shocked. As soon as the woman started to turn around, he quickly extinguished the fire.

"You two," Gunz roared, waving his hand at the petrified demons, "run, if you want to live."

He hated to let demons go alive, but he couldn't reveal his true nature in front of this woman. Especially not now, when he needed to blend in and go to the martial arts school where she appeared to be a student.

Gunz wasn't sure that the demons recognized the Fire Salamander in him, but they surely recognized a power mightier than theirs. One of them raised his hand up and mumbled, "Sorry, man, we have no quarrel with you—"

"I said leave before I change my mind," he growled. Then he noticed that the other demon that was lying on the ground got up and tried to follow his friends. Gunz seized his shoulder and shook his head. "Not you, you stay here. I need to have a word with you."

The two demons took off running right away, but the one that Gunz was holding froze in place, his face contorted by fear. Gunz took in his appearance, carefully scanning his aura. His first impression was correct. There was a weak white glow of a human soul, suppressed by the demonic energy in him. The demon was a lot taller and Gunz had to squeeze his shoulder, forcing him to his knees.

"Demon," he whispered quickly into the man's ear, "leave this body now without harming the human and I promise not to set your shady ass on fire. At least not now."

The demon whimpered, twisting in Gunz's deadly drip. "Fire Salamander, you can't use your power in front of this girl," he hissed quietly. "And even if you use your power in front of her, you'll kill the owner of this body..."

Gunz knew that the demon was right, but he wasn't about to give up. He gave the demon an arched stare and the corners of his lips quirked up. "Are you willing to bet your miserable existence on this assumption?" he asked, redirecting a small amount of fire into his hand, burning the demon's shoulder.

The demon decided not to tempt his fate. He didn't answer, but Gunz saw a dark shadow separating from the man's body and soundlessly dissipating into the air. The man moaned and bent forward, dropping on all fours.

"Where am I?" he asked, looking around without a sign of recognition in his eyes.

The woman approached him and stared down. "Why did you attack me?" she asked frostily, putting her hands on her hips.

The man raised his eyes and noticed her bloodied face. His eyes widened. "I did that?" he asked. "I would never hit a woman... I don't remember... how did I get here?"

The man rubbed his forehead like he had a headache. Probably he did. *Who knows how long that demon was wearing his body,* thought Gunz.

"Can I call anyone for you?" asked Gunz, helping the man to his feet.

The man patted the back pockets of his jeans and pulled a cell phone out, showing it to Gunz. "Thanks, but I have my phone. I'll call my wife." He turned around and walked away slowly without looking back, picking up speed at the edge of the parking lot.

As soon as the man was gone, the woman walked to Gunz. She stopped right in front of him, her hands on her hips and threw him a scorching gaze. Gunz looked down at her with a light smile. She was tiny, a few inches shorter than him and very young, by the looks, no more than eighteen. Her long black hair, tied into a ponytail on the back of her head, got untidy during the fight and a few strands fell over her face. She brushed her hair off, smudging the blood over her flushed cheeks.

"Who the hell are you?" She lashed out at him, pushing him on his chest. "Who the hell asked you to get involved into my business?"

"Whoa! Take it easy," said Gunz, suppressing laughter, backing away from her with his hands up. "I'm just an innocent bystander who saw a young lady being attacked by four big bad men."

"Lady?" shouted the girl, stepping forward and pushing him again. "Do I look like a frigging damsel in distress who needs your help, Lancelot? I was doing just fine without you."

"Be reasonable. He had you in a choke hold—," started Gunz, but quickly changed his mind. "Forget it. I'm sorry if I ruined your evening promenade. We obviously started on the wrong foot." He extended his hand to her, smiling. "I'm Zane and you are?"

"Late for my Taekwondo lesson," she growled ignoring his hand. She strolled by him to her car where she grabbed her sport bag and a brown McDonald's paper bag and set off toward the school at a fast pace.

Gunz shook his head and followed her. "Hey, are you training at the Elements Martial Arts?" he asked. "That's where I was going."

She stopped and turned around to face him with a scolding glare. "Zane? Is it? Why would you need a martial arts school, when you can bring an adult man twice your size to his knees with one hand."

Gunz sighed. He didn't sleep thirty-six hours straight, didn't eat since morning and an unplanned use of power to fight the demons got him a little drained. "As far as I recall, *modesty* is a part of the Black Belt Creed," he said tiredly. "I believe that there is always something one can learn. No matter how good you are at what you're doing, there is always a place for improvement."

She pursed her lips and gave him another once-over. "Fine," she said finally, gesturing to him to follow. "Let's go, my mini-hero. I'll introduce you to Master McGrath."

~ ZANE BURNS, A.K.A. GUNZ ~

*G*unz followed the young woman to the martial arts school. By the door, he halted and bowed, giving his respect to the dojang before entering. She walked inside, put her bags on one of the chairs and waved at him to sit down. Then she quickly disappeared behind the door of the Lady's room and came back a minute later, cleaned up.

Inside, the *Elements Martial Arts* school was spacious and was brightly lit by numerous lights. The dojang floor was separated from the lobby by a glass wall. In the center of the wall there was a granite counter with a large opening above it. All the children were gone and only a few adults in martial arts uniforms were practicing inside the dojang. The characteristic hollow sounds of kicking bags and short barking kihaps were bouncing against the tall ceiling.

Gunz smiled sadly, thinking how much he missed all this. It had been at least a couple of years since he had a nice sparring session with his friends. He practiced with Jim and a few other FBI agents, but it just wasn't the same. And right now, seeing the dojang floor, hearing the familiar sounds that could be heard only inside a martial arts school, he felt homesick. Everything inside him was screaming, begging him to take his shoes off and step on the soft floor.

A young man in an instructor's uniform passed through the lobby. He waved at the woman with a boyish grin on his face. "Hey, Tessa," he said without stopping, "you're late again. And you're bleeding... again. Master McGrath will have a few words to say." He winked at her, humorous sparks shining in his dark eyes.

"Don't worry, Angel, I'm fine. Thanks for asking," she replied sarcastically, sitting down on the chair in the lobby and reached for the paper bag with her food. "I'll be on the floor in a jiffy."

"I'm no angel, Tessa. The name is An-hhh-el," said the young instructor, slowly pronouncing his name in Spanish. He laughed and winked at her again, before bowing at the entry into the dojang and walking away.

Gunz studied Instructor Angel with interest. The young man wasn't human, at least not entirely human. Gunz was positive that Angel wasn't evil, there was nothing dark about his aura, but while his energy signature somehow felt a little familiar, he couldn't quite place it. Wondering if the rest of the instructors in this dojang were supernaturally endowed, Gunz got up and was about to approach the counter, when another young man walked into the lobby.

The man was also dressed in a white instructor's uniform. A thick black belt with Korean writing on it and seven white horizontal stripes was wrapped around his slim waist. He was tall, at least six feet two and athletically built, which was a given, considering the Seventh Dan black belt he was wearing. He stopped in front of Tessa and folded his arms over his chest, his bright blue eye gazing at her reproachfully.

Tessa put away the McDonald's bag and got up. "Master McGrath," she said, greeting him with the traditional Taekwondo bow.

"Ms. Donovan, you're late again," he said, shaking his head and bowed back to her. He had a light Irish accent that was giving his speech a sing-song quality.

"I'm sorry, Master McGrath. We had an accident at work. A patient died during the procedure," she explained.

Master McGrath's eyes slowly moved from Tessa to Gunz and his eyebrows drew together. Gunz met his heavy gaze and drew in a sharp breath. Whoever this man was, he had some serious magic and the energy of power was surrounding him like a thick wall. Gunz was sure that Aidan McGrath wasn't just a wizard. He never felt so much power and magic in a single person before, not even in a Master of Power. And that was saying a lot, because Masters of Power were considered to be one of the most powerful magical beings. Besides magic, Gunz also sensed the elemental power in him – Fire and Water. That explained the logo of the martial arts school.

Master McGrath stared at Gunz without blinking, his eyes glowing with a soft white light. For a moment, Gunz felt dizzy and disoriented, like the man was scanning his insides, turning him inside out. Slowly the white light in his eyes dimmed down, and Gunz took a rugged breath, instantly feeling better.

"Tessa," said Master McGrath without taking his eyes off Gunz, "why do you insist on bringing junk into my dojang?"

Gunz mouth fell open in shock, but he didn't say anything. At this moment he wasn't sure if he should laugh or be upset at the way he was treated. *Is it just me, or it seems like since yesterday everyone is on my case.*

"I'm sorry, Master McGrath, but the junk-food was the only option on my menu today," said Tessa, gazing at him with an innocent smile and then switched her tone. "Come on, Aidan, give me a break. I didn't eat since morning and I was trying not to be late, because I knew that you would chew my ass out for that. And I wouldn't be late if four morons didn't attack me in the parking lot behind the school."

"Language, Tessa, you're in my dojang," said Aidan dryly,

shaking his head. "And this one?" He jerked his chin toward Gunz. "Is he one of those... morons that attacked you?"

"This one?" asked Tessa, throwing a sarcastic glance at Gunz. "No, Aidan. He's a completely different type of moron. He actually thought that I needed his help. Can you believe it? He's my knight in shining armor."

Aidan McGrath stared at Gunz for a few moments silently. "What are you doing here? What do you want?" asked Aidan finally with so much frost in his voice that Gunz shivered.

He had no doubt that Aidan knew what he was and didn't love the idea of a Fire Salamander being in his school. Gunz raised his hands up and smiled, hoping that his smile looked natural and sincere.

"Relax, I came in peace," he said without breaking his eye contact with Aidan, still wondering what he was. "I was looking for a martial arts school. Need some practice."

"U-huh," hummed Aidan. "And what style of martial arts does a cre— um... a man like you practice?"

"Kickboxing, Jiu-Jitsu, Sambo, Systema," replied Gunz calmly. "I knew that you were teaching Taekwondo and I wanted to learn something new."

Aidan narrowed his eyes, hooking his thumbs at his belt next to the knot, looking like a man who was trying to decide what to do next. "Well, let's see what you're good at," he said smirking. "I need to test you, to see what level I can place you in. A short sparring session, perhaps?"

"Bring it on," said Gunz with a half-shrug.

Aidan turned toward the dojang and yelled, "Uri!" A tall man walked into the lobby and bowed to Aidan. "Uri, can you please get this man a beginner's uniform?" he said, giving Gunz a quick once-over. "Check the kids' section... Maybe a kids medium size would fit him."

Gunz grunted but decided not to say anything. Obviously Master McGrath not only disliked the fact that he was a Fire Salamander, but he didn't like his height either. With a friendly smile, Uri put his hand on Gunz's shoulder. "Let's go," he said with a rolling Russian accent, "I'll find something that fits you in the adult section. What's your name?"

"Zane," exhaled Gunz, swallowing hard. "My name is Zane Burns."

Uri's touch sent a smoldering wave of fire through his body, as he scanned Gunz's presence like Aidan did a few minutes ago. Uri was wielding the Fire, but his power wasn't elemental and Gunz didn't know what he was either. *What kind of place is this?* he thought warily. So far he met three creatures of magic here, but he couldn't recognize the energy signature of either of them.

* * *

GUNZ PUT a new uniform on and tied the white belt around his waist. The fabric felt stiff and a little rough against his skin. Gunz made a few quick moves to make sure that the uniform was fitting him right and then followed Uri into the dojang. He bowed at the entry and stepped inside, enjoying the feel of the soft floor under his bare feet.

Besides Aidan, Uri and Angel, there were just two more instructors inside the room. As soon as Gunz walked in, Aidan stopped the practice and approached him. "Please give us the floor," he said calmly to his students and instructors. "I'll spar with this one myself."

Uri and Angel exchanged a quick look but walked outside, leaving only Aidan and Gunz on the floor. All of them, including Tessa, gathered behind the glass, waiting for the fight to begin. Aidan didn't seem to be in a rush. First, he walked to the window and closed it, completely isolating the two of them inside the dojang. Then he approached Gunz, smirking down at him.

"What would you like me to do, Master McGrath?" asked

Gunz. He was fighting to stay calm and respectful, but this man's arrogance was driving him up the wall.

"I want you to survive for three minutes, little man," said Aidan, his lips curved in distaste. "Just three minutes fighting me like a man, and not like the little reptile you are."

Gunz raised his hands, getting into the guarding stance. "Fine. No power, no magic," he growled, staring at Aidan over his fists. "But don't you think it's kind of unfair that you know what I am, but I don't know what you are, Master?"

"It's above your pay grade." Aidan laughed and moved forward, starting the fight with a quick roundhouse. Gunz stepped to the side, blocking the kick and redirected his body into a powerful hook, connecting his fist with Aidan's side.

"Not bad, lizard," hissed Aidan, quickly regrouping and returning the favor.

As much as Gunz disliked Aidan at this point, he had to admit that he was an expert fighter. Light on his feet, he was moving fast and fluid, and Gunz had to employ all his skills to stay on his feet. He was moving around Aidan, carefully avoiding his kicks and punches, waiting for the right moment to attack.

Aidan checked, making Gunz step back. Using the opportunity, Aidan stepped forward, and moved into a back spin hook kick. Gunz didn't react fast enough, and Aidan's heel caught him in the side of his head. Gunz fell back, but quickly hopped to his feet, breathing hard.

"It hasn't been three minutes yet, but your ass already landed on the floor, little man," muttered Aidan, quickly advancing at him.

"It's not the size—," breathed out Gunz, breaking through Aidan's defense and punching him in his jaw.

Aidan staggered back, looking furious. "If you say, 'it's how you use it', I'll turn you into a tiny lizard and put you into my aquarium," he mumbled, quickly switching into an open stance and crushing Gunz's chest with his roundhouse. "I always wanted to have a pet lizard."

"It's not what I was going to say, Master McGrath. But I like your train of thought." Gunz chuckled, dancing around Aidan and carefully probing his defense.

Furious, Aidan lost his concentration for just a moment. He threw another round kick, but Gunz anticipated it. At the moment of the kick, he stepped forward, quickly closing the distance, and sent Aidan flying backward with a powerful uppercut. Aidan fell on his back, his chest rising and falling with laborious breaths. Gunz approached him and extended his hand to help him up.

"I was going to say – it's not the size of the dog in the fight, it's the size of the fight in the dog," he said smirking down at Aidan.

"Who would think, eh? An educated little lizard, aren't you? Quoting Mark Twain," muttered Aidan.

Ignoring Gunz's hand, he twirled on the floor, swiping his long legs and tripped Gunz down. In a split-second the situation had changed, as Aidan locked Gunz in a kneebar, applying severe pressure on his Achilles tendon.

"Submit, lizard. If you know anything about martial arts, you know that you are done for. Tap out, or I swear, I'll break your leg!"

Aidan applied a little more pressure and Gunz cried out, tapping his hand on the floor. Even though Gunz tapped out, Aidan didn't release him, keeping the pressure on.

"You won," groaned Gunz. He was in considerable pain, but he refused to use his power, keeping true to his original promise to fight as a man. "I submit. Please stop."

Aidan exhaled and released the pressure a little, still holding Gunz's leg in a lock. "Tell me why you are here, Fire Salamander," he demanded, his fingers readjusting, ready to apply the pressure again.

"I told you the truth," said Gunz quietly. "I was looking for a martial arts instructor who was better than I am. I think I found what I was looking for, Master McGrath."

"How old are you?" asked Aidan.

"Twenty-eight."

Aidan stared at him in wonderment and finally released his leg completely. "You're very young for a Fire Salamander. How long has it been since you discovered the Fire in you?"

"Couple of years," replied Gunz, sitting up and massaging his ankle. "Give or take."

"Who trained you, boy?" asked Aidan. "I was driving you crazy, but you didn't lose your control even once."

"Kal," replied Gunz, unwillingly.

"Kal?" asked Aidan, incredulous. "The Fire Elemental? The Great Salamander himself was your mentor?"

"Yes, sir," said Gunz, sighing. "Are you done with your questions yet? I had a very long day." He leaned forward, resting his arms on his knees tiredly.

"For now," said Aidan rising and offering his hand to Gunz. "Get out of my dojang, Salamander. We're done for today. Come back tomorrow after all the children are gone. Elite team's training starts at 7 PM sharp. Don't be late."

"Yes, sir," said Gunz, bowing to him.

"And take this white belt off," added Aidan smirking. "Doesn't suit you."

Gunz headed toward the exit but stopped at the door. "Hey, Master McGrath," he said turning around, "you may want to know that those four morons that Tessa was fighting on the back of your school were demons."

"Are you sure?" asked Aidan, suddenly alert.

"Yes, sir," answered Gunz. "I killed one and expelled one. The human inside the body was still alive. But I had to let the other two go. I couldn't use my power in front of Tessa."

"It's been a bit hectic lately. All the creatures of the dark came out of their closets and are walking freely in the daylight like they belong there," said Aidan, shaking his head. "Including the little Fire reptile."

"Interesting," murmured Gunz. "That's what I've heard. Any idea why they feel so fearless?"

"No," replied Aidan, "but I intend to find out."

"Count me in, if you need help, Master McGrath," said Gunz, putting his hand on the door handle.

Aidan chuckled, raking his fingers through his golden-blond hair. "Don't get ahead of yourself, lizard. I'm still not sure about your place in all this," he said. "But thank you for helping Tessa. I'm sure she didn't show you any gratitude."

Gunz nodded to him and walked out of the dojang.

~ ZANE BURNS, A.K.A. GUNZ ~

*O*n the way home, Gunz stopped at Publix and picked up everything he needed to take care of his kitten. It was late and the only thing he wanted was to get home and fall on his bed. He didn't even feel hungry. His whole body was buzzing with exhaustion and his ankle was painfully sore after the sparring with Aidan. Of course, he could easily heal himself, but to do it, he needed to get into his natural state. The natural state of a Fire Salamander was deadly to humans. The blast of the fire energy originated by the process would instantly obliterate any human within a few hundred yards around him into ashes.

Living surrounded by humans, the only place he could allow himself to relax to a degree was inside his house. The house was made impervious to fire by a Master of Power. The walls and everything inside the house were infused with magic to contain his fierce natural state. Also a few complicated wards, seals and protection spells were placed around the house and the backyard not only to contain his natural state but also to make sure that no one could break into his house, catching him off guard. But even inside his house, he could never fully relax, always keeping in the back of his mind the possibility of what could happen if his wards would fail.

Gunz parked his car in the driveway and shut it down. He grabbed the few Publix shopping bags off the passenger seat and opened the door. The loud ring of his cell phone split the silence of the evening. Gunz flinched and pulled the vibrating device out of his back pocket. He looked at the display and cringed. Jim. He forgot to call him with the report.

He clicked the green button, answering the call. "Hello, Agent Andrews," he said bracing himself for Jim's wrath.

"Hey, Gunz," said Jim. He didn't sound upset or angry. "How did your visit to the martial arts school go?"

"It was fine. I think I'm in," replied Gunz, giving Jim a quick overview of everything that he found out by examining the bodies of the victims and then everything that happened in the dojang. Jim was listening to him silently, and Gunz could almost see him sitting in his office, clicking his pen on and off, and nodding at everything he was saying.

"That's good. We need to move quickly," said Jim with a sigh, sounding tired and upset. "We have one more death that fits our case. So, six now."

"When did it happen?" asked Gunz, his sleepiness instantly evaporating like from a shot of a double espresso.

"Just a few hours ago, in some small dental office," replied Jim. Gunz heard something clicking on Jim's side. "I just emailed you all the information on the new victim. Take a look. This victim's background and associations may present a problem."

Gunz switched his cell to a speaker and opened his email. He stared at the photo of the victim, thinking that this man's face looked oddly familiar. "Dmitry Koval," he read aloud, scratching his head. "Isn't he the right-hand man of —"

"One and the same," interrupted Jim. "So, you understand why we need to move fast, before Mr. Koval's boss would start searching for the killer himself. His methods of investigation could be less than savory, if you know what I mean."

"Yes, sir, I understand," replied Gunz, closing the email and switching his phone off speaker. "I think I developed a bit of a toothache after our last conversation. I'll go to that dental office in the morning and see if I can get an emergency appointment. Since the man was killed just a few hours ago, I hope to sense some traces of magic that did him in. I want to see if I can recognize what killed Mr. Koval."

"Thank you. Get in touch with me tomorrow as soon as you get out of the dental office."

"Yes, sir."

"And Gunz… listen…" said Jim. He took a pause and Gunz could feel the air of discomfort on the other side of the line. "Listen… I wanted to apologize…"

"You don't have to, Agent Andrews," said Gunz flatly. "Actually, I prefer to know where I'm standing."

"It's Jim… And listen… I *am* sorry." Jim sighed.

"Apologies accepted, Jim. I'll talk to you tomorrow." Gunz hung up the phone and got out of his car.

He walked up to the front door, holding the shopping bags in his hand, but froze as soon as he touched the door handle. The wards around his house were down and all the protection spells were gone. He put the bags on the steps in front of the door and turned up his senses, scanning the area around the house. He felt an unfamiliar human presence in his backyard. The question was, how a pure-blood human could disarm the complicated wards a Master of Power had placed on his house.

Gunz walked down the steps, but instead of following the fence around the house, he hopped over the shrubbery and quietly walked toward the backdoor, hiding in the shadows. The backyard was dark, but with his sharp vision of the Fire Salamander, he could see a man sitting on the steps.

Leaning at the wall, with his empty hands folded on his lap, he looked relaxed, almost bored. And since Gunz couldn't sense any magical energy in him, he was sure that the man wasn't a creature of magic. The man seemed to be unarmed. While no mortal weapon could kill a Fire Salamander, in his human form Gunz still could get hurt. Cut with a knife or shot with a bullet, he was bleeding red – hence he could feel the pain like any other person.

Things like decapitation or being shot in the head or in the heart would be extremely painful, but it wouldn't kill him. In the state of human death, his fire power would run free, instantly restoring his body and obliterating every human around him within visible distance. So, attempting to kill a Fire Salamander in his human form, for a mortal person was like committing suicide.

Gunz walked out of the shadows and headed toward the man, secretly hoping that the uninvited visitor didn't bring any firearms with him. As soon as he saw Gunz walking toward him, the man got up. He wasn't tall and had a slight build. In his late fifties, he had a full head of gray hair and attentive dark eyes behind thin prescription glasses. He was dressed in plain blue jeans and despite the warm weather, he wore a light jacket over his shirt. By looking at him no one ever could guess how rich, powerful and dangerous he was.

Gunz stopped a few steps away from the man and shoved his hands into his pockets. He didn't need an introduction. The man in front of him was Anatoly Karpenko, the head of the local Russian mob. Gunz heard enough about him to know that this man was holding in his hands the strings to many shady under-ground operations that were going on all over the country. Seeing him in his own backyard wasn't giving Gunz a warm and fuzzy feeling.

"Good evening, Mr. Burns," said Anatoly, smiling like he was greeting his best friend. "I hope you're doing well."

"I was doing well before I found you in my backyard," replied Gunz calmly, displaying his complete indifference to Anatoly's influence and status. "What are you doing here, Mr. Karpenko?"

While Gunz wasn't scared of the Russian mobster, he didn't like the idea that this dangerous man was able to bring down his wards and invade his territory uninvited.

"You know who I am, eh? Wonderful, wonderful." He smiled, rubbing his hands together. "That should make our conversation so much easier and hopefully pleasant for both of us."

"A conversation?" huffed Gunz, folding his arms over his chest. "I have nothing to talk to you about. Please leave, Mr. Karpenko, you're trespassing."

"I see. I was hoping that it wouldn't come to that. I prefer peaceful resolutions and mutually-beneficial business agreements to violence and intimidation. But we'll do it your way."

Anatoly moved his hand up and slid it into the inside pocket of his jacket. Gunz tensed, expecting to see a gun. The mobster noticed his reaction and smirked.

"Relax, Mr. Burns," he said, pulling a cell phone out of his pocket and showing it to Gunz. "I was reaching for my phone. Like I said, I came here to talk. Not to fight. Besides, killing you would be equivalent to killing myself, and I'm not in a rush to see what's behind the veil, Mr. Fire Salamander."

Gunz held his breath for a moment. It wasn't common for humans to know or even believe in the existence of the supernatural, but this man knew what he was, and it didn't seem to worry him in the slightest. *How did he find out? How was it possible?* Gunz was sure that until his visit to the martial arts school a few hours ago, besides himself, Jim and Angelique, no one knew about his existence.

Anatoly pressed the home button, unlocking his phone and shuffled through the photos until he found the picture he was looking for. He waved at Gunz to come closer and offered the phone to him. Without taking his eyes off Anatoly, Gunz took the phone out of his hands. Slowly he lowered his eyes and peered at the screen. His chest tightened with fear.

On the photo, he saw his two best friends, Sergei and Sasha.

They were sitting outside of some small restaurant. Their surroundings suggested that the photo was taken somewhere in Russia, probably recently. Sergei and Sasha were not just his friends, they were more like brothers to him, the only family he had. They served and fought together for years, trusting each other with their lives.

Gunz's hand shook and he squeezed the phone, raising his eyes at Anatoly. The fear and anger boiled up in him before he could suppress them. Responding to his emotions, the fire flared up in his chest and dancing red flames went up in the depth of his eyes. Anatoly met his burning gaze without blinking, scarlet flares of fire reflecting in his glasses.

"Cool down, Mr. Burns," said Anatoly, taking the phone out of his hands. "Or shall I call you Gunz?" Gunz stiffened, small flames running up and down his arms. Anatoly chuckled, putting away his cell phone. "You didn't think that I would come to a meeting with you without doing my homework first? I know what you and your friends did a few years ago in Belarus. Destroying a full branch of my organization in a matter of a few hours? Not too many people could pull it off. I received a full report and I must tell you, I was impressed. I wish the three of you were working for me."

"What do you want?" asked Gunz quietly, his voice hoarse.

"Oh, good, I see you're ready to talk now," said Anatoly and waved at the door. "Would you like to invite me in?"

"No, not really. I don't have a cross and holy water readily available to invite in a blood-sucking creature like you," muttered Gunz dryly, reaching for the keys. "But it seems you left me no choice." He opened the door and allowed Anatoly to pass through into his kitchen.

Anatoly sat down at the kitchen table and waved at the chair across from him, inviting Gunz to join him. Gunz sighed but sat down.

"Tell me what you want from me, Anatoly."

"Yes, of course, Mr. Burns."

He reached in his jacket pocket again and pulled out a photo. Gunz took the photo out of his hands and frowned. It was a photo of a young woman. She had long blond hair that was running down to her chest and back in soft waves. With her large blue eyes, high cheekbones, and coral-red lips, she was undeniably beautiful. But at the same time, her face had some unexpected hardness that was making her expression look almost sinister. Gunz didn't know this woman. He threw the photo on the table and it slid back into Anatoly's hands.

"Keep it," said Anatoly, moving the photo back to Gunz. "After all, you should know how the person you are going to kill looks like."

"Excuse me?" asked Gunz shocked, slowly rising. "I'm not an assassin. I'm sure you can find someone who is more qualified for this job in your own organization."

"Sit down," barked Anatoly, slamming his hand on the table. "Remember, your friends are alive only for as long as I want them to be alive. And don't get any bright ideas. If I don't call my people in an hour, your friends are dead." He ripped his glasses off, sharply pulled a clean handkerchief out of his pocket and wiped his glasses before placing them back on the bridge of his nose. Then he sighed and switched to his normal soft and polite way of speaking. "You're a sharpshooter trained by Belorussian special forces and a Fire Salamander, Mr. Burns. And since this woman is not human, there is no one in my organization who is qualified for this job more than you."

Gunz dropped back into his chair and propped his elbows on the table, hiding his face in his hands. He sat quiet and Anatoly didn't bother him, giving him the space to process the information. Gunz didn't think – there was nothing to think about. His past caught up with him, and no matter what, he couldn't let his friends down. He just needed some time to calm down and come to terms with the situation. A few minutes later, he lowered his hands and pinned Anatoly with a heavy gaze.

"If I do what you want, can you guarantee me that you leave me and my friends alone?" he asked quietly.

"I'm a man of honor, Mr. Burns. You have my word," said Anatoly, his face calm and serious. "You do what I ask, and I'll never bother you or your friends again."

A man of honor? Gunz suppressed the desire to roll his eyes – how much could one trust the word of a mobster? Especially a Russian mobster and an ex-zek judging by the tattoos on his hands. All ex-inmates of Russian prisons had special type tattoos and Anatoly's hands looked like an art gallery. But he had no choice. If he didn't comply, he had no doubt that Anatoly would kill his friends.

"Tell me about this woman. What is she to you and why you want her dead?" he asked taking the photo back.

Anatoly's phone jingled softly, and he pulled it out. He read the text message and shook his head. Then he switched his attention back to Gunz.

"I assume, you're in the working mood now, Mr. Burns. It's late, and I hope you understand that I'm a busy man," he said, tapping his fingers on the smooth screen of his phone irritably. "So, let's spend my time productively. I'll tell you what I know, and you'll be listening quietly."

"Fine," said Gunz, squeezing his hand into a fist under the table.

"This woman showed up at my place of work last week. As soon as she walked in, all my magic detectors went crazy," started Anatoly but noticed Gunz's move and raised his hand to stop the interruption. "I'm sure, working as an FBI consultant, you're familiar with the modern technology that allows us, mere mortals, to detect the energy of magic, Mr. Burns?"

"Yes, I saw the magic detectors before, but myself I don't need them," said Gunz with an indifferent shrug of his shoulders. "I can see the energy of magic and the flow of the elemental power. I was just a little surprised that you have one of those in your possession. I thought that so far only the government had this experimental technology."

"Mr. Burns." Anatoly chuckled, shaking his head. "You're wasting your talent working for the government. I would pay you ten times what the FBI pays you. Work for me and I'll make all your wildest dreams come true."

"Thanks, but no thanks. I like my job and I'm exactly where I need to be. Please proceed," said Gunz dryly.

His kitten Mishka showed up in the kitchen and meowed, demanding to be picked up. Gunz picked him up and Mishka climbed to his shoulder, settling there. Anatoly stretched his hand to pet the kitten, but Mishka hissed and snapped his paw, thin sharp claws extended.

Anatoly pulled his hand away and laughed. "I would never think you were a cat person, Mr. Burns, but this little fellow seems to fit right with you."

"Please continue, Anatoly," said Gunz, petting the kitten. "It's late. I need to feed my cat and I'm very tired."

"Right, right, let's continue," agreed Anatoly, getting serious. "So, like I said, she came in and all my magic detectors went crazy. She demanded to meet with me immediately. But I thought that it would be better if I met with her while both my wizards were in the office, next to me. You know, it sounded like a good idea at the time to have some magical defense. So, I made her wait for fifteen minutes or so and when I finally called her in, she was a little upset.

"She stormed into my office and her eyes registered the presence of my wizards at once. She waved her hand and both of them fell unconscious. After that she sat down and told me that her name was Eve and she wanted me to do something for her. She didn't offer her last name, Mr. Burns, and I was too stunned to ask anything," he said anticipating Gunz's question.

"What did she ask you to do that you want her dead?" asked Gunz.

Anatoly chuckled. "Yes, a very good question. She wanted me to get rid of a person. A very powerful and influential person, even scary, in my opinion."

"What? Someone who is scarier and more influential than you?" asked Gunz, sarcasm dripping out from his every word. But Anatoly ignored his sarcasm.

"Yes, a lot more powerful than I am," he said, nodding. "But this man is not in the same line of business, if you know what I mean. On the surface he is keeping a low profile, just a regular law-abiding citizen. But he is surrounded by mystery, and he has connections that make him extremely powerful and influential. I tried to investigate him once but found nothing incriminating on him. Honestly, sometimes I wonder if he's human or something else entirely, but I can never get close enough to him to use my magic detector.

"What struck me as weird was that Eve didn't ask me to kill this man. She wanted me to force him to leave the state and if possible, leave the country. I told her that it wasn't possible, and she didn't like my answer. She told me that I have a week to start working on this. If I didn't do as she demanded, she would start killing everyone who is dear to me, one by one. And she said that she would kill one person every few days for as long as that man was still remaining in Florida.

"I told her again that I can't do what she asked. She got up and left. And earlier, my right-hand man Dmitri Koval dropped dead. With no apparent reason. I guess, it would be safe to assume that Eve killed him. I hope you understand the predicament I'm in, Mr. Burns. As scary as this bitch is, I still prefer to have a war with her than with the man she wants me to get rid of. I hate to place you under this awful duress, but I need this woman, or whatever she is, out of my life as soon as possible."

"Who was the man she wanted you to get rid of?"

"I don't think that it's relevant to your assignment, Mr. Burns," said Anatoly coldly, rising.

"Fine. Where can I find this Eve," asked Gunz, getting up and gently lowering Mishka on the floor.

"Well, that's the challenge," replied Anatoly, heading toward the front door. "I have no idea. You need to find her. If you decide to get help from your boss, Agent James Andrews or his little witch, I don't mind. Just don't mention my name. Surely you understand that I'm not very comfortable around FBI."

Gunz opened his front door and followed Anatoly outside. He walked to the end of his driveway and stopped there. "How much time do I have?" he asked.

Anatoly turned around and stared at him over the rim of his spectacles, his eyes cold and calculating like the eyes of a snake. "You don't have any time, Mr. Burns. I'm not giving you a deadline. You must get Eve out of my life as soon as possible. The longer you take, the more people will die. And if you think that she would kill only my employees and business partners, you're mistaken. She will go after my family, friends and acquittances who are not involved in my business. Innocent people will suffer, you know? Including your friends in Russia."

Gunz nodded. With a heavy heart he watched Anatoly getting into a black Audi, parked a few yards away from his house. He hated to do any work for the Russian mob, but at least there was some silver lining in all that – Anatoly gave him information that could help with the paranormal case he was working on with Jim.

Now he had a photo and the name of the person who killed the last victim. He needed to check the dental office and the body of Dmitry Koval to see if it was the same dark magic that killed the other five victims. All he had to do was find this Eve, find out what kind of monster she was and vanquish her.

Piece of cake?

~ AIDAN ~

*A*idan pulled a jar with Turkish coffee from the kitchen cabinet, carefully measured one tea spoon of the fine brown powder and put it inside of a copper ibrik. He added just a little bit of sugar and poured one demitasse of water into the ibrik. After mixing everything together, he put the ibrik on the stove and sat down.

Making the Turkish coffee by hand was taking time and patience, but he liked the process. And the coffee he was making couldn't be compared to anything that was made in regular coffeemakers or bought in Starbucks. Just the rich and slightly bitter aroma of Turkish coffee foaming on the stove was spellbinding.

Once the coffee was ready, he poured it into the demitasse, careful not to destroy the foamy light layer at the top. With his coffee in one hand and iPad in the other, he walked out to the balcony. Living in a penthouse of one of the Ft. Lauderdale high-rises had its perks. The view of the ocean was spectacular.

The sun was slowly rising over the ocean, painting the rippling surface of the water with soft bursts of light. A pleasant cool breeze touched Aidan's silk robe, wrapping it around his legs. He loved living close to the ocean and the sunrise was his favorite time of the day. The pink flares of the early morning sun, reflecting in the dark surface of the ocean as always were giving him an elated feeling of good things to come, a hope for a better future.

He put the coffee on the table, sitting down and opened the Sun-Sentinel website on his iPad, but no matter how hard he tried, he couldn't focus on the news. His thoughts were circling back to the strange events of last evening.

Four demons attacked Tessa right next to his school. That was a first. Demons and other evil creatures knew better than to come in such close proximity of his territory. And the mere thought of demons hurting Tessa made his every muscle tense. He knew Tessa since she was just twelve years old – a tiny, quiet girl, mercilessly bullied by her mean classmates.

* * *

THAT DAY WAS ETCHED in Aidan's memory forever. He was on his way to his martial arts school when he heard a noise coming from a small parking lot behind the building. He ran there and saw three boys pushing around a little girl. She huddled into a corner, crying, but still fighting them tooth and nail. As soon as Aidan approached them, the bullies – cowards as most of the bullies are – ran off, leaving the girl sitting on the ground, her arms still covering her head.

She lowered her arms slowly, exposing her bleeding nose and bruised eye, and stared at Aidan with her big brown eyes filled with tears. He helped her to her feet and offered to give a call to her mother, but she threw her arms around his waist, hiding her bloodied face in his shirt and cried silently. Aidan lifted her off the ground and she wrapped her trembling arms around his neck, clinging her whole tiny body to him. He took her to his school where she finally calmed down and gave him the phone number of her mother.

When Tessa's mother arrived, Tessa was cleaned up, changed in a brand-new white martial arts uniform, and was furiously attacking the kicking bag. Aidan invited Tessa's mother into his office and offered to get Tessa into a martial arts program for free. She agreed right away, strongly believing that the only way to help her daughter with the bullying problem was to teach her how to defend herself. However, she gracefully rejected Aidan's offer of free lessons and paid for every single lesson her daughter took until the day she passed away.

Tessa was the best student he ever had. Focused and determined, she put her entire self into the training, spending all her free time in the dojang. Unlike with the other children in his school, Aidan made sure to train her himself, giving her extra lessons in the after hours.

With time, Tessa blossomed, transforming from an awkward, terrified child into a confident young woman. She wasn't beautiful by the generally-accepted standards. Short and slender, she had long black hair that constantly was falling over her face, covering her angular features. But it was her large brown eyes, soft and velvety, that made her appearance truly special and captivating.

She could walk into Aidan's office and ask him for just about anything, and as long as she was gazing pleadingly at him with those deep-brown cherries, he could never say no to her. Tessa knew that and wasn't afraid to use it.

After her mother passed away, Tessa became withdrawn and was spending even more time training, staying away from other students and instructors. Aidan was the only person, she was open with, not worried about showing him her true feelings. And he was there for her every moment through the grieving, gently supporting and leading her toward recovery.

Aidan didn't notice how it happened, but over the course of six years, Tessa became a true necessity in his life, and he couldn't imagine spending a day without seeing her. He wasn't sure what he felt toward her, but he knew that he would do anything for her, to make sure that she was safe and happy.

* * *

AIDAN SHUT down his iPad and slowly sipped his coffee. Between the demons' attack on Tessa and the unexpected appearance of the Fire Salamander in his school, everything felt wrong. How could it happen that he didn't know that a Fire Salamander was living in his city? This man had to be suppressing his elemental power every second of the day, otherwise Aidan would feel his presence.

And the way Tessa looked at this short man when she said that he was her knight in shining armor... She was sarcastic of course, but there was something in the glance she threw at that Salamander... Aidan wasn't sure why, but at that moment he felt a painful jolt. And he didn't like it.

He got up and drew a complicated rune with his finger. The rune hung suspended in the air, glowing with a bright white light. Aidan touched it and whispered a summoning spell. A few minutes later, the air shimmered with a soft red glow and Uri materialized in front of him. His hair was untidy, and he looked like he just woke up.

"Good morning, Uri," said Aidan, gesturing at a free chair. "Coffee?"

"Morning," replied Uri, his voice slightly hoarse and sat down. "Yeah, thank you. I'm not sure if I'm fully awake yet."

Aidan snapped his fingers, manifesting a fresh cup of Starbucks coffee. Uri took the cup and inhaled the bitter smell of hot beverage before taking the first sip.

"I'm sorry to summon you here so early in the morning," said Aidan, "but I need you to do something for me."

"What do you need?" asked Uri, staring at Aidan over his coffee cup.

"The Fire Salamander," said Aidan, his brows pulled together over his blazing blue eyes. "I don't like him, and I don't trust him. He showed up uninvited and it worries me that I couldn't feel his presence earlier."

"You don't like him, or you don't like the way Tessa was looking at him?" asked Uri with a wide grin.

Aidan sighed and scratched his head. "Both?"

Uri laughed. "Aidan McGrath is jealous," he said, shaking his head. "I never thought that I'd see the day... You're a bad boy, Aidan. Falling for your student?"

"Ugh, Uri," muttered Aidan, throwing his hands in the air. "I'm not jealous or falling or anything else. I feel responsible for Tessa. She has no one to take care of her except me."

"You know that she has her uncle, right?"

"The uncle that is under his wife's heel? The wife who can't stand Tessa and did everything to get her out of her house and her husband's life. That uncle?" asked Aidan, anger and bitterness in him bubbling up to the surface. "Why do you think Tessa moved back into her mother's condo as soon as she hit her eighteen's birthday?"

"Hey, Aidan, calm down," said Uri, raising his hand up. "I know that her situation is a bit too close to home for you, but I don't think that Tessa is in any trouble right now."

"Uri, I don't like this Fire Salamander. You know how dangerous his natural state can be to humans. And Tessa is human," said Aidan, squeezing the demitasse in his hand.

"Are you sure, she is human?"

Aidan thought for a moment and shook his head. "No, I'm not sure. She seems to be human. I can't sense any magic in her, yet her aura has a hardly noticeable trace of some kind of energy that I can't recognize. Anyway, it's neither here nor there... The Fire Salamander could be dangerous to her. Period."

"You want me to check his background?" asked Uri and Aidan nodded. "Already did. I have to tell you – he has been around this city for over a year. If you couldn't sense his presence, it means he's in complete control of his power. I don't think you need to worry about the safety of any humans next to him."

"What else did you find out?"

"Not much," said Uri, taking another sip of his coffee. "His name is Alexander Burns, but he introduced himself as Zane Burns. There is very little information on him in the system. Slightly over a year ago, he didn't exist. No credit cards, no utility bills on his name, not even a library card. Nothing. I don't think that he's in some kind of witness protection program. So, my best guess, he's working for some government agency – FBI, CIA, NSA... Whatever letters of the alphabet you like. Take your pick."

"Why would you think that he works for the government?" asked Aidan, troubled. "I have never heard of any creature of magic working with any governments. He could be anything, a conman, using fake documents and Zane Burns could be just one of his aliases."

"I don't think so," objected Uri. "When he was in the school, I scanned him with my light and there was no darkness in this man. I couldn't see any evil in him."

Aidan fell silent. He knew that if Uri couldn't see any darkness in the Fire Salamander, the man couldn't be evil. But for whatever reason, he couldn't accept it. "He told me that he was just twenty-eight," said Aidan finally. "Where was he for the other twenty-seven years, before he got here? Can you find that out?"

"Very young for a Fire Salamander," muttered Uri. "If I'm right and he works for one of the government agencies undercover, it'll be very hard to find out anything."

"You have my permission to utilize any of my connections," said Aidan rising. "I want to know everything there is to know about this man."

"Fine," said Uri. He gulped the rest of his coffee and got up.

"But wouldn't it be easier just to ask him a few questions? You told me that he answered every single question you asked him, and you didn't detect any lies. Think about it, Aidan. With his Fire power, he could be a welcome ally in your war. Don't make an enemy out of him."

Aidan nodded, and Uri waved his hand, instantly vanishing from the balcony.

Questions? Well, and the questions I shall ask, thought Aidan as he walked out of the balcony, leaving the unfinished demitasse with coffee on the table.

*I*t was a relatively quiet day for a busy dental practice. After the unfortunate events of the last evening, Dr. Davis took a few days off to recover. As a result, all her patients were rescheduled for the next week. Tessa stared at the computer screen, checking the schedule of Dr. West. He had a cancelation and the next patient didn't arrive yet. All rooms were prepared, the instruments were sterilized, and the office was breathing with cleanliness.

Tessa leaned back in the chair and allowed herself to relax for a few minutes. Her thoughts slowly traveled to the dojang. Between everything that happened there yesterday, she didn't get a chance to talk to Aidan. In her mind, she re-played the sparring session between Aidan and that new guy, Zane, wondering what came over him. In all the years that she knew Aidan, she never saw him so aggressive and merciless in sparring. Especially not with the new people. She remembered the look of pain on Zane's face when Aidan got him in the kneebar. Zane seemed like a nice guy and she couldn't understand what Aidan had against him.

The door into the office opened up and a tall man walked inside. He was dressed in black jeans and grungy Metallica t-shirt.

With his shoulder-length dark hair and dark overgrown stubble, he looked like a biker. Even though he was inside the office, he didn't take his dark sunglasses off.

The man stopped at the front desk counter and smiled, demonstrating his perfectly healthy dental anatomy. Tessa threw a quick look at his sparkling teeth, asking herself why this man would need services of a prosthodontist. Claudia, the patient coordinator, got up to greet him. The man came prepared. He had all the new patient's forms filled online and Claudia opened his file on her computer screen to review them.

Since there was no need to make him wait, Tessa checked his name in his file and invited him in. "Please come in, Mr. Vargas," she said, opening the door for him. "Second room on your left."

Once she seated Mr. Vargas, Tessa walked out of the room and checked the long hallway, searching for Dr. West. She found him in his office at the far end of the hallway. He was sitting at his desk, looking at the x-rays of one of his patients. He was so engrossed in his work that he didn't notice Tessa's arrival and she had to touch his shoulder to get his attention. Ryan turned around and looked at her, his eyes lingering on the fresh scar on her lips.

"Tessa, what happened?" he asked with concern. "Don't you know, we're in the business of fixing teeth in this office, not breaking them."

"Speak for yourself, Ryan," she replied, chuckling. "I'm in the business of making the new business for your office – hence, breaking teeth."

"You're such a troublemaker, Tessa," said Ryan, rising. "Do I need to check yours?"

"Nope, I'm fine," she answered, heading toward the door. "Your new patient, Mr. Vargas, is ready for you in the room two. By the way, he looks like he just jumped off his bike and I couldn't get him to take his shades off. Have fun with this jackass."

Ryan just shook his head and followed her through the hall-way. He entered the room and approached Mr. Vargas, introducing himself. Not without amusement, Tessa registered that the patient still didn't take his sunglasses off. Ryan put his mask and gloves on, grabbed the explorer and mirror off the tray and sat down next to the patient.

"Okay, Mr. Vargas, let's see what's going on with your teeth," he said, readjusting the unit light. "But before we start, may I ask you to take your sunglasses off?"

Mr. Vargas pursed his lips, but pulled his sunglasses off, carefully hooking them to his jean pocket. Tessa glanced at his face and started to understand why he didn't want to take his glasses off. His eyelids were red and puffy, and his eyes were bloodshot and glassy, like he didn't sleep all night. He caught her gaze and his lips stretched in a cold smile, giving him a resemblance with an alligator.

"Allergies," he explained with a half-shrug. "Bright light bothers me."

For whatever reason, Tessa didn't believe one word this guy was saying. There was something bone-chillingly unsettling about this man. Standing next to him was like standing next to an open freezer.

"Just bear with me, Mr. Vargas," mumbled Ryan, leaning slightly closer to him. "I'll try to do the exam as fast as I can. And then you can put your sunglasses back on. Open please…"

Mr. Vargas opened wide, showing off his flawless set of choppers. For a moment Ryan stared at his patient's teeth, his eyebrows slowly rising. Then he blinked a couple of times and proceeded with the exam. Still uncomfortable in the presence of this man, Tessa watched Ryan working without taking her eyes off.

A soft ding of the intercom system made Tessa flinch and turn around. She got up and picked up the phone. Claudia was letting her know that Dr. West had an emergency patient and she already seated him in room one. By the time Tessa hung up the phone and turned around, Ryan was done with the initial exam.

"Well, Mr. Vargas, I can't see anything wrong with your teeth. As a matter of fact, the only place I saw teeth as perfect as yours was in the book of dental anatomy," he said, chuckling. He put away the tools and took his gloves off. "I'm going to let Tessa take a full set of x-rays and if everything checks out, we can schedule you for a prophylactic cleaning."

Ryan pushed the button, setting the chair in an upright position, but Mr. Vargas held Ryan's hand, already a familiar frosty smile lingering on his face. "Are you s-s-s-sure that you checked all my teeth, Dr. West?" he asked, his voice sounding deeper with an added light hiss. "Pleas-s-s-s-e take a look again... I don't want you to mis-s-s-s anything..."

Something is not right. A thought flashed in Tessa's mind as she bolted toward the chair. Only two-three steps were separating her from Ryan, but she wasn't fast enough. Mr. Vargas opened his mouth again. His normal teeth were gone, replaced by a set of sharp fangs. His every tooth was elongated and shaped into a sharp point, a thin web of saliva stretched between his unnaturally wide-open jaws.

Ryan gasped and started to back away, but the man's hand struck forward with a blurring speed, seizing his neck. The man was moving so fast that he was leaving a motion trail in his wake. In one lightning motion, he pulled Ryan closer, lifting him off the floor like the two-hundred-pound dentist was weighing nothing. He forced Ryan's head to the side, exposing his jugular and sank his terrifying set of fangs into his neck.

The raiser-sharp fangs easily penetrated his skin and a thick stream of blood, spilled down Ryan's neck, dripping on Mr. Vargas' shirt, but he didn't seem to care. His eyes were half-closed as he sucked the blood like it was his morning protein shake, his blood-stained lips smacking.

A thick copper smell drifted in the air and Tessa froze for a quick moment, fighting nausea. She came back to her senses a split-second later and grabbed Ryan's shoulders trying to tear him away from Mr. Vargas' grip. The man growled like a wild animal, a low sound rumbling in his throat as he continued sucking the blood.

Tessa snapped her arm back and punched Mr. Vargas in the side of his head. The man lifted his eyes and his bloodstained lips stretched into a carnivorous smirk over Ryan's neck. It seemed that Tessa's punch didn't leave a lasting impression on him.

"Can't say no to dessert," he hissed. His free arm flew forward and wrapped around Tessa's waist. He pulled her to his side, without stopping what he was doing, and Tessa couldn't understand how he managed it, but she was almost completely immobilized by his hold. As she was helplessly struggling against the man's deadly grip, her eyes fell on Ryan's face and silent tears burnt behind her eyes. Ryan was losing too much blood. His face was drained of color, his body feeble and limp.

He is killing Ryan, thought Tessa in despair, everything inside her crumbling into dust and ashes. *Ryan is dying... no...* "Help!" she yelled putting whatever strength she had left in this desperate cry. "Help!"

The door flew open like someone kicked it with their foot and with a loud bang hit the wall. Tessa moaned, lifting her eyes, struggling to see over Mr. Vargas' shoulder and her mouth fell open. In the doorway she saw Zane. He was breathing hard and his eyes were glowing red. He didn't run into the room but stopped at the door and waved his hand muttering something under his breath. Tessa couldn't hear what he was saying, but the room got flooded with a soft yellow light and the habitual white noise of the city that was coming through the window got muffled.

Before Mr. Vargas got a chance to react, Zane crossed the distance between them and seized his long hair, wringing it around his wrist. He yanked his head back roughly, forcing him to release Ryan's neck. The man dropped both Tessa and Ryan and roared, frustration making his fingers curl into claws. Tessa fell on the floor and huddled to the wall, shaking. She watched Zane punching out Mr. Vargas and quickly shoving Ryan's body closer to Tessa.

"Apply pressure to the wound," he said, his voice a low growl. "See if you can stop the bleeding."

Zane's glowing eyes swept from her to Ryan and he shook his head. Tessa could swear that he whispered the word *"humans"* as he spun around, switching his attention back to Mr. Vargas. The man was back on his feet, his shoulders hunched, and his arms outstretched forward giving him a resemblance with a predator, ready to attack. His upper lip was curved into a feral snarl exposing his horrendous fangs and his bloodshot eyes narrowed into angry slits.

"Ignius!" shouted Zane. He made a circular motion with his hand, pointing at Mr. Vargas.

What the hell? Is it even a real word? thought Tessa as a circle, blazing with smoldering flames erupted around Mr. Vargas. The man shrieked, his voice suddenly high-pitched and jumped up on top of the dental chair, crouching there and ready to launch at any moment. His narrowed eyes were following the flow of the fire with unmistakable fear.

Zane turned back to Tessa and squatted next to her. He tapped her shoulder gently. With an effort, she tore her eyes off the dancing flames and stared at him, speechless.

"Call an ambulance," he ordered, rising. "Dr. West needs medical attention."

He walked to the opposite wall and took a picture in a wooden frame off, smashing it against the table. The glass shattered, and the frame broke into four pieces. He picked up one of the longer pieces of the frame and squeezed it in his hand like it was a knife. In no rush, he walked through the fiery circle. Tessa gasped – not only was he not burnt by the fire, the flames wrapped around his body, licking and kissing him like he was their lover.

As soon as Zane passed inside the circle, Mr. Vargas screamed and pounced at him. Zane didn't blink an eye. His arm shot forward, and he caught Mr. Vargas' neck, stopping him in midair. With one move, Zane flung the man back on the chair and forcefully drove the piece of frame into his chest, piercing his heart. Mr. Vargas cried out, grabbing the piece of wood with both hands. He pulled the wood out and fell back, motionless.

Tessa couldn't see every little detail through the wall of fire, but everything she saw was enough to raise multiple questions. Zane was in good shape, but he was short. How could he hold a man twice his size in the air with one hand? And didn't he just kill him? As far as she knew, a wooden stake through the heart was considered to be a fatal wound. She got up, gently lowering the unconscious Ryan to the floor and stepped closer to the fire circle, ignoring the scorching heat.

Zane was standing over the body of Mr. Vargas, shaking his head in disbelief. To her horror, Tessa noticed that even though there was a giant black hole in Mr. Vargas's chest, he wasn't dead. Slowly he was rising, pressing his hand to the hole. And his wound wasn't bleeding.

"Hell's bells," muttered Zane, scratching his head. "I was so hoping that you were just a vampire…"

Vampire? With everything that happened in the last few minutes, Tessa felt shocked and confused.

In the meantime, Zane reached into his jean pocket and pulled out a Swiss army knife. Mr. Vargas barked laughing.

"Really? A tiny Swiss army knife?" he spat between the wild bursts of laughter. "What are you going to do with that, MacGyver?"

Zane didn't answer, but a crooked smirk appeared on his face. He held the knife in his hand and whispered a single word Tessa couldn't recognize. The knife started to grow, expending into a long sword. The weapon looked like a medieval sword and was blazing with smoldering flames.

Mr. Vargas hissed and shifted away from him, hitting the

dental chair with his back. Surrounded by fire, he had nowhere to run. With one fluid motion of his arm, Zane swung the sword and ran it through Mr. Vargas' neck, instantly decapitating him. The head rolled over his shoulders, hitting the floor with dull thud. The body stayed in place for a few more seconds, the dead fingers grasping at the air. Zane pushed the body down next to the head and put the tip of his flaming blade to Mr. Vargas' chest.

"Ignius Amplio," he muttered, and a steady stream of fire escaped his sword, setting Mr. Vargas' body ablaze. In a matter of a few seconds, the body was gone like it was never there. Zane said another word that sounded like gibberish to Tessa and his sword turned back into a tiny Swiss army knife. He put the knife back into his jean pocket and finally looked up.

"Tessa, did you call 911?" he asked calmly like he didn't kill and burn into ashes a man (or whatever Mr. Vargas was – a vampire?) just a second ago.

Tessa swallowed and nodded. Her throat felt uncharacteristically dry and she couldn't bring herself to say a word.

"Okay," said Zane. "I need to leave now. Let me get rid of all this fire."

He approached the fiery circle and put his hand directly into the fire. He didn't say anything, but the flames slowly subsided and finally disappeared. He approached Tessa and halted a few steps away, scratching his head. Then he sighed and looked at her.

"I'm sure that after everything you just witnessed, you probably have a few questions," he said evenly.

"No shit, Sherlock," croaked Tessa, her speech finally coming back to her. "You're goddamn right, I have a few questions."

"And I promise to answer your questions as soon as I can. Just not right now." Zane headed toward the door, but then stopped and turned around. He waved his hand again and the soft yellow light disappeared. "Do you know which hospital they will take Dr. West to?"

"Broward Health in Coral Springs, most likely," said Tessa,

lowering herself down on the floor to check on Ryan. He was abnormally pale, and an ugly deep bite mark, overflowing with blood was shining on his neck. But she found a weak pulse in his wrist and that gave her hope that he would be all right.

"I'll see you there in an hour," promised Zane and walked out of the room.

~ TESSA ~

An empty hospital waiting room was shockingly freezing. It smelled of sterility, and the flickering light of the fluorescent lamps was throwing cold shimmering shades on perfectly neutral walls. Everything inside this room was painted in soft, muted colors. Possibly it was supposed to be relaxing, but Tessa was anything but relaxed.

Since there was no one in the room besides her, she pulled her feet up on the neutral-colored chair and hugged her knees with her arms. She always hated hospitals. Let's face it – unless you're a hospital employee and that's the way you're making your living, no one likes to be here. But Tessa had an entirely different reason for that. Since she was a child, she always felt an unpleasant vibe as soon as she was crossing the threshold of any hospital. It was like a jolt of electricity inside her, something that pulled her nerves on alert, making her jittery and a little paranoid.

After the encounter with Mr. Koval's spirit, Tessa started to understand why the hospital atmosphere was affecting her this way. Here, she was surrounded by pain, suffering, death and sorrow. Death... It meant the spirits of people who recently passed away could be somewhere right next to her. She shivered and looked around, almost expecting to see someone appearing in the room, surrounded by a white light.

She glanced at the clock on the wall and sighed. Almost an hour had passed since the ambulance drove Ryan and her to the Broward Health Hospital. He lost a lot of blood and needed surgery to fix the damage to his neck. The doctor said that Ryan was in critical condition and promised to send a nurse with an update as soon as he knew anything. Where was the nurse? Tessa got up and circled the small waiting room a few times, hoping to calm her nerves.

It didn't work, and she sat back down. Tessa didn't want to think about anything, but her thoughts were stubbornly coming back to Zane. She had no explanation to what she witnessed, but she wasn't afraid of him or what he was. She caught herself thinking that she actually wanted to see him again.

I just want to ask him a few questions, she said to herself, trying to compromise with her own standards of right and wrong. *That's all. Anyone would be curious after seeing his fire-show. I just need to know.*

Deep inside, she realized that there was more to her desire to see him than just plain curiosity. Tessa recalled the fierce flames on the bottom of his eyes and the way the fire obeyed his every command. He was different. Not like other people. He was a freak, just like her. And she liked that. She liked his igneous eyes and his lopsided smile. She sighed, struggling to admit even to herself that she liked the way his smile brought up that single dimple on his cheek, setting his whole face alight. She liked him from the first moment when she saw him in the bright lights of Aidan's dojang. Something like this had never happened to her before.

The door of the waiting room opened up and Tessa got up, expecting to see a nurse with an update on Ryan's condition. But it wasn't the nurse. Zane was standing in the doorway. He met her eyes and a shy smile transformed his face. She gazed at him wondering how he could be so different. She remembered the way he kicked the door into the room back in the dental office, his every step driven by deadly purpose and self-assurance. Now he was standing, uncomfortably shifting from foot to foot, looking like a person who wasn't sure if he was welcome here.

"Zane, you're here," she exhaled, surprised that he kept his word and came to the hospital. For some reason she was sure that she wouldn't see him until the next Taekwondo lesson, assuming he would show up at all after the way Aidan treated him.

"I promised," he said with a light shrug. He walked up to her and sat down in the chair across from her. "How is Dr. West?"

"Critical," she said with a sigh. "Still no updates from surgery."

"I'm sorry about your boss," he said uncomfortably, and Tessa could see that he didn't really know what to say.

"He's not just a boss. Ryan is more like a friend to me," said Tessa quietly, turning away so he wouldn't notice tears gathering in her eyes. "You saved both of us, Zane. Thank you."

He looked away and sighed. "I guess, I owe you an explanation, Tessa," he said finally, still staring down at his hands.

She glanced at his hands – calloused and rough, these were the hands of a man who was used to physical work and practiced marital arts for years. And for some reason, she could hardly contain her desire to touch these hands. She looked up. His eyes were no longer glowing red. They were silvery-grey, the color of steel. And for a moment she wondered if what she saw earlier was just an illusion, a play of light or deception created by her mind, overpowered by fear.

"You don't owe me anything," she objected, leaning back in her chair. "But if you don't mind answering just one question..." He gave a her a short nod and she continued, "What was that man? A vampire?" Saying the word *vampire* like it was a real thing didn't come easy for her. "How is that possible? It can't be real."

"It's real, alright," he replied with a smirk. "There are many things that go bump in the night that are real. You wouldn't believe me even if I tried to tell you. But this man wasn't a vampire. I wish he was. It would be a lot easier to get rid of him."

"What was he?" Tessa repeated her question, feeling the small hairs rising up on the back of her neck. She saw the spirits of dead people and she talked to them. So why wouldn't she believe in the existence of vampires and whatever else was sneaking around in the dead of night.

"Upir," explained Zane calmly. "It's like a vampire on some serious steroids. You can kill a regular vampire with a wooden stake through his heart or by decapitating him. Not that simple with upir. But you saw it yourself. With an upir, you need to cut his head off and then burn his body, otherwise he still can come back. Upirs can walk in the daylight and they look absolutely normal. It's been a while since I've seen one…"

"Wow," mumbled Tessa, not quite sure who was the craziest person in the room. "Upir… I didn't even know that there was such a thing. And you're what, like a friendly neighborhood *Buffy, the vampire slayer?*"

"What?" he asked looking lost for a moment but then laughed. "No, I'm not Buffy. I'm Lancelot. The bravest and noblest of them all, ready to save any little damsel in distress."

Tessa giggled and punched him in the shoulder. "I'm no damsel, you moron."

Zane smiled but all of sudden tensed up staring somewhere over Tessa's shoulder. She followed his gaze and noticed a weight-less semi-transparent cloud that was softly glowing with a pure white light, slowly drifting through the wall, entering the waiting room. For a moment, the view of the room switched to negative and then back to normal. She didn't need to guess – it was a spirit. Tessa looked back at Zane and by the expression on his face, she was positive that he could see it too. The realization that she wasn't the only one who could see spirits of the dead gave her unexpected comfort.

She got up with a sigh and approached the blob of energy. The spirit finished crossing through the wall and came to focus in front of her eyes. It was a young man. He looked disoriented and sad.

"Where am I?" asked the spirit, his voice distant and hollow.

"In the Broward Health Hospital," replied Tessa, trying to sound as comforting as she could.

The spirit stared at her for a moment, furrowing his brow. "I think I'm starting to remember something..." He fell silent and his glowing body shimmered like he was ready to vanish, but then he came back into focus and stared at Tessa intently. "I remember an accident. This driver... he just rammed straight into our car. Head-on collision at full speed and I had no time... My wife! She was in the car with me and she was pregnant! I need to find her. I hope she's okay... the baby too..."

The spirit turned away from her and headed toward the door. *Spirits don't use doors. He probably doesn't realize that he's dead,* thought Tessa and rushed after him.

"Wait," she called after the spirit. "Before you leave, I need to tell you something."

"What is it?" asked the young man.

"I'm not very good at being diplomatic," she said apologetically. "So, I'll just tell you straight. I think you're dead."

"Excuse me? You're crazy," he said with assurance in his voice which made it obvious that he didn't believe anything she said.

Tessa searched the room and picked up a magazine from the coffee table. She offered the magazine to the spirit. "Take it. If you are not dead, you'll have no problem holding it, right?"

"You're crazy," repeated the sprit but extended his hand to take the magazine. His fingers slid though the magazine. He tried again to no avail. He raised his eyes at Tessa and stared at her mortified.

"I'm sorry," she said quietly, sadness gripping at her chest.

"But why?" he whispered like he didn't hear her. "Why now? I was happy, we were going to have a baby... Why me? It's not right..."

"You're right," she replied. "It's not right, not fair, but it is what it is."

"But if I'm dead, how can you see me, talk to me?"

"I don't know," replied Tessa. "I just can."

"So, what do I do now?" He twirled around like he was searching for the proverbial white light. "Should I go for the white light or look for a door or something?"

"I'm not sure. I'm new to all this. But one other spirit told me that the next step is to cross behind the veil," she explained, throwing a quick look at Zane. He was sitting in his chair, seemingly relaxed, like nothing out of ordinary was happening in the room right next to him.

"Veil? Is that like heaven or hell?"

"I don't know what's behind the veil," said Tessa. "I never died before and I never met anyone who returned from behind the veil. But that's what you need to do. And I think I can help you with it if you're ready." She extended her hand to him.

The spirit looked at her hand indecisively. "How about my wife? Is she dead too?"

"I don't know, but I can't see her anywhere around. So hopefully, she is alive."

"Good..." whispered the spirit. He visibly relaxed and put his hand into Tessa's. "Thank you..."

As soon as she touched his hand, the spirit shone brighter and a few seconds later, he disappeared, leaving a few floating sparks of white lite slowly drifting in the air. Tessa walked back to her chair and sat down without looking at Zane. She was afraid that he was going to ask some questions she wasn't prepared to answer. But he wasn't saying anything – no questions, no statements, nothing.

"You know that I wasn't talking to myself," she said finally, gazing at him tentatively.

He smiled and met her eyes. "Of course, I know that. Was it a spirit of a dead person?"

Tessa nodded. "You could see it too, couldn't you?"

"I could see, but I'm sure what I saw was a lot different than what you saw. I can see the energy that the human soul emits. Usually it's a light, bright white or golden. But I can't see the actual ghosts and definitely can't talk to them or hear them talking."

For the first time in years, hope rose in her soul. Maybe Zane could help her answer these questions that were bothering her for years – why could she see the dead? What was she?

"Zane," she said, her heart thundering in her chest, "do you know what I am? Why can I see spirits and talk to them? Why can they talk to me?"

"No, not yet, but let's see if we can find out." He got off his chair and squatted in front of her, staring up into her eyes. "Don't get scared. My eyes may glow red and try not to touch me. My skin may get a little hotter than normal."

"Go for it, Lancelot," she said with a sarcastic smirk.

Tessa calmly observed as his eyes started to glow red and then small flames manifested in the depth of his eyes. She felt the wave of heat his body was emitting, but she didn't move allowing him to do whatever he was doing. A minute later, he got up and sat on the chair next to her. He was sitting quietly, thinking, and Tessa was afraid to ask.

"So, what did you see?" she dared to ask finally, staring straight forward.

"I don't know... I'm not sure what I saw," he replied slowly. "You have a pure human soul, so that would make you human. Normally, I can see the energy of magic and elemental power, but you don't have either. I can also see the dark energy of demons and other evil beings, like vampires, upirs, werewolves, you know... But you don't have any dark energy in you either. So, you're not evil —"

"What a relief!" She interrupted him, rolling her eyes. "I knew that I wasn't evil without you telling me that, moron."

Zane chuckled and shook his head. "Having said that, you're not a pure-blood human either. The energy of your soul is a lot brighter than the energy of a regular human. It's warm and kind and pure... but I can't recognize it. I've never seen anything like this before."

"Wow, nice..." Tessa pursed her lips. She tried not to laugh, but the corners of her lips quirked up. "So, I'm a covert paranormal freak. And my cover is so good that even other paranormal freaks can't recognize me."

"You're not a freak," objected Zane. "We just need to find out what you are. I'll do what I can to help you."

"Do you know what you are?" she asked without looking at him and held her breath for a moment.

"Yes."

"How did you find out?"

"The hard way," he replied. His eyes drifted to the side like he was looking back into his past. "But I had my friends by my side. And they helped me through the transition. I also have a great mentor."

"You had friends?" asked Tessa. "Where are they now? Are they alive?"

"Yes, they're fine, but they're far away from here and I came to terms with the thought that I'll never see them again."

For a moment he looked so sad and lonely that Tessa's throat tightened, like she could feel his pain. Her first instinct was to touch him, comfort him somehow and she moved her hand to him, but a wave of heat around his body made her stop. *What am I doing?* she thought, surprised by her own actions. *I don't do touchy-feely.*

"I have only one true friend – Aidan," she said quietly, her voice hoarse. "But I never told him anything. He's so... I don't know… Normal? He would never believe in anything supernatural. And I didn't want him to think that I was crazy."

"Aidan? As in Aidan McGrath? He doesn't believe in the supernatural?" asked Zane. He looked so shocked that Tessa frowned, wondering why he would think otherwise.

"Yes, Aidan McGrath," said Tessa dryly. "He doesn't know anything, and I want to keep it that way."

"If he is your true and only friend, don't you think he deserves your honesty?" asked Zane with a lopsided smirk. "You never know, he could be more open to the idea of supernatural than you think."

"No!" Tessa got up, fear surging through her. "No, please. I don't want him to know anything."

"I won't tell him about you, if you don't tell him about me," said Zane winking at her.

"I'm serious, Zane. I'm not going to tell him anything about you. I was unconscious and didn't see anything. But if you say one word to Aidan, I swear, you'll regret it!"

Zane raised his hands up, grinning. "Tessa, relax. I wasn't going to tell him anything. I'm not that close with Aidan to have a heart-to-heart. The man hates me."

"He doesn't hate you, Zane. He just doesn't know you and Aidan is not a very trustful person. You need to deserve his trust first." She sighed and finally touched his hand lightly. His skin felt like he was running a high fever, but it didn't burn her. "Listen, can I count on you? Can you help me find out what I am?"

"Yes, of course. I already told you that I will," he replied right away. "Can I have your cell for a moment?" She glanced at him surprised but gave him her cell phone. He quickly punched in the numbers. "Here is my phone number. If you ever need my help – call me."

She stored his phone number in her phone's contact list. "Why would I need your help?" she asked, giving him an arched stare. "You saw me in action. I can take care of myself."

"You never know." He shrugged, getting up. "You may have an infestation of upirs or an invasion of walking dead. I don't know. Since you refuse to tell the truth to the only friend you have, when paranormal knocks on your door, who are you going to call?"

"Aw, I'm sorry. My first assumption was incorrect. You're not Buffy, you're an uncredited ghostbuster..." She snickered, getting up, patting him on his shoulder. "But on the serious side, Zane. May I ask you what you are?"

"Yes, you may ask," he agreed, an evil grin on his face, "just don't expect me to answer." But he quickly changed his mind. "Fine, I'll tell you. I am —"

He didn't get to finish what he was going to say, as the door opened and a man in medical scrubs walked inside the waiting room. He looked tired and serious, and Tessa felt a spike of fear tearing through her heart. She took a step toward the doctor and stopped.

"Ms. Tessa Donovan?" he asked. "I'm Dr. Alister. I wanted to let you know that Dr. West is doing well. He lost a lot of blood, but we performed a successful surgery to fix the damage to his neck, and he's stable now. We moved him to ICU and you can see him any time you're ready."

"Thank you, doctor," mumbled Tessa, instantly feeling relief.

"Do you know what bit him?" asked Dr. Alister. "It looked like a bite of a large animal, but in my years of practice I had never seen anything like this. We'll have to treat him for rabies."

"I don't know," said Tessa, terrified of the idea of telling the truth to the doctor. "I didn't get a chance to see the attacker."

"Well, you can go to the nurses' station and they'll tell you where you can find Dr. West," said Dr. Alister and left the room.

As soon as the doctor was out of the room, Tessa turned back to Zane. "I got to go," she said. "Can you do me a favor?"

"What do you need?"

"Can you tell Aidan that I'm in the hospital with Ryan? I don't want him to worry about me, so please go to the school as soon as possible and let him know. Don't wait until the evening training. Okay?"

"Don't worry, I'll tell him." He raked his fingers through his short hair. "I'll have to find a way to explain to him how I know that you're in a hospital with your boss."

"Good point," said Tessa narrowing her eyes at him. "What were you doing in my dental office, huh?"

Zane laughed and opened the door out of the waiting room, gesturing at her to pass through first. "I had an emergency appointment. Toothache."

"Yeah, right. If only I believed you." She scolded him with her eyes as she walked past him, pushing him with her shoulder. "And don't you dare open doors for me, little man. I don't need your assistance... Friggin' knight in shining armor."

"My lady." Zane laughed and bowed to her. It wasn't a traditional martial arts bow, more like a bow of a medieval knight. And even though his bow was full of mockery, Tessa couldn't shake off the feeling that it wasn't the first time he bowed like this.

This man is full of secrets, she thought walking away toward the nurses' station. *And there is nothing I love more than unravelling a good mystery. He's my kind of puzzle.*

~ ZANE BURNS, A.K.A. GUNZ ~

*G*unz left the hospital and walked through the busy parking lot, searching for his car. It didn't take him long to find his white *Mercedes*. He sat down in the driver's seat but didn't start the car right away, thinking about Tessa and the mystery that surrounded her. She could see and communicate with spirits, but he didn't think that she was a medium. He came across a few mediums before and they all had a different aura about them. Their aura included some energy of magic. Tessa had none of that and the brightness of her own energy was unprecedented.

He remembered the first time when the Fire Salamander in him reared its flaming head and the torture he went through until he learned to control his power. He didn't know what was happening to him, and even though his power didn't manifest in its full potency right away, he still hurt those closest to him – his friends who stood by his side, no matter how hard it was.

Now that he learned how dangerous his natural state was to humans, he was thanking God for not letting him gain his pure Fire Salamander state until much later on. By the time he grew into the full power of a Fire Salamander, he was under control of his mentor – Kal, the fierce Fire Elemental, the magnificent Great Salamander.

At the beginning, Gunz hated Kal. He was terrified of Kal's ability to control him and suppress his freewill. The knowledge that at any moment Kal could make him do anything he wanted was making Gunz sick with fear and anger. But with time, he realized that everything Kal did in the beginning was done to teach him how to control the dangerous power within him. And now that Gunz was in complete control of his power, he no longer feared or hated Kal. He started to appreciate everything the Great Salamander did for him and respect him as a mentor, valuing his help and advice.

Tessa didn't know what she was and there was no way to say what kind of possible powers or magic her slender body was harboring. Keeping in mind all the troubles he went through in the beginning, when he didn't know what he was, Gunz couldn't let Tessa go through it alone.

He started his car and drove toward *Elements Martial Arts*. He wasn't looking forward to having a conversation with Aidan. However, since Tessa asked him so nicely and he foolishly agreed, there was no way of avoiding it.

Gunz pulled out his phone and dialed Angelique's number. She answered almost right away, her voice mostly cheerful with slight shades of concern.

"Zane, is everything okay?" she asked. "Are you coming in?"

"Hi Angie, everything is fine," he replied, suppressing his smile. On the phone, she sounded like a teenage girl. Besides, she didn't call him Vladislav and that was a step in the right direction. "And sorry, but I'm not coming in, not yet. I still need to go to that martial arts school. But there are some new developments in the case and I need to talk to Jim about it. So, I'll try to stop by his office tomorrow."

"Oh," she exhaled, a breeze of disappointment in her voice.

"Angie, can I ask you a favor?"

"Sure, what do you need?" she asked right away with that undying eagerness and cheerfulness she always had.

"I met someone —"

"You met someone?" she parroted, interrupting him, all the cheerfulness gone.

"Angie, relax, not that kind of someone," he said chuckling.

"Oh... sorry... please continue."

"Anyway, I met someone with power or a magic signature I couldn't recognize," he continued his explanation. "She's a young girl. Eighteen at the most. And she doesn't know what she is. I was wondering if you could do a reading for her."

Angelique stayed quiet for a few seconds, but then cleared her throat and said, "Yes, you can bring her over whenever you're ready. I'll do the reading. Where did you meet this girl?"

"At Elements Martial Arts," said Gunz. "She can see and communicate with the dead."

"She is a medium," said Angelique immediately sounding dismissive.

"I assure you, she's not a medium. Let's do a reading. But we need to meet somewhere outside the FBI building. I don't want her to know that I'm working for the FBI."

"No problem," said Angelique and in his mind, he could see her waving her hand. "We can meet at my apartment. Just let me know a few hours before you show up with your new... um... supernatural friend."

"Thank you, Angie. I owe you one."

"You owe me a lot more than one," she replied grumpily. "Be careful out there, Zane. Immortal or not, you still can get hurt."

She hung up the phone and Gunz smirked, throwing his cell on the passenger seat. Angie was always worried about him no matter how many times he proved to her that he was quite capable of taking care of himself in a combat situation, but it was nice to know that someone actually cared if he was dead or alive or hurt.

A few minutes later, he parked his car in front of Aidan's school. He glanced at the clock on the dashboard. It was still early, and the kids' lessons weren't over yet, but delivering a message from Tessa was a good opportunity for him to check out the school and the instructors in the day time. After a few minutes of consideration, he decided to go in and talk to Aidan right away.

Gunz walked inside the school and halted, surprised how different the school looked in the daytime. The spacious lobby was filled with children and their parents. The dojang floor was occupied by at least twenty little students, their age varied from seven to twelve. A few instructors were taking care of children, running the practice session. He recognized Angel and Uri, but he didn't know the third instructor. He wasn't as tall and looked slim, compared to the other two.

Gunz looked around the lobby but didn't notice Aidan anywhere. He walked closer to the counter and searched the floor. At the far end of the dojang, he found Aidan. He was kneeling next to a little boy. Holding the boy's leg gently in his hands, he was showing him how to kick properly. The boy was laughing, trying to repeat the move and it seemed that both of them had fun.

It was only the second time that Gunz saw Aidan McGrath, but the contrast in the way Aidan behaved yesterday and the way he was right now, was striking. Gunz looked at the warm smile on Aidan's face and the way he was with this little boy, realizing that Aidan loved working with kids, and that was making him more human than he originally thought.

Gunz decided not to bother him and was about to leave the school when Aidan got up and turned around sharply. His gaze, now cold and heavy, bore into Gunz, pinning him in place. Aidan crossed the floor and put his hand on the counter heavily. His jaw tightened, and his hand clenched into a fist.

"My office. Now!" he hissed, pointing at the door behind the front desk and stormed away toward his office.

Gunz sighed, mentally getting ready for a beating. He walked through the side door and ended up in the back of the dojang. Aidan was standing in the doorway of his office, his arms crossed over his chest, his whole body locked up with rage.

"Get in," said Aidan, pointing at his office.

"Master McGrath, let me explain —," Gunz started to say, but Aidan grunted and shook his head stopping him. He covered the distance between them in two long strides, grabbed Gunz by the back of his neck and pushed him inside the office, slamming the door shut behind them.

"*Oprimenta Amnia,*" mumbled Gunz, placing a concealment spell over Aidan's office.

Aidan checked the soft yellow glow of the spell and a cold smile stretched his lips. "Perfect. A Fire Salamander with magic," he whispered, and his eyes shone with a bright white light. "God-dammit, Salamander, what are you doing here in the daytime? I thought I made it clear to you. You can be here only after all the children are gone."

"Master McGrath, I assure you that I'm in complete control of my power. The children are not in any danger, or I would never show up here," said Gunz calmly.

"I don't give a damn what you think!" shouted Aidan, slamming his hand on the wall above Gunz's head. "If you want to take lessons here, you will do as you're told. Am I clear?"

"Yes, sir," replied Gunz calmly. Aidan looked fearsome in his anger with his glowing white eyes and bulging muscles, but it didn't bother Gunz. "I would comply with your orders, sir, but I had to deliver an urgent message to you and I was asked not to wait until the evening."

"Oh? Now you're also a messenger boy, puny lizard?" huffed Aidan, the white glow in his eyes slowly fading away. He walked around the desk and sat down in the leather chair. "Who is the message from?" Gunz hesitated for a moment considering all possible exit strategies, but Aidan waved his hand dismissively. "Go on. Normally I don't kill the messengers."

"The message is from Tessa, sir," said Gunz quietly, taking a tentative step back.

"From Tessa?" growled Aidan slowly rising. He slammed his hand on the table and his eyes lit up with the blinding light again. "What the hell were you doing around Tessa?"

Gunz shuddered inwardly. He still couldn't recognize the source of Aidan's magic, but he was undeniably powerful, and his anger spiked the magical energy field around him with incredible strength. But besides the pure rage, there was something else that Gunz noticed on Aidan's face – a deep concern about Tessa, bordering with fear. The kind of worry that one can have only about a person he deeply cared about or loved.

"Please, sir," said Gunz peacefully, "let me finish."

Aidan took a deep breath and waved his hand at Gunz, allowing him to proceed.

"Tessa is fine, sir," said Gunz. "She's in the Broward Health Hospital with her boss, Dr. West. He was attacked and severely injured. She wanted me to tell you that she'll be late for the lesson, if she even makes it here at all tonight. She asked me to deliver this message to you right away, so you wouldn't worry."

Aidan dropped back in the chair and put his hands to his face, tiredly rubbing the corners of his eyes. "How did you know about it? Were you with Tessa when the attack happened?"

"I was in the office —"

"What were you doing in Tessa's office?" asked Aidan. He didn't sound angry, but his every word was infused with a silent threat. "And think well before you answer that question, reptilian."

"I didn't know that it was Tessa's office," explained Gunz patiently. "I needed to see a dentist and I made an appointment to see Dr. West. I had no idea that Tessa was working there. When I came to the office, I heard Tessa screaming for help."

The color drained from Aidan's face and sweat glistened on his forehead. "Who attacked her?"

"Not who, sir. What," said Gunz. "Dr. West was attacked by an upir and by the time I ran into the room, he was nearly dead, and Tessa was completely subdued by the monster. They both were lucky that I happened to be there."

Aidan closed his eyes and shook his head with a heavy sigh. "Upir in a dental office? What did he need? Crowns for his fangs? What the hell? Please tell me you didn't use your elemental power in front of her, Zane."

Gunz's eyes widened – it was the first time Aidan used his name, instead of calling him a lizard, Salamander or reptilian. A step in the right direction.

"No, Master McGrath, of course not," he said with a half-shrug. "But I had to use my magic though. It was an upir and fire was the only way to kill it. But Tessa didn't see anything." He quickly recounted everything that happened in the office, omitting a few details.

"Zane, thank you," said Aidan, lowering his blazing eyes. "I can't imagine what would happen if you weren't there and I appreciate you stepping in. Nevertheless, I don't want you anywhere next to Tessa or my students. I'm sorry, but I can't risk their safety."

"I understand, sir," said Gunz rising. "I'm leaving right now."

"No, wait." Aidan waved his hand, placing another spell over his office. "If you want, you can stay here until all the children are gone. Today only."

Definitely a step in the right direction, thought Gunz, watching Aidan leave his office.

~ ZANE BURNS, A.K.A. GUNZ ~

*B*y the time his Taekwondo training was over, Gunz was no longer sure that he progressed in his relationship with Aidan. And the so called step in the right direction didn't feel so right any more. Besides him, there were three more students at the Elite team training. Tessa didn't make it and Gunz was wondering if everything was okay with Dr. West.

Aidan started the training by introducing Gunz to his team. He didn't bother to say his name, but right away called him a Fire Salamander exposing his true nature to everyone who cared to listen. He didn't bother introducing the other team members to him either and jumped straight into the training. Saying that Aidan was merciless with him, driving him to the point of exhaustion with his non-stop drills, would be saying nothing. He was far worse than Gunz's drill-sergeant during special forces training.

Gunz couldn't help but notice that Aidan was patient and respectful with the other members of his team, and it was only him whom he was driving up the wall with snide remarks and endless sarcasm. By the end of the two-hour training, between the physical exhaustion and constant mental strain to keep his emotions at bay, Gunz was at the end of his rope.

When Aidan finally announced that the training was over, he dropped on the dojang floor, breathing laboriously, his uniform soaked with sweat, and closed his eyes. A few minutes later, he felt a light touch to his shoulder and cracked his eyes half-open. Instructor Angel was squatting next to him, staring at him with a wide grin.

"You survived, little man," he said with his light Spanish accent, offering his hand and pulled him up. "I wonder if we'll see you tomorrow after Aidan's warm welcome." He laughed, and the other men joined him.

"I've been through worse. So, trust me, you'll see me tomorrow, Angel," muttered Gunz, wiping sweat off his forehead with the back of his hand. "And the day after tomorrow and the day after that."

* * *

BY THE TIME he walked out on the street, he could hardly move, his every muscle sore. The freshness of the evening air enveloped him, and he inhaled enjoying the cool touch of a light breeze to his hot skin. The restaurant was still opened, but his car was parked right in front of the school and this part of the parking lot was mostly vacant. He opened the door and heavily dropped on the driver's seat. He didn't start the car and for a few minutes, stared blankly at the dashboard, not sure if he had enough strength left in him to press the pedals.

The only thing he could think of was going back to his house and letting his guard down, allowing his power to run free. He needed to heal his aching body, but mostly he needed to relieve this constant pressure of keeping his emotions under control. He needed to unwind. He thought of *Missi's Kitchen* and how much he would love to have a shot of vodka right about now. Or three…

Gunz glanced back at the school. All the windows were dark, no one was inside. He smirked tiredly. He didn't see anyone walking out of the school. It could mean only one thing – every single man of the Elite team, including the owner of the establishment left the building by teleporting or by using a portal. All of them weren't human.

He reached toward the dashboard, ready to press the start button when he noticed a slight movement in the dark alley that was curving around the building toward the small parking lot behind the school. Gunz sharpened all his natural and supernatural senses. He still couldn't see clearly, but something was definitely moving in the shadows. He sighed and opened the car door. Since yesterday he encountered four demons on that same parking lot, he couldn't leave the area without checking it out first.

Quietly he slipped out of the car and softly closed the door, manually locking it. Trying to produce as little noise as possible, he stealthily ran toward the building. Luckily it was the night of a new moon and the plaza was mostly dark. Cautiously, he moved toward the alley, probing the area ahead of him. The closer he was getting to the dark alley the heavier he felt the presence of something dark and vicious.

Gunz reached the alley and stopped. There was nothing there, at least he couldn't see anything, but he could clearly feel the evil presence somewhere right in front of him. He sent some of his fire toward his hands, getting ready to fight and walked through the empty alley toward the parking lot.

He halted at the edge of the parking lot, pressing his back to the rough wall of the building and carefully peeked inside. The stench of dark magic was so intense that his stomach clenched and spasmed painfully. A menacing, multi-voiced growl carried through the deserted parking lot, making him shiver like from a cold wind. The whole space of the parking lot was filled with animals. Giant wolves of all colors were standing shoulder to shoulder, packed like anchovies in a can.

Even though it wasn't necessary, Gunz scanned the roaring

pack. It was obvious that these beasts weren't your regular run-of-the-mill wolves. *Werewolves?* he thought but right away dismissed this thought. It wasn't a full moon and these animals looked different than any werewolf he encountered before. *If not werewolves, then what?*

One blast of his full fire power and all these monsters would be gone. He glanced around to make sure that there were no humans anywhere in the area. A soft laughter broke through the continuous low growl of the pack and he heard more voices. People were leaving the restaurant, heading toward the alley to cross to *the Coral Grove*. He had just a few second to get rid of the pack. In fear of hurting innocent people, he let go of his elemental power and turned to his magic.

"Ignius," he shouted, and the stream of fire escaped his hands.

At the same time, the front row of beasts charged at him. They leaped in the air, their furry bodies taken by fire in an instant. For a moment they lingered in the air, looking like flaming torches in the darkness of the night and then softly fell on the ground in piles of ash.

Gunz pushed forward, unleashing one blast of smoldering fire after another on the howling pack. Once he made his way through to the other end of the parking lot, he turned around and ran. The monsters' hungry growl rose in the air, making it thick with an evil intent, and the infuriated pack charged after him. He remembered that close by there was an empty construction zone, and this was where he led the monsters.

He ran as fast as he could, once in a while glancing over his shoulder to make sure that the pack was still following him. Gunz reached the construction zone and hopped over the fence, ignoring the *No Trespassing* sign. The wolves didn't care to obey the local laws either, and they followed him like a howling dark tidal wave. Some of them jumped over the fence, but the rest of them just broke through it, demolishing it on their way.

Gunz zoomed through the construction zone, jumping over

the small holes in the ground and piles of construction materials, and avoiding the bigger obstacles. The hungry pack was following him closely, scurrying just a few feet away. Finally, he found what he was looking for and stopped. Right in front of him, there was a large hole in the ground. The excavation was completed, but the foundation of the house wasn't laid yet.

He probed the area for any human presence and since he didn't sense any, he jumped inside the hole, landing softly on his feet. He just had enough time to channel as much power as he could when the pack of monsters rained down on him. Gunz yelled, placing a protection spell over the hole in the ground to contain his fire and let his control go, reverting to the natural state of a Fire Salamander. His body dissolved into scorching flames and an obliterating wave of magical fire energy and real fire spread around him like a blast wave of a bomb. In a split-second every single monster was gone, burnt into ashes.

Gunz moaned and fell down on all fours, breathing laboriously with his open mouth. His body finally stopped aching, healed by his natural state, but at the same time he felt exhausted and completely drained. He fell flat on his stomach, feeling the coolness of the soft ground under him and closed his eyes. He didn't think that he had enough strength left in him to walk all the way back to his car and then drive home.

Slowly, Gunz scrambled to his feet and waved his hand, unrolling the fire-curtain of his portal. He got up with an effort and stepped through the curtain. He walked out in his backyard facing the backdoor to his house. Hardly moving his feet, he moved toward the door, thinking that finally he was home and he could relax when a gut-wrenching feeling of a dark presence assailed him. He snapped around and couldn't believe his eyes.

"Dammit," he swore quietly and added a few more choice words in Russian, frustration surging through him with unbelievable strength. He took a few breaths to calm down. He couldn't allow his power to escape his control and he needed a clear mind to think.

Just a few yards away from him, reeking with the dark energy of evil magic, there was another pack of wolves, just as big and vicious as the pack he was fighting behind the martial arts school. His whole backyard was infested with monsters. They were shifting, slowly advancing at him, and pushing him closer to the house.

He had no place to run. Living on a busy street, he couldn't think about using his natural state to destroy the pack and he was too exhausted and drained to use magic. Slowly he moved his hand down to his pocket and pulled out the key to the house. He was afraid that if he would turn his back on the pack just for a second to put the key into the keyhole, the pack would attack.

Pressing his back to the door, Gunz moved his hand behind his back and found the keyhole. Even any tiniest move he did was greeted by the pack with loud howls and hungry growls and by the time he managed to put the key into the keyhole and turn it, the pack was no more than a few feet away from him.

He pushed the door inside and staggered through the doorway. The pack launched at the same moment. Gunz pushed the door shut and locked it in one motion. The wolves impacted the closed door with a loud thud.

Breathing hard, Gunz opened himself to the magic checking the wards and protection spells around his house and couldn't contain a cry of aggravation. Everything was working against him. When Anatoly Karpenko visited him the other night, he brought his wards and protection spells down and Gunz didn't get a chance to restore everything yet.

Now, he was defenseless and whatever these wolves were, they weren't real animals and they weren't about to give up because of something as trivial as a locked door. The non-magical doors and locks were built to stop normal people from entering. They weren't going to stop professional burglars and for sure they were useless against anything that was magic.

Gunz heard people talking somewhere on the street next to his house. He had to make a choice and he had to make it quick. He was too drained to use magic and he couldn't use his natural state without killing everything human within a few hundred yards radius. But if wolves would break through the door and tear him apart, killing him, these innocent people on the street would die anyway.

Catch-22.

"Dammit! Dammit! Dammit!" Gunz squeezed his head with his hands, his fingers digging into his scalp, his brain working on overdrive.

He heard a set of loud bangs as the wolves pounded at the door with a mighty force. The walls of the house trembled at the impact and the plates in his kitchen cabinet jingled drearily.

What are these wolves? Not werewolves for sure. What the hell am I dealing with?

The next impact of the bloodthirsty furry monsters left a crack in the door and the walls of the house shook again. One more strike like this and the door would shatter into a million splinters. The unsuspecting people were laughing and chatting peacefully somewhere on the street right in front of his house...

Screw catch-22, he thought, trying to gather at least some magic in his drained body. Nothing.

No magic, no power, no strength. Gunz opened the drawer and pulled out a gun. He checked the magazine and threw the gun back into the drawer. He laughed bitterly, a short painful sound.

The bullets weren't silver.

~ ZANE BURNS, A.K.A. GUNZ ~

*T*he next impact came almost immediately and with a crashing force of a wild rhino. The door moaned but somehow withheld the pressure one more time. The bottom panel cracked nearly falling out, but the door was still hanging on its hinges. The wolves roared and seemed to get smarter. They regrouped, pulled back a little and attacked with reinforced strength, this time targeting not only the door, but also the large kitchen window.

Clever furry bustards! Gunz pulled his Swiss army knife out of his pocket, transforming it into a flaming sword. He wasn't going to give up without a fight. The door finally gave in under the pressure, shattering inward into a cloud of dust and slivers of wood. At the same time, with an ear-splitting noise, the window broke, spraying everything with pieces of glass.

He brought his sword above his shoulder and swung it at the first monster that jumped through the door. His sword slashed through the wolf, splitting him in two and setting his fur ablaze. But an avalanche of monsters already flooded the kitchen. They were coming through the unhinged, dismembered door and through the glassless window frame.

Pressing his back against the wall, Gunz screamed, desperately swinging his sword without aiming, cutting through and setting as many furry bodies on fire as he could. But he knew that he was just delaying the inevitable – he would be killed, and with him every human in the immediate vicinity would die too.

Gunz cried out as one of the monsters sank its fangs into his shoulder and another one bit into his leg but didn't drop his sword. However, the sharp pain made his control over the power waver and he almost lost it. As the fire flooded his tortured body, he took a ragged breath, struggling to regain full control. Something moved above him, and he felt the fire energy field spiked up all around him. He knew that it wasn't him, he was still in control, at least partially.

For one second when his attention faltered, it was enough for the monsters to take over. Sharp teeth captured his wrist and he dropped his sword. One heavy body after another landed on top of him, pushing him down to the ground. Gunz collapsed and curled into a tight ball, protecting his neck and face with his arms. The twinges of multiple bites fused into a continuous torment. He groaned, disregarding the agony of his body as his flesh was torn apart piece by piece, and focused on his mind, repeating the same words over and over like a mantra.

Don't die...

Don't pass out...

Stay in control...

Like through a wall, he heard someone yelling a joyful *"Yeeha"* and with the corner of his eye, he saw a fiery inferno unfolding above him. The fire ignited under the ceiling and then moved down, assaulting the monsters, igniting their furs. The foul stench of burnt hair and flesh hung heavily in the air. The wolves panicked, squealing in pain and fear. As some of them were dying devoured by hungry flames, the rest rushed out of the house creating a deadly stampede, crushing each other in the narrow doorway.

Through the broken door, Gunz saw something flaming zooming around the perimeter of the backyard and soon a wall of fire rose all around, blocking all the ways in and out. In a matter of a few minutes, every single monster was gone, and only piles of steaming ashes remained of a once formidable pack. The fire in the house and around the backyard subsided, leaving grey smoke and a burnt stench behind.

Gunz was lying down motionlessly, sprawled on the floor in a puddle of his own blood. He couldn't move even if he wanted to. He had no strength and the nonstop pain of the wolves' bites was stretching his control over the power to the limits. He moaned, thinking about that panic button on his watch that Jim installed for him. Without the wards and protection spells, he couldn't revert to his natural state to heal his anguished body, so maybe Jim could take him somewhere where there were no people... He tried to lift his arms to press the button, but he had no strength even for that and this small move just increased the pain tenfold, sending a wave of nausea to his throat.

"I need help... Kal..." he moaned, calling to his fierce mentor. He knew that without the fire he couldn't summon the Fire Elemental. But even though Kal wasn't a god, in his mind he was the only god he believed in, the only god worth praying to. And in the moment of desperate need, he prayed to his mentor, asking for help.

"The help is here, baby Salamander. What can I do for you?" He heard a high-pitched voice above his head.

Gunz raised his eyes and his mouth fell open. A small creature, about size of a house cat, with webbed wings and a long tale was hovering right above him. The creature looked like a miniature dragon, but he was sure it wasn't a dragon even though it had the distinct fire signature about it. It had only two paws and its long tale was ending in an arrow-shaped tip. Its body was covered in shiny red scales and its leathery wings shone with gold.

"What are you?" whispered Gunz flatly, too hurt and exhausted to sound surprised.

"I'm the mighty wyvern who is about to save your fireless ass," announced the little creature, spitting out a few tiny fireballs. "Kal sent me a while ago to keep an eye on you."

"Mighty what?" mumbled Gunz, incredulous.

"Wyvern," repeated the mini-dragon indignantly, cocking its head. "Don't you know your brothers in element, baby Salamander. Wyvern or Dragonet or Fire-drake. Any of these names ring the bell?"

"No... why would Kal send you... Did he run out of a full-size dragons?"

"Full-size dragons for full-size Salamanders," huffed the Wyvern, pouting like a little girl. "A mini-dragon for a mini-salamander."

"Fine, fine... I got the point... Sorry," whispered Gunz closing his eyes for a moment as the next wave of nausea enveloped him. "Do you have enough magic in you to restore the wards and protection spells around the house?"

"I have more magic and fire in me than you ever dreamed of," muttered the wyvern, jerking his wing toward the backyard. "Didn't I just cleanse your backyard off all those nasty mutts?"

"You sure did... I need my wards and all the spells restored... please..."

"Count to ten, boss," sang the wyvern and disappeared, leaving a hardly visible fire-trail behind.

The wyvern came back exactly ten seconds later and softly landed on Gunz's chest. Even this light pressure resulted in more pain and Gunz groaned, "Get off... hurts..."

"Your wards and spells are up and more powerful than they ever were, boss," announced the wyvern proudly, hovering in the air above Gunz's chest. "These Masters of Power... always multitasking between all the elements instead of learning how to use one properly. Did you know that the latest research shows that multitasking actually lowers your productivity?"

Gunz ignored the last statement of the chatty wyvern and probed the wards. The wyvern was right – the protection spells and wards around the house were more powerful than ever. The wyvern smiled, exposing his tiny sharp fangs.

"Believe me now, boss?" He landed on the kitchen table and waved his wings. "Come on, baby Salamander, show me the fire! Heal yourself."

Gunz sighed and let go, reverting to his natural state. The fire engulfed everything inside, quickly spreading through the house and filling everything within the walls of protection spells with a blistering heat. A few minutes later, it was all over. The fire slowly sizzled down and disappeared without a trace like it was never there in the first place. Back in his human form, Gunz pushed himself up, leaning his back against the wall. The pain was gone, but he felt dizzy and weak.

He pulled his phone out and dialed Jim's number. Jim answered right away, his voice thick with worry.

"Gunz," he said right away, "is everything okay?"

"No, not really," replied Gunz tiredly. "Some weird shit is going on. I need to come in, Jim. Just not right now. Can we meet tomorrow?"

"Yes, of course. 11 AM in my office?" asked Jim. "Just don't use your portal. Pretend that you're a normal human being and walk in."

Gunz chuckled weakly. "Yes, sir. I'll try to remember how to do that."

"See you tomorrow," said Jim and hung up the phone.

Gunz dropped the phone on the floor, his eyes closed, and he fell asleep.

* * *

THE MORNING SUN was beating through the broken window and door, shining directly into Gunz's face. He rubbed his eyes and blinked a few times, trying to understand where he was and how he got there. The events of the last night flashed in front of his eyes and he remembered everything. His bloodied sword was still on the floor next to him. He picked it up, turning it back into the knife and put it in his pocket. Pushing himself up with his arms, he got up. He was fine, no pain, no dizziness. Other than the intense craving for caffeine, he felt absolutely normal.

Gunz glanced at his wrist watch. It was only 8 AM, so he had more than enough time to get ready and make it to Jim's office by 11 AM. He swiped the splinters of glass off the kitchen counter and placed a new k-cup into his coffeemaker. Taking in his surroundings, he sighed. *Goddamn monsters,* he thought, shaking his head. Now he needed to clean everything in his kitchen and fix the door and the window. And he would need to place enchantments on the new door and window to make them fire-proof. With gratitude he thought of the Master of Power who insisted on teaching him how to do it on his own.

What were these monsters and why the hell were they so set on killing me?

"Good morning, boss!" Gunz turned around and found the wyvern sitting on top of the kitchen table. "I hope your morning is a lot less adventurous than your evening was." The wyvern grinned at him, displaying his white fangs and stretched his golden wings, basking in the warmth of the morning sun.

"Hey," said Gunz waving his hand at the wyvern. "Thank you for your help last night." The wyvern nodded. "By any chance do you know what kind of monsters those wolves were?"

"Don't you?" asked the wyvern, an exaggeratedly shocked expression in his round eyes.

"No, I don't," admitted Gunz, "otherwise I wouldn't be asking, would I?"

"Volkolaks, of course," said the wyvern, looking heavenward.

"A lot of them. I had never seen so many volkolaks in one place. That was some serious dark magic at work. I hope you know that unlike regular werewolves, volkolaks are created by a dark spell, not by some random bite."

"Yes, of course, I knew that. I just never came across one before," mumbled Gunz, wondering who wanted him dead.

To turn a man into a volkolak wasn't easy. It wasn't just any dark magic. The one who wielded it, had to be extremely power-ful, and considering the size of both packs, whoever wanted him dead was a power to be reckoned with. Gunz cringed, thinking that every one of these volkolaks at some point was a person. Even though he scanned both packs and didn't feel the presence of humanity in any of the monsters, he still felt remorseful. He kept asking himself if there was still a chance of reversing the dark magic, saving all those people.

"Well, thank you for the information and for your help," said Gunz again, but since the wyvern didn't move, he added, "You can leave and go home any time you want."

"No can do. Kal sent me here to take care of you. I do what Kal says," he said lightly, his eyes shifting to the coffee cup. "The coffee is ready."

Gunz took the cup of steaming coffee and inhaled its refreshing scent. The wyvern flew up and landed next to the coffeemaker, staring at Gunz sternly.

"Now what?" asked Gunz putting the cup down.

"Aren't you supposed to offer some coffee to your honored guest first?" he scolded, shaking his head reproachfully. "Where are your manners, Salamander? I should have a word with Kal. How was he teaching you?"

"Um, I'm sorry," mumbled Gunz, placing the coffee cup in front of the wyvern. "I didn't realize that mini-dragons drink coffee."

"Jeez Louise," huffed the wyvern, "I don't understand how the Great Salamander lets you run free in the human realms when you're such an ignoramus. He told me that you needed a body-guard. He never mentioned that I would have to play teacher too." He lowered his head into the cup and sampled the steaming coffee, closing his eyes joyfully. "Mmm, that's good. At least one thing you know how to do right."

Gunz sighed, getting the second cup of coffee ready. He got used his solitude and he wasn't sure that he needed this chatty and unbelievably invasive little roommate. But he wasn't about to start arguing with Kal. It was never a good idea to argue with a person who has complete control over you.

"What's your name?" asked Gunz. "Since you're not leaving any time soon, you might as well tell me how I should call you."

"You already know it," replied the wyvern dryly between slurps. "Mishka."

"I called my kitten Mishka —," started to say Gunz but then cut himself short. "Wait a minute…"

"Meow," said the wyvern grinning, sounding like a man who was trying to imitate a cat.

"You can shift? You were the kitten?"

"Ding-ding-ding," sung the Wyvern, sarcasm in his every word. "That was when I thought that I needed to guard you only in your home at night. But now that I know what kind of doofus you are and how amateurish you are when it comes to the elemental power and magic, I believe that I need to guard you every moment of the day."

"And how do you imagine doing that?" asked Gunz with a lopsided grin. "I'm not going to walk around the city with a tiny dragon on my shoulder. People are going to think that I'm some kind of crazy *Game of Thrones* castaway. Father of Dragons." He rolled his eyes and took a swig of his coffee.

"Father of Dragons my ass. You wish," muttered the wyvern. He lifted one of his legs, carefully balancing on the other and pointed at a small bracelet made out of some red stone that Gunz didn't notice before. "You see this? Magic… lets me shift into anything I want." Gunz moved his hand to touch the bracelet but the wyvern hopped back. "Hey, you, no touchy. Keep your hands to yourself."

"Fine," said Gunz, pulling his hand away. "Enlighten me. How are you planning to camouflage yourself?"

Mishka soundlessly vanished from the kitchen counter and the next moment, Gunz felt a sharp pain in his left ear. He slapped his hand to his ear and felt something hard and round under his fingers.

"What the hell?" he mumbled staring at his reflection in the dark glass of the cabinet. A large diamond stud earring was shining in his ear. "What the hell! Mishka, get out of my ear. I'm a man! And I'm not a pirate either. I don't wear earrings."

"*Sheesh, we're so touchy!*" Gunz heard Mishka's grumpy voice in his head and almost jumped. "*Fine. I'll come up with something else... I'm a man, hear me roar... Macho!*"

The next moment the earring vanished and Gunz felt a burning pain in his chest. "Mishka, are you exploring my pain barrier today?" he groaned, tearing the leftovers of his shirt off his chest. The reflection in the dark glass showed a fresh tattoo on his chest. It was depicting a dragon or perhaps a dragonet surrounded by dancing flames.

"Aw, hell no!" shouted Gunz, slamming his hand on the counter. "A tattoo? Not a chance. I treat my body like the temple and I don't need graffiti on my temples' walls."

"*Oh, for Fire's sake!*" yelled Mishka in his head. "*You already have some scribbling on your temple's wall. What's wrong with mine? You're just prejudice against my creative and imaginative expressions.*"

"A scribbling? This is my special forces tattoo!" exclaimed Gunz, running his fingers over his upper arm. "And this is the only tattoo I'll ever have. Am I clear?"

"*Fine,*" said Mishka and the tattoo vanished from his chest.

Gunz braced himself for the next spike of pain but nothing

happened. "Mishka, where are you?" he asked carefully, not quite sure that he wanted to find out.

"What time is it?"

Gunz glanced at his watch and took a sharp breath. The normally white face of Jim's watch was sporting a red outline in the shape of a wyvern with expended wings. Gunz brought the clock to his ear, hearing a soft ticking sound.

"Please tell me, you didn't break Jim's watch, you little varmint," hissed Gunz.

"Well, let me see," said Mishka, sarcasm overflowing, *"GPS, so your local pet owner could keep close tabs on you – check. The panic button, so you can cry for help like a little baby – check. Watch, the only useful functionality in this device – check. No, everything seems to be intact."*

"Damn, Mishka," mumbled Gunz, heavily sitting down on the only surviving chair, "why are you so acidy? What did I do to you to deserve this attitude?"

For a few seconds, the wyvern remained silent. Then Gunz heard him clearing his throat. *"It's in my nature. Deal with it, Salamander. I'm not going to change who I am to fit your needs."* But his voice softened up. *"So, can I ride in your watch then?"*

"Is it still going to show the right time?"

"At least twice a day it will," replied Mishka snidely.

Gunz sighed and went upstairs to get ready for the meeting with Jim.

"That's going to be an interesting ride," he muttered under his breath, thinking of his new companion.

"I heard that!" shouted Mishka, and Gunz felt a jolt of an electric shock in his wrist under the watch.

~ AIDAN ~

$\mathcal{I}$t was just eight in the morning, but Aidan was already in his office at the Elements Marital Arts. Uri and Angel were sitting in the room with him, displaying all the symptoms of infinite boredom. Uri was silently staring at his phone and it wasn't clear if he was reading something or was avoiding Aidan's eyes. Angel was leaning back in his chair, lazily throwing a tennis ball up in the air and catching it.

Aidan ignored their presence, nervously moving some papers around his desk. He picked up one of the documents and tried focusing on reading it but couldn't and dropped it back on the desk, slamming his hand on top.

"It's eight," he muttered, checking his watch, aggravation rising in him. "Why can't he be on time for once?"

"I didn't realize that it was such a vast emergency. Hello, everybody." A young man materialized in the office and raised his hand, greeting them. He was a little shorter than Aidan, and his figure, while well-shaped and athletic, was slender. He approached the desk and peered at the flower pot with a half-dead orchid in it, disapproval on his face.

"You forgot to water your flowers, Aidan. Again." He touched the flower with his finger and it bloomed under his touched, dried dead leaves replaced by fresh thick greenery, beautiful white flowers expending their tender petals.

"Sven. Thank God," muttered Uri. He shut down his phone and put it back in his pocket. "I don't think I could tolerate Aidan's killer mood for another minute."

"You're welcome! Oh wait... Which god were you thanking, Uri, if I may ask?" said Sven, an innocent look plastered on his round face, but his oversized turquoise eyes betrayed his mischievous intent.

"The one true God, of course," grumbled Uri, glaring at him warningly.

Sven laughed, ruffling his spiky blond hair with his hand. "Really? And was your one true God as nice as I am and said, *you're welcome* to you?" He winked at Uri and added, "Would you like to get deeper into the meaning of *one* and *true* —"

Aidan listened to them bickering and could hardly contain his annoyance. He got used to hearing their friendly arguments, it wasn't anything new, but today he was on edge and everything and anything was setting him off.

"We're not here for theological debates," cut Aidan short, rising. "Let's get to business. Uri, please tell us what you found out."

"I was right," said Uri, shrugging his shoulders. "Your young Salamander is working for the FBI. He's an FBI consultant, part of Agent Andrew's team. And we all know what Agent Andrews' specialty is, right?"

"Ahhh," exhaled Aidan, rubbing his stubbled chin with his hand tiredly. "Agent Andrews... He specializes in being a pain in my neck. I was so hoping that you were wrong, Uri. But I'll deal with it. Did you find out anything about his past? Where was he for the last twenty-seven years? What was he doing before he awakened the Fire Salamander in him?"

Uri sighed, his lips set in a straight line. He got up and stepped closer to Aidan. "Listen, Aidan. Can you just trust me? The boy is not a threat neither to you nor to Tessa. Be reasonable, old friend..." He put his hand on Aidan's shoulder squeezing it lightly. "He's just twenty-eight. Compared to any of us, he hardly even exists. Besides, he's Kal's boy... And you know how overprotective the Great Salamander is when it comes to his children. You don't want to mess with him. And your mentor is not going to appreciate it, if we get Kal hot under the collar."

"Are you talking about that little Fire Gecko that I met yesterday in the dojang?" asked Sven, his sandy eyebrows rising. "Twenty-eight? He's in his infancy. Why are you so worried about him, Aidan? You can kick his ass even without using your magic. Just show him a good fire extinguisher and he'll run for the hills, leaving his tail behind." He chuckled, and a bright phosphoric light ignited on the bottom of his large blue eyes. "Angel, what do you think?"

Angel remained silent, his dark gaze burying into Aidan. "It's up to you what you want to do, Aidan. You know that we all support you, no matter how crazy your ideas are," he said finally. "But myself, I would prefer to have this little Salamander as a friend, not as a foe."

"Why?" asked Aidan.

"I was watching you torturing him yesterday during training," replied Angel frowning. "You were abusing him, my friend. That wasn't like you at all and I was going to stop you a few times. Yet he remained calm and respectful all the way through training and he didn't lose control of his power even once. For someone so young and inexperienced, he's strong and focused. I don't think you have any reason to worry about him."

Aidan looked at his friends, his gaze slowly drifting from one face to the next. Inside, he knew that they were right, but he couldn't help feeling threatened by this young man. He wasn't afraid for his life or safety. He was afraid of losing Tessa. In his mind, he saw her gazing at this young man with curiosity in her brown eyes. What if she falls for him? A spike of jealousy struck through his heart and he felt blood draining from his face.

Through all his very long existence, he never let himself get attached to anyone. The way he felt about Tessa was confusing and frustrating, and her interest in this young Salamander, as slight as it was, was hurting him. He never felt like this before and he wasn't sure how to deal with it and what to do next.

"Uri, please," he said quietly, dropping back into his chair, "tell me everything you found out. I'm not going to do anything with this information, I swear. I just want to know what kind of a person we're dealing with... I want to be prepared. Just in case."

"We're dealing with a good man, Aidan," started Uri. "It wasn't easy to find out his background because the FBI covered his tracks well. But like you said, your connections are more powerful than the FBI." Uri smirked, sitting back down. "His real name is Vladislav Kirilenko. Alexander Burns is the alias that the FBI gave him. He was born in Belarus and lived most of his life there. He served in the spetsnaz – Belorussian special forces. Sniper. Multiple tours of combat duties. Besides high school, no college education —"

"I want to know who he's hiding from and why the FBI is covering for him," said Aidan, softly interrupting his friend.

"It's a good story, you may actually like it," said Uri smirking. "Zane and two of his friends, without any support, destroyed a full branch of the Russian mob. In a matter of a few hours, they killed them all, blew up four SUVs and burned their house. Just the three of them. Both his friends were wounded, and Zane pulled them out of the house before burning everything to the ground. My guess is that this was when he discovered his Fire. It happened slightly over two years ago."

"Yeah, that's what he said," murmured Aidan, mindlessly playing with a silver coin, twirling it between his fingers, "about two years ago... Something still doesn't add up... If he is in

Florida slightly over a year, where did he spend that one year between him discovering his power and moving here?"

"I couldn't find anything concrete on this period of his life, but it's not hard to guess," said Uri. "Zane told you that Kal was his mentor, right?" Aidan nodded. "Do you know where Kal resides most of his time?"

"Yes, of course," said Aidan with a light shrug. "Outside our realm, in Kendral."

"So, my guess, he spent this year in Kendral with his mentor, learning how to control his Fire," continued Uri. "And from what I see, Kal trained him well. As far as the FBI – they cover for him because he helps them keep this city safe from things that go bump in the night. Aidan, Zane is a good man, stop torturing him."

"Agreed," said Angel, joining him.

"Okay, I'll promise to be nicer to him. That's assuming that he'll show up tonight," agreed Aidan, getting up. "But let's see how strong and focused he really is."

Aidan approached Sven and put his hand on Sven's shoulder. Then he bent down and whispered something in his ear. Sven's jaw dropped, and humor reflected in his large eyes.

"Are you sure you want to do it?" asked Sven, staring up at Aidan. Aidan flicked his eyebrow at him, suppressing a smile, but the corners of his mouth lifted a little. "I think I'll have fun with it."

"Wait!" exclaimed Uri, jumping to his feet, stretching his hand to Sven to stop him, but he wasn't fast enough. The young man just snickered and vanished from the room. Uri turned to Aidan, his eyes glowing with golden light.

"Aidan," he growled, throwing his hands in the air, "please tell me you didn't just send the trickster after Zane."

"Maybe," replied Aidan with a sly wink and vanished from the room.

* * *

AIDAN MATERIALIZED in his penthouse apartment. Even after everything that Uri told him, he still felt uneasy. Something was bothering him, but he couldn't put his finger on what it was. This dreadful feeling was going far beyond his worries about Tessa's safety or her possible affairs of the heart. There was something else going on, and he was still trying to figure out how all the moving parts were tied together – Tessa, the Fire Salamander, demons attack, and an upir in the dental office. There had to be a connection.

He walked into his closet and quickly undressed, changing into light linen pants and drawstring white shirt. At first, he was going to teleport to his favorite part of the beach but then changed his mind. It was close to 9 AM and he was sure that the beach wasn't empty.

Aidan pressed the elevator button and waited until the doors softly opened. He walked inside and clicked *G/L* on the computer screen. The elevator moved down fast and soundless. A few seconds later, Aidan walked out of the building and crossed the patio, heading toward the beach.

Despite the pleasant weather, the beach was relatively empty. Just a few people were relaxing on beach chairs here and there, and a young couple was on their morning run. He walked slowly along the shoreline, looking for a place where there were no people at all. Soon, he found a secluded area between two trees. Their branches were so low that they were almost lying down on the sand. The sandy area wasn't large in this place, most of the beach devoured by the hungry ocean.

Aidan sat down on the sand and pulled his knees to his chest, resting his folded arms on his knees. For a while, he sat quietly, staring wistfully at the ocean. The waves softly rushed to the shore, getting his shoes and his pants wet, but he didn't seem to notice. He listened to the gentle whisper of the waves, enjoying the touch of the light morning breeze.

"My sister," he whispered into the wind, his voice merging with the murmur of the ocean. "My fair-shouldered sister... I miss you so much." Sadness crushed him, and his throat tightened for a moment. "I wish you were here with me, my darling sister. I feel so lost..."

No one answered. Nothing broke the silence around him – just the same even rush of the waves, whisper of the wind and piercing screeches of seagulls. He bowed his head, hiding his face in his folded arms and sighed.

A sudden splash of water and a touch of a cold wind made him raise his head. The weather was quickly deteriorating before his eyes. Aidan tried to get up, but the next wave rolled over him, drenching him in the salty water from head to toe. He jumped to his feet, coughing and surveyed his surroundings. He couldn't see anything, but he knew that something wasn't right. Natural weather could never change that fast.

He channeled the magic, and his eyes shone with a bright white light. He still couldn't see anything, but he detected a strange icy presence somewhere next to him. It wasn't strong enough for him to recognize what it was, but his heart thundered against his chest with an expectation of trouble.

"Aiiii-dannnnn..." He heard a soft whisper in his head and his every muscle tensed at this unexpected invasion. "I see you, boy..."

The voice disappeared, and the sun was shining again.

~ ZANE BURNS, A.K.A. GUNZ ~

The elevator stopped softly on the eighth floor of the FBI building. Gunz walked out of the elevator and opened the glass double door of Jim's office. He surveyed the large room with a few desks and a couple of small offices at the opposite wall. It had been a while since he met with Jim in his office, almost a full year, but nothing had changed here. A few agents were standing around one of the desks, talking about something quietly. As soon as he walked past them, they broke their conversation and stared at him with curiosity.

Gunz proceeded to Jim's office and knocked on the door. A moment later, he heard a loud "come in" and walked inside the room. Jim was sitting at his desk, scowling at the computer screen like it was his worst enemy. He hardly glanced at Gunz over the top of the monitor and waved at an empty chair.

"Hey, Gunz," he mumbled, without pulling his eyes off the screen. "Is everything okay? Yesterday you sounded like a train ran you over."

"Oh yeah?" asked Gunz. He didn't sit down but stopped in front of the wall with a city map and pictures of victims from the case he was working on. "Well, maybe a train did run me over... at least it felt like that yesterday."

"Very good... Tell me about it," murmured Jim, his attention elsewhere, his fingers furiously clucking at the computer keyboard like he was trying to knock nails into each key. "I'm... listening..."

"I see that you're giving me your full and undivided attention," said Gunz, biting his lip to contain his laughter.

"Yes, of course." Jim nodded absentmindedly and waved his hand to proceed. Gunz leaned on the wall, folding his arms over his chest and stared at Jim with a lopsided smirk.

"Well, I thought I would walk into the main hall of the Diplomat hotel during one of the business conventions and turn myself into a Fire Salamander in front of all the people there. Do you think it's a good idea?"

"Uh-huh," mumbled Jim, nodding.

"And maybe, I'll bring a few dragons from Kendral to do a little fire show there too. What do you think?"

"Dragons... yeah..." repeated Jim, shuffling through the open windows on his computer screen. "Sounds interesting... What? Dragons? Excuse me?"

Jim finally pulled his attention off the screen and looked up at Gunz, meeting his eyes, sparkling with humor.

"Okay, you got me," said Jim chuckling. He pushed the button on the computer screen and shut it down. "Sorry. I'm listening now."

Gunz reached in his pocket and pulled two pictures out. Then he took a couple of pins from the desk and secured both pictures to the wall with the pins. He tapped at the photo of Anatoly Karpenko with his finger and turned to Jim.

"Guess who visited me in my own house a couple of days ago?" he asked.

Jim paled, his face getting that cold look that was reserved for urgent situations that everyone in his team knew so well.

"He came to you alone? What did he want?" he asked, getting up and approaching the wall with the map.

"He wanted me to be his personal assassin. And he asked me so nicely that I just couldn't say no," replied Gunz through gritted teeth. He pointed at the picture of the young woman that he pinned to the wall above the photo of Anatoly. "He wants me to kill her. Agent Andrews, meet Eve."

As concisely as he could, Gunz gave Jim all the important details of his conversation with the head of the Russian Mob. Then he covered everything that happened from the moment Anatoly left his house, including the fight with the upir in the dental office and the double attack of volkolaks.

"Do you know anything about this Eve?" asked Jim, his fore-head creased as he observed the photo.

"Except her name and the fact that she is a creature of magic, I know nothing," replied Gunz, pulling the chair out, sitting down. "Well, I also know that she's one evil bitch. I checked out the dental office where Dmitri Koval was killed, and I must tell you, since I became the Fire Salamander, I have never sensed such a dark and malignant energy signature as hers."

"Do you know what she is?" Jim opened his computer again and was quickly typing in some notes.

"No. I can tell that the residual energy of her magic had traces of demonic presence. So, possibly she's a demon. But not a garden-variety demon. I'm sure that the upir in the dental office and the attack of volkolaks were her handy work. Whatever she is, she's so powerful that she could turn hundreds of people into volkolaks. I don't know anyone who has this kind of power."

"Let me run her photo through the facial recognition program," suggested Jim. He got up and snapped a photo of Eve's picture with his cellphone. "Let's see if I can find out anything about her. I'll get Angelique to check her out too."

"Thank you, Jim," said Gunz, twisting an FBI pen in his fingers. "I doubt that you'll find anything in your FBI database on her. But maybe you can give me some information on Aidan McGrath, the owner of *Elements Martial Arts* and Tessa Donovan, his student. I still don't know what or who Aidan is, and I have a feeling that Tessa is somehow connected to everything that's going on. So, anything you can give me would help."

Gunz got up and put the pen back on the desk. He was going to say his goodbyes to Jim when the phone on his desk rang. Jim raised his hand, asking Gunz to stay and picked up the phone.

"Agent Andrews." He listened to someone on the other side, nodding. "When did it happen... Yes, please forward everything you have... Yes, and forensic files too... Everything."

Jim listened for a few more minutes, his hands squeezing the phone and then hung up. He raised his eyes at Gunz, troubled.

"I think you can expect another visit from your Russian friend," he said quietly. "Last night, Vasyli German was found dead in his house. No sign of forced entry or any kind of foul play. Matches the offender's M.O. on the other six cases we have so far. Vasyli was another close friend and um... colleague of Anatoly Karpenko."

"Eve doesn't take her time," muttered Gunz, biting his lip. "I thought she was supposed to give Anatoly a full week before she started killing off his people."

"Gunz, we need to move faster, or more innocent people will die," said Jim.

"You mean, innocent gangsters?" Gunz chuckled humorlessly and his steel eyes got darker. "I need to move faster, Jim, or my only friends are as good as dead. You understand that? And I have no idea where to look for this woman or how to fight her."

"I'm sorry, Gunz, you're right," said Jim. "For you, it's personal."

Gunz closed his eyes for a moment, his lips pressed tight together. "Jim, do you know who this highly-influential and powerful person is? Eve wants him out of the picture because she's afraid of him. Possibly he could be the key to fighting her."

Jim shook his head no. He came back to the wall and pinned two more cards on the map. A card with a large question mark on it, he placed next to the photo of Eve and a card with the name "Vasyli German", he put next to the photo of Dmitry Koval.

"At least now some connections are starting to take shape," he said quietly.

Jim took a red thread from his desk and wrapped it around the pins, connecting the photo of Eve with Anatoly, and the photo of Anatoly with the picture of Koval and the card with Vasyli German's name on it. Then he connected the photo of Eve with the question mark. Gunz observed the wall and took two blank cards from Jim's desk. He wrote a name on each card – Aidan McGrath and Tessa Donovan.

"Here," he said, offering both cards to Jim. "I don't know where these two would fit in, but I'm sure, both of them are involved somehow."

Jim pinned two new cards to the wall, connecting them with each other and turned to Gunz, staring at him with narrowed eyes. Then he took a few of the yellow cards from his desk and wrote: upir, four demons, two packs of volkolaks.

"Something tells me that your name should be on this wall of fame too, Gunz," muttered Jim, pinning the yellow cards to the wall. "You were present during all these attacks. Tessa Donovan was present only at two."

Jim connected Tessa's card with the cards that said "Upir" and "Four Demons". Gunz took a white card and wrote his name on it – Zane Burns. Then he took a yellow card and wrote "Succubus". He pinned both cards to the wall, connecting his name with all the yellow cards and also with Anatoly's, Tessa's and Aidan's cards.

"Succubus?" Jim asked, trying not to laugh. "A succubus attacked you? I'm sure it was terrifying."

Gunz glanced at him and rolled his eyes. "I hope you realize that succubi are demons and they can be deadly to a man, Jim. Don't underestimate them. Just because it'll go for your crotch instead of your throat, it doesn't make it any less dangerous. And it didn't attack me. It tried to seduce me using its magic. Why I found it strange, was because succubi are extremely sensitive to the energy of magic. But this one didn't recognize the Fire Salamander in me."

Jim took a couple of steps back and observed the wall like an artist observing his work. Then he tapped Gunz once on his shoulder.

"I'm sorry, man," he said, true regret underlying his voice. "I got you involved and forced you right in the middle of this mess. If you want out, you're free to stop the investigation any time you want. Despite what your intimidating mentor wrote to me, you're a free man. I don't want you to feel like you're obligated to obey my every command. I had no right to put you in harm's way."

"I know that, Jim. First of all, you didn't force me," objected Gunz. "Second, it's a lot safer for me to be in the middle of this magical mayhem than for you. I'm immortal after all. I'll survive. And last, I don't know what Kal wrote to you and I don't give a damn. I work with you because I love my job. I spent many years in the military and I learned to respect the chain of command. But I comply with your commands because I agree with your decisions. Having said that, you can't force me to do anything I don't want to." Gunz winked at him and got up.

"Uhhh, you're in so much trouble, little Salamander. I heard what you said about your master." Mishka's voice rang in Gunz's head and he cringed inwardly. He totally forgot about the little spy that was hiding inside his watch. *"I'm so going to tell Kal everything."*

"I'll deal with you later, little rat," whispered Gunz, raising his watch up, like he was checking the time. Right away an electric shock pierced his body, originating in the watch and traveling all the way to his toes. Gunz grunted and squeezed his hand into a tight fist, fighting the desire to smash the watch together with its pesky passenger into pieces.

"Did you say something?" asked Jim, gazing at Gunz with curiosity.

"I was saying that it's time for me to go," replied Gunz, pointing at his watch. "I still have a few things that I need to take care of before I go for my next Taekwondo training tonight. Unfortunately, last night after the fight with the first pack of volkolaks, I left my car in the parking lot in front of the martial arts school. So, I have to use Uber all day today. It slows me down a bit."

"What do you need to do?" asked Jim, opening the door for him.

"The volkolaks destroyed my backdoor and broke the kitchen window," explained Gunz, maneuvering between the desks. "I need to go to Home Depot and get a new door and glass to install. And then I need to place the spell on all the new stuff to make everything fire-resistant. Luckily I learned how to do it myself and I don't need to ask a Master of Power for help."

"You can install a new window glass on your own?" asked Jim, his dark eyebrows rising.

"Yeah, I've done that a few times. I can do it on my own." Gunz smirked. Jim seemed to be more shocked by the fact that he could do a handyman's job than that he knew how to place his own fire-proofing spells that were normally performed by the Masters of Power.

"Fine," said Jim, shaking his hand. "At least bring me your receipts for the Home Depot shopping and for your use of Uber. Let the Bureau reimburse your expenses."

The elevator door opened with a soft hissing sound and Gunz walked inside. "Thank you, Jim," he said, giving Jim a quick nod as the elevator door closed.

~ ZANE BURNS, A.K.A. GUNZ ~

*I*nstalling a window and a new door ended up being a lot harder than Gunz expected and quite a few times he cursed Eve, her volkolaks and everything else associated with any dark magic. By the time he finished with the installations, made everything fire-resistant and cleaned up the mess, he hardly had enough time to take a shower and call Uber.

Ignoring the unusually talkative Uber driver, Gunz checked his watch. The traffic was heavier than usual, and he was running late for his training. *Oh, shit... Aidan is going to skin me alive for being late. It's not like he was gentle with me before,* he thought, staring at the bumper-to-bumper traffic ahead. *Next time I see Kal, he better teach me how to teleport.*

As soon as the car stopped in front of the martial arts school, Gunz threw a few bills into the driver's hands, grabbed his bag with equipment and ran inside the building. Gunz opened the door and bowed before entering the dojang. The training already started. As soon as he stepped on the floor, everyone stopped what they were doing and stared at him, some with surprise, some with sarcastic smirks, and only Tessa's face lit up with a friendly smile.

Aidan McGrath strolled across the floor, his expression betraying no emotions, and halted in front of him. Gunz braced himself for his usual snide remarks, but still gave him a traditional Taekwondo bow, showing his respect.

"I'm sorry, I'm late, Master McGrath," he said calmly. "My job responsibilities held me longer than I expected, sir."

Aidan stared down at him for a moment but then smiled. A smile coming from Aidan McGrath? Gunz wasn't sure if it was a good thing for him or a bad one.

"Don't be late again," Aidan said calmly, returning his bow. "Join the training, Zane. Let's don't keep the team waiting."

That can't be good, thought Gunz, stepping in line with Instructor Uri, *I'm sure he'll show what he really thinks during the training.*

But it didn't happen. It seemed that Aidan made a hundred-eighty-degree turn. He treated Gunz just like everyone else, with patience and respect. The only thing he noticed was that Aidan kept Tessa as far away from him as he could. Through the duration of the two-hour long training, he wasn't able to exchange a word with her. After the training was over, Aidan pulled Tessa into his office and when Gunz was leaving, they were still there.

To Gunz it was obvious that Aidan had feelings for Tessa. The way he looked at her, and the way he reacted when Gunz told him that Tessa was attacked by an upir and was in the hospital. Mighty Master McGrath was wearing his heart on his sleeve and anyone with eyes could see how he felt about Tessa.

Anyone but him and the object of his affection, thought Gunz as he walked to his car.

What wasn't clear to him was why Aidan thought that he was a threat. Tessa was a nice girl and he had to admit that he would like to have her as a friend. But he knew her for too short of a time and there couldn't be anything between them except friendship. He never gave Aidan any reasons to think otherwise.

He sat down in his car and pushed the start button, thinking that he was done with Uber forever. The engine screeched and with a loud bang, the car jerked and fell silent.

"What the hell?" mumbled Gunz and pushed the start button again.

The engine barked, something clapped and banged inside the car and a light white smoke swirled up from beneath the hood. Gunz cursed quietly, slapping his hand on the steering wheel and pushed the button to open the hood. As soon as the hood popped open, a cloud of white smoke puffed up and hung above the car.

He walked around and waved his hand to get rid of the hot cloud. He peered inside, checking for any visible defects but couldn't see anything out of the ordinary.

"God damn these new cars," he muttered closing the hood, "nothing is visible from outside."

The car wasn't even hot. It was sitting on the parking lot doing absolutely nothing for over twenty-four hours. Where did this hot smoke come from? He decided to try again. As soon as he pushed the start button, the whole car jerked, something knocked loudly under it and clanked inside.

Gunz pulled his cell phone out and punched in the AAA number. At least he got lucky with that. There was a AAA truck not too far away and his wait time was only fifteen minutes. He sat inside the car with his eyes closed. He wasn't sleeping, just tired and frustrated. When the AAA driver knocked on his door, he jolted up, hitting his head on the ceiling. He gave the driver the address of his mechanic's shop and watched the tow truck leaving the plaza with his vehicle.

At first, he was going to call Uber again, but as soon as he turned his phone on and saw the icon of the Uber app, he changed his mind. He didn't think that right now he could tolerate another long drive with another chatty driver or talkative people.

Gunz jogged around the school to the small parking lot in the back and quickly surveyed the area. There was no one here. The parking lot was dark and pleasantly empty. He waved his hand, opening the fire-curtain of his portal and walked through it, counting seconds to the moment when he could finally lie down and close his eyes.

He walked out of the portal and yelped in pain. Instead of standing in his own backyard, he found himself in the middle of his neighbor's swimming pool, up to his chest in cold, well-chlorinated water. At the touch with the cold water, his whole body got twisted with dull pain and as if that wasn't enough, an electric shock struck through him, making all his muscles spasm.

Mishka rushed out of his watch and was hovering over him, angrily spitting fireballs in his direction.

"What's wrong with you, Salamander!" he yelled, hopping up and down over his head. "Decided to go for an evening swim without taking your watch off? Don't you know that water hurts?"

Gunz exhaled and didn't say anything, slowly moving toward the edge of the pool. His skin was burning at the touch with the cold water. He was exhausted, drained and pissed, so he put all his efforts into keeping his cool and controlling his power. He finally made it out of the pool and stood still for a moment, water dripping down off his shivering body.

Slowly he made it out of his neighbor's backyard and crossed over to his own. He mumbled a quick spell checking his wards and protection spells and walked inside the house. After he locked the door, Gunz re-enforced his wards, making them stronger and rushed upstairs, where he stripped all his soaked clothes off, dropping them on the floor in a wet pile. Standing absolutely naked in the middle of his bedroom, he channeled some fire, heating up his skin. The water slowly evaporated, surrounding him with soft swirls of hot steam.

Mishka materialized in the bedroom and sprayed him with fire. At the touch of his element, Gunz sighed and relaxed. At least the nagging pain was gone. He picked up his pants, dripping with water and pulled out his wallet, cellphone and FBI consultant badge. His cellphone was fine, thanks to the waterproof case, but everything inside his wallet and his FBI badge were soaked with water.

He cursed again and dropped down on the bed, hiding his face in his hands. How did he manage to open his portal to a wrong location? Thank God, no one saw him. It never happened to him before. He couldn't count how many times he opened a portal to his backyard and he never missed the right location even by a foot. Something wasn't right.

"Why don't you relax, boss," said Mishka peacefully, landing on his shoulder. "Don't take it hard. Happens to the best of us."

"Doesn't happen to me," growled Gunz, rubbing his temples with his fingers. "It's just that I've been under a lot of stress lately."

"Sure, you were," purred Mishka sympathetically into his ear, stroking his hair with his wing, "you just need to try it again and I'm sure you'll perform just fine. You were opening this portal while you were tired, upset about your vehicle and stressed a little... Plus it was your first time opening the portal in front of me, probably the performance anx—"

"I do not have performance anxiety," roared Gunz, wiping the wyvern off his shoulder with one move of his hand. "Someone is messing with me! And you know what, Mishka, why don't you go annoy someone else for a change. I need my rest!"

"But why?" asked Mishka, pouting. "I like annoying you. It's fun!"

"Ugh." Gunz fell on his back and pressed a pillow over his face, hugging it with his arms. He moaned into the pillow. "Please... I'm begging you... go away... Please!"

"Fine, boss, I got it," said Mishka, pulling the blanket from under Gunz. "You need your beauty sleep. Now lie down..."

Gunz sighed and pulled himself up on the bed, putting the pillow under his head. Mishka threw a blanket over him and disappeared. Gunz closed his eyes and slowly started to drift asleep when he heard a soft humming. Unwillingly, he half-opened his eyes and saw Mishka sitting on the pillow next to him, singing.

"Mishka... I thought you were gone. What are you doing now?" he mumbled.

"Singing you a lullaby, so you sleep better, of course," said the wyvern proudly. "I have an amazing singing voice, don't you think?"

"Yeah... You're the next *American Idol*," muttered Gunz, feeling at his wit's end. "Now shut the hell up, you little flying rat, before I exterminate you."

Mishka huffed indignantly and vanished from the room.

"Next time I see Kal, remind me to give him my piece of mind..." Gunz mumbled, turning to his side and fell asleep almost immediately.

* * *

DIFFERENT PEOPLE REACT DIFFERENTLY to the sound of a gunshot. Some people stare into the black abyss of the gun barrel, consumed by panic so intense that their mind and body freezes in place, devoured by terror. They can't move, can't think and even the instinct of self-preservation can't rip them out of this state. Some people panic, run around, scream, cry, unable to think rationally and do anything to protect themselves.

And then there is one more category of people, whose mind reacts to the gunfire or any kind danger by becoming sharp and focused. The clarity of their mind and the speed of thinking increases exponentially, and their body becomes a cold, precise instrument of their highly-alert brain.

The dry sound of gunshots filled Gunz's ears, immediately tuning his mind into a state of extreme vigilance. A thunderous sound of an explosion overlapped the barking of guns and immediately, three more explosions followed. He stared in the direction of the sound, trying to sort out everything that was going on.

Where am I and how did I get here? A thought flew through his mind and disappeared as he had no time to think about it.

"Gunz! Cover me!"

He recognized the voice of his friend Sasha in the communication system and pulled the scope of his sniper rifle to his eye. He saw Sasha fighting his way toward a house, surrounded by a few hostiles. Everything looked excruciatingly familiar – a blast from the past. From his past.

"Gunz! Are you sleeping?"

Good question. Gunz aimed at the man closest to his friend and softly pressed the trigger. His rifle jerked back against his shoulder and the man fell. He aimed at the next hostile and pressed the trigger again, sending another man tumbling down, clearing the path for his friend.

"Gunz, Sergei is inside. I'm going in..." He watched Sasha disappearing behind the door of the house and he remembered what he did next. He got up and ran downhill toward the house, holding his rifle in his hand.

What am I doing? It can't be real. I'm dreaming...

Gunz clearly remembered falling asleep in his house in Florida and everything that happened before that. He had to be sleeping. But everything felt so real – the rocketing of the gun fight, the thunderous booms of explosions, the smell of gunpowder mixed in with the stench of burnt car oil.

He came to a sharp halt right next to the house and surveyed the area. It was just a dream, it had to be. He was reliving one of his most painful memories – the time when he discovered the fire within him. He didn't want to... no, he couldn't go through all that again.

It's a dream, concluded Gunz. *Dammit! Why can't I just scream and wake up?*

A man jumped in front of him. The gun in his hand flared with bright light, spitting fire, and Gunz felt a push in his shoulder, followed by a burning pain. Reactively, he raised his rifle pointing it in the man's direction and pressed the trigger without aiming, killing him instantly. The kickback radiated through his body, followed by an agonizing pain in his wounded shoulder. He clasped his hand to his wound, staring at the warm streams of red thick liquid running down his fingers with shock.

He was bleeding. Real blood. And the pain was more than real too.

Gunz reached for the fire but couldn't find it. His magic was gone too. *What's going on?* The pain was becoming too much to handle. He screamed and spun around, searching for anything that would help him escape this nightmare. A loud buzzing filled his ears and bright flares of light, green and red, followed.

For a split-second, everything went dark and when Gunz was able to see again, he found himself on the floor of his bedroom. He jumped to his feet and a sharp pain in his shoulder responded to his move. He groaned and touched his shoulder tentatively. His hand was covered in blood. The gunshot wound was real.

How is that possible? Gunz turned around searching for Mishka, but the wyvern wasn't in his bedroom.

"Mishka!" he yelled, and the wyvern materialized in front of him right away.

"Boss, you're bleeding," acknowledged Mishka. He cocked his head, staring at him with interest. "Did you shoot yourself?"

"Ahh, of course not!" yelled Gunz, clasping the bleeding wound on his shoulder. "I was going to ask you if you noticed anyone coming in or out while I was sleeping? Or a presence of any kind of magic, other than mine?"

"I was downstairs, hunting. One has to eat," said Mishka, scratching his head with his golden wing. "Didn't notice anything or anyone."

"Hunting? Where?" mumbled Gunz.

"In your refrigerator, of course," replied Mishka, shrugging his wings.

"But of course." Gunz chuckled, carefully probing the wards

and protection spells. All his spells and wards were in place. So, if someone was messing with him, he or she had to be powerful enough to do it, bypassing all his defensive magic.

The pain in his shoulder was making him nauseous. Gunz let go, reverting to his natural state and quickly healed the wound. When he came back to his human form, he heard the *Enter Sandman* ringtone blasting in his bedroom, accompanied by a loud rumbling of vibration. This ringtone meant that the caller wasn't in his contact list. He grabbed his cell phone from the bed stand and stared at the screen.

3:23 AM.

Coral Springs, FL.

A phone number he didn't recognize.

*B*y the time Aidan walked Tessa out of his office, it was close to 10 PM. Everyone left earlier, and their steps were echoing loudly on the marble tiles of the empty lobby. Aidan wanted to walk Tessa to her car, but she gave him one scorching gaze and he backed off right away. He didn't even try to open the door for her, but she noticed that he stayed in the lobby, watching her until she got into her little Honda and started driving away from the parking lot.

As her car moved through the evening city streets, she rehashed her conversation with Aidan. It wasn't the first time she stayed behind to talk to him, but something was different about this time. Aidan was different. He was stressed and looked tired. He asked her about Dr. West and what happened in the dental office. When she told him her side of the story, he kept interrogating her, digging into every little detail until she got tired and cut him off.

The biggest challenge was explaining to him what Zane was doing in her office and then in the hospital. And at the end, he demanded that she stay away from Zane, telling her that he couldn't be trusted. She was still boiling about that. *Who is he to tell me who I can or cannot associate with?* Tessa thought furiously as she drove through the gates of her condominium community.

She remembered the look on his face when she yelled at him for trying to control her relationships and her life. He looked sad and a little desperate. Then he tried to apologize and tell her that the only reason he mentioned that was because he was worried about her safety.

As she walked out of the car and the cool evening breeze brushed through her long hair, Tessa sighed, regretting her behavior. Her hot blood started to cool down and now she was looking at everything in a slightly different light. Come to think of it, Aidan didn't do anything wrong or out of character.

Since that memorable evening, when he carried her into his school in his arms, he always cared about her wellbeing and did everything to make sure that she was safe and had everything she needed. He was like her overprotective older brother – ready to come to the rescue at the first sign of trouble. Tessa decided that tomorrow she'd talk to him and set it all straight.

She walked up to the door of her condo and reached into her bag for the key. At the same time, her neighbor Mrs. Rosenberg opened her door and slowly walked outside with her little old Pomeranian Daisy. Both the old lady and the dog were tiny, had fluffy yellow-orange hair, and biddy round eyes. She noticed Tessa and waved her hand.

"Hello darling," she said, her brown eyes smiling kindly.

"Hi Mrs. Rosenberg, what are you doing outside this late?" asked Tessa smiling back at her. She liked this little old lady and her little old dog. Since Tessa moved back into her mom's condo, Mrs. Rosenberg always found a reason to stop by and bring freshly baked cookies or invite her for dinner.

"Aw, it's nothing, darling," she said, waving her wrinkled hand dismissively. "Daisy is a bit restless tonight. She keeps squealing and crying, and I thought I'd take her out to get some fresh air."

She sighed, massaging her left shoulder with her fingers deformed by arthritis. "But to be honest with you, my joints are bothering me today more than ever. I won't be surprised if the weather will start changing tomorrow... Well, you have a good night, honey. And do come by for dinner before your karate practice tomorrow..."

"Thank you, Mrs. Rosenberg," said Tessa, but as she watched the old lady shuffling away, slowly and heavily stepping on her sore feet, she sighed and rushed after her. "Why don't you go home, Mrs. Rosenberg. I'll walk with Daisy and bring her back in a few minutes."

Fifteen minutes later, Tessa returned Daisy back to Mrs. Rosenberg and finally walked into her apartment. She took a quick shower and climbed into her bed, feeling her every muscle throbbing with tiredness.

A half hour passed but Tessa still couldn't sleep. In the quietness of her bedroom, she could hear Daisy howling and the wooden floor moaning under Mrs. Rosenberg's heavy steps. Tessa turned to her side and pressed a pillow over her ear. Little by little her exhausted body won the war with her overly vigilant mind, and she fell asleep.

* * *

TESSA WOKE UP WITH A START. She sat up right and searched around, her heart beating heavily against her rib cage. The room wasn't dark – she always kept a nightlight on, but in the dim light of her starry globe, she didn't notice anything unusual. Except for the semi-transparent form of Mrs. Rosenberg, glowing with a soft white light, that was levitating right above her bed, everything else was as usual.

"Holy mother of pearl!" she yelped, jumping off the bed. "Are you dead or something?"

"Or something," replied Mrs. Rosenberg dryly, slowly gliding down to the floor, now levitating in front of Tessa. "What do you think?"

"Oh, no... Mrs. Rosenberg," whispered Tessa, sadness constricting her throat and filling her eyes with tears.

Probably the most adaptive species in nature are human beings. People can get used to pretty much anything. Tessa remembered how terrified she was when she started to see the spirits of the dead. But now she felt nothing but deep sadness. She was still uncomfortable with her ability, but mostly because she didn't know what it was and how to use it. She didn't know what she was and why she had this power. But after seeing what Zane could do and realizing that she wasn't the only supernatural freak in this universe, she started to feel better and the fear slowly melted away.

"Don't Mrs. Rosenberg me, Tessa," said the spirit of the old lady sternly, shaking her semi-transparent head. "I'm not here for a social call."

"I can see that," said Tessa, stretching her hand to the spirit. "I'm so sorry about your death. Let me help you, Mrs. Rosenberg."

The spirit flew up to the ceiling avoiding her touch and glowered down at her indignantly. Tessa stared up, her jaw dropped. She never saw such a strange, irritable spirit before and she wasn't sure if the behavior of Mrs. Rosenberg was funny, frustrating or scary.

"Don't you dare touch me, missy!" the spirit shouted, folding her arms over her chest. "I still have some unfinished business, and this is why I'm here."

"Oh," mumbled Tessa, the first time in her life lost for words.

"Oh?" repeated the spirit, an air of sarcasm swirling around her. "That's all you can say, Therasia Donovan?"

"Okay, Mrs. Rosenberg, let's take it down a notch on your sarcasm. You were never like this when you were alive, so let's don't start it in your afterlife."

"Afterlife, huh?" huffed Mrs. Rosenberg. "Darling, I can't start on my way to the afterlife until I deliver a message to you. And you're wasting my precious time here."

"A message?"

"Do I hear an echo here?" asked the spirit, throwing her translucent hands in the air. But then she sighed and waved toward the door. "Follow me, child. Let me show you something."

The spirit glided out of the bedroom into the living room and Tessa followed her. They crossed the living room and the spirit halted in front of a small den. The den was so small that a floor-to-ceiling bookshelf filled with books and a small sofa was taking most of its space. It was Tessa's favorite spot in the house. Any free moment she had, she was spending in this den, curled up with a book on the sofa.

"Tessa, darling," said the spirit, her voice suddenly soft and kind like it used to be in life, "you've been to my place before. Our apartments' floor plans are supposed to be identical. Now, look carefully at your den and compare it to mine. Do you see any difference?"

In her mind, Tessa visualized the den in Mrs. Rosenberg's apartment. It was turned into Daisy's kingdom, filled with doggie toys, blankets and Daisy's accessories. And it was two times bigger in length. The color drained from Tessa's face and she approached the bookshelf, trying to take a peek behind it.

"Wait, darling, not like this," said Mrs. Rosenberg. "I see you noticed the difference. So, let me give you a message from your mother before I show you how to open her secret room."

"My mother had a secret room?" whispered Tessa, more to herself than to the spirit, but then added louder, "Mrs. Rosenberg, my mother sent me a message from behind the veil? With you? How is it possible?"

"She didn't send a message from behind the veil, sweetheart," replied Mrs. Rosenberg. "She left it with me a few days before she passed away. And she asked me to deliver it to you when you were ready. I'm not sure that you're ready yet, but since I'm kinda dead here, there will be no better time to deliver this message to you than now."

Tessa stared at Mrs. Rosenberg, her heart in her throat. Did her mother know that she was going to die, and this is why she left a message for her with Mrs. Rosenberg? Why didn't she show her this secret room herself? And what was she supposed to be ready for?

"What was her message?" she asked, her voice hoarse.

"She asked me to show you this secret room, darling," said Mrs. Rosenberg. "She said that inside this room you won't find all the answers to your questions, but it'll be a good start. Tessa, it may come as a shock to you, but I have to tell you some truth about your mother. The rest you'll have to discover on your own."

"What is it?" Tessa's voice was hardly above a whisper and her hands were trembling. She didn't know what this old lady was going to tell her, but freezing fear was slowly squeezing her heart.

"Your mother was a witch," said the spirit flatly, sounding so calm and even, like she was telling her that her mother was a librarian. "Not just any witch. She was a Guardian. I never knew all her secrets and what exactly she was guarding here. It was way above my pay grade. I was just a witch practitioner, you know."

"A Guardian Witch?" mumbled Tessa. "What do you mean? My mom was a police officer and the only thing she was guarding was the law."

The spirit chuckled softly. "Sweetie, you're communicating with the spirit of the dead. I'm sure you're realizing that not everything is black and white in this world. If not, then here is a rude awakening – supernatural is not that *super* in this world. It's mostly natural. Magic, elemental powers, and monsters under your bed – everything is real. You need to process this information fast, Tessa, because I must move on and I must do it soon."

Tessa swallowed hard. Of course, she knew that the supernatural existed. To a degree. After meeting Zane, it became evident.

But the idea that her sweet, down-to-earth mother was a witch still didn't sound real to her. She cleared her throat.

"Yes, of course, Mrs. Rosenberg, I realize that," she said. "I'm ready. Please show me the secret room."

"Darling, I don't know what you're going to find behind this bookshelf," said the spirit. "Your mother never let anyone inside. And even though, I was the only one here who knew her true identity, she never let me in either. So, I'm not going to break her rules by entering now. You'll have to go in alone."

The spirit approached the shelf and pointed at a small book without a name on the cover.

"Pull this book out. It's the trigger that opens the room," explained Mrs. Rosenberg. "But before you do it, I want to bid my farewell, darling. I'm sure that no matter what you find there, you can handle it." Tessa nodded, now tears flowing down her ashen cheeks. "Call my daughter before you open the room. Please let her know of my passing and ask her to take care of Daisy. I'm afraid that if you go inside the room first, you'll be too busy, and you'll forget to do it."

"Of course, Mrs. Rosenberg, I'll do it right away. I have Lisa's phone number."

"Thank you," said Mrs. Rosenberg. "And please, be careful, darling. I've heard that something dark is rising on the border between the realm of life and the world of spirits. So, watch your back." She extended her hand to Tessa and sighed. "Now, I'm ready to go..."

"Goodbye, Mrs. Rosenberg," said Tessa, gently touching her hand. A soft smile appeared on the old lady's face. The white light shone brighter and the spirit slowly dissipated, as her last words lingered in the air a few moments longer.

"Blessed be..."

* * *

AFTER THE SPIRIT of Mrs. Rosenberg was gone, Tessa went back to her bedroom and found her cell phone. For a moment, she stood quietly, thinking how to present this sad news in the best possible way. After all, she couldn't just tell Lisa that the spirit of her dead mother visited her, so she needed to find a good way to explain how she knew about Mrs. Rosenberg's passing.

In the end, she told Lisa that she heard Daisy's howling and went to check on Mrs. Rosenberg. But no matter how hard she knocked on her doors, no one answered, so she called Lisa because she was worried. Lisa thanked her and said that she was going to leave immediately to check on her mother.

With her cell phone still in her hand, Tessa went back to the den. She sat down on the sofa, staring at the bookshelf and sat like this for a while. She didn't know what she was going to find inside this hidden room and she was terrified and hopeful at the same time.

Part of her couldn't wait to open this door and walk into this new life. The unknown world filled with magic, elemental powers and supernatural beings. This part of her wanted to learn all there was to learn. But there was the other part of her that desperately resisted everything that was hidden in this room, the little part of her soul that wished to be normal, to have a normal supernatural-free life.

She didn't realize how long she was sitting there. A loud knock on the door brought her out of her emotional stupor. She opened the door to find Lisa telling her that her mother passed away and thanking Tessa for calling her. Tessa didn't remember the words of support and condolences she said to Lisa.

Like in a dream, she made her way back to the den and stopped in front of the bookshelf. She wasn't going to wait another minute. She was done double guessing herself. She had to know the truth. Tessa raised her hand and carefully pulled the book with the blank cover.

Something clicked behind the shelf and it moved forward

slightly, creating a small opening in the wall behind it. Tessa pulled on the shelf to widen the opening and slipped into the dark room hidden behind it.

It took a few seconds for her eyes to adjust to the darkness. Once she was able to see again, Tessa noticed a lamp installed on the wall next to the door. She pulled the string and a soft yellow light filled the small room.

After what Mrs. Rosenberg told her about her mother being a witch, a Guardian Witch to boot, Tessa was ready to see pretty much anything – witchcraft books of spells, crystal balls, tarot cards, maybe dried out herbs and weird animal parts in glass jars.

She observed the room, with relief noticing that there was nothing especially creepy here. The walls of the room were covered with weird symbols, possibly runes or sigils. None of these symbols looked familiar or meant anything to her. At the far end of the room, there was a small table and a single chair next to it.

Tessa approached the table and sat down on the chair, thinking how many times her mom was probably sitting here, alone, doing God knows what. Everything on the desk and inside the room was well-organized, just like anything her mom ever touched. She found a few folders filled with papers, a small blue box sitting on top of folders, an old book in leather binding and a notebook.

She opened the old book and stared at the first page in wonderment. She recognized her mom's concise handwriting, but she couldn't understand anything that was written in the book. It wasn't written in English. She scanned through the book, but everything was written in the same weird language. There were a few pictures, mostly symbols similar to those on the walls and a few sketches of strange creatures. But nothing inside this book told her anything about what her mom was doing.

Tessa put away the old book and took the notebook. It was

worn out and looked like it was used quite frequently. Carefully she opened the first page and read the first paragraph.

"September 12, 2010 – Still didn't find anything that could help me figure out what happened ten years ago. I followed the trail all the way to Chicago and lost it there. I can't spend too much time away from my Tessa. Even though I know that Sarah is taking excellent care of her, I can't tolerate another minute without my little sweetie..."

Tessa stared at her mom's handwriting, tears burning in her eyes. It was her mom's diary. Probably not the first one since the first record in this notebook was dated September 2010. Her cheeks flashed at the thought that she was reading her mom's diary. It was private. No one should be reading other people's diaries. She closed the book, putting her hand on top of its cover. The cover felt soft and warm, and for a moment Tessa felt like she was touching her mom's hand.

She put away the diary and opened the blue box. Inside the box there were two more thick notebooks. She quickly checked each one of them. These were her mom's earlier diaries. Tessa put them back in the box and closed the cover. Even though her mom was gone, she didn't think that she had any right to read her private thoughts.

Tessa pulled the first folder with some paperwork out of the stack and opened it. The first page in the folder looked like some official Certificate with a golden seal and gothic writing. She pulled it out of the folder and moved closer to the light, carrying the certificate in one hand and the folder in the other.

"Certificate of Adoption," she read and stopped, her hands trembling, her body slowly filling up with lead. "This is to certify that Therasia Reagan Doe was formally adopted into the Donavan family..."

Tessa dropped the folder and a few more papers fell out, gliding on the floor. She picked them up – more legal documents confirming her adoption. She stared at the words on the paper but couldn't understand anything. Numb inside, she slid down to the floor, leaning her back on the wall. Her thoughts were tripping over each other in her head and she couldn't stop and think clearly. Bitter tears gathered in her eyes and spilled down, but she didn't bother wiping them.

The room around her swayed and something dropped on the floor with a soft thud. Tessa blinked her tears away and stared down. It was her cell phone. She picked it up and the first well-formed thought flashed through her mind. She was thinking that she needed to get out of this house. She needed a few hours of being away from all this, so she could calm down.

For the first time in a long while, she didn't want to be alone. After her mother passed away, she always felt lonely. Even when she lived in her uncle's house, she felt alone. It never bothered her before. But right now, she desperately needed someone by her side. Someone, who could understand. She didn't need this person to comfort her or tell her that everything was going to be fine. The silence was fine, as long as it wasn't silence in solitude. Maybe later on she would need some alone time to figure things out, but not now.

Tessa tried to get up, but her legs felt weak and shaky, and she had to sit back down. She unlocked her phone and opened the contact list. For a moment she was considering calling her uncle but then quickly changed her mind. She didn't think that she could tolerate his wife's attitude at this moment.

Aidan... He was the only person she could call. But how was she going to explain this room to him? He would be... She had no idea how he would react to the fact that her mother was a witch. She just knew that she couldn't tell him that. She couldn't show him this room. He would think that she was off her rocker. And then he would never see her in the same light again. No, she couldn't call him, she couldn't talk to him about all this. Aidan was the normal part of her world. He was the definition of normality and strength, and she loved it about him. She couldn't take even the tiniest chance of losing it, losing Aidan.

Tessa scrolled through her short list of contacts. Her eyes stopped on the name she was looking for. Zane Burns. He was the complete opposite of Aidan. To her, he represented everything Aidan was not. He was her connection with the world of the supernatural, the part of her life she feared and was hiding from everyone. She hardly knew him, but for some reason she felt that she could trust him. She could trust him with everything outside the normal. He was the only one who could help her sort out all this mess.

3:23 AM. She pressed the dial button next to Zane's name.

~ ZANE BURNS, A.K.A. GUNZ ~

*G*unz dressed as quickly as he could and ran out of the house, just to remember that he didn't have a car. Frustration simmered up in him ready to boil over. He punched the air, cursing brutally and jumped over the fence into his own backyard. The last few days were a complete disaster. He forgot when he had a full night of sleep; he was drained magically, and he desperately needed some decent shut-eye to restore his strength.

It seemed that the rest wasn't anywhere in his foreseeable future. First, he needed to figure out a way to get to Tessa. She called him at three in the morning, asking if he could come over right away. She wasn't crying, but her voice was empty and lifeless, and when he asked her if she was okay, her answer was no. His car was at the mechanic shop and calling a cab at this time would take an extra thirty minutes to an hour. He was sure that Tessa wouldn't call him in the middle of the night without a good reason, and he didn't like the idea of leaving her on her own for such a long time.

There was another question burning in the back of his mind.

Why did Tessa call him instead of Aidan McGrath? She said it herself – Aidan was her one and only true friend. But she thought that Aidan knew nothing about supernatural. The only reason she would call him was because something supernatural was going on and this thought made his blood run cold.

He re-read the address Tessa texted him, committing it to memory. He knew this neighborhood well and there were enough of dark corners and alleys where no one would see him walking through his blazing portal. *Screw it,* he thought, opening the fiery curtain of his portal, *if someone will see me walking through the fire, they will need a few extra therapy sessions.*

Gunz walked out in the dark backyard behind Tessa's condominium building and immediately ran into an oak tree. He hit his forehead so hard that his eyes watered, and he staggered back almost falling. Carefully, he touched the bump on his forehead and winced, noticing blood on his fingers.

"I swear there was no tree here. I know this area," he groaned, wiping his forehead with the back of his hand. But he had no time to contemplate on that. He ran toward a thin road that was circling the building. As he was turning the corner, he glanced back and came to a screeching halt. The oak tree he had the head-on collision with was gone. *Someone is messing with me,* concluded Gun, as he walked around the corner toward the entrance into Tessa's building. *If I find out who it is...*

Tessa lived on the first floor. Gunz stopped in front of her door and pushed the doorbell button. No one answered. He knocked on the door and waited a few seconds, listening intently. The dead silence behind the door sent chills through him. He put his hand on the door handle and turned it carefully. The door was locked.

"*Recludius,*" he whispered a spell and turned the door handle again. With a soft squeak the door opened up. Gunz walked inside and stopped, probing the house for any supernatural presence. He didn't sense anything alarming, but there was a light hint of protective magic lingering in the air. The living area was dark and only a thin yellow strip of light was cutting through the dark floor, coming from a den at the far end of the room.

"Tessa?" called Gunz, moving toward the light.

She didn't reply. Gunz walked into the den and stopped. The light was coming from behind a bookshelf. He approached the shelf and pulled on it, expending the opening behind it. Hidden behind the shelf, he found a small room. Tessa was sitting on the floor, hugging her knees with her arms. Her head was bowed down to her knees and the dark mane of her hair was obscuring her face. She looked so small and helpless that something inside him shattered. A few documents were scattered on the floor around her.

His first instinct was to walk inside the room and see if Tessa was okay, but he decided to err on the side of caution and probed the room for wards and protection spells. Immediately he knew that he couldn't cross the threshold of this small room. At least not right away.

"Tessa," he called louder. She lifted her face and a hardly visible smile touched her red eyes.

"Zane," she said, "you're here. You came..." Her voice trailed away as her eyes moved to the papers on the floor.

"You called," Gunz replied. "What's going on, Tessa? What is this room?"

She got up slowly, holding her hand on the wall to stop herself from swaying. Her glassy eyes made a dazed circle around the room and then fixed back on his face. Her lower lip trembled, and she bit it.

"This is my mom's secret room," she whispered bitterly. "Zane, I lived my whole life with my... this woman and I have never known her... She wasn't even my real mom." Her eyes darted down to the documents on the floor.

Gunz followed the direction of her gaze and noticed the Certificate of adoption. He quickly reviewed the sigils and runes on the walls and he had no doubt that besides the fact that Tessa's mom wasn't her biological parent, she was also a witch. A supernatural witch, not a Wiccan practitioner.

"Tessa, that's not true," he said quietly. "You didn't know some areas of your mother's life, but you knew the woman who raised you, who loved you and took care of you for most of your life. Supernatural or not, adopted or biological, it doesn't matter. Just because she didn't give you birth, it doesn't make her any less of a mother."

"She lied to me my whole life…"

"She didn't lie to you. Do you think that possibly, your mother didn't want to reveal this side of her life to you because she was trying to protect you?" asked Gunz. This wasn't the most comfortable subject for discussion for him and he wasn't the right person to talk to her about that. "We all have our secrets. And you should know that better than anyone else, Tessa. I still believe that you need to tell the truth to Aidan."

"Zane, she was a Guardian Witch," said Tessa. "Do you know what that is? A Guardian? What was she guarding?"

Gunz frowned. He'd heard of the Guardians before, but he knew nothing about this ancient organization. "I'm sorry, I can't answer these questions. I don't know," he said, shaking his head slightly, thinking that possibly Kal would have an answer.

"Come here, take a look yourself," she told him, moving toward the table.

"Wait, Tessa," called Gunz. "I can't walk into this room. At least I don't think I should."

"What do you mean?" She turned around to face him.

"Your mother placed some serious wards and protection spells over this room," he explained, pointing at the runes and sigils on the walls. "I think, she placed them in the way that only you could safely cross the threshold. I don't know what I would trigger if I walk in, and I don't think that I should try to bring down the wards... assuming I can. This is kind of a magical panic room for you. If something happens, you're always going to be safe here, supernatural attack or otherwise."

Tessa kept quiet for a few seconds, observing the drawings on the wall. Then she walked out of the room and shut down the light. She pushed a blank book that was half out back into the shelf and the bookshelf glided back soundlessly, concealing the hidden room. She leaned her back against the shelf and looked up at him.

"Zane, I don't want to be here. I just can't," she said, her fingers gripping at the books behind her back. "I need a little time to process all this and think what to do next. And I can't do it here so close to my mom's secret life."

"I understand," replied Gunz, "where do you want to go? Do you have any relatives that I can take you to?"

"Where do you live? Can I stay with you for the rest of this night?" she asked, staring directly into his eyes.

Gunz hesitated, feeling a little uncomfortable with her request.

"Do you live alone?" she asked, noticing his hesitation.

"Yes, I live alone," replied Gunz, making a quick decision. He didn't want her to be alone and obviously she wasn't ready to talk to Aidan about the supernatural side of her life. "You can stay in my house tonight. A small problem though... My car is at the mechanic's shop and I had to travel here by portal."

Tessa smirked and shrugged her shoulders lightly. "Well, that would be another new experience for me today. Go ahead, open your portal."

Gunz waved his hand, unfolding the fire-curtain. She approached the wall of blazing flames and quickly stepped back.

"It's fire," she said, giving him an arched stare. She didn't look concerned or scared, just curious.

"Are you going to punch me out if I attempt to lift you and

hold you in my arms?" he asked, unable to conceal the sarcasm in his voice.

"That depends," she replied dryly. "Try something funny and you'll find out."

"Nothing funny, cross my heart," he promised. Carefully he lifted her, holding her against his chest, thinking that holding her was like holding a child, so weightlessly light and as tiny as she was. "As long as you're with me, the fire is not going to harm you."

"I trust you," she replied simply, hiding her face in his shoulder, wrapping her arms around his neck.

Right now I don't trust myself, he thought, wondering if he would end up in the middle of his neighbor's swimming pool again.

"Let's hope that whoever is messing with me is on a coffee break," murmured Gunz and stepped through the portal.

* * *

GUNZ WALKED out of the portal, recognizing his backyard with relief. No swimming pools, trees or any other pranks. Gently, he lowered Tessa to the ground and brought down his own wards. Then he unlocked the backdoor of his house and opened it, gesturing for her to come in.

"Don't you dare open the door for me," she warned, folding her arms over her chest. Involuntarily, his lips stretched into a smile as he recognized that she was getting back to normal.

"You're in my domain now. My place, my rules," he said grinning.

"Fine," she grumbled, heading toward the door. "Friggin' Lancelot."

"After you, my lady," he said with a light bow, letting her through the door.

Gunz closed the door and restored his wards. Tessa stood next to the kitchen table. Now she looked a little uncomfortable, like she no longer was sure in her decision to spend the rest of the night in his house.

"Tessa, you're absolutely safe here," he promised with an encouraging smile. "I'll never let anything happen to you and I would never do anything to hurt you myself."

"Yes, of course," she mumbled, smiling weakly. "Otherwise I wouldn't be here."

"Can I get you anything?"

"A place to lie down?" she asked, awkwardly playing with her phone. "Do you have a couch?"

"How about a guest bedroom? Would that be acceptable?" he asked, gesturing at the door that was leading into his living room.

Gunz led her through the living area to the second floor and showed Tessa to the guest bedroom. She sat down on the bed, staring at him like she was expecting him to say something.

"Make yourself at home. If you need anything, I'll be in the room next door," he said, ready to leave.

"Wait," she said, her voice strained, and that vibe of awkwardness flared around her again. "I don't want to be alone... Zane, please... stay..."

Gunz froze, thinking how unbelievably wrong it would be for him to stay in the same room with her at night.

"I'm not sure that it's such a hot idea—," he started to object.

"Come on, Zane," she pleaded. "What century were you born?"

"The same century you were born," he told her back, frowning. "I just don't feel comfortable with the idea of spending a night with you in the same room."

"Jeez, Zane, can you drop your code of honor for a few hours. I trust you not to lay your hands on me or any other parts of your body for that matter," she said wryly, but then her voice softened as she pleaded with him, "I don't want to be alone... I can't... You understand? Not now. Please?"

Maybe Tessa was right and living in modern days, there was nothing wrong with spending a strictly platonic night with a young woman in the same room. But between his upbringing, military training and all the medieval knight's morals that Kal instilled in him, he didn't feel right doing it. He glanced into her glassy eyes, recognizing the signs of fear and despair in her gaze and sighed.

"Fine." He walked to the small armchair that was sitting next to the closet door and sat down. "Lie down, Tessa. I'll stay in the room with you."

"But you'll be uncomfortable in this tiny chair—," she started to object, but he cut her off.

"It's either this, or I'll be in the room next door."

She nodded and slid under the comforter, shifting to the edge of the bed, closer to where he was sitting. Gunz got up, opened the closet and pulled out a throw blanket. He sat back down on the armchair, stretched his legs and covered himself with the blanket.

The door into the guest bedroom cracked open and a small grey kitten strolled into the room. He hopped on the bed and turned on his engine, purring loudly.

"Mishka!" hissed Gunz, not sure what to expect from the wyvern. "What are you doing here?"

"Relax, loverboy, I'm here to help," reassured Mishka, softly rubbing against Tessa's arm. *"Haven't you heard? Cats are therapeutic. We can relieve stress and trigger a feeling of happiness."*

"Zane, you never told me that you have a kitty," said Tessa, softly running her fingers through the kitten's soft fur. "He's so little." Mishka flipped on his back, allowing Tessa to rub his belly.

"Yeah, little... It's not a kitty, it's a little monster. Just a stray I picked up on the street," muttered Gunz. "Still considering if I should give him to the Humane Society."

Mishka purred louder, throwing an angry scowl at him, and Gunz gave him an evil grin back when Tessa wasn't looking.

"I would keep him if I were you," said Tessa, coddling the kitten to her chest. "He's so sweet and purry."

"Oh yeah, she's going to keep me and give you to the Humane Society." Mishka snickered in his mind and Gunz rolled his eyes.

"I'll see how he behaves," murmured Gunz, watching Mishka settling down next to Tessa, his head lying down on her breast. "Now, try and get some sleep, Tessa."

"Jealous?"

Gunz heard Mishka's snide question in his head but decided to ignore him. He'll deal with the pesky wyvern tomorrow when Tessa wasn't around.

Tessa just nodded and closed her eyes. A few minutes later, her breathing became deeper and she appeared to be asleep. Gunz observed her relaxed face, thinking that it would be a good opportunity to take Tessa to Angelique for a reading. He decided to talk to her about that when she woke up in the morning.

His thoughts slowly drifted to Aidan and Tessa's entangled relationship with him. She really needed to talk to him, tell him the truth. Gunz didn't know what Aidan was, but it was obvious that he wasn't new to the world of magic and most likely he knew a lot more about it than Gunz did. He wished he could talk openly to Aidan and ask him a few questions. That would make many things so much easier. Gunz sighed. Aidan built a wall around himself and Gunz had no idea how to breach this wall.

In the meantime, he secretly hoped that Aidan would never find out that he spent a night in the same room with Tessa. It wouldn't help his cause. He wasn't afraid of Aidan, even though magically-speaking Aidan was a lot more powerful than he was. Despite the fact that so far Aidan didn't show much kindness to him, Gunz respected him and he wanted to avoid getting into any kind of confrontations with him – magical or physical.

As tired as he was, Gunz couldn't fall asleep for a while, his restless mind keeping him awake. Everything was happening too fast, too many moving parts and unknowns. He had no time to organize his thoughts and process everything calmly.

Most of the night he spent sitting in his chair, keeping an eye on Tessa. Her sleep wasn't restful either. She was crying and moving in her sleep. After a while Mishka got tired of her constant movement. He assumed his true form and sat down on her pillow, softly humming some kind of spell. Tessa sighed and finally relaxed.

Only when the first rays of the morning sun touched the sky, did his tired mind quiet down and he slowly drifted to sleep.

~ TESSA ~

he large red numbers of the alarm clock were showing 9:48 AM. Tessa sat up on the bed and looked around. The window blinds were open, and the bedroom was bright with the morning sun. Indifferent to the bright light, Zane was sleeping, sitting in the armchair. His head was tilted back, and his arms were folded on his chest. Even in his sleep, he didn't look relaxed.

Tessa slid off the bed and quietly approached him. For a few seconds, she just stood, silently studying Zane's face. Noticing the blanket at his feet on the floor, she picked it up and carefully covered him. She was hoping that the touch of the blanket to his arms wouldn't wake him up. His lips parted a little and he turned his head to the side, avoiding the direct sunlight but didn't wake up. Tessa tiptoed her way to the window and pulled on the string, closing the blinds. After that, she grabbed her phone from the nightstand and quietly left the room.

She walked downstairs, and first thing called her office. Even though Ryan was still recovering after the attack, and Dr. Davis was still off, the dental office wasn't closed. Claudia answered the phone and Tessa told her that she had a family emergency and she would need a few days off. Since it was the middle of the week, she told Claudia that she'll be back at work on Monday and hung up the phone.

Even though she could get a ride home with Uber, Tessa didn't want to leave. She was still shaken by everything she found out last night, but it wasn't the only reason why she didn't want to go. She didn't know Zane that well, however, in these few short days, she learned to trust him, and that was quite unusual for her. Not very social, normally she kept everyone at arm's length. She never shared her private life with anyone and trusting didn't come easy for her.

Zane was different. She smiled thinking about his archaic chivalry and the way he managed to be there for her, every time when she needed him. *"You called."* That's what he said when he showed up in her apartment in the middle of the night. He said it like it was the only possible option. Tessa smirked. She was sure that if she called her uncle, with his wife hissing into his ear, he would find a thousand excuses why he couldn't come right away. And probably anyone else would also tell her to wait until morning.

Well, Aidan would show up too, she admitted to herself. But she couldn't let herself drag Aidan into all this. He was her anchor, her safe place, the small island of normality in the midst of this supernatural storm.

A soft meow pulled her out of her thoughts. Tessa looked around the kitchen and found Mishka, Zane's kitten, sitting on the kitchen counter between the coffeemaker and a small tray of K-cups.

"K-cups. That's easy," murmured Tessa, adding a cup of water into the coffeemaker. A few minutes later the coffee was ready, and its bitter warm aroma wafted through the kitchen. Tessa was ready to take the cup, but the kitten put his paw on her hand and meowed again.

"Wait," said Tessa, her eyebrows slowly climbing up. "You want coffee?"

"Meow," replied Mishka, nodding.

Did the cat just nod at me? thought Tessa and asked aloud, "Milk and sugar?"

The kitten nodded again.

For a moment, Tessa stared at him flabbergasted, but then laughed and moved the coffee cup toward the kitten. "Figures," she muttered, adding some milk and a spoon of sugar into his cup, "even his pet is a freak of nature. I'm not going to be surprised if this kitten can speak English."

"Why only English?" She heard a high-pitched voice and twirled around. The kitten was licking the burning-hot coffee and talking to her. "I speak most of the local languages. I can even speak the Dragon tongue."

"Holy shit!" gasped Tessa and clapped her hands. She wasn't scared and now that she got over the initial surprise, she actually liked the idea of a talking feline. "You really are a talking cat. That's so cool!"

"Uh-huh, I'm Mr. Cool," said Mishka proudly between licks. "But I can purr too, if that's what you prefer. Meow-meow."

"I think talking is a lot better than purring," admitted Tessa, stretching her hand to pet the kitten but stopped halfway. "Hmm... since you're not a regular cat, would it be okay for me to pet you?"

"For you, babe? Any time." Mishka lifted his head and a wide feline grin spread on his face.

Tessa giggled, petting Mishka's grey fur. He stretched under her touch and arched his back, just like a normal house cat.

"Well, Mishka, I see you drink coffee," she said, searching through the kitchen cabinets. She found the box with the pancake mix and pulled it out. "Do you also eat pancakes for breakfast?"

"Do you know how to make pancakes?" asked Mishka, pulling his head out of the coffee cup again and staring at her with curiosity in his round reddish eyes.

"Oh yeah," sung Tessa, reaching into the refrigerator for the milk and eggs. "I'm the best."

"Then everything you cook is mine," replied the kitten matter-of-factly. He traveled between the plates on the kitchen counter and rubbed his head against Tessa's elbow. "You know, prrrr, who loves you the most... prrr... Zane can wait until some other breakfast. Maybe tomorrow morning."

"Aw, Mishka, don't be greedy." Tessa smiled, petting the kitten. "I'll make enough pancakes for everybody."

A half hour later, a stack of fluffy golden pancakes was towering in the middle of the table and the smell of coffee and freshly-baked goods dominated the kitchen. Tessa took one of the pancakes and put it on a small plate.

"Here is the best one for you, Mishka," she said, putting the plate in front of the kitten. "I'm going to get Zane. Try not to eat everything."

"Sorry, I can't promise that," replied Mishka, starting to get personally acquainted with the hot pancake on his plate.

Tessa wagged her finger at the purring kitten warningly and headed to the second floor. She walked into the bedroom and found Zane in the same position in the armchair. She came closer and gently touched his shoulder. The moment her fingers connected with his shirt, he woke up.

Tessa gasped and backed away. She had never seen anyone waking up like this. He didn't move, but his eyes flew open and every muscle in his body tensed, his face a stone mask. The flames lit up on the bottom of his eyes and his body radiated an unbearable heat.

"Zane, it's okay, it's just me," she said soothingly.

"Tessa," he exhaled, visibly relaxing. The red glow in his eyes dimmed down and he got up. "I'm sorry, I didn't mean to scare you." He folded the blanket and put it away in the closet.

"You didn't," said Tessa trying to sound nonchalant. "I just wanted to tell you that breakfast is ready, and we should go back to the kitchen before Mishka eats it all."

He stared at her for a moment with a shocked expression, but then raked his hand through his short hair uncomfortably and looked away.

"Thank you," he said, his voice a little hoarse. "Give me a few minutes to clean up and I'll be right down."

Tessa returned to the kitchen and noticed that Mishka didn't manage to devour all the pancakes in her absence. He was still working on the first one, chasing it down with his coffee. She quickly set up the table for two and put another k-cup in the coffeemaker. By the time Zane walked into the kitchen, everything was ready. He halted at the door, giving her that shy lopsided smile that she liked so much.

"Sit down," she told him, waving at the empty chair. She put a small stack of pancakes on his plate and offered him a cup of coffee. "Your breakfast is served."

He sat down, taking the cup from her hands and threw a quick glance at her. And again, she caught a touch of surprise in his eyes. "Thank you," he said, "you did all this cooking for me?"

"No, silly, she did it for me," purred Mishka. "You can leave any time you wish, Mr. Third Wheel."

Tessa laughed and petted the kitten, but Zane frowned, throwing a scorching gaze in his direction and mouthed something that Tessa read as "You're talking".

"What?" huffed Mishka innocently, catching a pancake with his tiny claw and pulling it down from the stack on Zane's plate. "She loves the talking kitty. My kind of girl."

Zane just sighed and started to eat. After he was done, he got up and quickly cleaned the table. He didn't let Tessa do any work, and washed all the dishes, cups and the frying pan, stacking everything neatly in the dish rack that was sitting next to the sink. Once he was done, he turned around and leaned against the kitchen counter, gazing at her.

"Tessa," he said after a quick pause, "do you need to be anywhere today? Work? Home?"

"No," she replied and held her breath. She was hoping that he didn't need to go anywhere either. She liked it here, with this shy, slightly awkward man and his cheeky talking cat. She felt safe and comfortable, and for the last few hours she allowed herself to forget about all her problems and unanswered questions. Zane glanced at his watch and her heart skipped a bit, as she thought that he was late somewhere.

"Perfect," he replied, and Tessa exhaled, realizing that she was holding her breath all this time. "If you remember, I promised to help you figure out what you are. So, if you're up for it, we can visit my friend today and hopefully, she'll be able to tell us what's going on with you. What do you say?"

"Of course!" Tessa's heart lit up with hope. "Let's do it."

"Okay." He glanced at his watch again. "Give me thirty minutes. I need to get my car. My mechanic left me a message, saying that I can pick it up at any time today."

* * *

AN HOUR LATER, Zane parked his SUV in front of one of the high-rises on Ocean Drive. Tessa watched him walking around the car and rolled her eyes – he was seriously going to open the door for her. *Oh no, you don't,* she thought, watching his progress, *you open this door and I'll kick your ass.*

Zane opened the door and offered her his hand, a boyish grin on his face accompanied by a mischievous twinkle in his eyes. Tessa looked around and since few people were standing right next to them, she gritted her teeth and silently accepted his hand, walking out of the car.

"You see? It didn't hurt at all." He winked at her.

"It'll hurt you," growled Tessa, squeezing his fingers in her hand. "Never again."

"Ouch, ouch…" He groaned mockingly. "Never again… my lady."

Tessa stared at him for a moment, and then started to laugh. "Promise me that one day you're going to tell me where you acquired all your medieval manners."

"I promise, my lady." And there it was again – that bow that she saw only in the movies about the Middle Ages. This archaic, courtly bow that seemed to come so natural to him.

They walked into the building and took the elevator to the 3rd floor. Zane stopped in front of the door with the number 313 on it and knocked. A young woman in a business suit opened the door. In her high heels, she stood a little taller than Zane. She threw a curious gaze at Tessa, her eyes going up and down like she was sizing her up. Then her gaze moved to Zane and she smiled. Her smile was sweet and a little shy, and her fingers fidgeted with her long ponytail, as a faint blush colored her cheeks.

"Please, come in," she said stepping to the side to let them walk in. She turned to Tessa and held out her hand. "My name is Angelique." Tessa shook her hand, introducing herself.

"Angie," said Zane, "Tessa is the girl I told you about."

"Yes, of course," said Angelique, gesturing toward the couch. "Please sit down. I'll be right back."

She walked out of the room and came back a minute later with a small box in her hand. The box had a tiny antenna and five light-bulbs at the top. She waved at Zane impatiently.

"Zane, come on. You know how this works – stand behind me. Your presence will drive this machine crazy. I want to check Tessa only."

Angelique turned on the device, pointing it at Tessa and peered at the gage. At the beginning, the arrow on the gage remained still, but a few seconds later, the device buzzed angrily. The arrow zoomed all the way to the right and all five lightbulbs went up with the bright red light.

"Wow!" exclaimed Angelique, shutting down the device and

staring at Tessa in awe. "You're so... Wait, what are you?" She turned to Zane. "You were right. She's not a medium."

Another dead-end, thought Tessa, rising. She glanced at Zane but quickly averted her eyes, a heavy weight of disappointment settling in her heart.

"Tessa, hold on, don't give up hope so easily." Zane walked up to her and bent down slightly to find her eyes. "We're not done yet. That was just a magic detector. So now we know that you have magic and your magic is powerful. But we still need to find out what you are."

"That's right." Angelique came to the rescue immediately. "Sit down, Tessa. Let's do the reading now. I'm sure, between the three of us, we'll figure it out."

Tessa threw a gaze at Zane and he nodded encouraging her to do what Angelique was asking. She sat down on the couch and spread her hands.

"Okay, I'm sitting," she said, "now what?"

"Now, put your hands palms up on the table and relax," said Angelique. She pulled a small stool and sat down across the table from Tessa.

Tessa put her hands on the table and Angelique lowered her hands, holding them just an inch above hers. Tessa felt a soft stream of heat exiting Angelique's hands and traveling down into her palms and then higher, up her arms and shoulders. The warmth was pleasant and calming and Tessa wanted to close her eyes and relax.

As if reading her thoughts, Angelique smiled and said, "Close your eyes, if you want. I need you to completely relax and let go."

Tessa closed her eyes. The warmth was slowly traveling through her body, accumulating somewhere in her chest and it felt so good and so comforting, she never wanted it to end.

"Relax... relax... let it go... let it all go..."

Tessa heard Angelique's soft voice and smiled. It sounded like a lullaby. Memories of her mom flashed in her mind. She saw herself, a five-year-old girl, her mom tucking her into bed, singing that song... What was that song? Tessa wanted to remember the song her mom used to sing, but her mind was traveling too fast down memory lane and she knew that she wasn't the one who was behind the steering wheel... Now she was a teenager and she was talking with her mom about her future, college, and dental school. How much she wanted to come back to this time... Her life was perfect. She was living a dream and she didn't even realize that.

The heat wave rushed through her body and Tessa exhaled, the feeling was so intense that her breath came out almost like a gasp. The heat accumulated in her chest, expending wider, circling somewhere around her heart. Her hands were getting warmer and warmer, almost burning hot. She remembered Zane waking up this morning, his body surrounded by smoldering heat and smiled. What she felt right now was almost like as if she touched him...

The change came unexpectedly, brutally ripping Tessa out of her sweet oblivion and tossing her back into the paranormal nightmare of her current life. She felt Angelique's hands tremble, now touching her open palms. Tessa opened her eyes, just in time to see a bright lightning bolt originating in her hands and striking Angelique on her chest. Angelique was thrown off her stool. She flew back a few feet, hitting the wall. Zane rushed to her side, quickly checking her pulse.

Tessa gasped and ran to Angelique, who was unconscious on the floor. "Zane, I don't know what happened!" she panted, having a hard time speaking as anxiety clawed its way into her throat. "I swear... I didn't do anything."

Zane raised his eyes to her and she didn't find anything there except understanding and concern. "Calm down, Tessa," he said, his voice soft and composed. "I know you didn't' do anything wrong. Angelique is going to be fine... look... she's coming back."

Tessa knees shook, and she had to sit down on the floor next to him. Angelique opened her eyes, her hands traveled to her chest and she moaned. Zane carefully lifted her off the floor and sat her down on the couch, putting a pillow behind her back for extra comfort.

"Angie, are you okay?" he asked squatting in front of her and taking her trembling hands into his.

Tessa watched him taking care of Angelique, holding her hands in his and she caught herself thinking that she wanted him to care about her as much. She wanted to know how it felt to have someone worry about her, hold her hand when she was hurt or comfort her when she was crying.

Angelique sat up and gently stroked his cheek with her delicate fingers, her eyes caressing his face with a lot more affection than her fingers. "Zane, I'm fine, don't worry," she said, her voice raspy and still a little constrained. She glanced at Tessa and her brows drew together. "Tessa, I couldn't finish the reading. I'm sorry, but you and your powers are guarded."

"Guarded?" echoed Tessa.

"You have a Guardian who is shadowing your power and protecting you," explained Angelique.

"She had a Guardian," corrected Zane quietly, rising. "I think Tessa's mom was a Guardian Witch. Do you know anything about them?"

"Was?" asked Angelique, her expression surprised and troubled at the same time.

"My mom passed away a couple of years ago," explained Tessa.

"I'm sorry," said Angelique, sympathy in her gaze. "I don't know much about the Guardians. It's an ancient secret order of highly-gifted and powerful witches. They act upon orders of the Destiny Council and the only person they communicate directly with is the Destiny Keeper. They don't accept into their circle just anyone with magic. One has to be an extremely powerful and talented witch to be considered. But one thing I know for sure. If a Guardian is no longer able to perform their duty, a second Guardian is sent.

"So, after your mom passed away, I'm sure that the Guardians sent another witch to shadow your powers. Maybe she's not doing the same work as your mom used to do, but I still couldn't read you. As soon as I got closer to the source of your magic, I got zapped. Someone is definitely guarding you. The questions still remain – what you are and why the Guardians think that it's important that neither you nor anyone else find the answer to the first question."

"How can we find this other Guardian?" asked Zane.

"I don't know," said Angelique, shaking her head. "It would be someone who either lives or works close to Tessa's home. But other than that, there is nothing that can help you to single out this person in a crowd. The Guardians are the masters of disguise and even a powerful magical being like you are, Zane, won't be able to sense the Guardian's magical energy. After all – making things invisible is their core skill, right?"

"Right," said Zane, his expression closed up. He turned to Tessa. "I guess, we should start looking for your Guardian, Tessa. This is the only way to find out anything about what you are."

Tessa turned her face away. She didn't want Zane to see how she felt at this moment. For the first time since she found out that her mom was a Guardian, she asked herself this question. What kind of scary magic did she have in her that an ancient secret organization of witches had to hide her power not only from the world but even from herself. Was her power evil? Was she evil?

"Zane," she croaked, "am I evil?"

"What?" he muttered, frowning. "Come on, Tessa. I already told you that I can't sense any dark energy in you."

"What if the Guardians are shadowing the evil in me? You wouldn't be able to sense anything, would you!" she yelled, her voice breaking on a high-pitched note.

"Tessa..." Zane moved his hand to touch her, but she staggered back, away from his touch. If she was evil, she shouldn't be anywhere next to him or next to any people she loved and cared about. She was putting all of them in danger. Tessa was barely able to breathe as she stared at Zane, her eyes wide with fear.

"Tessa, stop," said Angelique, seizing her arm. "You're not evil. I'm hundred percent positive. The Guardians would never send their people to guard any evil being. That I know for a fact. They guard people whose powers are highly caveated in the world of magic. These people's powers could be dangerous, but never evil. Do you understand me?"

Tessa wasn't sure that she understood everything that Angelique just said to her. But the part where the Guardians do not guard evil people was enough to get her to start thinking clearly.

"Thank you, Angelique, for everything," she said, smiling weakly at her. Angelique just nodded to her, warmth of sympathy gleaming in her eyes.

Tessa turned to Zane and took his hand in hers. She didn't know why she expected that he would pull away from her touch, but he didn't, and a small spark of happiness ignited in her heart.

"Zane, can we go now?"

He nodded.

"Just not my home, okay?"

He gave her a half-smile and nodded again.

~ ZANE BURNS, A.K.A. GUNZ ~

*G*unz took the 595, driving back toward Coral Springs. Tessa wasn't asking where they were going, and he decided to take her to *Missi's Kitchen* for a quick lunch. The atmosphere of the restaurant was always relaxing, and he thought that Tessa could use a few minutes of peace after everything that just happened.

Angelique's magic wasn't enough to break through the Guardian's spells. The only other person who he could ask for help was Kal. Gunz sighed, biting his lip, thinking about summoning the Great Salamander tonight after he took Tessa back home.

He parked his *Mercedes* in a small parking lot on the back of the restaurant and walked around the car to open the door for Tessa. Before he got around, she opened the door, jumped out of the car and stuck out her tongue at him. He just smiled and shook his head. She was so young, just a child. Why at such a young age she was already up to her ears in this supernatural chaos? Why her?

"I thought we could do with a quick lunch," he said pointing at the restaurant. "I like this place. Food is nothing special, but it's quiet and relaxing."

"I'm starving," said Tessa. "I'll eat just about anything right now."

They walked through the parking lot and entered the semi-dark room. After the blistering heat of the midday sun in combination with the sticky South Florida humidity, the coolness of the air-conditioned space felt like a blessing. The restaurant was almost empty. A few people were sitting at the back table, but the rest of the tables were unoccupied.

Gunz made his way to the bar and stopped there, waiting for Missi to come out from the kitchen. He could hear her voice behind a half-open door, giving some instructions to her chef.

"Do you usually sit here?" asked Tessa, sitting down on one of the bar stools.

"Yes," replied Gunz, "but if you prefer to take a table or go outside, we can do it."

"The bar is fine. I can see why you like it here," said Tessa, turning her barstool around and leaning her back against the counter. "The place has this vibe of calmness and silent acceptance. You know what I mean? It's like you can just be yourself and no one ever would ask a question or judge."

Gunz smirked, throwing a quick glance at her. "You got all that from being here for a whole two minutes, oh wise one?"

Missi walked out of the kitchen, tucking a fresh white towel behind her black apron. She stopped in front of Gunz and nodded to him. Then her gaze shifted to Tessa and her eyes widened for a split-second. The change in her expression was so momentary that normally no one would notice it, but Gunz caught this small transformation and a warning flag went up in his mind. Why was Missi so shocked? Is it because he was here with Tessa? Or was there something else? With the kind of lifestyle he lived, it could never be a normal explanation. There was always a supernatural catch.

This is my supernatural-free place, thought Gunz, forcefully folding down all the red flags, *the place where I can live a resemblance of a normal life. For once, there should be a normal explanation.*

Like an answer to this thought, Missi smiled and wiped the bar counter, placing the menu in front of Tessa and him.

"Good afternoon, Mr. Burns," she said with her usual cheerfulness, "I was a little shocked to see you accompanied by a woman. You're always alone. That's a welcome change." She winked at Tessa. "Who is this beautiful young lady that finally tamed the beast?"

Gunz chuckled. *Here is my normal explanation,* he thought with relief.

"Hi Missi. This is Tessa," he made an introduction. "Just don't call her *lady*, if you want to live to see another day."

Tessa smiled uncomfortably, throwing a killer look at Gunz. He caught her gaze and raised his hands up, grinning. "Hey, I just said the truth. No need to get violent."

"I guess it would be too early to order your usual, Mr. Burns?" asked Missi checking the wall clock. "What can I get for you?"

"It'll be a while before I can order the usual again," said Gunz, throwing a wistful look at the bottle with Russian vodka. "Just get me a hamburger and French fries, please."

Missi wrote his order on her small notepad and turned to Tessa. "And for you, Tessa?"

"The same for me, please," said Tessa, smiling shyly, giving her back the menu.

Missi put the menus away in a plastic holder and walked away to the kitchen. As soon as she was gone, Tessa touched Gunz's hand gently.

"Mr. Burns?" she asked, giggling. "So, what is that usual that you can't have for a while and why can't you have it?"

Gunz glanced at the shelf with alcohol wondering how he should answer this question. He didn't like lying to his friends, but sometimes it was necessary to protect them. In the case of Tessa, he decided to stick to the truth as much as was possible.

"Vodka," he replied unwillingly, waving his hand at the shelf. "I usually come here in the evening to get a drink. After work and martial arts training, sometimes I feel like I need to unwind a little. So, I drink."

He was expecting her to get surprised or disgusted or at least say something, but she didn't. She just nodded, staring straight forward.

"Aidan is overly tough on you," she murmured. "I don't know what came over him. The way he treated you, I'm not surprised you needed a drink."

"Yeah, no... It's not about Aidan. He doesn't like me, and he probably has his reasons for that," Gunz said, thinking back to the last Taekwondo practice. "I've been coming here for almost a year. My job is a bit on the stressful side. And the latest assignment requires me to have a clear head twenty-four seven. So, no vodka for me for a while."

"You know, you never told me what you do for living," said Tessa, meeting his eyes in the reflection in the mirror behind the shelf.

Missi arrived from the kitchen sporting a large round tray with their food. Gunz watched her unloading the plates, thinking that he was saved by the bell. He wasn't sure that it was a good idea to tell Tessa that he was working for the FBI. He couldn't take a chance of her telling Aidan about that. First, he was supposed to be undercover, hence no one should know that he was an FBI consultant. Second, that could complicate his already strained relationship with Master McGrath.

* * *

IT WAS LATE AFTERNOON, when they left *Missi's Kitchen*. Gunz could feel that Tessa was doing everything to postpone the moment when he had to take her back home. She was eating slowly, without looking at him and at the end she didn't object him paying for their meal. After they were done with their food, she asked him if he wouldn't mind going for a walk and they spent a while just sauntering along the canal. She looked pensive and he didn't want to bother her, silently walking by her side. By the time they finally got in the car, it was close to 5 PM.

As they neared Tessa's condominium building, the tension inside the car became palpable. Gunz threw a glance at Tessa's face and sighed. Clearly, she didn't want to go home. He drove the car and parked it next to her building. She threw one tortured gaze at him but didn't say anything and pushed the door open, ready to leave.

"Tessa, hold on," said Gunz, taking her elbow. She looked at him over her shoulder, a question in her deep brown eyes. "I can see that you're not ready to go back home. Am I right?"

She nodded, sliding back into the car seat but leaving the door open. Her head was bowed down to her chest and she looked like a little girl, ready to cry.

"Listen, you can stay at my place one more night," offered Gunz. Everything inside him was screaming that he was making a mistake, but he just couldn't say no to her silent plea. "Let's go to your apartment and get whatever you need. Okay?"

Her face lit up with happiness in a momentary change of mood. They went to Tessa's apartment and she twirled around the place like a hurricane, quickly collecting everything she needed for the night. In less than five minutes, she assembled a small bag and couldn't wait to be out of her apartment.

"Hold on," said Gunz, stopping her at the door, "don't you have Taekwondo training tonight?"

"Not tonight," she said, gazing at him pleadingly, "please, I just want a quiet evening."

"At least call Aidan and let him know," suggested Gunz, as they walked outside, and Tessa locked her door. "And do me a favor…

If you don't want to see me dying a very painful and violent death, please don't tell him that you're with me."

"No problem, Mr. Burns," said Tessa giggling, climbing into his car, "I like seeing you alive."

"At least someone does," muttered Gunz under his breath, driving away from the condominium complex.

* * *

SINCE GUNZ MOVED to Coral Springs, it has become a part of his everyday routine. Even though he had powerful wards and protection spells placed on his house, every time when he came back home, before he opened his door, he had to probe the house and the backyard for any supernatural presence.

He approached the door and closed his eyes, relying on his Fire Salamander sense. The house was clean, but there was something off in the backyard. He wasn't sure what it was, but something felt off.

Gunz opened the door and walked inside first. He scanned the house again and only after he was sure that everything was clear, he let Tessa in. He told her that he needed to step out for a few minutes and asked her to stay inside until he came back. She snatched the purring kitten into her hands and went upstairs, seemingly unconcerned with anything else. A minute later, he heard her walking around the bedroom, discussing something with Mishka.

Cautiously, he opened the backdoor and stepped outside. As soon as he passed the threshold, he heard a loud whistling sound. He could never mistake this sound for anything. His military training kicked in and he dropped on the ground, covering his head with his arms. A missile whizzed through the air and a powerful explosion rattled the ground beneath him.

The downpour of sand and debris dropped on his back, covering him from head to toe. He coughed, swallowing dust, and scrambled to his knees. Everything around him was spinning, his head was buzzing, and something was ringing in his ears, rendering him deaf. He struggled to his feet and took a couple of unsteady steps forward. A moment later, his visions steadied, and he froze in place.

He wasn't in his backyard. He was standing on top of a hill, holding his sniper rifle in his hand. From this elevated position, Gunz could see a half-destroyed city a short distance away. Partially demolished houses were staring at him with empty eyes of glassless windows. Piles of bricks and debris were blocking the roads. As his hearing slowly started coming back, the distinct barking sound of gunfire broke through the constant ringing in his ears and the air got filled with the roaring of airplane engines. All this looked painfully familiar.

What the hell? thought Gunz and spun around, still disoriented.

Another missile shrieked through the air and Gunz fell on the ground, pushed by someone's strong hand. A man fell on top of him, covering him from the explosion.

"Gunz! For the love of God, man, what are you doing?" He heard a voice in his ear and he recognized it right away.

"Oleg?" he mumbled. "But how?"

"Sasha, Sergei... I found him. He's fine." He heard Oleg's voice and struggled to his feet. A few yards away he saw his friends, partially concealed by a camouflage screen. Behind them there were a few more soldiers. He knew them all, they used to be a part of his unit. Used to be... Gunz shuddered. He recognized where he was, and he remembered what was going to follow next.

"Oleg, incoming!" Sasha's desperate voice rang through the communication system.

Oleg cried out like from pain, and a powerful shield enclosed the area around them. Another blast rocked the ground, as a missile blew up just a few feet away from them. The explosion propelled the dirt in the air, like a thick black fountain, carrying death and destruction in its wake. Oleg's shield got impacted by a powerful blast but withheld it. A moment later everything was over. Oleg let go of his shield, his knees buckled, and he dropped to the ground, breathing laboriously.

Gunz didn't need to look. He already knew. Sergei, Sasha, and Oleg – his friends, his brothers – they were alive. To save his friends, Oleg exposed his magic for the first time in his life. But everyone else around them were dead. Gunz squeezed his head with his hands, his fingers digging into his scalp, and screamed.

No, not again, no... Gunz counted to ten, slowly getting in control of his spiraling emotions and spun around, quickly surveying the area. *Someone is messing with me. All I need to do is find something that doesn't belong here.*

He found what he was looking for almost immediately. A tall oak tree was growing just a few yards away from where he was standing. Gunz snarled, an overwhelming anger and cold determination making his blood boil.

"Ignius," he hissed, extending his hand toward the oak tree.

A tight flaming circle surrounded the tree. Gunz ran to it, his whole body now engulfed in flames. Stepping into the fire, for a moment he dissolved into his element. The tree trembled, the leaves falling to the ground and the surroundings started to change. A moment later, Gunz was standing back in his backyard.

"Who are you?" he roared, stepping closer to the tree, setting the ground around it on fire. "Show yourself, or I swear to God, I'll reduce you to ashes."

The tree spun in place, the air around it twinkled with green lights, and a slender young man manifested in its place. The man folded his arms over his chest and laughed, throwing his head back.

"Hello, Fire Gecko," he said, a mischievous gleam in his glowing phosphoric eyes. He put his hands on his hips and tilted his head slightly. "Game over, you won. You got me."

"You motherf—," exhaled Gunz, choking on anger. His shaking

hands clenched into fists. "Game? You, asshole... you made me relive the most painful memories of my life! It's a game to you?"

"Oh yeah... sorry about that," the man said, raising his hands in the air. "Nothing personal. I just needed to play a few pranks on you... How did you like your swimming pool fiasco or the car troubles? The smoke in a cold car was a nice touch, eh?"

Gunz stared at the man, incredulous. "Son of a bitch... I think I know you..." he whispered. "You're Sven. One of Aidan's men."

"Ta-dah!" sung Sven, clapping his hands. "And the prize goes to the fried lizard!"

Gunz took a few deep breaths, extinguishing all the fire within him, leaving only the burning circle around Sven.

"Sven," he whispered. "These glowing eyes... I can't believe I didn't recognize what you were the first time I met you. You're Svyatobor, aren't you? Slavic god of nature. You're a god! Did Aidan put you up to it? Why?"

From what Gunz remembered, Svyatobor was one of the high nature deities in Slavic mythology. He was a god of forests and all forest dwellers. In the old days, people believed that he had the power over their lives and their destiny. But they also knew that he was a mischievous trickster and they used to do anything just to appease him and get on his good side.

"Good for you! You're a smart little reptile, know your Slavic pantheon and all. I'm honored." He threw a mocking bow in Gunz's direction.

"Why, Svyatobor? Just tell me why Aidan hates me so much?" Gunz repeated his question quietly. His anger slowly simmered down, leaving him tired and resigned.

Svyatobor stopped laughing, quickly sobering up. He pursed his lips, taking in his appearance and sighed.

"That's something I can't tell you, Zane. You need to talk to Aidan and sort things out with him," he said, shaking his head. "I did only what he asked me to do. And I'm truly sorry, I put you through hell. But you have to understand... This is how my power works – I can only create an illusion out of things that are already in your memory. When I agreed to play a few pranks on you, I had no idea what kind of horrors were stored in your brain..."

Gunz touched the burning circle, ordering the fire to cease. "You're free to go. Please leave," he said quietly, his voice painfully hoarse.

Svyatobor started to say something but then changed him mind. He snapped his fingers and vanished, leaving a few oak leaves behind.

Gunz turned around and slowly moved toward the house. The old, painful memories that he worked so hard to push far away in the depths of his mind, now resurfaced with agonizing clarity. He opened the door and walked inside the house. Not fully realizing what he was doing, he passed through the kitchen and stopped in the middle of the living room.

He looked around, his gaze empty, everything inside him hollow. He knew where he was, but the memories of the war were playing in front of his eyes, making him dizzy and disoriented. Mechanically, he opened the wine cabinet and pulled a vodka bottle out. With shaking hands, he opened the bottle and froze, staring at the clear liquid.

Tessa and his wyvern were somewhere on the second floor. He couldn't drink... He shouldn't... He must keep his mind clear... He grunted but closed the bottle and put it back inside the cabinet. Something fell upstairs with a loud thud. Inside his clouded mind, he knew that it was probably Tessa dropping something, but his body reacted to the sound on its own.

Gunz dropped to the floor, covering his head with his arms.

~ ZANE BURNS, A.K.A. GUNZ ~

*T*he darkness surrounded him, embracing him with its cold menacing touch. It wasn't soft and relaxing. It was harsh, painful and violent. It was ripping his flesh apart, while the sounds of war were ravaging his frazzled mind. The shrieking and whistling of missiles, the earth-crashing blasts of explosions, the dry cough of automatic weapons – everything was mixed into one giant cacophony of sounds, excruciating, nonstop, gut-wrenching racket. And over all that, he still could hear the voices – screams of pain, cries of terror, the shouting of commands – fear and adrenaline almost palpable in the air.

He breathed in the suffocating stench of war – sweat, burnt flesh, and blood. His hands smelled of gunpowder, bullet lubricant and the metallic odor of ammunition. He couldn't see it, but he could feel the stock of his sniper rifle pressed against his shoulder, and the trigger under his finger.

Gunz cried out and squeezed his head with his hands. He tried to fight the darkness, somewhere in the back of his mind realizing that all this wasn't real, but he was too weak, too tired and the darkness was winning. *Open your eyes, wake up,* he ordered himself, but he couldn't. It was too painful, too hard…

He felt a soft touch on his shoulder. Someone was talking to him, calling his name. A welcomed voice was pushing the sounds of war away and down. The touch became stronger, more persistent. It was destroying the horrors of war that were alive only in his memory, shattering them into pieces.

Gunz flinched and opened his eyes. For a moment everything around him was blurry, but slowly his vision came to focus, and he saw Tessa. She was kneeling on the floor next to him. Pulling on his shoulders, she was trying to turn him onto his back. Her eyes were wide with shock and worry.

"Zane, are you okay? Say something." He heard her voice, filled with concern, and he tried to sit up. She helped him up, supporting him with her arms and he leaned back against the cabinet.

"I'm fine," he replied, hardly recognizing his own voice. "Just give me a moment and I'll get up."

Slowly, he managed to scramble to his feet, still a little disoriented, and sat down on the couch, hiding his face in his hands. He felt Tessa sitting down next to him, her hand gently stroking his back and shoulders. She wasn't talking to him, wasn't asking anything, and he appreciated the silence. For the first time in the last year, he felt like he wasn't alone, and it felt good.

Gunz lowered his hands, exposing his face glistening with cold sweat. His eyes fell on the open wine cabinet. He wanted it, just one shot of vodka to help him relax and forget. No, he needed it – desperately and agonizingly, to help him bury these unwanted memories somewhere in the darkest, deepest corner of his mind, so they would never break free again.

Tessa got up and walked to the wine cabinet. She picked up the open bottle with vodka and turned to him, holding it in her hands.

"Do you need it?" she asked quietly.

"Yes, but I can't," he croaked, lowering his eyes.

"Zane, you were in a war zone before, weren't you?" she asked, putting the bottle back in the cabinet and closing it. "You have PTSD." She made a pause, but he didn't answer. "I recognize the symptoms. I saw it a few times before. My uncle had it after he served in Afghanistan."

"I'll be all right," said Gunz, trying to smile. He wasn't sure that it looked like a smile, just a grimace resembling one. "Yes, I did a few military tours back in my country, but I never had PTSD... Someone was messing with my mind and brought all this darkness forward. It's over now. Thank you, Tessa."

He relaxed back in the couch, little by little his sanity and much needed focus returning back to him. Tessa sat down, staring at him with curiosity.

"Back in your country? You're not from here?" she asked, astonished. "You have no accent in your English. Where are you from?"

Gunz didn't reply right away. His eyes found a large digital frame that was sitting on the shelf next to his TV. Photos of forests, rivers, lakes, city streets were slowly sliding through the screen. He watched the pictures changing inside the frame and sighed.

"I moved here slightly over a year ago," he said, pointing at the digital frame. "Originally, I am from Belarus. The reason I don't have an accent is because in reality, I don't speak English. I use magic to speak and understand. A long time ago, someone told me that magic doesn't have language barriers. It's true."

Tessa approached the frame and stood there for a few minutes, watching the pictures until they went full circle. Then she turned around and smiled warmly.

"Your land is beautiful. Are these photos of your city?"

Gunz nodded. Sadness tightened his chest as he looked at the sliding photos. He missed his land, these endless rivers, deep lakes, the dark greenery of forests. He could spend hours just sitting at the lake, fishing, or doing absolutely nothing, just enjoying the view. This wild land was always his sanctuary, a place where he could forget everything and relax, body and soul.

But even more than his land, he missed his friends. With all his heart he wished they were here now, standing by his side as they always did. Everything would be so much easier... He swallowed and stared down at his clenched hands.

He came to terms with his situation. He was never going to see his friends or come back to Belarus again. His life was here now. And this digital frame with the photos of his past was just a small reminder, his safe place when he felt the need to forget the present for a few short moments.

"You're homesick," whispered Tessa, staring at him, her eyes widened, filled with surprise.

Gunz chuckled softly, putting his arm behind his head, relaxing. "No, Tessa, I'm not homesick and I don't have PTSD. I'm fine, believe me. But you're not. So, let's talk about you."

"What's there to talk about?" she said with a light dismissive shrug. "You already know about me more than anyone else. But you did promise to tell me what you are, magically speaking. I'm still waiting."

Gunz glanced at her and shook his head. She was so very young, just a little curious girl. For her young age, she seemed to be strong, definitely no *damsel in distress* as she put it herself. But right now, she needed help, even if she didn't realize or admit it yet.

"How about we make a deal," proposed Gunz, winking at her. "We talk about you a little and then I tell you what I am and even give you a little magic show. Deal?"

As soon as he finished talking, Tessa lit up with glee. It was like a lightbulb going up somewhere inside her and she glowed with excitement.

"It's a deal!" she exclaimed. "Can we do your part first?"

"Nice try," said Gunz, suppressing laughter, but then changed back to serious. "Tessa, it's important that we talk about your situation. You probably don't realize it, but right now you're hiding. By staying here, in my house, you're hiding from what you need to do, procrastinating or delaying the inevitable. And unfortunately, the kind of reality you and I live in, the truth will catch up with you sooner or later, no matter how hard you try to avoid it. So, from my experience, it's better to face it right away and deal with it on your own terms."

Gunz was expecting objections and arguments. He was expecting the rougher side of her personality to come through and tell him to mind his own business, but she didn't.

"You're right," Tessa said, playing with the edge of her shirt, avoiding his eyes. "I am hiding here. I'm hiding because I'm too scared to go back and face the truth. I'm scared to learn what I am and why the Guardians are interested in me. And I hate it! I hate feeling scared and helpless. It's not me!"

"Tessa, you have to do it. You can't hide here forever." He took her chin with his fingers and gently lifted her face. She glanced at him, her eyes deep and dark with sadness. "You need to go back home, open your mom's secret room and read every single document, book or paper you find there. The more you know about yourself the safer it'll be for you."

"There are my mom's diaries there. Three of them," whispered Tessa, averting her eyes. "I can't read those. It's not right... it's hers... personal. You know?"

Gunz shook his head, biting his lip. "You're looking at it the wrong way, Tessa. Your mom is dead, and you can't just come home and ask her questions. So, the only way to find out why the Guardians sent her to shadow you, is to read her diaries. The way your mom placed the wards and spells on her room was done so you could safely walk in. Only you, Tessa, and no one else. Don't you think that perhaps everything she left in this room was for you to find and use? Including her diaries?"

She remained silent for a few moments. Then her eyes met his and she nodded. "You're probably right. I will read her diaries and everything else there. Well, almost everything else."

"What do you mean?"

"There is one ancient book there that looks like a book of spells. A Book of Shadows or a Grimoire. I couldn't understand anything that was written there. Even the letters didn't look like the English alphabet."

"Oh," said Gunz, "it's probably written in Dragon tongue – the original language of magic."

"Can you read it?"

"Unfortunately, no," replied Gunz. "I learned a few spells and words in Dragon tongue, just enough to be dangerous. But I had no time to learn the actual language. I'm too new to all that. But if you'll need to read it, I can always ask someone who's fluent in Dragon tongue. I know a few people."

"Okay, tomorrow morning, as soon as I get back home, I'll go to my mom's secret cave and start with light reading." Tessa smiled shyly. "You don't mind me hiding out one more night in your house, do you?"

Gunz rubbed his forehead tiredly but shook his head no. He still felt that it was wrong for her to be here at night, but he couldn't send her away either.

"Just one more night, Tessa, and then you do the right thing."

"Scout's honor!" she said, raising one hand up, three fingers extended. "Now your turn to keep your word. Show me what you are."

"Not yet," objected Gunz. "There is one more thing we need to discuss."

"What else?" whined Tessa, sounding disappointed.

"Aidan," said Gunz straight. "You must talk to him and tell him the truth. You said that he's your only friend. We do not lie to friends, Tessa. Lies have a bad habit of coming back and biting you on your butt. They always do. No matter how long you twist and spin the lie, sooner or later the truth will come out and you'll be the one facing the consequences."

"I can't, Zane," whispered Tessa, gazing at him pleadingly. "Aidan is so normal. He'll think I'm crazy and I'll lose him forever. You understand? I can't lose him! Not Aidan. Please don't make me tell him about all this…"

Gunz suppressed a sigh. He didn't like the way this conversation was going, and he was afraid that if he would push Tessa more, she would start crying. He wasn't very comfortable dealing with tears.

"Tessa, I can't make you do anything. I can only recommend. Think what would happen if Aidan finds out about all this some other way? Then you would definitely lose him. At least give him a chance. If he really is your true friend, he'll understand, and he won't judge. He'll support you no matter what. Give him a chance, Tessa. Don't lie to him."

"Okay," she said so softly that he could hardly hear her. "I'll talk to Aidan, but not today. I need to read everything in my mom's room first. Once I know and understand a little more about all this magic stuff, I promise, I'll talk to Aidan."

Gunz exhaled a sigh of relief. Now that he knew that a Slavic deity Svyatobor was working with Aidan, he was more than ever positive that Aidan McGrath wasn't your every-day wizard. Who knows, he could be some kind of ancient god himself. Hopefully, Aidan knew more about the Guardians and he could protect Tessa better than he ever could.

"Now my turn," he said, and Tessa finally looked up at him, curiosity back in her giant brown eyes. "I'm a Fire Salamander, Tessa. I can wield the elemental power of the Fire. I also have magic, so I can cast spells and enchantments, but I'm not very experienced with all that. It has been only two years since I discovered the fire in me."

"Fire Salamander?" asked Tessa, staring at him in awe. "You're a lizard?"

"Do I look like a lizard?" he asked, laughing. "I'm an essence of Fire."

He got up, standing in front of her, and directed some fire toward his hands. A small flame ignited in his palm. Tessa stood up and moved her hand close to the fire but quickly pulled it back, recoiling from the heat.

"Wow, the fire is real," she mumbled.

"Of course, it is." He channeled more power allowing the small flames to start running up and down his arms. "I'm the fire."

"Amazing…" she whispered, gazing at him intently. "You are—"

"A lizard?" he asked with a smirk. "I can take the shape of a lizard too – a fire salamander to be precise."

"Really?" Now she definitely looked like a ten-year old girl, her eyes twinkling with expectation of something new and amazing. "Can you show me?"

"I can try, I'm not very good at it yet and I hardly ever do it," he said, awkwardly pulling his shirt off and taking his shoes and socks off. "Sorry, the less clothes I have on me the easier it is for me to transform."

Gunz channeled more power, allowing the fire to run freely inside his body and spun in place, transforming into a fire salamander. Tessa gasped and squatted down, to see him better.

"I've never seen anything like this," she said stretching her hands to touch him. "What would happen if I pull on your tail?"

"I don't recommend doing it-s-s-s," hissed Gunz, backing away from her. "I have no idea-s-s-s what would happen-s-s-s, but I'm s-s-s-ure, it won't be pleas-s-s-ant."

"You're so cute, when you're a lizard," said Tessa, giggling, gently running her finger over his back. "And you have this hissing s-s-s when you speak."

Gunz spun in place again, taking back his human form. He stood, breathing hard. The process of shifting into the salamander form was still taking a lot out of him. Tessa straightened up and carefully touched his unclothed chest with her fingers.

"I think you're a lot cuter when you're a man," she whispered breathlessly, taking in his appearance. "A perfectly proportional... well-shaped... mini-man..."

"I'm not that small, Tessa," he said, taking her hands off his chest. "I'm five-foot-six-inches, a lot taller than you are."

"A pocket-sized man. Very convenient." He heard Mishka's voice snickering in his head and ignored him.

"No, you are not small..." she whispered, her eyes gliding up and down his muscled body.

Gunz caught her eyes and bent down to pick up his shirt, but she stopped him, gently taking the shirt out of his hands, putting it on the couch. She ran her hands over his shoulders to his neck and slowly moved her fingers down. It had been a while since he felt the touch of a woman's hand and everything inside him awakened with need. He sucked in a sharp breath, not expecting her to be so forward and froze under her touch.

"Oh yeah, ah-ha," sung Mishka's voice in his head, *"you work it, loverboy. Show her who's the teacup man here."*

"Tessa, don't," he said, putting his hand over hers to stop her.

"Why?" she asked absentmindedly.

She took a half-step forward, closing the space between them. Her firm breasts pressed against his chest, teasing him and his breath caught. She stretched up a little and pressed her lips against his. His lips parted, and he answered her kiss, before he realized what he was doing.

No, stop! I need to stop her. I can't do it. His mind was shouting and fighting. This girl was a child compared to him, and Aidan was obviously in love with her. He couldn't do it to her and he shouldn't be doing it to Aidan. It wasn't right.

Yes! His body was screaming, making summersaults of joy. *About time!*

"You go, boy!" Mishka was cheering in his head. *"Show her the fire!"*

Gunz seized Tessa's shoulders with his hands and pushed her

away. She stood, her lips slightly opened, shock staring at him from her fogged eyes.

"Tessa, no," he growled, his voice deep and heavy, his body still not quite complying with his mind's demands. "I can't do it. I'm sorry."

"You can't?" she asked, her eyebrows rising. "I'm sorry... Are you... Do you prefer boys?"

"What? No, I'm not gay," he replied, his mind slowly getting in control. "But it doesn't change anything. I can't do it with you."

"Why, Zane? What's wrong with me? Not your type?"

"Tessa, please," he said, taking another step back. "You're a wonderful girl, but—"

"A girl?" She interrupted him, throwing her hands in the air. "Is that what you see when you look at me? An innocent needy girl, who begs for your help and protection? A little virgin in distress?"

"Tessa, please listen to me—"

"Hell no! Now you listen to me! I'm not a virgin and I'm definitely not a damsel in distress that needs a big strong man to save her ass on a daily basis. I make my own choices. Am I clear, you moron?"

"Tessa, I don't care about all that. But I still can't offer anything except my friendship and support," said Gunz firmly. "If you need my help to learn more about the Guardians and who you are, I'm here for you. You call me at three in the morning and I'll come over, no questions asked. But don't ask for anything more than friendship. Please."

He stepped back to the couch and picked up his shirt. All of a sudden, a strange wave rushed through him and he stiffened, probing his wards. Everything seemed to be in place and functioning, but something was still off. He probed the area around the house and held his breath. His whole house was surrounded with a thick cloud of magical energy the likes of which he had never sensed before. Channeling his fire, he got ready to fight and turned to Tessa.

"Tessa, something is coming, run…"

The entrance door swung open with a loud bang and a blinding white light flooded the house.

~ ZANE BURNS, A.K.A. GUNZ ~

*T*he walls trembled violently, and the windows on both floors imploded, flooding the house with splinters of broken glass. With an earsplitting bang, the wards collapsed, leaving the entry unprotected. The blinding white light slowly dimmed down and Gunz saw a dark outline of a tall man in the doorway.

The magical energy was wrapping around him, flowing through him uninterrupted. Except for his eyes that were glowing with a brilliant white light, Gunz couldn't see his features. As the remnants of the wards and protection spells crumbled, the man passed through the threshold and stopped.

"Aidan," exhaled Gunz, recognizing him.

"Aidan?" mumbled Tessa, staring at the man, incredulous. She grabbed Gunz's arm and he felt her fingers digging nervously into his bicep.

Aidan was standing just a few feet away, his rage almost tangible. His chest was rising and falling with heavy breaths, his jaw set in a straight line. In his anger, he didn't bother concealing his magical energy. Not only his eyes, his whole body was radiating a brilliant white light. He took one more step forward and the floor trembled like from an earthquake.

This idiot, thought Gunz, fury flaring up in him, *he just exposed himself as a creature of magic to Tessa... She had no idea.*

Gunz stepped forward, shielding Tessa with his body and let go of his power, raising his hands up. He wasn't sure why Aidan was here and what drove him to this insane level of fury, but he would rather find out what was going on and resolve the situation peacefully than fight. Especially, he didn't want to get into a confrontation with Aidan in front of Tessa. She already had enough of nasty surprises for one day and he didn't want her to watch Aidan using his magic against him. But if push came to shove, he was ready to hold his ground and defend himself.

"Aidan, tell me what's going on," said Gunz, keeping an eye on the fluctuations of magical energy around him. "I don't want to fight you. Let's talk."

"Who said anything about fighting, lizard?" thundered Aidan, his hands clenched into fists. "I'm not planning to fight you. I'll just kill you right away."

The magical energy spiked around Aidan's arms and a bright ray of white light erupted from his hands. Gunz was ready. In one move he channeled the fire and magic, raising a glowing power shield between them. The ray of light impacted the shield but didn't penetrate it. Gunz grunted, straining to hold Aidan's attack.

"Aidan, please..." he hissed, sending more magic into his shield, as Aidan stepped closer, increasing the flow of his power. "Stop... you'll hurt... Tessa."

Aidan stopped the flow of his power and narrowed his eyes. "Speaking of Tessa," he snapped, and the magical energy spiked around him again. "What is she doing spending a night in your house, lizard, and why are you half naked?"

"It's not what you think, Aidan," said Gunz, dropping the shield. "If you would stop trying to kill me for a moment, maybe I can explain. She needed my help —"

"She needed your help? How dare you lie to me!" shouted Aidan. "If Tessa needed help, she would call me, not you! Why would she call a tiny man whom she knows for less than twenty-four hours?"

In one fluid motion, he conjured an energy ball and threw it at Gunz. Gunz failed to raise the shield fast enough and the energy ball struck him in his side, burning through his flesh. Gunz cried out in pain, clasping his hand to his side. Aidan conjured another energy ball. It was twirling in the palm of his hands, crackling with electric discharges. As he was getting ready to send it flying, Tessa jumped in front of Gunz. She spread her arms wide, shielding Gunz with her slender body. Aidan grunted and got rid of the energy ball, in fear of hurting Tessa.

"How dare *you!*" she yelled, fearlessly taking a step closer to Aidan. He was blazing with the energy of his magic, his eyes were burning with fury, but at this moment it seemed, Tessa couldn't care less. "You lied to me for years! All this time, I thought that you were a normal human being. But you're neither normal nor human. I called Zane for help because my problem was supernatural. That's right – super-natural." She pronounced the last word, breaking it into two parts. "He didn't hide the truth from me. I knew what he was, and this is why I called him. If you didn't lie to me about what you were, I would probably call you, jackass!"

"I did not lie to you, Tessa!" yelled Aidan, anger spiking the magical energy around him with unbelievable strength. "I didn't want to expose you to the world of magic. I was trying to protect you. You didn't even give me a chance! At the first opportunity, you jumped into his bed."

"Whoa... Stop right there, Aidan," said Gunz stepping forward. "Nothing like that happened or could ever happen between me and Tessa."

"Silence, lizard!" snarled Aidan. He snapped his fingers and Gunz felt an invisible collar wrapping around his neck, squeezing his windpipe. "I wasn't talking to you."

Automatically, his hands moved to his neck as he struggled to breathe. He channeled as much fire through his body as he could without reverting to his natural state, obliterating the restraints of Aidan's magic.

Tessa jumped forward, stomping her foot angrily. "No, you shut up!" she yelled, punching Aidan in his chest. "Who the hell are you to tell me who I can or cannot sleep with? You're not my father. It's none of your business, you jerk. Unlike you, Zane doesn't lie to me. He is exactly what he says he is."

Aidan grabbed Tessa's wrists, pulling her closer. "Is he now? Are you sure he told you everything?" he hissed, staring at her with his unnerving white eyes. Then he glanced at Gunz and smirked. "Do you want to tell her what you are, Gunz, or should I?"

"God knows what *you* are, but I know exactly what he is, Aidan. He's a Fire Salamander!" shouted Tessa, twisting her hands, trying to get free from Aidan's grip. Then Aidan's words dawned on her and she stared at Gunz over her shoulder. "Wait... Gunz? Why did he call you that, Zane?"

"Because it's my nickname," said Gunz with a sigh. "That what my friends used to call me back in Belarus."

"Tell her about your daytime job, Gunz," suggested Aidan snidely.

"How is that relevant to anything?" asked Gunz, fighting a losing battle with anger.

"Let me do the honors." Aidan laughed, his face remaining cold. "Tessa, your reptilian pet here is an FBI agent. He was undercover, investigating all of us, including you." Aidan let go of Tessa's wrists and she slowly turned around to face Gunz.

"Tessa, I'm not an FBI agent. I'm a consultant, working with the paranormal division of the FBI," explained Gunz.

He reached in the pocket of his pants and showed her his FBI consultant badge. She glanced at the badge and lowered her eyes, shaking her head. The disappointment was exuding from her every move. With regret Gunz realized, that no matter what he was going to say, his relationship with Tessa was most likely ruined and the person who would suffer the most, was Tessa.

"Yes, I was undercover, but I wasn't investigating any of you," said Gunz, stepping closer to her, but she staggered back, away from him and held her hand up to stop him. "Not you, Master McGrath, not you, Tessa. I was investigating five paranormal homicides that were committed in the area... As of today, it's already seven homicides... I'm sorry, I didn't tell you about that. But the work I do with FBI is classified."

Tessa backed away toward the door, her eyes darting from Gunz to Aidan, a pained expression on her face.

"Gunz... or whatever your name is... You're an FBI consultant," she whispered, gazing at him reproachfully.

"Tessa—," started Gunz, but she didn't listen to him. Slowly she turned to Aidan, tears silently running down her pale face.

"Aidan, I don't even know what you are... You were my only friend, my stronghold, my safe place... You were my everything, Aidan... But now, I don't know you anymore..." She shook her head, her lips quivering. "I don't want to see either of you." Tessa pivoted on her heels and stormed out of the house.

"Tessa, wait," said Gunz, taking a step forward.

"Stay still," commanded Aidan frostily and the energy of his magic wrapped around Gunz's body, pinning him in place. "I'm not done with you."

"But I'm done with you!" growled Gunz.

The fire rose in him, burning out the chains of Aidan's magic. He pulled the fire into his hands and redirected a smoldering stream of flames at his opponent. Aidan laughed and blasted Gunz with the blazing ray of his magic. The red beam of fire collided with the white ray of pure magical energy with a thunderous bang. Gunz reached for more fire, now his whole body ablaze.

Aidan extended his arm up, shouted something and icy rain fell from the ceiling. Gunz cried out, the touch of freezing water and icicles to his skin sent him into the abyss of pain. Ignoring the pain, he let the fire take over, bordering with reverting into his natural state. The water started to evaporate at the touch with his scorching skin, hissing loudly. The swirls of steam rose in the air.

Despite all that, his stream of fire didn't waver, and Aidan howled in rage. He intertwined the elemental power of water with the stream of his magical energy. The ground quacked. The water clashed with fire, filling the house with hot steam. The room looked like a battlefield, but neither Aidan nor Gunz were willing to stop.

Mishka assumed his true form, yelled something to Gunz and vanished. A few minutes later, a fire curtain manifested in the living room and a giant man walked through it. Fire was burning in the bottom of his deeply set eyes and his flaming red hair was flowing to his back. He folded his brawny arms over his wide chest and for a few seconds, he was standing still, observing the reenactment of the doomsday prophesy that was unfolding in the living room of the small suburban house. Neither Gunz nor Aidan noticed his presence, until it was too late.

"Cease!" shouted the man. His voice strong and deep reverberated from the walls of the room. The fire obeyed his command, ceasing immediately. Both Gunz and Aidan stopped the fight and stared at the man.

"Kal," whispered Gunz, breathing hard.

"Great Salamander," said Aidan, bowing.

"Silence!" shouted Kal, anger setting his arms and hair into scorching flames. He turned to Gunz and extended his hand to him. "Fire Salamander, down! You're grounded until the end of your days, boy!"

The tight grip of Kal's control, twisted Gunz's body. He collapsed to his knees, bowing low to the floor. Gunz knew that it was useless to fight against Kal's control, but he couldn't help but struggle. "Kal, please, let me explain," he pleaded.

"I said, silence!" boomed the Great Salamander and turned to

Aidan. "Aidan McGrath, stop the water. You're destroying the house that belongs to the Mistress of Power."

Aidan waved his hand, stopping the flow of water. Kal frowned at him and shook his head.

"Aidan McGrath, you're over two thousand years old, but you are behaving like a hormonal teenager," yelled Kal, throwing his hands in the air. "Jealousy scrambled your brain to the point that you can't see what's right in front of your eyes!"

Kal turned to Gunz, his eyes blazing with fury.

"And you, my Salamander, I'm so disappointed," he shouted, stamping his foot. "Did I teach you nothing? You are still punching first, asking questions later!" He stopped talking, breathing hard, glaring at Aidan and Gunz with reproach. "What's wrong with both of you? Don't you see? You two have a common enemy! But the two of you prefer to turn your powers against each other instead of combining them to fight your adversary!"

Kal approached Gunz and lifted him with one arm, easily throwing him over his shoulder. Then he turned back to Aidan.

"Aidan McGrath, out of respect to your mentor, I'm not going tell my Salamander who and what you are, even though you didn't think twice before exposing his identity. I'll let you think about everything and when you're ready, you need to find Gunz and do it yourself. You two must find a way to put your petty differences aside and work together if you want to survive and give a chance of survival to all the humans of this world. Get in touch with your mentor, Aidan, and talk to him. It's important. Do you understand me, boy?"

"Yes, my lord," replied Aidan with a respectful bow.

Kal waved his hand, unfolding his fire portal and walked up to it with Gunz's limp body hanging over his shoulder. Gunz couldn't move, completely subdued by Kal's control. Kal stopped next to the portal and turned to Aidan again.

"And Aidan... I'll let it slide this time, but I swear, you try and put your hand on my Salamander again and even your mentor won't be able to help you against my wrath. Only I can reprimand my children. No one else. Am I clear, Aidan McGrath?"

"Yes, my lord," replied Aidan quietly.

Gunz snickered inside. He wished he could see Aidan's face at this moment, but he was immobilized to the point that he couldn't even move his eyes.

* * *

KAL WALKED through his portal and gently lowered Gunz down on the floor. Gunz was still controlled by Kal. He couldn't get up, but his body was trembling violently, a thick blue vein pulsing on his neck. It wasn't fear that was making him shake. Kal controlled him even though he swore that he would never use his power against him. He made him kneel in front of this asshole Aidan McGrath. And right now, a raw rage was tearing through him, making him quiver with indignation.

"Gunz, my Salamander, I'm sorry, I had to control you. I had to give a show to Aidan McGrath and let him think that I was upset with you," whispered Kal, kneeling next to him. "Don't be afraid. You didn't do anything wrong and I'm not here to punish you. You may rise, my child."

As soon as Kal released him, Gunz exploded up, reverting to his natural state and rising to the same height as Kal. His rage was fueling his power and the fire wrapped around him like a scorching spiral.

"I'm not scared of you, Kal, I'm pissed! You controlled me!" shouted Gunz, punching the air, and his voice infused with fire, bounced off the tall ceiling.

"I love to see you so powerful, so fierce," said Kal unphased by Gunz's outburst, a light smile curving his thin lips. "Maybe I should control you more often?"

"Ugh," Gunz growled, going back to his human form and his

normal height. "Kal, you're just unbearable, infuriating… Why did you bring me here? And where are we?"

Gunz looked around, not recognizing the place. He was in a large room that looked like a bedroom suite of some luxury five-star hotel, furnished with expensive modern furniture and decorated in contemporary style. He walked to the window and separated the vertical blinds. An unobstructed view of the ocean unfolded before his eyes.

"You're not far from home, my child," said Kal. "This is one of my residences in this world. Fire-proof and protected, for the humans' sake of course. You can safely stay in your natural state here if that's what you want."

"Why did you bring me here," asked Gunz, searching for a chair. After everything that happened, he felt exhausted. He found a chair next to a small round table and sat down.

"I brought you here because you needed a break," said Kal. "The last few days got you exhausted as a man and drained you as the Salamander. You still have a lot to learn, my child. After you sort this mess out, you should come back to me and spend some time learning and training."

He stopped behind Gunz and put his hand on his head, slowly circulating the Fire energy through him. Gunz sighed and closed his eyes, enjoying the flow of his element.

"Thank you," he mumbled drowsily.

Kal stopped the flow of power and sat down on a chair across from him. Gunz stretched his arm on the table and rested his head on top of his arm.

"Gunz, I'll let you take a rest in a few minutes," promised Kal, "but let's have a quick talk first."

"Okay…"

"I have to tell you the same thing I already said to Aidan – you must put your differences aside and work together."

"I already tried to work with him – didn't work," muttered

Gunz, his eyes closing. "I can't do it. He's an insufferable, arrogant jackass."

"I'm sure that after Aidan will have a talk with his mentor, he may change his attitude a bit," said Kal, snickering.

"Who is his mentor," asked Gunz without opening his eyes, his mind drifting on and off. "What is he? Can you tell me?"

"I know who Aidan is and I know his mentor very well," replied Kal, tapping on Gunz's hand to wake him up. "But I promised that I wouldn't tell you. His mentor believes that Aidan needs to do it himself."

"Whatever..."

"When you get back home tomorrow, I need you to meet with Aidan," said Kal. "I know that you don't want to, but you must. Do you understand me, Salamander?"

"Yes, sir..." Gunz lifted his head tiredly and looked at Kal. "I need to get some rest, I'm sorry. I forgot already when I had a decent sleep."

"Gunz, you and Aidan need to find Eve and stop her," said Kal, rising. "She is more powerful and a lot scarier than you think. She must be stopped. Am I clear?"

"How did you know about Eve? And what do you know about her?"

Gunz got up, swaying and stared at Kal, surprised. He didn't remember saying anything to Kal about his conversation with the Russian mobster. Before he finished saying it, he remembered about Mishka. Of course, the pesky wyvern was spying for Kal. He was probably the one who brought Kal in the midst of his fight with Aidan.

"Only what I just said." Kal pulled him toward the bed. "She's an unspeakable evil and whatever she's up to can't be any good. You must stop her."

"Oh good," mumbled Gunz falling on the bed, "we're on the same page then. I also want to find this Eve, very much... But I need to find Tessa and take care of her situation too."

"Forget about Tessa, Gunz," said Kal with a sigh, sitting down on the edge of the bed next to him. "Aidan is head over heels with her and his jealousy is driving this pointless confrontation between you two. Let Aidan take care of her. Besides that, she has a Guardian. At the moment, she's a lot safer than you or Aidan. He doesn't even realize yet in what kind of danger he is."

"Fine," agreed Gunz. He just had no strength to argue with Kal. "Do you know what Tessa is? Why the Guardians are protecting her?"

Kal threw his hands in the air. "It's like talking to a wall," he muttered under his breath, but Gunz heard him and the corners of his lips quirked up. "I'm not telling you anything. Forget it for now. You have a more important mission. Do you understand me, Salamander?"

"Yes, sir," said Gunz, raising his hand to his temple in a mock military salute.

"Ahh, you're a pain in the ass, Salamander," muttered Kal, rising. "Remember your mission. Nothing else matters."

"Yes, sir…"

"I'm leaving. When you wake up tomorrow, just open the portal to your house."

"Yes, sir… Thank you, Father…" said Guns hardly moving his lips and a split-second later, he was fast asleep.

~ ZANE BURNS, A.K.A. GUNZ ~

"*W*akey-wakey, lizard-head."

Gunz opened his eyes and jerked back. Mishka, the wyvern, was hovering an inch above his face. He waved his hand at the wyvern, like he was nothing but an annoying insect. Shrilling his battle cry, Mishka made a loop de loop in the air and swooshed down over his arm. With his sharp claws, he caught the edge of the blanket and ripped it off Gunz.

"Hibernation is over," announced Mishka zooming in front of Gunz's eyes.

"Hibernation?" Gunz sat up, rubbing his eyes. The window blinds were open, and the sunlight was flowing freely into the room. He glanced around, recalling his confrontation with Aidan McGrath and shuddered. Kal was nowhere to be seen, and Gunz wished that his mentor was here, so he could talk to him now, when he wasn't completely wiped out.

Kal didn't like to get involved in mortal affairs. Normally, to get any information from him was as hard as getting a vampire to sunbathe. The Great Salamander would speak in riddles, avoiding giving him a straight answer. But yesterday he was straight forward, ordering Gunz to work with Aidan McGrath. It could mean only one thing – dealing with Eve, whoever or whatever she was, was no joking matter. Kal was seriously concerned. And if his powerful and fearless mentor felt uneasy, Gunz should take this situation seriously.

He got off the bed and to his surprise noticed a clean set of his clothes by the bedside, including his sneakers. Kal cared enough to go back to his house in Coral Springs and deliver the clothes to him. After all, when Kal carried him here through the portal, Gunz had only his pants on. His cell phone was lying next to his clothes, fully charged. He picked up the phone and noticed three missed calls from Jim. The phone was showing ten in the morning, and he thought that he'd call Jim as soon as he got back home. Jim could wait a few more minutes.

Gunz went to the shower and turned the shower handle all the way to the left. The burning-hot water rushed down his body and he lifted his face up, enjoying the heat. Thirty minutes later, he walked back into the room, feeling refreshed and energized. The smell of freshly made coffee was floating in the air and he glanced around surprised.

Mishka flew closer to him, holding a fresh white towel in his paw. "Your coffee is served, boss," he announced, waving the towel in the direction of the table.

Gunz sat down, taking the hot cup. "Thank you, Mishka. I needed it."

"I bet you needed it after your hibernation," muttered Mishka, moving a plate with a piece of toast closer to him.

"You keep saying 'hibernation,'" said Gunz sipping his coffee, giving Mishka a wary look. "Why is that?"

"You don't know?" asked Mishka, landing on the table in front of him.

"What exactly am I supposed to know?"

"Remember, I'm just a messenger," said Mishka, pushing Gunz's cell phone toward him. "What date is it today, boss?"

Gunz grabbed the phone and stared at the screen. "Holy shit!" he exclaimed jumping off his chair, almost spilling his coffee. "Are you saying I slept almost forty hours straight?"

"I'm saying nothing," muttered Mishka, inching his way to the other end of the table. "Your phone is saying that. You should be mad at your phone, not at your loyal and wise wyvern."

"Why would I be mad at you, Mishka?" asked Gunz quickly downing the rest of his coffee. "Why didn't you wake me up yesterday morning?"

"Oh, I guess you should be mad at your Father then," replied Mishka. "Yesterday morning, Kal told me to let you get as much rest as you needed. He also said that he didn't know when you'll be able to sleep again. Well, you know me – I usually do what the Great Salamander says. So, I waited for you to wake up on your own, but I got too bored."

"Jeez, this sounds promising," muttered Gunz, getting up, putting his phone in the back pocket of his pants. He cleaned the table, took the cup and plate to the kitchen and waited until Mishka vanished from the room, camouflaging himself in his watch before opening the portal to his house.

* * *

GUNZ WALKED through the portal and halted, astonished. He was expecting to see his living room in ruins, destroyed by Aidan's magic, glass all over the floor and a demolished front door. In his mind he was counting how much money he would need and how much work he would have to do to fix everything and buy new furniture and a big screen TV. Instead, he found that a new door and windows were already installed, the furniture and TV were replaced, and the house was sparkling-clean.

A plain white envelope with his name written on it was lying down on the coffee table. Gunz recognized Jim's handwriting. He sat down on the new couch and opened the envelope. Inside the envelope he found a new set of keys for his front door and a short note.

"*Gunz,*

I know what happened and I know that you're okay, but please call me as soon as you come back home. We need to talk. Everything inside your house was fixed and I took the liberty of purchasing new furniture for your living room since your old one was completely destroyed by water. All expenses were paid in full by your mentor.

Call me as soon as you can.

Jim.

P.S. The Master of Power made everything fireproof for you. You're all set."

Gunz put the letter on the table and attached the new key to his keychain. He carefully probed the house to find that all his wards and protection spells were restored and improved. *Kal took care of everything,* thought Gunz gratefully.

Now it was his turn to keep his word he gave Kal and meet with Aidan McGrath. Gunz locked the house and got into his car. He pulled out of the driveway and using the handsfree system, called Jim. Right after a quick "hi, how are you" Jim told him that Kal paid him a visit, accompanied by a Master of Power. Apparently, the Great Salamander wanted to make sure that his child didn't get in trouble with his boss at work and made a point to apologize to Jim personally for Gunz's prolonged absence.

With awe, Jim told him that as soon as Kal walked into the office, Angelique's magic detector blew up in her hands. Neither him nor Angelique ever met anyone with such powerful magical energy as Kal. Even the Masters of Power with their legendary elemental power, weren't as strong.

Masters of Power were magical beings who could wield and control all four elemental powers. Besides that, all the Masters of Power were skillful wizards and they were considered one of the most powerful magical beings in the universe. But as rare as they were, Jim had met all three of them before. However, it was the first time that he met an Elemental, the mighty Fire Elemental to boot, and he wasn't hiding his excitement.

"Your intimidating mentor cares about you," said Jim and there was a suggestive silence after the statement.

"Why do I feel that there is a 'but' coming up?" muttered Gunz.

Jim cleared his throat. "But... there was something he said that was quite unsettling, at least to me." He fell silent again for a moment and Gunz heard the sound of crumbled paper and the soft thud of a paper ball thrown against the wall.

"What did he say?" asked Gunz calmly. "You can tell me, Jim. I know Kal well. He's not an idiot. He realizes that you will tell me everything he said. So, most likely whatever he said to you was meant for my ears."

"You're right," agreed Jim after another short pause and sighed. "After Kal reviewed the wall of fame, he told me straight that I need to let you fight Eve on your own and that I should pull all humans and even Angelique out of your way. In so many words, your mentor told me to leave you unsupported. And when I told him that I would never do it, he said that in this fight you're safer alone. He said that the presence of humans will hold you back."

"I see," said Gunz, wondering if there was something that Kal wasn't telling him about this Eve. Probably there was, and it was pissing him off. If Eve was so dangerous, Kal should have disclosed every bit of information he had on her.

"I can't do it, Gunz," said Jim. "I can't leave you without any support."

"Thank you, Jim. But Kal is probably right. This fight is not going to be your average confrontation with a vanilla werewolf. I don't even know who this Eve is and what kind of beasty she is. Honestly? I don't even know where to start looking for her."

"Start from the beginning," suggested Jim. "When my investigation gets into a dead-end, I usually retrace my steps, going all the way to the very beginning. Think, when was the first time that you noticed something off?"

Gunz thought for a moment. The first time when he noticed a weird behavior of the supernatural community in the city was that incident with a succubus at *Missi's Kitchen*. And then there were the demons attacking Tessa. And of course, Master McGrath and his mighty supernatural crew. He told Jim about that.

"I would start with that succubus. Visit the *Temptress* club. Most of their kind are working there. Have a talk, see what gives," suggested Jim. "As far as Aidan McGrath and Tessa Donovan, I got whatever I could on them. It's not much and there is absolutely nothing special there but stop by my office and I'll give you everything I have."

Temptress of the Night was a bar-style strip club run by one of the demonic rulers. There were a few of them, controlling different factions of supernatural beings in Florida. It was a more or less successful attempt of some of the members of the supernatural community to fit into the normal, mundane life without making their presence obvious to humans. While succubi and incubi were still feeding on human souls, they were curbing their natural desire to kill and were taking only a little bit of the soul energy at the time, keeping their clients alive and happy, and laughing all the way to the bank.

Jim and his team were always keeping a close eye on the establishments run by the supernatural rulers, but since no one ever was seriously harmed or killed in the *Temptress* club, they let them be. It was either that or dealing with the demons and monsters sneaking around in the night and killing people.

Not all the demons, monsters and creatures of magic were regulated and controlled by their organizations. Unfortunately, the majority of them were still living by the old rules where humans were on the bottom of the food chain. This is where Jim's team and a few of the rogue hunters had their hands full.

"I'm on my way to see Aidan McGrath," said Gunz, cringing inwardly at the thought. "Kal's order. I have to find a way to work with this self-important asshole. Anyway, I'll call you after I'm done with him and if you're free at that time, I'll stop by."

After Gunz hung up the phone, he thought about Tessa, fighting with the desire to call her. He was worried about her. She stormed out of his house, leaving behind the only two people who could help her. He lost Tessa's trust and unfortunately Aidan fell from his shining pedestal too. She was alone, with no one to call in case of trouble, supernatural or otherwise.

Gunz cursed silently, blaming himself for everything that happened, and pressed the handsfree button on the steering wheel, calling Tessa. The dial tone rung five times before the outgoing message of her voicemail started to play. He hung up before the beep, not sure if he should leave a message. After a minute of thinking, he redialed her number. Tessa didn't answer again, but this time he waited for the outgoing message to play out and for the beep.

"Hi Tessa, this is Zane. I know you're upset with me and I understand," he said, trying to sound calm and friendly, "but please, call me back when you get this message. We need to talk. It's important."

By the time he finished leaving the message and hung up the phone, he was already turning into the parking lot in front of Aidan's school. Gunz parked his car at the far end of the parking lot and was sitting for a few minutes observing the school. It was early afternoon and the school was filled with kids. He knew that Aidan wasn't going to appreciate his daytime intrusion, but at this point he couldn't care less.

Gunz walked out of the car and clicked the lock button on the remote. The car didn't beep. He turned around and pulled on the door handle to make sure that it was locked. The push in his back was so unexpected and forceful that he staggered forward, falling on the side of his car. Before he could react, a few pairs of hands twisted his arms back, immobilizing him. At the same time, someone grabbed his hair and brutally slammed his head against the side of the car.

A searing pain exploded in his head and everything went dark.

~ ZANE BURNS, A.K.A. GUNZ ~

*D*arkness, pain and movement. These were the first three things Gunz registered as soon as he regained consciousness. He remained calm and motionless, hoping that whoever kidnapped him wouldn't notice that he was awake, and quickly assessed his situation.

Darkness – a tight blindfold over his eyes.

Pain, a constant dull ache in his head – whoever abducted him probably banged his head a few times, even after he was out.

And the movement – no doubt, he was inside a moving vehicle. A slight smell of fresh lumber was lingering in the air. *Probably this vehicle was used for construction purposes. It had to be a commercial van,* decided Gunz.

He carefully shifted his hands, just to confirm that his wrists were bound behind his back. He smirked. The idiots didn't use handcuffs and bound his wrists with nylon ties. They probably had no clue who he was and what they were dealing with. Carefully, he scanned the vehicle with his Salamander sense. He registered the presence of three humans – one was a little farther away, in the driver's seat, and two more were right next to him. He rolled his eyes under the blindfold, keeping his head bowed down to his chest. Most likely, they were Anatoly's thugs. The men were speaking quietly in Russian and that confirmed his theory.

Gunz channeled some fire, directing it to his wrists. The nylon ties were gone a second later, and his hands were free. Without any rush, he brought his hands up and took the blindfold off. He was on the backseat of a large van with all the windows covered, and the two idiots that were supposed to guard him were so busy yammering away that they didn't even notice that he was restraints-free.

He leaned back in his seat and folded his arms over his chest. His every move was accompanied by a throbbing pain in his head. He brought his hand up and touched his forehead, feeling the stickiness of blood under his fingers. The back of his head was also sore, but he didn't bother checking it.

"Hello, comrades," he said in Russian, an uneven smile curving his lips. "Didn't Anatoly warn you that you need to treat me with TLC?"

Both men jumped up and spun toward him, their eyes bulging. They looked like brothers – both were tall, beefy, blond, with short military-style haircuts and five-o'clock shadows on their chiseled chins. Poster-children for the American stereotype of Russian thugs from the Cold War era, short of t-shirts with the hammer and sickle on their chests. One of them moved his hand down to his gun holster. Gunz pursed his lips and wagged his finger at him warningly.

"Don't bother," he said coldly. "It won't be necessary. I'll go with you willingly. Besides, I can kill you faster than you can pull that gun out of your holster."

"How the hell did you—," started to say one of the men, but fell silent, catching Gunz's sarcastic grin.

"No, seriously, boys," said Gunz, starting to feel frustration as the pain in his head increased. "Didn't Anatoly tell you how to treat me properly?"

The men exchanged a look and sat down. Even though one of them was still holding his hand on his gun, the second one looked completely at ease. Gunz decided to keep him in his happy oblivion for as long as it was possible. He preferred to be underestimated by his oversized opponents. Just in case.

"Yeah, Anatoly told us to bring a few fire extinguishers," replied the second man. He pulled a fire extinguisher from under his seat and brought it forward. Pointing at the dent on the canister, he snickered. "He didn't specify how to use them."

"That was absolutely unnecessary," muttered Gunz, lying down across the back seat of the van and put his hand under his aching head. "All you had to do was tell me that Anatoly wanted to meet with me. Do any of you, schmucks, have Tylenol? The headache you gave me is a bitch."

"You'll survive," huffed the second man with a cold smirk. He stepped forward and looked outside through the windshield. "We're just a short distance away from the final destination. And I'm sure, after you meet with Anatoly, you will need something stronger than Tylenol."

Gunz didn't answer. He put his arm over his eyes and relaxed, thinking why Anatoly would send two of his men to bring him over, instead of paying him a visit at his house like he did the last time. He knew that it would be a matter of a few seconds for him to knock out these two morons and escape the van. As frustrated as he was, now he wanted to meet with Anatoly and see what had changed, hoping to get more information on Eve.

The van came to a soft stop a few minutes later. Gunz sat down, staring at his entourage quizzically. One of them picked up the blindfold off the floor and showed it to Gunz.

"This is going back up and so is this," he said, pulling another nylon tie out of his pocket, a contemptuous smirk on his face. Gunz could see that the idea of restraining him again was pleasing this idiot. Obviously these two were too busy pumping iron when God was giving away the brains.

"You know that neither of these things can hold me for longer than a second," said Gunz frostily. "Assuming that you've got what it takes to restrain me against my will."

His statement wiped the smirks cleanly off their faces and the men exchanged a troubled look. The one with the gun stepped forward. "Come on, man," he said sounding almost pleadingly, fidgeting with the ties. "We're just doing our job. Rules are rules. You said, you wanted to talk to Anatoly? Well, this is the only way you can see him."

"Fine," muttered Gunz, extending his hands forward.

"Behind your back," ordered the thug with the nylon tie in his hand.

Gunz sighed but turned around and crossed his hands behind his back. The man bound his wrists. Gunz grunted and pulled against his restraints. The tie was applied too tight, cutting off his circulation. The second man put the blindfold over his eyes and everything went dark.

They helped Gunz out of the van and walked him through something that could've been a driveway. He heard the sound of an opened door and felt the coolness of an air-conditioned space on his skin. He was inside a house. One of the men warned him that they'll be taking the stairs to the second floor. Walking to the second floor blindfolded and with his hands behind his back wasn't very comfortable, but luckily the thugs weren't rushing him. One more door was opened for him and his escort finally stopped him.

"Take his restraints off." He heard Anatoly's soft voice and a second later his hands were free, and he could see the light of day again.

He was standing in the middle of a large room that was furnished as a private office. The heavy burgundy panels were concealing two large windows, preventing the sunlight from coming in. The room was illuminated by a large chandelier that was hanging from the ceiling. The dark-wood parquet floor was polished to perfection and shone like dark ice, reflecting the soft electric light of the chandelier. Anatoly was sitting behind a massive mahogany desk staring at Gunz over the rim of his glasses. His attentive eyes darted up and he frowned at the sight of the blood.

"Mr. Burns, please," he said gesturing at a leather armchair, offering Gunz to sit down.

Gunz sat down, noticing that the two thugs shifted a little closer, now standing behind his chair, glued to him like two unwanted shadows.

"Mr. Karpenko," said Gunz frostily. "I heard you wanted to see me?"

"Yes, Mr. Burns. The situation we discussed a few days earlier has escalated and I needed to make sure that we're on the same page," replied Anatoly. He entwined his fingers and Gunz noticed that he squeezed his hands together nervously, his fingernails digging into his skin.

"What's going on? Do you have anything new on Eve's whereabouts?" asked Gunz. He glanced over his shoulder at Anatoly's men. The idea of two jumbo-sized dimwits looming behind his back was making him edgy. He turned back to Anatoly. "You can let your people go. I guarantee your safety. At least for the duration of this meeting."

Anatoly stared at him for a moment and shook his head, his dark eyes becoming icy-cold. "No, Mr. Burns, they stay."

Gunz shrugged indifferently. "So, what was so urgent that you sent your people to abduct me and bring me here – beat up, unconscious and restrained? Do you really think that treating me like this will help your cause or make me move faster?"

Anatoly's eyebrows rose as he stared heavily at the two men. "Beat up and unconscious?" Both men shrunk under his gaze. Anatoly turned to Gunz and said, "I apologize, Mr. Burns. It wasn't my intent to hurt you."

"That's okay, Anatoly. I don't blame your employees," replied

Gunz with an evil grin. "I'm sure, when they were observing me from their height of six-foot-five my formidable frame of five-foot-six would have an extremely intimidating effect. They had no choice but to handle me quickly and roughly."

Anatoly grunted, and his thick brows pulled down over his eyes. "Mr. Burns, for what I have to discuss with you, I need your full and undivided attention, as well as a clear state of mind. If you're in pain and need to heal your wounds, I have a fireproof room here."

"Your room can't withstand my fire, and frankly, none of you can, so please proceed. I'm all ears," replied Gunz coldly.

"Fine, let's proceed," said Anatoly curtly. "Yesterday my daughter, Tanya, was kidnapped. My fourteen-year old child was taken from my own home!" He slammed his hand on the table and squeezed his fingers into a fist so tight that his knuckles cracked. He closed his eyes for a moment, his jaw clenched.

Gunz stiffened, bracing for whatever Anatoly was planning to unleash on him. It wasn't hard to guess that if Eve wasn't involved in Anatoly's daughter's disappearance, he wouldn't be here right now. Eve was growing impatient. She killed two of Anatoly's righthand men and now she took his daughter.

Things were moving too fast, becoming extremely personal for the head of the Russian mob. Just like any good father, Anatoly would do anything to see his daughter safe, back in his embrace. But with the ethics and resources of the Russian mob, his fatherly love was becoming a liability for everyone around him.

"Eve called me the same day and informed me that she had my daughter. She even let me talk to Tanya," continued Anatoly through clenched teeth. "She told me that if I don't do what was asked of me, seven days from now, she'll kill my daughter... my little girl..." His voice trembled and trailed off. "I hope you understand the gravity of the situation I am in, Mr. Burns. I need you to work faster."

"Anatoly, I'm truly sorry it came to this," said Gunz, "but trust me, I'm doing everything I can to find this Eve. And at this point, it's not only your blackmail that makes me look for her. There are other circumstances that are pushing me to work on this case."

"I don't care what makes you work on this!" yelled Anatoly, rising, slamming his fist on the table. He stood, rigid and tense, staring down at Gunz, his eyes blazing with fury. Gunz met his drilling gaze calmly. "I don't know what other circumstances you're talking about and I don't give a damn. But trust me, Mr. Burns! You're going to get cracking. Eve made it personal for me, and I had no choice but to make it extremely personal for you!"

Anatoly grabbed the monitor on his desk and sharply turned it around so Gunz could see the screen. Gunz glanced at the black-and-white video of the security camera and fear twisted his gut. A woman was sitting on a bed inside a tiny dark room with a small window under the ceiling, with an iron grille over it.

"Lena..." exhaled Gunz, cold sweat running down his back.

"That's right," said Anatoly. "This is Lena. But wait, I'm not done."

He pushed a few buttons on the keyboards and the video on the screen changed. Another tiny room with an iron-clothed window. A man was lying on the bed, his hands crossed on his stomach. Anatoly took his phone and dialed a number.

"Please give the phone to Mr. Shevchenko," he ordered coldly.

Sasha. Alone, thought Gunz, his brain on fire. *If he has Sasha and Lena, no doubt Sergei is somewhere there too.*

On the video, a tall man in all black walked into the cell and pushed Sasha's shoulder. Sasha got up and took the phone.

"Mr. Shevchenko," said Anatoly. "In a minute, I'll give this phone to the only person who can save yours and your friends' lives. I hope you can convince him to do what needs to be done."

Anatoly silently offered the phone to Gunz. He took the phone with unbending fingers and pressed it to his ear.

"Sasha," he whispered, "do you know where you are?"

"Gunz? You're the man who —," he cut himself off and swallowed. "I have no idea where I am. What do they want from you?"

"They want me to kill someone," replied Gunz, his throat dry. "Not a human... a creature of magic. I still don't know what she is and where to look for her."

The man walked back into the room and extended his hand, demanding the phone back.

"Gunz, I don't care what they will do to me," said Sasha, speaking fast, "but you can't let Sergei and Lena die. Gunz—"

The guard pulled the phone out of Sasha's hand and walked out. Gunz slowly raised his gaze, furious flames igniting in the bottom of his eyes. He couldn't speak, his throat constricted with anger and fear for his friends. The fire rose within him, wrapping his arms into the silky ribbons of flames. For the first time since he moved to Florida, he wasn't sure that he was in control of his power.

"Mr. Burns are we on the same page now?" barked Anatoly Karpenko.

Gunz swallowed, a muscle twitched in his jaw. He was afraid that if he would make a move or say a word, the fire would take him over. So, he remained silent and motionless, pinning Anatoly with his furious gaze.

"Mr. Burns, I promise that as soon as Tanya is back with me, your friends will be released, unharmed," said Anatoly quietly. He stared at Gunz, his expression blank and emotionless. "Now, I need you to get things rolling. Do you understand me?"

Gunz gave him a hardly visible nod, slowly getting in control of his power. "Anatoly," he whispered, his voice hoarse, "I will find this Eve and I'll save your daughter. But if anything happens to my friends..." He clenched his teeth and took a pause, forcing the fire in him down. "There will be no place in this world or any other world where you'll be safe. Do *you* understand me?"

"Yes, Mr. Burns," replied Anatoly, calm and unphased, "I wouldn't expect anything different from you." He turned to his men and waved his hand. "Please take Mr. Burns home and this time treat him with care. I need him in good shape."

One of the men approached Gunz, showing him the blindfold. Gunz pulled away, his upper lip curled in contempt. His first desire was to send this man tumbling down to the floor. The fire surged through him again, accumulating in his hands. He decided not to wait until he wouldn't be able to control his power anymore and waved his hand, opening his portal.

Before Anatoly's thugs were able to stop him, he walked through the fire curtain and vanished from the room.

~ ZANE BURNS, A.K.A. GUNZ ~

*G*unz stumbled through the portal, falling out into his backyard. He dropped on all fours, taking shallow, rapid breaths. His heart was beating in his throat and his stomach heaved. He grunted, fighting nausea and forced himself to his feet. Moving slowly, he unlocked the door and headed straight to the living room. He needed a breather, a momentary reprieve so he could settle the spiraling turmoil in his mind. He couldn't allow himself to panic. Not now, not when his friends' survival was dependent on him.

With shaking hands, Gunz opened the wine cabinet and pulled the bottle of vodka. The small shot glass that he always kept in the cabinet wasn't there. Frustrated, he grabbed the bottle and walked back to the kitchen, cursing Anatoly, Eve, and his magic that put his friends in harm's way. He placed the bottle on the kitchen counter and pulled a glass out of the cabinet.

For a moment, he was at a standstill, staring at the bottle with the clear liquid inside without blinking. He wasn't thinking, his mind finally blank. Slowly, the rage started to rise within him, replacing the last traces of panic. Gunz snatched the bottle off the counter and slammed it forcefully into the kitchen sink. The bottle shattered into countless sparkling pieces, the heavy smell of alcohol rising in the air. The shards of glass flew in every direction, slashing his arm in a few places.

Like in a trance, he watched the dark crimson fluid trickling down his arm, not registering the pain. A loud knock on the door broke him out of his stupor. He walked toward the entrance door and opened it. Angelique and Jim were standing outside.

"Oh, wow," said Jim, taking in Gunz's appearance, shaking his head. "Angelique, I owe you twenty bucks." He pulled out his wallet and gave Angelique a twenty-dollar bill.

"Do you mind if we come in?" she asked, putting the money away into her purse.

"I'm sorry, of course. Please, come in," mumbled Gunz, stepping aside. "What's with money?"

Jim walked into the living room and sat down on the couch, propping his elbows on his knees. Angelique stopped next to Gunz and gently touched his arm, checking the thin lacerations on his bicep.

"Well, Angelique said that something was going on with you and I didn't believe her," explained Jim with a light flick of his hand. "How could I know that she was crazy enough to keep a psychic connection with you? If I knew I wouldn't bet."

Gunz gaped at Angelique, a thousand thoughts flashing through his mind. He didn't ask anything, but she blushed under his gaze and looked away.

"I'll be right back," she mumbled uncomfortably and disappeared into the kitchen. A moment later, Gunz heard her picking up the shards of the glass off the floor and throwing them in the garbage.

Gunz walked closer to Jim and stopped across the room from him. He leaned against the wine cabinet, folding his arms over his chest. His panic and anger subsided, leaving him tired, and now he started to feel the stinging pain of the cuts on his arm. Jim gave him another once-over and pursed his lips.

"Would you like to tell me what's going on?" asked Jim, relaxing back in the couch. "Between Angelique's psychic alarms going off and your... sunny disposition, I would really like to know what happened to throw you over the edge."

Gunz sighed and told Jim about his meeting with Anatoly Karpenko. It took him less than five minutes to tell Jim everything, but it was enough to get his blood boiling again. A heat wave spread around him, and his eyes glowed bright red.

"Gunz, you picked the worst possible time to fall apart," said Jim dryly. "What you need to do hasn't changed. You still need to continue your investigation. You still need to find Eve and get rid of her. The only thing that changed was your deadline. It got a lot shorter. So, stop crying the blues and get moving, son!"

"I'm not falling apart—," Gunz started to object, but Jim wouldn't have any part of it.

"Oh yeah?" Jim got up and shoved his hands into his pockets, staring at him mockingly. "You're going from a state of panic into obliterating rage in a heartbeat. Your hands are shaking and you're bleeding. Your house reeks of alcohol! And let's even forget about your emotional roller-coaster for the moment, Angelique could sense your power storm from miles away!"

Gunz frowned, a deep vertical crease cutting through his forehead. For many years, his friend Oleg was running from the gangs back in Belarus. Oleg had magic and the gangsters would do anything to make his magic work for them. To help him, Gunz and his friends destroyed a full branch of the Russian mob, risking their own lives.

When Gunz discovered his magic and the fire, he decided to flee from Belarus, leaving behind the land he loved and the only people who were his family. Worried about the safety of his friends, he did everything in his power to severe any kind of connections with them. It wasn't easy, but he knew that they would be safer this way. Now, Anatoly had Sergei and Sasha, and the worst of all – he had Lena, Sergei's wife. Sergei and Sasha were trained military men, but Lena was a school teacher. She was an innocent in all this, her only fault was that she knew Gunz and cared about him.

"Jim, you're right…" Gunz lowered his eyes, staring at his hands, as shame stirred in him. "I don't know what came over me. I am —" He bit his lip, frowning.

Jim sighed and approached him.

"I know what came over you. And if the situation was different, I would probably be more sympathetic to your situation." He put his hand on Gunz's shoulder and slightly squeezed it. "But there is only one thing I can tell you right now. Cowboy up, kid! You don't have the luxury of panicking and falling apart. It's not only your friends' lives that depend on your ability to fight. The way your mentor put it – you're the champion of humanity in the fight against the darkness." He laughed, throwing his head back and gave a quick tap on Gunz's shoulder. "Oh, God, we're all gonna die."

"Jim!" exclaimed Angelique indignantly and both Gunz and Jim turned to her. "Would it hurt you to be a little nicer?" She approached Gunz and started wiping blood off his arm with a wet cloth.

Gunz smiled at her, thinking how light and tender her touch was. "Angie, thank you, but you know that I can heal myself. This is just a tiny scratch. It's nothing."

"Aw, Gunz," said Jim with a smirk, winking at him. "Just sit down and relax. Let her take care of you. I'll see you both later." He waved his hand goodbye and walked out of the house.

As soon as the door closed behind Jim, Angelique gave him an arched stare and slapped him lightly on his shoulder.

"You heard the boss," she said in no-nonsense tone. "Now sit your ass down on that couch and be quiet."

"Yes, ma'am," said Gunz, giving her a military salute and sat down on the couch.

She sat next to him and continued taking care of his cuts.

Gunz closed his eyes and lowered his head to his chest, enjoying the softness of her touch. Angelique was done a few minutes later and he sighed, opening his eyes unwillingly. She smiled and gently caressed his cheek with her fingers.

"You need to learn how to relax," she lectured him softly, gazing into his eyes. "You're always so tense. When I talked to Jim's goddaughter, she told me that a few years ago, when she met you for the first time in Belarus, you were a firecracker. You weren't taking anything seriously, including yourself. What happened to that man?"

Gunz shook his head and turned away, breaking their eye contact. She was talking about a time long gone, a time before the fire. The time when he had no idea that the world of magic existed. His life wasn't easy, and it wasn't perfect for sure, but he was happy, and he knew how to enjoy every moment of his imperfect life.

"The firecracker discovered the real fire," he said quietly, his fingers digging into the edge of the couch. "That man is gone and he's never coming back."

"But why?" she asked, her hand resting on his shoulder.

"Angie, you're a smart woman and you know all this supernatural stuff a lot better than I do," he replied with a half-shrug. "It's like what Jim said... If I inadvertently revert into my natural state – I'm a weapon of mass destruction. I'll kill every human around me. I can never relax. I have to be in control twenty-four seven. I don't relax even when I sleep."

"But why?" she repeated her question, sounding sincerely concerned. "Your house is warded and sealed to contain your natural state within these walls. Surely, you can let yourself relax here?"

Gunz shook his head no and rubbed his face with his hands. Even when he needed to heal himself, he checked every spell and every ward on his house to make sure that nothing would go wrong before he would allow himself to let go. Yes, he could allow himself to relax in his house to a degree, but never all the way. There was always a *what-if* thought on the back of his mind.

"No, I can't... I live in a suburb, surrounded by hundreds of innocent people. What if something goes wrong and the wards fail? I can't be responsible for the death of all these people. I just can't..."

Angelique gaped at him, her full pink lips open, shock imprinted on her tender face. "But it's impossible to live like this," she whispered. "I didn't realize... No wonder you're always stretched like a guitar string."

Impulsively, she threw her arms around his neck, pulling him closer. Gunz held his breath for a moment, relishing this unexpected embrace. His arms wrapped around her shoulders and he felt her lips softly brushing his cheek. He turned his face toward her and found her deep eyes gazing at him with warmth.

The corners of her mouth lifted in a slightly drunk, dreamy smile and she raised her arms, fixing his face between her hands. For a moment she studied his face and then her lips softly connected with his. Everything inside him was screaming for more, but he didn't return her kiss and gently pulled away.

"Angie, don't do it," he said quietly, lowering his eyes, his voice hoarse. "Kal once told me that the fire power makes me... um... sort of... sexually desirable to women."

For a moment, Angelique stared at him flabbergasted and then burst out laughing. "Fire power? What a bag of bullshit!" She laughed again and slid off the couch, squatting in front of him with one knee on the floor. "Look at me, Gunz."

She reached up and turned his head down a little. He bit his lip and finally met her gaze. She touched his lips with her finger gently, forcing him to let go and shook her head.

"Only men can be so blind to things that are right in front of them," she whispered. "Gunz, the way I feel about you has nothing to do with your power. Maybe Kal is right, but not in my case."

"Angie—"

"When you're troubled, you're always biting your lip," she continued, ignoring his attempt to stop her. She ran her fingers over his slightly parted lips. "Your eyes are grey right now, it means you're in complete control of your power and you're as close to the state of relaxation as you can be. When you're tense, or something bothers you, your eyes change color, glowing with a light red shine. And when you're happy or enjoying something, you smile... you have this shy lopsided smile that brings up a single dimple on your cheek. And I love seeing it... I know you, Gunz, and trust me, it's you I'm attracted to, not the Fire Salamander in you."

She pulled up slightly and gently kissed his cheek. A heat wave expanded in his chest and he drew in a short breath. He knew that he shouldn't be doing it, but it was becoming harder and harder for him to contain his desire.

"You drink, and now I know why, and I understand," she proceeded, slowly covering his face with short soft kisses. "This is your way of taking the edge off your always stretched nerves. And it's okay. You need to do whatever helps."

"Angie, please—"

His body throbbed at her touch and his mind got clouded as passion took him over. Gunz leaned forward and kissed her, hungrily crashing her lips with his. She moaned rising up on her knees. Without thinking about what he was doing, he found the lapels of her jacket and yanked it off her shoulders, throwing it to the floor. His arms encircled her slim waist and he pulled her fervently to his chest. The touch of her body to his, through a thin fabric of her silk tank top, electrified him. The heat surged through his veins, igniting the real fire within him. He made an effort and pulled away.

Breathing hard, he was staring down at her as she sat back on her heels, gazing up at him. She was so pretty, with her eyes fogged and her cheeks flushed. Her slightly swollen lips were parted, and her beautifully-shaped breasts were rising and falling with quick breaths. And she had no idea how hard it was for him to stop. He moved his hand over the thick mane of her dark hair and smiled sadly.

"Angie, you are..." His voice caught. "I can't, I'm sorry..."

"I see the flames dancing in your eyes and I can feel your fire energy rising," she whispered, gently running her fingers over his cheek. "And it's okay. You know that I'm a witch. Your fire energy can't hurt me."

"Maybe not the fire energy. But the real fire can still hurt you," he objected quietly. "My fire energy is what creates the deadly blast when I revert into my natural state. But besides that, there is also a real fire within me." He got up and spread his arms, allowing the fire to surface. The fire ignited brighter in his eyes and the small flames rushed up and down his arms. "You see it? This is what can happen if I lose control. You're not impervious to fire, Angie. I can burn you and I would never forgive myself."

She followed the flow of the flames on his arms and got up, standing in front of him. "I see it and I'm willing to take the chance. I trust you to control your fire."

Gunz laughed mirthlessly. "Angie, look what you did to me... With you, I don't trust myself." He shook his head, stepping away from her. "I can't take that chance. I can't do it. I'm sorry."

"Are you saying—," she started to say but cut herself off and cleared her throat. "Are you saying that you had never been with a woman since you became a Fire Salamander?"

"I'm not ready to talk about it," he said awkwardly, looking to the side.

"I guess it's a yes," she said. "Gunz, you need to talk to your mentor—"

"Really? You want me to talk to Kal about my sex life?" asked Gunz choking on laughter.

"Of course not!" said Angelique, putting her hands on her waist. "There has to be an easier way to suppress your fire... You can't live like this. This is what I want you to ask Kal about."

Gunz chuckled. Women can be persistent when they want something.

"There is a way," he said, extinguishing his fire. "But something tells me you're not going to enjoy the intimacy with a third person present in the room."

"Excuse me?" she exhaled, blinking at him furiously.

He laughed openly. "Kal or a Master of Power can control the fire within me, allowing me to relax my mind," he explained. "But never mind. I shouldn't be talking about all that. I shouldn't even think about it, especially now when..." His voice trailed away, and he bit his lip. Then he remembered what Angelique said about his habit of biting his lip when he was troubled and released it.

"Especially now? You never talk about your private life, Gunz." She picked up her jacket from the floor and brushed it off with her hand before putting it back on. "You're so shy and so guarded at the same time. It's practically impossible to pull you into any personal conversation."

Gunz thought that she sounded a little hurt and cringed, cursing himself for his awkwardness in everything to do with women.

"Angie, I'm sorry if I hurt you—"

She chuckled, interrupting him. "You didn't hurt me, silly. You're hurting yourself. You need to find a way to live a normal life, Gunz. You can't always be in control."

"I have to. I have no choice," he objected firmly. "But unfortunately, right now I'm not in control of anything. I feel like someone put a noose around my neck and squeezed it, pulling me into a hundred different directions. And neither of these directions are good. I can't breathe, Angie. But like Jim said, I need to *cowboy up*. And I need to do it fast." He smiled, raking his fingers through his hair. "It's not a good time for me to think about my personal life."

"It never is..."

Gunz waved his hand, unfolding the fire curtain of his portal.

"I need to get ready for my next move," he explained, hoping that he wasn't hurting her feelings by asking her to leave. "But before I take you home, can you promise me something?"

"I'll try. What is it?"

"Angie, I need you and Jim to do what Kal said," he said quietly. "I need you both to step away from all this and let me deal with it alone. I also need you to severe your psychic connection with me. Just until I sort things out and get everything under control. Eve is extremely dangerous, and things are escalating too rapidly. Both of you can get hurt. I would feel a lot better knowing that you're safe and I don't need to worry about you."

For a split-second, Angelique looked like she was ready to cry, but she nodded and approached the wall of fire. She glanced at him, her eyes reflecting the flames of the portal. "Gunz, listen… I care about you. If staying away from you will keep you safe, I promise to do it."

Gunz lifted her gently and she embraced him, softly kissing his cheek.

"You know where to find me when you're ready," she whispered into his ear. "And I know how to wait."

Gunz stiffened the sigh and carried her through the veil of fire.

~ ZANE BURNS, A.K.A. GUNZ ~

*T*he darkness took over the city, replacing the sunlight with the yellow gleam of electric lights and the bright headlight flares of the evening city traffic. Gunz drove into the parking lot of the *Temptress of the Night* club and stopped there, carefully surveying the area. Despite the gloomy, cloudy sky, the area in front of the club was illuminated by a few neon lights, giving the whole building a mysterious and inviting look.

At the door, he noticed two large men who were playing the roles of bouncers but most likely were personal guards of the owner of the club. Gunz had never met the Demonic Queen personally, but he heard enough to know that she never travelled without her entourage which included a few werewolves that served as her bodyguards. Normally werewolves were staying within their packs, considering that it was beneath them to serve other supernatural species. But the Demonic Queen managed to hire a few strays who lived outside the restrictions of any local packs and didn't mind making a few extra bucks.

Gunz quickly scanned the bouncers just to confirm his theory – both men were werewolves. He shuddered inside, thinking how much he hated dealing with their kind. He pulled his gun out of the glove compartment and checked the magazine to make sure that the bullets inside were silver. He clicked the safety on and stuffed the gun into his belt behind his back, hiding it under his shirt. Before leaving the car, he checked his pockets to make sure that his Swiss army knife was there and threw his FBI badge inside the glove compartment.

He was about to leave the car when he noticed a man approaching the guards. The man was obviously a human, but the guards stopped him and produced handheld metal detectors, quickly scanning him for weapons. While their metal detectors looked similar to the regular airport security metal detectors, even from this distance Gunz noticed some differences. He had no doubt that these devices could detect not only magnetic metals but silver as well.

Gunz grunted frustrated but pulled the gun out and shoved it back inside the glove compartment. A gun loaded with silver was the easiest way to deal with werewolves and he hated the idea of leaving his gun behind. On the other hand, he was positive that his Swiss army knife wouldn't set off the security detector since it was enchanted, and beheading would work on werewolves just as well as any silver bullet through the heart. Either way, it wasn't his goal to fight with the guards. He just needed to get inside the club, so he could search for the succubus he met at *Missi's Kitchen*.

He put up an unconcerned look on his face and strolled toward the club. As soon as he reached the entrance door the guards stopped him. Now that Gunz was standing close to them, he could appreciate their full grandeur. Both were over six feet tall with wide shoulders, massive chests and overly muscular builds that couldn't be concealed even by their black suits.

Werewolves in businessman's clothing, thought Gunz, snickering inside. *You don't see something like that every day.*

Brutal and short-fused by nature, werewolves preferred the freedom of movement and the heavy, constricting business suits wouldn't normally be their clothes of choice. But in this case, it was easy to guess that their attire was the choice of their boss, the infamous Demonic Queen.

"Stop!" growled one of the guards, his hand making a move toward his side betraying the presence of a concealed weapon beneath his jacket. "This is a respectable establishment. We don't let your kind in."

Gunz raised his hands up and chuckled, exuding the air of innocence and cluelessness. "Whoa, guys, what do you mean 'my kind'? What kind of *kind* is that?" he asked, winking at them. "I'm just another man, looking for a few hours of good time."

The guards exchanged an amused look and barked laughing. "You are not a man," said the second guard after he could finally contain himself. "I'm not sure what you are, but you reek of magic-shit and this establishment is for normal humans only. Get the hell out of here, little monster, before we break every bone in your body."

Gunz plastered a shocked expression on his face. "I reek?" He lifted his arm and pretended to sniff his armpit. "And here I thought I took a good long shower before coming here. Oh wait… Did you sniff my butt when I wasn't looking? I didn't notice you moving."

The guards exchanged an angry look and their lips curled into identical snarls. Both shifted forward, towering over him with malice. Gunz jumped back, putting some distance between him and the guards and snickered.

"I think we started on a wrong foot here, boys," he said peacefully, suppressing the overwhelming desire to laugh. "Let's try it again. I'm just a man, standing in front of two mutts, asking them nicely to let him through."

Both werewolves howled in rage and sprung forward. As fast as they were moving, they were no match for him. Easily avoiding their outstretched arms, Gunz slipped through the narrow space between their bulky bodies and stopped a few steps behind them, folding his arms over his chest. As soon as the werewolves realized that they were outmaneuvered, they spun around, ready to attack again.

"What's going on here? What's with all the commotion?"

Gunz heard a pleasant female voice and turned around. A tall woman in a dark business pantsuit was standing in the doorway of the club. He had never seen a business suit looking so sexy on any woman before. She had the height of a model, but her body wasn't a skinny straight-up-and-down type that some of the models had. Her flowing curves and delicate waist were accentuated by her jacket that was just a touch too tight around the chest area and its lapels were seductively pulled apart on her full breasts.

Her large brown eyes, deep and foggy, were slightly veiled by her long eyelashes. They promised all the pleasures of the world to any man who was lucky enough to catch their attention. Her full coral lips were open a little, and a soft blush was playing on her high cheekbones. Her obsidian black hair was falling freely to her back and was partially covering her chest. On the front, the long wavy strands of her hair were carefully styled to provide just enough visibility of her tastefully exposed breasts to make any man wish to see more.

"Your Grace," said both werewolves at the same time, bowing to her awkwardly.

The Demonic Queen waved at them with her well-manicured hand dismissively and her eyes darted to Gunz. She gave him a quick once-over and her lips stretched into a slow sensual smile that made her look even more attractive, if it was even possible. Without any rush, she sauntered toward him, swaying her shapely hips gracefully. Her every move was radiating a raw feminine sensuality so powerful that his mind got clouded before she even attempted to use her magic.

The queen stopped in front of Gunz, staring down at him with interest. He arched his eyebrow at her, but then decided to go with the flow and gave her a bow in the best style of a medieval knight as Kal taught him. She chuckled and lightly touched his shoulder, asking him to rise.

"Fire Salamander," she exhaled. The tip of her pink tongue moved over her upper lip from one corner of her mouth to the other. "I've heard that there was one in Florida, but I had a hard time believing."

Her seductive magic enveloped him, and he drew in a sharp breath. For a split-second, all the thoughts in his mind got scrambled as his body responded to her magic and there was nothing he could do to prevent it. But the queen let go of him right away, an uneven smirk curving her lips.

"You *are* a Fire Salamander," she said. "It's been more than a thousand years since I met the last one of your kind. You know how rare the real Fire Salamanders are?"

Gunz nodded, not quite sure that the gift of coherent speech was available to him yet. The queen stared down at him, enjoying his state of confusion. Her eyes moved to her bodyguards and she nodded at them.

"You can let him pass," she ordered. "He's human enough and I'm sure he's not going to cause any problems or create any fire shows. Are you, hon?" She gently lifted his chin with her fingers and Gunz met her eyes.

"No, ma'am," he replied, his voice cracked. "No problems, no fire."

"That's a good boy." She laughed, her hand caressed his shoulder while sending the next wave of her toxic magic through him. Then she switched her attention back to her bodyguards. "By the time my girls are done with him, the only thing that's going to be on fire"— her eyes slid down to Gunz's crotch — "is his loins. This boy hasn't touched a woman in ages. No wonder he has such shapely biceps – all the morning exercises he has to do in the shower..." She giggled, winking at Gunz, her fingers squeezing his upper arm appreciatively.

Gunz grunted, channeling some fire to cleanse his system of

her magic. The queen noticed his attempt and her eyes flared with playful twinkles.

"Just relax, Child of Fire," she said, gesturing toward the entrance. "Let my girls do their job. I promise – you'll enjoy it. I'll tell them to be gentle with you."

Gunz silently bowed to the Demonic Queen and walked inside the club. As soon as the door closed behind him, he stopped, leaning on the wall, trying to catch his breath. His head was still swimming, and he could feel the succubus' magic circulating in his system. He closed his eyes and focused on the fire within.

"Hey, boss, what did the lecherous queen mean by morning exercises in the shower that you do?" asked Mishka. The wyvern's high-pitched voice in Gunz's murky mind was so unexpected that he flinched. *"I've been with you for a while now and I've never seen you doing any kind of exercises in the morning."*

Gunz almost choked. "Mishka, I'm not going to discuss this with you," he whispered quietly, feeling his cheeks burning.

"Why not?"

"Because it wasn't nice of her to imply something like that."

"So?"

"And because it's personal," he hissed. "Why am I even answering your questions?"

"Oh, personal..." muttered Mishka. *"Do you mean she was talking about your intimacy issues?"*

"Mishka! Enough!"

"Fine, fine. Jeez, boss. You're so touchy," mumbled Mishka. *"I can never understand you humans. Everyone loves to have sex, but no one wants to talk about it. I bet humans are just so bad at it that they don't want to embarrass themselves."*

"No, Mishka. Because gentlemen do not kiss and tell," whispered Gunz. His mind cleared out and finally he was able to experience the world around him.

"Next time you spot a gentleman, let me know," said Mishka snidely. *"I have never seen one yet."*

Gunz rolled his eyes and didn't answer, focusing on observing the club. The main room was dimly lit with red and pink lights, with the brightest spotlight on the stage. The club was packed with customers, but luckily there was still an empty table at the far end of the room. Even though the table was away from the stage, it worked for Gunz perfectly. From this place he could easily see all the girls that were dancing, serving drinks and promenading between the tables.

He probed the room carefully. All the club employees were demons – and since it was gentlemen's night, most of them were succubi. But every single willing customer was human. The succubi were gliding between the tables, gently touching customers and infecting them with their magic.

Each succubus, sultry, alluring and deadly to a man, was hungrily craved and desired by the unsuspecting humans. The more magic succubi channeled, the more eager the men became, lust dripping from their every pore. They were cheering the dancing girls, throwing money on the stage, ordering drinks and begging for private dances. The club was swimming in cash and the air was thick with the energy of magic.

Just sensing succubi's magical energy was poisoning Gunz, making him weak and dizzy. His body was reacting in ways he never suspected was possible and he had to keep circulating his fire to keep his head in the game. He noticed a few girls taking customers to the side rooms for a private dance. He was sure that the majority of feeding was happening behind the closed doors of these private rooms. Nevertheless, Jim told him that no one ever got killed or injured here and Gunz switched his attention to searching for the fake blond he met at *Missi's Kitchen*.

A few minutes later, he found her. Tonight, she wasn't blond, sporting a short red wig, but Gunz recognized her right away. Her wrists were decorated by a number of heavy bracelets to conceal the fresh pink scars of recent burns. Gunz got up and waved at her, gesturing for her to come over. The succubus smiled to him seductively and moved toward his table.

She stopped in front of him and leaned forward slightly, either to hear him better over the music that was blasting in the club or to show off her ample bosom, readily available for his eyes.

"What can I do for you tonight, handsome?" she asked, her voice sultry and a lot more mysterious than her appearance.

Her skimpy outfit was leaving very little to the imagination and she looked like she'd been around the block a few hundred times over the span of a few hundred years. She softly touched his hand, her finger hardly connecting with his skin and he felt the zing of her magic spreading through his body. However, this time she seemed to recognize that he wasn't a pure-blood human and her eyes widened.

Gunz leaned back in his chair, putting some distance between him and her busy little hands and cocked his head. The succubus didn't recognize him. She was behaving like she had never seen him before. This was becoming more interesting by the moment.

"How about a private dance, beautiful?" he asked, unable to veil the sarcasm in his voice.

"One moment, sir," she mumbled, straightening up and adjusting her almost nonexistent bra. She searched around the club with her eyes. A few minutes later the Demonic Queen arrived. She smiled down at Gunz and turned to her employee.

"Rowan, darling, I want you to make this man happy," said the queen with a salacious smile. "He needs to experience the true pleasure that is not self-served. Use all your capable resources and don't say no to anything that is appropriate for our establishment." She gazed down at Gunz, gently brushing his cheek with her polished nails.

"Yes, Your Grace," said Rowan and curtsied.

"And Rowan, you're a clever girl, don't do anything I wouldn't do," said the queen suggestively, giving her an arched stare and added in a whisper. "Make sure you don't feed on him. If Kal finds out that someone was abusing his child, your life would be over in a heartbeat."

"Yes, Your Grace," said Rowan and curtsied again, but her face blanched.

The queen threw one more lustful gaze at Gunz and strolled away, leaving a sugary trail of her magical energy behind. Rowan smiled strenuously and waved toward the other end of the club.

"Please, follow me, young man," she said to him and headed toward the door into the private section of the club without looking back to make sure that Gunz followed her.

Gunz was sure that the succubus was petrified by the queen's warning. Now that she knew that she would be dealing with a Child of Fire and not some clueless mundane, her self-confidence was quickly dwindling down.

He followed Rowan into one of the private rooms and she closed the door behind him, turning the lock with a soft click. The room was small, no more than ten feet by ten feet. It had no windows, but the walls were draped with heavy red curtains. An L-shaped sectional sofa was sitting at the opposite wall and a few throw pillows were scattered all over it. Two small round tables were standing at either end of the sofa. The room was dimly lit by the wall lights and soft slow music was flowing through the air in dreamy erotic waves. Everything here was done with the emotional seduction and physical pleasure in mind.

"What's your name, handsome?" asked Rowan, little by little acquiring her normal demeanor and returning to her habitual modus operandi.

"Zane," said Gunz. "But listen—"

"Make yourself comfortable, Zane," said Rowan, waving at the sectional. "Would you like some wine or maybe something stronger?" She walked toward a small wine cabinet.

"Rowan, thank you but no," called Gunz. He walked to the couch but didn't sit down. "I don't need you to… um… please me. I just wanted to ask you a few questions."

She returned to him and pushed him back gently, forcing him to sit down. Then she leaned forward, placing her hands on either side of him and smiled.

"You wanted to ask a few questions, Zane?" she breathed out into his ear, her lips brushing his skin.

Gunz lifted his face. Her sizable breasts were right in front of his eyes. She ran her hand over her long neck down to her cleavage, hooking her finger on the edge of her bra and slightly pulling it down. He nodded, trying to push himself deeper into the sofa, away from her.

"Well, obviously you want me to answer your questions, handsome?" she murmured, her voice infused with erotic tranquility.

Gunz nodded again, bringing up some fire closer to the surface, just to be ready.

"How about we'll play a game?" she suggested with a tiny smirk on her face. She placed her hand on his cheek, probing him gently with her magic again and her smile widened. "I'll answer your questions and you'll let me do my job."

Gunz seized her wrist and pulled it away from his face. "How about you'll answer my questions and we'll skip on your job. You can just sit down right here"— he patted the couch next to him — "and I'm going to tell your queen that you were unforgettable."

The succubus laughed, her red hair flowing around her face in a fake plastic cloud. "It's impossible to mislead the queen. Each succubus has a unique energy signature and queen Aisling is so ancient and so powerful that she can feel our magical energy at work even when she's not in the same room with us. Sorry, hon, but if you want me to answer your questions, you will have to enjoy the process."

She put her hand on his crotch and applied a little pressure. "Mmm... you're good... and so ready... I like it..."

Gunz grunted and grabbed her wrist, but she wagged her finger at him warningly.

"Don't you know the rules, hon? You can't touch me." She snickered but let go off him. "So, what's your first question?"

Her hands went up to his shoulders and she drenched him with her intoxicating magic. He moaned softly as the heat rushed down his spine and his body arched involuntarily. He knew that he was supposed to fight her influence, but her magic was playing with his body entirely bypassing the feeble orders of his brain.

"Ahh... do you remember... meeting me a little while go... at Missi's Kitchen," he managed to ask, panting.

For a moment Rowan stopped what she was doing, searching his face but then shook her head. "Sorry, Zane, I've never seen you before. Trust me, I would remember eye-candy like you."

Rowan straddled him, perching herself on his lap and her body started to move in slow and fluid waves. Gunz moaned as she sent more of her seductive magic through him. His mind got foggy and the dark room around him spun. Responding to his emotions, the wave of fire rose in him, instantly burning out the succubus' magic.

"My next question..." he panted, his every cell aching for her touch. "We met before, Rowan, and it's not only that you don't remember our meeting... When you met me, you didn't recognize the creature of magic in me. How was that possible?"

She halted, gaping at him, her eyes wide open. "It's not possible. You project such a strong fire signature that it would be impossible for someone like me not notice it... Are you sure it was me?"

Gunz took her hand in his and pulled the bracelets down, pointing at the scars on her wrists. "Do you remember how you got these scars?"

"No..." she whispered.

"I gave you this burns when you tried to use your magic on me."

"But it can't be... it's impossible—"

With a soft click of the lock, the door opened and the Demonic

Queen herself walked inside the room. "But it's possible, darling," she purred softly. "Rowan, please leave us. I would like to take care of our honored guest myself." A soft smile tugged at her lips as she approached Gunz and put her hand on his forehead.

Uh-oh, thought Gunz, cringing inside, as the Demonic Queen started to wield her magic. "Please don't..." he mumbled lethargically, but she wasn't listening. This time her magic was different. She wasn't trying to seduce him or give him sexual pleasure as Rowan did. At the touch of her magic, his body went numb and his mind got soft and mushy... Slowly the world around him went dark and he fell asleep.

* * *

A STRONG CURRENT of fire through his body woke him up with a start. Gunz opened his eyes and found himself inside the same private room of the club, lying down on the couch with a pillow placed under his head. The succubi were gone and he was alone in the room. Only Mishka was hovering over him, thrusting one fireball after another through his heart.

"Mishka," croaked Gunz, still feeling slightly disoriented, "thank you for waking me up, buddy. You can stop now."

"Finally," muttered Mishka grumpily, shaking his head. "That slutty queen did a number on you, Salamander. You weren't ready for her magic. Be happy she didn't kill you."

"She couldn't kill me," muttered Gunz.

"Oh, that's just great," huffed Mishka, rolling his angry eyes. "She couldn't kill you. Big friggin' deal! She could have put you on a short leash, bewitch your mind, force you to do her bidding against your will. Any of these options sound better to you?"

"I know, Mishka, you're right," said Gunz, lowering his head. "It was stupid of me to show up here like this. I wasn't ready at all. Not magically, not physically. Lesson learned."

His eyes fell on the corner table that was moved in front of the couch. Except for a business card there was nothing else on the table. Gunz picked up the card and turned it in his fingers. One side of the card was red, and a short note was written on it by hand.

"If you wish to know the truth, see me tomorrow at 8 PM."

There was no signature. Gunz flipped the card over. The opposite side of the card was black. A Ft. Lauderdale address and the name of the company "EverSafe Security, Inc." were printed on it. There were neither name nor phone number printed anywhere on the card, but Gunz knew exactly who this security firm belong to and the idea of meeting with another supernatural ruler didn't sound too enticing at the moment.

Gunz got up and put the card in his pants pocket.

"Mishka, did you see who left this card here?"

"Sorry, but I also sort of... dozed off," replied the wyvern sounding a little embarrassed and vanished from the room, hiding in Gunz's watch.

"Well, whatever didn't kill me today, surely will give another try tomorrow," muttered Gunz, walking out of the room.

~ TESSA ~

"*My investigation hit a dead-end. I tried all the leads I had, but the last trail went cold just like everything else I tried before. I'm failing the Guardians and my girl.*

After considering all my options, yesterday, I decided to visit Father Collins, but didn't make it all the way. As soon as I pulled out of the condominium gates, I noticed a dark SUV with tinted windows. After I made a few turns, I had no doubt that they were after me. I have no idea who they were and why they were following me, but I felt like the circle around me and Tessa was getting tighter.

No matter what, I need to find a way to meet with Father Collins. I'll try again tomorrow.

R.D."

"R.D." – Reilly Donovan. Tessa closed the diary, her eyes swimming with tears. She put her hand on top of it. The soft leather of the notebook felt warm and soft, and she stroked it gently with her fingers, feeling almost like she was touching her mom's hand. That was the last record in her mom's diary. She wrote it the evening before the accident that claimed her life.

Who was following her mom and why?

Was her death an accident or did the people in the dark SUV kill her?

She couldn't find the answers to these questions in her mom's diary. And she had no one to ask for help. Tessa thought back to that day at Zane's house when she found out that Aidan had magic. Aidan – the only person she believed to be normal, the only person she trusted, no questions asked. He lied to her for years.

And Zane... She just didn't know him. Tessa shuddered. What in the world made her believe that she knew him well enough to trust. She actually thought that she was attracted to him. *What came over me?* she scolded herself bitterly. *I don't need either of them. I was always fine on my own. Nothing has changed.*

Tessa put the notebook in the box and slowly walked out of her mom's secret room. As she closed the door, her eyes fell on the wall clock in the living room. It was showing ten to four in the morning. She didn't realize that she spent all night reading.

She walked into her bedroom and flung herself on the bed without taking the bedcover off or undressing. She fell asleep almost immediately and when she woke up, it was ten o'clock in the morning. After a quick shower, Tessa got dressed and headed to the kitchen. She didn't feel hungry, so she made a cup of coffee and sat down, thinking what to do next.

After reading her mom's diary, one thing became clear to her – her mother's death wasn't an accident and she needed to find out who did it and why. Just to visualize her thoughts, she took a piece of paper and started writing everything she wanted to do.

"1.Find out who killed my mother and why."

Possibly finding the truth about her mother and the assignment she received from the Guardians, would help her learn why the Guardians were interested in her. Thinking back to her conversation with Angelique, she wrote the second item on her list.

"2.Find my second Guardian and talk to her or him."

She looked at her writing and pursed her lips. Even if she finds this second Guardian, what if she or he refuses to answer her questions. She drew a giant question mark at the end of the sentence. Maybe before she starts looking for the second Guardian, she should find out who these Guardians are and what their true mission is.

"3.Learn more about the Guardians."

But even if the Guardians refuse to help her, there was always another source of information about her origins and possibly her power. She knew that it wasn't going to be easy to find them, but she had to try. She couldn't go on living like this, not knowing what she was and who she was.

"4.Find my biological parents."

Tessa picked up the paper, looked over everything she wrote so far and threw it back on the table. It all looked perfect on paper, but she had no leads and she had no idea where to start.

Or maybe I do? Tessa got up and ran back into her mom's secret room. She pulled her third diary out of the box and opened the last page. Father Collins. Her mother wanted to meet with this priest. She thought it was important and most likely she died when she was driving to meet with him. She checked every single paper inside the secret room but didn't find any information on how to contact Father Collins.

Her mother was Catholic, and she raised Tessa believing in the existence of God. But she wasn't very religious, and they weren't observing the holidays or going to church every Sunday. From her earlier childhood memories, Tessa recalled her mother taking her to an old church. The church was too far away, south of Miami, and her mom took her there maybe two-three times at the most. Is it possible that she was meeting with Father Collins there?

Tessa locked the secret room and went to the master bedroom which used to be her mom's. Since her mother's death, Tessa never opened the door to this room. Too many memories were associated with this place. She knew that every little thing there would remind her of her mother and she didn't want it. She didn't want to remember. She didn't want to feel the crippling despair and pain of loss again.

For the first time in the last two years, she opened the door and crossed the threshold. Everything in the room was untouched, just the way her mother left it that day. Tessa swallowed her tears, forcing herself to stay focused on her mission. She walked toward the dresser where her mother used to store some of her personal papers.

A thick layer of dust covered everything in the room. Tessa sighed, thinking how much her mother hated dust and decided that she should clean this bedroom even if she wasn't planning to use it. Carefully she picked up the chest that was sitting on the dresser and sat down on the bed, placing the chest next to her.

Inside, there were a few letters, a bunch of business cards held together with a rubber band and a stack of post cards. Tessa recognized the cards and her vision blurred. These were all the birthday and Mother's Day cards that Tessa gave her over the years. Every single one of them. With unblinking eyes, Tessa stared at the cards scattered all over the bed. She was afraid that if she would blink, she'd start crying and she wouldn't be able to stop. Ever.

She took a deep breath and rubbed her eyes with her hands, wiping the unwanted tears away. "I'm going to stay strong," she whispered. "I'm not going to cry… I promise, I'll find whoever did it to you, mom. And when I find them—" She clenched her teeth so tight that they squeaked. "They will pay for what they had done to you. I swear…"

Tessa grabbed the stack of business cards and pulled the rubber band off. Patiently, she checked one card at the time and finally, her determination was rewarded. The last card in the stack had the name of Father Collins printed on it in an embossed gold font. There was no phone number, but the address of the church was printed on the back. *Church by the Sea* – she read the name of the church, thinking that it was quite an unusual name for a place of worship.

Tessa got up, hope blossoming in her heart – she found what she was looking for and now she knew what needed to be done next. It took her a minute to put everything back in the chest and return it to its place. Squeezing tightly Father Collins' card in her hand, Tessa walked out of the room and shut the door.

* * *

THE DRIVE to the Church by the Sea was an unnerving blur of stop-and-go traffic during the lunch hour on the southbound freeway. Her fervent belief that she would find some answers in this church was making Tessa impatient and she drove fast and reckless, like she had never driven before. As her little car was swinging between lanes, she was muttering under her breath, cursing bad Miami drivers who didn't know how to use their turn signals, South Florida tourists who had no idea where they were going and the chronic rush hour on the southbound ninety-five.

Following the directions of her GPS, she exited the freeway and took a small side street. Turning left and right on different streets, drives and parkways, Tessa slowly left behind the suburban area. The last street merged into a small two-way road that was going through the forest. After fifteen minutes of drive, the obnoxiously cheerful GPS-lady announced that her destination was on her right. Tessa stopped the car and took in her surroundings. There were the usual Florida thickets on both sides of the road and there was nothing anywhere that looked remotely like a church. Since it wasn't a dead-end, Tessa decided to keep going, following the path.

After another few minutes of drive, the road came to a dead-end at the ocean side. There was a small space clear of greenery that looked like a parking lot and two cars were parked there. Tessa stopped her car and walked toward the ocean. As she reached the narrow strip of a beach and glanced to the right, she finally saw the church. The building was facing the ocean, but it's back was enclosed by a grove. It wasn't clear if it was a park that belonged to the church or a real wild forest.

Tessa stopped, gaping at the building with her mouth open. She hardly recalled this place from her childhood memories, and most of her memories retained the way the church looked inside. Even if she remembered how the building looked from the outside, as a child she wouldn't be able to truly appreciate its beauty and the uniqueness of its architecture.

Tessa didn't have enough knowledge of history and architecture to identify the century it was built. But she had no doubt that the church was ancient and by the looks of it, merciless time took its toll. The walls were constructed of large, roughly-cut stone blocks. The blocks were worn down and crumbled in places by years of tropical winds and rains, and their surface was covered in patches of dark moss and slithering green vines.

The whole church looked like a miniature version of a medieval cathedral. It had everything any medieval cathedral had – pointed arches, high roofs and towers, stained glass windows, and even flying buttresses. The facade of the building was decorated by statues. Most of the sculptures suffered the unforgiving effects of time and weather and were mostly destroyed, but the statues of two gargoyles on both sides of the door, looked almost untouched, as though they were carved just yesterday.

Tessa stared at the gargoyles with interest. From her history lessons, she remembered something about gargoyles being used to take the water away from the building walls during rains. But these two didn't look like rain gutters. Tessa stepped closer, craning her neck to see them better. The gargoyles had the body of a lion with webbed bat-like wings and the face of a dog from hell. Their mouths were opened in a grotesque snarl, their terrible fangs exposed, and their snouts were distorted by rage so realistic that Tessa felt goosebumps rising on her skin.

As she walked toward the front door, she couldn't get rid of the feeling that the gargoyles' furious eyes were following her. She stopped in front of the heavy wooden double-door and pulled on the door handle. Despite the heavy look, the door opened easily and quietly. Gingerly Tessa stepped over the threshold and walked inside the church.

Inside, the church also reminded her of a medieval cathedral with its tall vaulted ceilings and stained-glass windows. It smelled of candles and oils, which was normal for a Catholic church. Besides that, a light, hardly noticeable scent of flowers and freshly cut grass was lingering in the air.

There was no one inside, so she walked between rows of benches and sat down somewhere closer to the exit door. For a moment, she stared at the altar with a large crucifix behind it. She didn't pray or think of God.

After her mother was taken away from her, she never questioned or blamed God for what happened. She accepted things for what they were – accidents happen, and good people have bad things happen to them all the time. For her, it was never about God or his mighty angels. It was about life. And in real life, when shit happens, you have to deal with it and not count on divine intervention. You're on your own. In her mind, there was no more place for faith and God. The moment she threw the handful of dirt on her mother's coffin, she buried her faith together with the body of her mother.

Tessa sighed and folded her arms on the back of the bench in front of her. She lowered her forehead on her folded arms and closed her eyes. She sat like this for a while, tired and sleepy. After she returned back home from Zane's house, she went straight to the hidden room and spent every minute of the day and night reading her mother's diaries, books and documents. The sleepless nights finally caught up with her, and she dozed off.

A soft touch to her shoulder woke her up. Tessa raised her face and blinked a few times to adjust her vision. A young man dressed in black pants and black shirt with a white clerical collar was standing next to her.

"Can I help you, young lady?" he asked with a soft smile and Tessa realized that all this time she was just rudely staring at him. It's not like she hadn't seen a Catholic priest before, but she could never imagine a priest that looked like this man. For her it was easier to imagine him on a runway than behind the altar.

She cleared her throat, lowering her eyes uncomfortably. "Are you Father Collins?" she asked. Noticing that her voice was still hoarse, she cleared her throat again.

"No, I am not," he replied calmly with a heavy French accent. "My name is Father Raoul de Beaumont. But Father Collins should be here in a minute."

"Thank you, Father Beaumont," she said. "I'll wait for Father Collins here then."

"I'll leave you to your prayers, my child," he replied with a light bow and walked away.

My child... right, thought Tessa, rolling her eyes. She couldn't give him more than twenty-five.

She heard the entrance door open and turned around. A man in his late seventies, dressed in black robes of a priest entered the church. He was short and stout, with a full head of silver-gray hair and matching beard. His eyes fell on Tessa and his thick silver eyebrows climbed up. The priest made his way to Tessa and she got up to greet him.

"Hello... Are you Father Collins?" she asked, observing his aged face with heavy wrinkles around his eyes. A deep scar was crossing his left eyebrow, disfiguring his cheek and disappearing under his beard. If she wasn't looking at a priest, she would think that this scar was left by a knife or maybe even a sword. Tessa couldn't help but wonder where a peaceful Catholic priest could receive this kind of injury.

"Yes, my child," replied Father Collins. His voice was deep, maybe a little too deep for his height. "And you are Therasia Reagan Donovan, Reilly's little girl."

"Yes, Father," replied Tessa. Last time she was here, she was about seven years old. She glanced at the priest wondering how he could remember or recognize her.

"When I learned about Reilly's death, I was expecting that I would see you sooner or later," said Father Collins with a sigh, waving at the bench. "Sit down, Tessa. Tell me what brought you here. What are you looking for?"

Tessa sighed. "No offence, Father, but one thing I'm not looking for is God," she said. She glanced at the crucifix, but then turned away and met Father Collins' grey eyes.

"I wasn't offering you a prayer, my child," replied Father Collins calmly. "Unless you need it, of course…" He took a pause, but Tessa shook her head no and he continued, "I'm sure, since your mother is no longer protecting you, you discovered the existence of the supernatural."

Tessa's eyes flew open. This was the most unorthodox priest she'd ever met. "You believe in the supernatural, Father?"

"Why yes, of course." The priest smirked, his lips stretching under his white mustache, crinkles gathering around his eyes. "As far as I'm concerned, anything that exists in the world is natural, even if it can't be explained by modern science." He chuckled. "And who is to say that something is real or not, can or cannot exist? Believe me, some myths and legends carry a lot more truth in them than some of our historical records."

"So, you believe that witches, vampires and werewolves… All these could be real? And my mom, the Guardians… this is all true?" Tessa held her breath, expecting his answer.

"And a lot more," murmured Father Collins, his eyes drilling into Tessa. "Your mother wasn't just a witch, child. She was the highest level mage among the Guardians. Powerful, beautiful woman. I'm so sorry for your loss, Tessa." He lowered his head and pressed his hand over his eyes.

"Mage…" mumbled Tessa. "Ever since I found out that she was a Guardian, there wasn't a minute in the day when I didn't wish that she told me the truth and explained everything to me herself."

"How did you find out that your mother was a Guardian?"

"That's a long story," said Tessa, her fingers playing with the car keys that were still in her hand. "But to make it short… My neighbor passed away and her spirit gave me my mom's message and showed me a hidden room with her diaries and her spell books. At first I didn't want to read all of them, but my friend changed my mind. So, I've been doing some light reading the last few days."

"I know your neighbor. She was a witch practitioner," said the priest. "But may I ask the name of your friend? You told him who your mother was?"

Tessa chuckled, shaking her head. "No, Father. His name is Zane Burns and I didn't have to tell him about who my mother was. Once he saw the pictures on the wall of the hidden room, he knew. He told me about the world of magic and was trying to help me with my research. After everything that happened, I had to know what I was."

"Aw, Zane Burns, of course… I've heard of him. Remarkable young man. Quite unique, I might say… I'm glad to hear that you have such powerful friends – Zane Burns and Aidan McGrath. Now that your mom is not around, you may need both of them by your side…"

Tessa suppressed a sigh. *Both of them by my side? Well, that would be tricky, since I just told both of them to go to hell…* She didn't expect that the priest knew about Aidan and it left her mind in chaos. He obviously knew what Zane was. But did he know what Aidan was? Was it possible that he knew what she was? Who was he that he knew all this stuff? The questions were creating a wild stampede in her mind and she couldn't organize her thoughts.

"Father," she said finally, "how do you know all this? Who are you?"

The priest didn't answer right away, deep in his thoughts. "I guess, you're not going to stop until you learn the truth, so I better tell you," said Father Collins. "I'm a Warden."

"A churchwarden?"

"No." The priest smiled. "More like a knowledge Warden. I'm a part of the ancient organization that was established thousands of years ago by the Destiny Council. We gather and guard the knowledge and wisdom of different worlds and generations, human and supernatural."

"So, you're like a glorified librarian?" Tessa felt a twinge of disappointment. All this time she thought that there was something special about Father Collins. That he was more than just a priest. If her mother, who was a Guardian mage, needed his help, he had to be a powerful wizard or at least a mighty warrior.

"Yeah, like a librarian, if librarians were studying the art of war and magic, various combat skills, and were guarding the most dangerous spells, enchantments and incantations known to the world," said Father Collins, chuckling. "Humans say that knowledge is power. And it's a relatively true statement, relative to how well you apply your knowledge.

"But the knowledge we guard is the purest form of power and magic, not a figure of speech. We're the Wardens of the wisdom of many, collected over thousands of years and preserved by the Destiny Council. Trained warriors, we operate alongside the Guardians, providing them with the support and information they need to do their job. I was working with your mom for years..." His voice trailed away, and a shadow of sadness darkened his face.

"Father Collins, there is a lot that I don't understand," said Tessa quietly, "and I would love to learn as much as I can about the world of magic. But right now, I have only one question for you. And with all my soul I hope that you have the answer."

"What's your question, Tessa?" asked the priest, his expression hardened as he grew more serious, his fingers squeezing the crucifix on the silver chain around his neck. "I pray I can answer it."

"I can communicate with the spirits of the dead. I'm not human. What am I, Father?" whispered Tessa, her voice trembling. For some reason she felt afraid to voice her question out loud.

"Oh, child..." Father Collins sighed, scratching his white beard. "I was afraid that you would ask that. This is the only question I can't answer... Your mother spent over a decade trying to answer this question and everywhere she looked, she came to a dead-end."

"Then why did the Guardians decide to shadow me, or my power," she said, her voice breaking as tears of disappointment gathered in her eyes.

"The magical energy spike that accompanied your birth was so powerful, that anyone who had an ounce of magic in them could feel it," explained Father Collins. "Your biological parents abandoned you on the steps of a church. This church." Father Collins waved his hand around. "Only people privy to the Knowledge were aware of the existence of this church and the Wardens. So, there was no doubt that your parents weren't new to the world of magic. With you, they left just a little note that had nothing but your name – Therasia Reagan. Not even a last name.

"Our seers examined you and all of them agreed that you had magic, but no one could say what kind of magic you had and what you were. Nothing about your essence and energy signature looked familiar. So, the Destiny Council and the Wardens decided to assign a Guardian to you, to protect you and shadow your powers until we would learn more about who your parents were.

"Your mother fell in love with you the moment she laid her eyes on you, Tessa. She was the most powerful mage the

Guardians had, and she had a promising future in the organiza-tion. But she wouldn't hear of it. She left everything behind, adopted you and dedicated her life to protecting you, not only as your magical Guardian, but also as a loving and caring mother."

"Father, I need to know what I am," said Tessa quietly. "My mom died protecting me. She learned something and was on her way here when she was killed. I'm sure that her death wasn't acci-dental, and I can't rest until I find whatever or whoever killed her."

"I never thought that Reilly's death was accidental," muttered Father Collins. "No car accident can kill a powerful mage like her. And I can understand your need to learn who you are, and I support it. But I have to warn you – the path of revenge will bring you nothing but more pain and disappointment, my child."

Tessa tilted her head, staring at the priest, and smirked bitterly. "Revenge? Who said anything about revenge, Father? I'm just trying to repay in kind. I don't like to be in debt."

"Tessa," said the priest putting his hand on her shoulder, "Father Beaumont and I will do everything we can to help you in your search. We'll start where your mother left off and we'll work together with you, until we uncover your origins. I hope you will change your mind about seeking the vengeance for your mother's death. I'm sure she wouldn't approve of it, and neither would —"

Father Collins stopped talking in midsentence and slowly rose. For a moment fear shadowed his features and his shoulders tensed. Tessa also got up, but she couldn't hear or sense anything. Suddenly, the ground trembled and a thick cloud of dust fell from the ceiling. A split-second later, an ear-piercing howl, hostile and malevolent, rambled through the church. Tessa never heard a sound so bone-chilling and terrifyingly evil. She pressed her hands to her ears, barely able to breath. A cold wind swept through the church and windows exploded inward showering them with colorful shards of glass.

The priest grabbed Tessa's hand, pulling her toward the altar.

She ran after him, trying to keep her balance as the ground kept rattling and swaying under her feet.

"Father, what the hell is going on?" she yelled over the noise.

"Language, you're in the house of the Lord," barked the priest, pulling her forward faster and shouted louder over the overwhelming discord, "Raoul, now! NOW!"

Father Beaumont stood in front of the altar. Tessa caught sight of him and gasped. The peaceful priest was gone. Raoul de Beaumont was holding a long sword in his hands, his body clad in a real medieval knight's armor, chainmail and all. She reached the altar and Father Collins muttered something under his breath. A long sword, similar to the one Raoul was holding, manifested in his hands and the armor wrapped his body. He put his hands on Tessa's shoulders and shouted in her ear.

"Tessa, something truly evil is coming. The howling you hear are the gargoyles trying to protect the entrance. Whatever it is, they won't be able to hold it for much longer. You need to run." He waved at a small door in the sidewall. "Go through this door. It'll lead you into an underground tunnel that will take you outside. Raoul and I will try and give you a few minutes. God be with you, my child."

"Father, you and Raoul need to go with me," begged Tessa, cold sweat running down her back. "It'll kill both of you!"

"No! Tessa, run!"

The ground shuddered, and she yelped, grabbing Father Collins' arm. The entrance door blasted open and the dark, dirty fog entered the church. Quickly devouring the distance, it moved toward them emitting the stench of evil magic. Father Collins pushed Tessa toward the sidewall and raised his sword.

Tessa ran forward. There were only a few feet separating her from the door and the safety of the tunnel. At the moment when she put her hand on the door handle, the dark, sinister cloud enveloped her, suffocating her with its hatred and malice. She couldn't see anything around her except for filthy swirling dark air. Fear tore through her, freezing her in place. She brought her arms up to shield her face and screamed at the top of her lungs. In the last moment, with horror she saw a beam of bright white light erupting from her hands as lightning split the darkness. And everything dissolved into oblivion.

~ ZANE BURNS, A.K.A. GUNZ ~

*G*unz parked his car in the business district of Ft. Lauderdale and walked inside one of the newest high-rises. He approached the security guard and told him that he had a meeting with the owner of *EverSafe Security.* The guard picked up the phone and dialed the phone number of *EverSafe* front desk to confirm his appointment. The meeting was confirmed immediately, and the security guard called an elevator for him.

EverSafe Security was owned by the queen of vampires, a.k.a. the Scarlet Queen. The queen was famous for holding her subjects in hand, controlling everything to do with vampires' and upirs' affairs in her territory. However, just like with any other supernatural organizations, there were quite a few of their kind who didn't care to play by the rules.

The Scarlet Queen was the eldest supernatural ruler in Florida and she learned to appreciate the quiet and stable lifestyle she was living, without being hunted by different groups (human or otherwise) and rogue hunters. If any of the so called "loose" vampires were accidentally getting within the reach of the queen, they were dealt with swiftly and without mercy.

Cold and ruthless to the rule breakers, she was always taking good care of her loyal subjects, making sure that they had good housing, well-paid jobs within her multiple enterprises and enough blood to go around. She established underground dealings with the blood banks and a group of willing humans who didn't mind getting bitten by vamps. All of them were cognizant of supernatural existence and paid well for their silence and donations of blood.

No one knew exactly how old the Scarlet Queen was. But the rumor had it that she was turned when she was just twenty-one, and it happened sometime during the late Jōmon period of Japanese prehistory. The period of late Jōmon spread anywhere between 1500 BC to 300 BC, and no one knew exactly which year or even century she was born in. She was known by the name Akira Ida, but of course no one could say if it was her real name or one of her aliases. The Scarlet Queen was the most mysterious and secretive ruler of the supernatural community. Not even all vampires and upirs got a chance to meet with her face to face.

The elevator stopped on the forty-second floor and Gunz walked out into a spacious lobby. He looked around uncomfortably, realizing that in his black jeans and plain shirt he was slightly underdressed for this place. Just slightly – maybe by a few thousand dollars or so.

The interior decorator didn't spare his time and the queen's money. The lobby was breathing with a modern extravagant design, technology and luxurious comfort. The walls were decorated with contemporary art and a large marble board with the company name was hanging behind a massive, well-polished front desk. Soft leather furniture was strategically positioned around the room, surrounded by plants and decorative elements to create a relaxed and lavish atmosphere.

As a private security firm, the *EverSafe* was targeting wealthy and famous clients, providing twenty-four seven security service with complete secrecy and strict non-disclosure policy. The employees were under absolute obligation to conceal their true nature from the clients – no ifs, ands, or buts about it.

Despite that, Gunz was sure that there were some occurrences where a question or two could have been asked by clients, but no one ever said anything. There were no reports of anyone ever getting hurt by the company employees and having a strong, fearless bodyguard who was endowed with extra strength and faster-than-normal speed sounded attractive. The clients never asked any questions and paid without objections, no matter how many zeros there were in the total amount on the invoice.

The night services were provided by vampires and upirs. But the daytime requests were covered by upirs only, since they weren't as sensitive to the sunlight as vampires were. Sometimes Gunz was wondering if those rich and famous were aware that they were hiring vampires and how would they react if they would find out. Well, first they would need to actually believe that such a thing as a vampire could be real.

As soon as Gunz walked inside the lobby, the secretary that was sitting behind the front desk got up and walked around to greet him. She looked young, no more than twenty in human years, but Gunz could sense her vampiric energy signature and he knew that looks could be deceiving.

"Mr. Zane Burns?" she asked with a formal smile.

"Yes, ma'am."

"Ms. Ida is expecting you, sir," she said, gesturing toward the hallway on her right. "Please follow me."

Gunz followed her through the long, well-lit hallway all the way to the end, where she stopped in front of a polished, light-maple door. She asked him to wait a moment and opened the door letting the queen know that Mr. Burns was here. Gunz felt slightly troubled by the fact that no one checked him for concealed weapons, and except for a slim vampire-secretary, there were no giant bodyguards in front of the door.

He walked inside the queen's office and stopped at the door.

The office was large, decorated in the same modern style but with Japanese influence. At the far end of the office, he noticed a beautiful four-tier wall mount with four katana swords fitted inside. Gunz didn't know much about Japanese swords. However, these four blades didn't look like something you could buy at the local flea market, and he assumed that the queen wouldn't keep a cheap "Made in China" knockoffs in her office. The swords had to be real-deal ancient samurai katanas.

Out of the furniture, there was only an office desk and a couple of leather chairs. A few plants and decorative elements were placed sporadically around the office, but the rest of the space was unoccupied. The queen was sitting behind the office desk, but as soon as Gunz stepped inside her office, she rose and smiled. She was short and willowy, no more than five-foot-tall, and it was amazing to think that this tiny woman was holding in fear every single undead that was roaming the streets of Florida.

Even dressed in a modern business suit with a tight pencil skirt, Akira had this unmistakable exotic charm of an oriental woman. Her face, a delicate oval, had a porcelain whiteness of vampire skin, deprived of sunlight. Her eyes were blue which was rare for Japanese women and had a sharp angular cut. She lifted her small hand with bright red nails and quickly fixed a loose strand of her long black hair that was pulled in a tight bun on the back of her head.

"Mr. Burns, good evening," she said gesturing at the leather chair in front of her desk, her lips forming a delicate smile that didn't reflect in her glacial eyes. "Please come in, make yourself comfortable."

"Good evening, ma'am," said Gunz, bending forward in a formal bow to show his respect. She arched her eyebrow, visibly surprised by his greeting style and lowered her head in a light nod as her eyes warmed up just a touch. He sat down in the chair and looked at her, expecting her to start the conversation.

"Mr. Burns—," she started to say but then sighed and smiled.

"May I call you Zane? Sometimes all these formal salutations just don't feel right to me."

"Yes, ma'am, of course," replied Gunz, noticing that he was smiling back at her, mesmerized by her clear voice and sweet disposition. He couldn't help but wonder if it was her vampire powers that had this effect on him or it was her natural charm.

"Thank you. You don't need to call me ma'am or your majesty either," she said with a dismissive wave of her delicate hand. "Akira would be just fine. Every time someone calls me ma'am or your majesty, I feel extremely old."

She feels old. This is priceless coming from an ancient vampire who is a few thousand years old, thought Gunz.

"Akira, yesterday you left me a message, asking me to visit you," started Gunz. "I assume you have something to tell me?"

"Yes, Zane. I know you have been looking for some answers and I think I have what you've been looking for," she said, her blue eyes gazing calmly at him.

"You know something about Eve?" asked Gunz before he could stop himself.

The left corner of her lip twitched a little in a quick smirk and Gunz cursed himself in his mind. He had to be more careful. He can't allow himself to get indebted to a vampire queen.

"Yes, Zane. This is exactly why I invited you here," she confirmed, lowering her head gracefully in a nod.

Gunz didn't reply right away, considering his every word. "What would this information cost to me?" he asked finally, holding her blue gaze.

"You'd owe me nothing," she said rising sharply. She turned away and walked to the wall with the swords. Her fingers slowly followed the shape of one of the blades. After a moment she turned around. "I'll do my best to answer all the questions you have, and I expect nothing in return. The only thing I want from you is to do your job and free our realm from Eve's malignant presence, hopefully forever."

"Why?"

The Scarlet Queen wasn't known for her charitability and any favor she ever did had to be returned in kind.

"Normally, we're representing the opposite teams, but I believe the time has come for us to put aside our difference and start working together. Eve is our common adversary," explained Akira calmly, but the thin arches of her dark eyebrows pulled together above her blazing eyes. "It's the enemy-of-my-enemy situation."

"I was investigating a few homicides and I believe Eve killed these people, but all of them were humans," said Gunz.

"Eve doesn't discriminate between the mundane and supernatural," said the queen softly. "She does something to my children, forcing them to act in strange and unnatural ways. And not only upirs and vampires. I believe Queen Aisling had the same problem. Besides that, since Eve made her presence known in my territory, many of my loyal subjects have gone missing."

"Missing?" asked Gunz.

"Yes, missing," said Akira, shaking her head. "I had a report of two large packs of volkolaks. And a few of my spies reported that Eve enchanted my vampires, a few demons and even a couple of stray lycanthropes, turning them into volkolaks."

"That's not possible," muttered Gunz. "I thought that only humans could be turned into volkolaks."

She smiled at him kindly and walked toward a bonsai tree that was sitting on a small wall shelf. She touched its leaves, carefully adjusting them.

"There are a lot of things that you think is impossible," she murmured without looking at him. "You're too young, Zane, and your knowledge of the world is limited. Of course, your youth is just a tiny disadvantage that will disappear with time..." She flicked her fingers over her shoulder at him.

"This Eve must be an extremely powerful witch to pull something like this," mumbled Gunz. He turned in his chair, following Akira's progress across her office.

"Powerful... Yes, that she is," confirmed Akira airily. She remained calm and seemingly unconcerned. "But she's not a witch. Not anymore..."

"What is she?"

"Her real name is Aoife and she is an ancient air demon with the powers of a war goddess," stated Akira serenely. She walked back to her desk and sat on the edge in front of Gunz. "At some point in her life she was a witch, trained by druids. But for her evil deeds, an ancient Irish god, Bodb Derg, King of the Tuatha Dé Danann, cursed her by turning her into a terrible air demon, hoping that she would disappear forever." The queen stopped talking and closed her eyes for a moment, looking like she was exploring the memories of those old days.

"Seems like another case of good intentions gone wrong," muttered Gunz. "The King was hoping that the evil witch would disappear, instead he armed her with dangerous power and magic... Anyway, what does she want? What is she doing here after all these years?"

"Ah, that is a very good question," said the queen. She glanced down, twisting a diamond ring on her right hand before continuing. "I'm not sure what she wants. But whatever it is, it's not going to be good neither for humans nor for vampires. I like the balance we have on my territory right now, Zane. My children do not harm humans and your team does not exterminate my children just because their dental records are slightly different than yours."

"Speaking of dental records," said Gunz. "A few days ago, an upir attacked people in a dental office. Was it one of yours?"

"Yes, he was – Diego Vargas. He was abducted and enchanted by Eve," she confirmed Gunz's suspicions. "I was following Eve's steps to try and guess her intentions, but nothing she does makes any sense. I followed all the bread-crumbs, but it seems like she keeps changing her directions, jumping from one end to the other... I'm not sure, but possibly she feels that someone is on her tail and it's her deception technique... But whatever it is – it surely is working. I'm unmatched at the art of war, studying it for years, and I still can't put two and two together."

"Someone told me that Eve wanted to force one person out of the state. I was never told who he was. The only information given to me was that this person was extremely powerful and influential," said Gunz. "Do you know who this man is?"

Akira laughed, her laughter sounding like little silver bells. "I figured she would want him out of the way. She's afraid that he has become powerful enough to stop her. And I didn't think that she would attempt to kill him, again. After all, it is for cursing this man and his three siblings she got punished in the first place."

"Who is he?"

"I can't tell you that, Zane, as I'm bound to protect his true identity." She sighed, softly patting his hand. "You need to talk to your frenemy Aidan McGrath about it. He can tell you everything there is to know about this person."

As soon as Akira called Aidan his frenemy, a few red flags went up in Gunz's mind. Akira knew about his disagreements with Aidan. It could mean only one thing – the Scarlet Queen was well informed about all his moves and he didn't like the idea of the vampire queen keeping tabs on him.

"I'm not Aidan's most favorite person at the moment," he said dryly, "I doubt he would talk to me at all. Can you tell me anything else about this person?"

"All I can tell you is that this highly influential and powerful person is Eve's stepson. Aidan will have to give you more details."

"Fine," agreed Gunz, understanding that Akira wouldn't say anything else. "How do I kill Eve?"

"You can't. She is an immortal air demon. And when I say immortal – I mean it. There are no known ways to kill her," explained Akira with a light shrug. "But if you join with Aidan McGrath, between the two of you, you may find a way to defeat her and vanquish her from this realm. Unfortunately, this is all the information I can give you on Eve. If I come across any new information, I will contact you."

"Understood, ma'am. Thank you for your help," he replied, forgetting that she asked him to use her first name. Assuming that the meeting was over, he got up ready to leave but she gestured at him to wait.

"One more question," she said, walking toward the wall and pulling one of katanas off the rack. "How good are you at the swordplay? Do you know how to wield a sword?"

"A sword?" He stared at her incredulous. "Why?"

"I understand that with your fire power, you are the ultimate weapon against any vampire. But I do not believe for one second that you showed up for the meeting with the Scarlet Queen otherwise unarmed." She smirked down at him, and when he didn't move, she laughed and put her sword on top of her desk. "Zane, at the moment, I believe you're my ally and as such you have no reason to worry. I just wanted to see your blade. Indulge my curiosity. Please."

Akira said "please", but even this humble word sounded like an order, coming from her. Gunz sighed and reached into his pocket. He pulled out his Swiss army knife and touched it, turning it into a long medieval sword. She gasped and stretched her hands toward the blade but halted an inch short of it.

"May I?" she asked breathlessly.

He nodded and held out the sword in his both hands, offering it to her with a light bow. Akira took the sword and brushed her fingers over the blade, turning it to check the balance and weight. She made a few moves, the heavy blade in her delicate hands cutting through the air with a soft swoosh.

"What a beautiful weapon," she whispered. "A little too heavy like all medieval blades. I still prefer my katanas. But it's perfect for a strong man like yourself." She gave him the sword back and picked up her katana from the desk. "Care for a little exercise?"

Gunz glanced around the room, wondering if she wanted to

spar with him right here, inside the office. His eyes shifted to her tight business skirt and high heels, and he wondered how she was planning to spar dressed like this.

"There is more than enough space here," she confirmed. "I want to see how good a modern man can be with an ancient weapon. Are you game?"

"No vampire's speed and glamor?"

"No Salamander's fire?"

"Deal." Gunz chuckled and assumed the guarding stance, holding his sword to his shoulder.

Akira winked at him and raised her katana. True to her word, she wasn't using her vampire speed or strength, but even her uncomfortable attire didn't help Gunz to win. She was light and fluid, dancing circles around him and during the course of a few minutes, her sword found its way to his neck a few times.

After three five-minute rounds, she stopped him, lowering her sword. While Gunz was breathing faster, his forehead covered in beads of sweat, the fifteen-minute sparring match had no effect on Akira. Her skin remained porcelain-white and her cold face carried no traces of perspiration.

"Your swordsmanship is not terrible, Zane," said the Scarlet Queen. She walked toward the rack with the swords and carefully sheathed her katana, placing it back on the rack. "But you're lacking the finesse and strategic thinking of an experienced swordsman."

Gunz nodded at her. He transformed his sword into the Swiss army knife and put it back into his pants pocket. He had no illusions about his swordsmanship and was positive that Akira with her perfect manners was trying to make him feel better by complimenting him.

Akira smiled. It wasn't even a smile, just a tiny twitch of her small puffy lips. "I'm sure you've heard this one before... Probably from your master or whoever trained you." She walked around her desk and sat down, pointing with her hand at the chair across from her.

"Yes, ma'am," replied Gunz, sitting down. "I was trained by Kal and the Ancient Master of Power. But I don't think I had learned enough. The Ancient Master told me once that I use my sword like a woodcutter and I would be better off with an axe."

Gunz smiled sadly thinking that he should have stayed longer in Kendral and got more training, not only in his swordsmanship and martial arts but also in magic and Dragon tongue. His fiasco with the Demonic Queen made him realize that he needed to learn a lot more about his power and magic and how to use them effectively.

"Aw, that's not true, Zane. The Ancient Master was teasing you. He's famous for his mean tongue." She laughed exposing her small, perfectly straight teeth. Gunz cringed inwardly reminded of the second set of teeth she had that wasn't visible at this moment, thinking how many thousands of people she ripped apart with her fangs. "If you wish, I can give you a few lessons in swordsmanship myself. That's if you promise not to turn your sword against me, of course."

Gunz chuckled, shaking his head. "With all due respect, Akira, I can't promise you that. If you step outside the line, it's my duty to this city to stop you."

"I like you, Zane, you're respectful and honest, unlike most of the modern youth." Her eyes narrowed at him, turning into two thin angled slits. "And you have the makings of a great Bushido warrior. What you failed to understand is that there are no clear lines between good and bad. At the best, they are faded, blurry, sometimes even nonexistent." She fell silent for a few moments. "It's nice to be young, when everything is so simple – black is always black and white is always white, and there are no grey territories... As a Fire Salamander, you will forever keep your youthful appearance, but your soul will get older and you will grow wiser. And when we meet a few hundred years from now, I'll remind you of this conversation."

"Maybe you're right, Akira, and there is no well-defined border between what's right and what's wrong," said Gunz. "But Kal taught me the old code of honor and I embraced it. Based on that, I created my own lines and I prefer to stay within these lines as much as I can. So, as much as I'd like to take a few lessons from you, ma'am, I can't promise you complete immunity. If you or your children hurt any people on my watch, I will turn this sword against you. That I can promise."

The queen pulled back in her chair and gazed at him, slightly tilting her head to the side.

"Child of Fire," she said finally, "you have the fire in you in more ways than you know. But also, you're very human. With time Fire Salamanders become more Fire than human, tired of loss, pain and the burden of human emotions... Immortality has its drawbacks. You'll learn... with time.

"Anyway, I believe you are a man of honor and I respect it. Your honesty must be rewarded. So, I will give you the swordsmanship lessons. Once a week. Until I believe that you are ready to face the Ancient Master in single combat, without living through the shame of defeat. No strings attached. No debt involved, if that's what you're worried about. Assuming, we are both still alive."

Gunz got up and bowed to her. "Thank you, ma'am. I gratefully accept your offer."

She rose and gave him back a light bow. "I will teach you the ancient kenjutsu, the art of swordsmanship. The one that wasn't tainted by the modern western civilization. I haven't taught anyone for many years and I think I'll enjoy teaching you, Zane. Just remember one thing. For two hours once a week, you're not a Fire Salamander and I'm not a Scarlet Queen. I'm your master and you're my student. And for these two hours of training, you belong to me, body and soul."

"And during these two hours, there will be nothing but training?" asked Gunz carefully. "Akira, you will never demand of me doing something against my beliefs, would you?"

"Of course not, Zane," replied Akira with a sigh. "You have no trust. I would not do anything to dishonor you or myself."

"In this case, I accept your conditions, ma'am," said Gunz.

"We'll start after you're done with Eve," said the queen, walking him toward the door of her office. "I don't think you'll be able to spare any time for this now."

"Yes... Assuming we all survive," he said with a nod. "Thank you again for your help."

Gunz bowed to the Scarlet Queen and walked out of the office.

~ TESSA ~

he world was nothing more than a continuous sequence of black and white stripes. Blurry black and white stripes. The white stripes were unpleasantly bright. They were hurting Tessa's eyes, making them water. She raised her hand and spread her fingers, trying to shield her face from the brightness of the white light. Little by little, her vision got restored, but her head was still pounding with a dull throbbing headache.

Slowly, her memories came back to her. She remembered her visit to the church and her conversation with Father Collins. With painful clarity, she recalled the attack on the church – a malignant swirling fog rushing at her. She remembered Father Collins and Father Beaumont, in armor, with swords in their hands, fighting to give her a few seconds so she could run. With all her heart she hoped that both of them survived... And then she remembered the darkness taking hold of her, vanquishing her strength, her will to fight. Taking her whole being over.

Tessa turned her head from left to right and winced as the headache got sharper. She was lying down on a cold concrete floor inside a large cage. Flickering florescent lights were installed alone the length of the dirty-grey ceiling. The iron bars on top of the cage were creating the effect of black and white stripes that she saw when she first opened her eyes.

With an effort, she pushed herself up with her arms. Sitting down on the floor of the cage, she pulled her knees to her chest and looked around, carefully surveying her surroundings. She was in a large room without any windows and without any visible doors – grey dirty ceiling, four grey dirty walls and a concrete floor.

On her left and on her right, she counted eight glass boxes. Glass walls were running from the floor to the ceiling. Inside each box, there was a person, but she couldn't say if either of these people were alive. Their eyes were closed, and they were completely motionless, hanging lifelessly like in suspended animation. Their bodies were sprawled in midair, but no matter how hard Tessa was staring, she couldn't find anything that was supporting these people inside the glass boxes.

Across the room from her, Tessa noticed another cage, just like the one she was in. A girl dressed in a dirty wrinkled private school uniform was sitting behind the bars. Her back was rested against the back wall of the cage and her eyes were closed. Tessa noticed an even movement of her chest and assumed that she was sleeping.

The girl appeared to be no more than fourteen-fifteen years old. Her blond hair was an entangled mess and her face was covered in dust and dirt. A few lighter paths were running down her cheeks, undoubtedly left by tears. But at least she was alive and breathing. It meant that Tessa could ask her a few questions.

Tessa searched around her cage and found a small stone, most likely a piece of concrete. She approached the bars and threw the stone at the girl. She got lucky. The stone made it all the way to the other side of the room, flew between the bars and hit the girl on her arm. The girl woke up with a start and looked around wildly. Then she noticed Tessa and her face reflected disappointment.

"Oh, it just you," she mumbled tiredly. "You're finally awake."

"Finally?" asked Tessa. "How long has it been since I was brought here."

The girl shrugged her shoulders indifferently. "Do you see any clocks here?"

"Just give me an idea. Approximately," said Tessa, pursing her lips. The girl was nothing but a cynical teenager and she wasn't going to get down to her level.

The girl shrugged her shoulders again and rolled her eyes. "Does it really matter? Neither you nor I are going anywhere any time soon, so who cares..."

"I care," muttered Tessa, irritation starting to bubble up in her.

"I would say"—the girl looked to the side, her lips moving like she was counting in her mind— "at least twelve hours if not more. Eve brought you here herself."

"Who the hell is Eve?"

"Don't worry, you'll meet her soon enough," promised the girl, relaxing her back against the bars again. "She brought me here too."

"Do you know why this Eve brought us here?" asked Tessa. "What does she want?"

The girl sighed and pursed her lips. "I have no idea," she said finally. "At first I thought that she was going to send a ransom note to my father or something like that. I thought she was... you know... like after my father's money. My father would pay anything to get me back and since I'm still here, I don't think that she ever contacted him. So, yeah... I have no idea what she wants."

She is a fountain of useful information, thought Tessa as desperation was slowly expending in her chest. The only information she got was that the evil bitch that was running the show had a name. And her name was Eve.

"What's your name?" asked Tessa.

"Tanya," replied the girl. "Tanya Karpenko."

"I'm Tessa Donovan," said Tessa with a light wave of her hand. "Tanya, do you know who all these people in the glass boxes are? Are they alive?"

"They were already like this when Eve brought me here," replied Tanya quietly. "I think I've been here at least three days if not more, but I've never seen these people move... So creepy, right?"

Tessa nodded and fell silent. Tanya didn't know anything, and she didn't feel like talking. She didn't know how long they were sitting silently and after a while Tessa dozed off. She woke up with a start and jumped to her feet. Something wasn't right. She checked the room but didn't notice anything different.

Tanya was gazing at her with curiosity and was about to say something, but Tessa raised her hand stopping her. She sharpened her ears and heard soft, hardly-audible steps. There was someone in the room with them. Someone invisible.

"I know you're here," hissed Tessa, her hands grasping at the rough surface of the iron bars. "Show yourself!"

She heard a silvery laughter and a woman materialized in the room, hardly a foot away from her cage. Tessa gasped and staggered back, away from her. The woman was tall and shapely. She had large blue eyes and long wavy blond hair with slightly red tint. Given different circumstances, Tessa would probably find her attractive. But as it was, she didn't have to guess that this woman was no other than Eve, and nothing would make Eve look beautiful in her eyes.

The woman was dressed in a long elegant red dress, and Tessa thought that the bloody-red color of her outfit in combination with her scarlet lipstick was giving her an ominous vibe. She looked like a repulsively evil version of Jessica Rabbit.

Eve stopped laughing and slowly ran her fingers with sharp red nails over the bars. "Hello, darling," she said, her voice bright and musical, "welcome back. Finally, we have the pleasure of your company."

Tessa crossed her arms over her chest and ran her eyes up and down pointedly slow, like she was sizing Eve up. Then she tilted her head to the side slightly and smirked.

"How about this for the pleasure of my company, bitch," said Tessa, defiantly, flipping the bird at her. "What do you want from me?"

"Bitch? Really?" huffed Eve and guffawed, putting her hands on her curvy hips. "I got to give it you, child, you have nerve talking to me like this."

"What do you want from me, Eve?" Tessa repeated her question, dryly. "Why did you bring me here?"

Eve snapped her fingers and a chair manifested next to her. She pulled the chair closer to the bars of Tessa's cage and sat down, leaning back in it, crossing her ankles in front of her. Tessa sighed and also sat down, facing her. Inside her, everything was twisted with fear, but she wasn't going to show it to this woman.

"Well, darling," purred Eve, "you see, in the beginning, I had an interest in you personally. Just like I was interested in these pitiful creatures." She glanced around the room and waved her hand nonchalantly, gesturing toward the glass boxes. "But a little while ago, I came across something a lot more interesting and useful to my plan. More interesting than you, dear, and more useful than them. So, I hope you don't hold it against me, but my plans have changed."

"Oh, goody," drawled Tessa, gazing heavenwards, "if I'm no longer of interest, why don't you open this cage and let me go."

Eve hooted with laughter again, clapping her hands together. "I think I'll keep you here for pure entertainment value." Eve stopped laughing and since Tessa didn't say anything else, she continued, "Well, my plans did change, but I still need you and this other little creature." She flicked her hand over her shoulder at Tanya's cage. "Both of you make perfect hostages. Between her father and your lover, they will deliver me exactly what I need. Once I have what I want, I'll let you both go. I promise."

"My lover?" mumbled Tessa flabbergasted. "I don't have a lover. No lover, no boyfriend, not even a male friend. What are you talking about?"

Eve's eyes narrowed, and her eyebrows pulled down. "Are you serious, child, or are you mocking me?"

"I'm not mocking you, Eve!" yelled Tessa, jumping to her feet. "You got me mixed up with someone else. I have no lover! I swear!"

"Oh, wow…" mused Eve, her eyes twinkling derisively. "This idiot really never told you, did he? I have to wonder if he is afraid of rejection or he's just afraid to show anybody that he can have real human feelings."

"Who are you talking about, Eve?" Tessa grabbed the bars with both hands and shook them.

"Aidan McGrath, of course," said Eve coldly. "Are you blind, child? The man is so in love with you that he would give his own life to save yours. How can you not see it?"

Tessa fell silent, her arms dropped by her sides dangling powerlessly, and tears gathered in her eyes. Eve was lying. Aidan could never be in love with her. She grew up next to Aidan. He was always like the older brother she never had, watching over her, helping her, taking care of her. And when her mother was gone, he was her only family. He couldn't be in love with her. It made no sense. He was her friend, her brother, her family.

"You're mistaken, Eve," she whispered. She was so shocked that she forgot to be angry at Eve. "Maybe Aidan loves me, but not that kind of love. No, it's impossible."

"Oh, poor child. You really have no idea and he never said anything to you. So, let me open your eyes." Eve sighed and shook her head. She was no longer laughing or mocking Tessa. She looked dead serious. "I know Aidan McGrath longer than I would like to admit. And I'm telling you – Aidan can't live without you.

Right now, if I tell him to cut his chest open, rip his beating heart out and give it to me, he would do it. To save your life, he would do anything. No exceptions. You are his biggest weakness, possibly his only weakness. And I'm going to exploit it to get what I need."

Tessa pressed her hand to her mouth and swallowed, pushing her tears back. She had no doubt that Eve was telling her the truth and that scared her more than anything else. What did Eve want Aidan to do? What was that "thing" she wanted him and Tanya's father to deliver? And most importantly why? Whatever Eve wanted, it couldn't be good. And if she was right, Aidan would be stupid enough to give her what she needed for her evil plan to succeed.

"I see you finally believe me," said Eve rising. She waved her hand and the chair vanished from the room. "Well, goodbye now, Tessa. Hopefully, the next time when I see you, it would be to exchange you for what I need and give you back to your lover."

Before Tessa could say anything, Eve snapped her fingers and vanished from the room.

~ AIDAN ~

A dirty grey fog surrounded him, touching his skin with its sweltering icy fingers. Each touch sent a jolt of pain through his body. Aidan waved his hand, trying to get rid of the fog to no avail. He stopped moving and extended his arm forward. It disappeared into the murky swirls. Something touched his back and he felt another spike of pain. Aidan cried out and bolted forward, fear coiling inside him like a tight spring. He couldn't see anything behind the thick veil of the fog, but he couldn't stop running.

Driven by fear and blinded by the fog, he ran until the ground disappeared under his feet and he started falling, his body twirling helplessly in the air. The fog wasn't as thick here and he could see the rocky sea shore beneath him. It wasn't the warm Florida ocean. It was a stormy northern sea. High waves were rising and falling, breaking into myriads of sparkling droplets on the dark rocks. Aidan gaped at the rocks, knowing that he was about to die and there was nothing he could do to prevent it.

NO!

He couldn't just die. He needed to see Tessa... He had to tell her that—

Tessa!

He screamed her name and a hollow echo painfully bounced in his ears. Aidan cried out, his heart crumbling in his chest. In the last moment, before his body shattered and fell forever motionless on the sharp rocks by the cold northern sea, he whispered her name again.

Aidan woke up and jolted upright, breathing hard. Cold sweat was covering his forehead, running down his back. His shirt, soaked with sweat, clung to his body. He leaned forward, wrapping his arms around his knees and closed his eyes, taking a few deep breaths to help himself calm down.

"Hush, wee lad." Someone spoke to him in a quiet voice with a soft Irish accent and stroked his back gently. "It was just a nightmare... mama is here... shh..."

Aidan flinched at the sound of this musical voice and jumped off the bed. His back hit the wall, and he froze, hardly able to breath. Fear and anger combined into an explosive mixture, boiled up inside him and he roared like a cornered wild beast, his hands clenching into tight fists.

"Eve, you were never my mother then and you're not my mother now. Get the hell out of my house before I throw you out!"

"Now-now, lad," said Eve sternly, wagging her finger at him. "Is that the way to talk to your dear mother. Didn't Lord Hunter teach you any manners, boy? I shall have a word with him first chance I get. He took a sweet little lad and turned him into a giant jackass."

She waved her hand and before Aidan could do anything, his body got numb and he was thrown on the bed. Thick ropes wrapped around his ankles and wrists, binding him to the bed frame. He pulled against his restraints, but his body wouldn't obey, and after a few seconds of futile attempts, he gave up.

"Did I get your attention now, son?" asked Eve frostily, staring down at him.

"Eve, I'm going break these restraints and I—"

Eve snapped her fingers and another rope wrapped around Aidan's neck, strangling him. His mouth opened as he was gasping for air, struggling to breath.

"Are you ready to shut your mouth and listen?" asked Eve, an icy smirk playing on her sinister face. "Nod for yes."

Aidan nodded faintly, and Eve waved her hand again, releasing the rope around his neck a little, so he could breath.

He coughed, taking deep breaths, trying to fill his lungs with air. "What do you want?" he asked when he could speak again, his voice hoarse.

"Aw, who is a good boy now, Aidan," sung Eve in a high-pitched voice that pet owners usually reserve for their pets, patting his cheek. "What a good boy you are."

Aidan grunted, her touch felt like the caress of a venomous snake, but he didn't turn away. She raised his shirt up holding it with two fingers and took in his appearance.

"You shaped up nicely with age, my child," she said, pulling his shirt back down.

"Eve, just tell me why you are here and get the hell out of my house," said Aidan quietly. He pushed against the ropes one more time, but his body felt weak and heavy and he gave up.

"Fine," agreed Eve, shaking her head. "Listen, lad, I hate seeing you tied up to a bed." She stared at him for a moment and then barked laughing. "Aw, who am I kidding? I love seeing you like this – sprawled on the bed and helpless. You look so cute and vulnerable. But I must admit – it feels a bit inappropriate. After all you are my son. So, where is the fun in restraining you in the bed? Swear that you'll stay down like a good wee boy, and I'll let you go. I promise, I just want to talk to you."

Aidan sighed and rolled his eyes. "You can untie me, Eve. I can't fight you even if I tried. What did you do to me?"

Eve snapped her fingers removing all the restraints, leaving just the noose around his neck. Aidan brought his arms down and rubbed his wrists. He tried to push himself up to an upright position but felt weak like a baby and fell back down. Eve snickered mockingly and helped him to sit up, resting his back against the headboard of the bed.

"Don't worry, Aidan," she said dryly, patting his shoulder. "It's just a spell. It is draining your magic. I picked up a few tricks over the years too and learned how to deal with little freaks like you and your master. The effect is temporary. As soon as I leave, you'll get back to normal."

Feeling too tired to speak, Aidan nodded faintly. The only thing he wanted was for this evil monster to be gone from his house and hopefully from his life too.

"I guess I won't be able to get rid of you until you tell me what you want from me, Eve," he said flatly. "Just say what you need already, so I can tell you no and watch you leaving."

"We'll see about that." Eve snickered and leaned forward. Her long hair fell on his face and he jerked his head to the side, avoiding her touch. She lowered down and whispered a few words into his ear. As soon as she was done, she sat up straight, observing his reaction.

"Are you out of your damn mind!" yelled Aidan. He wished he could get up and tear this woman apart limb from limb, but he could hardly move. He was surprised that he had enough strength in him to scream. "I can't do it, Eve! I won't do it! I would never do such a low and despicable thing!" He pinned her with his angry gaze, breathing heavily.

"Are you done shouting?" asked Eve coldly. She got up and stared down at him. "You can, and you will. You don't think that I'm giving you a choice on this matter, do you?"

"What are you talking about? What did you do?" he hissed, his voice cracking and faltering, as everything inside him twisted with the expectation of something awful.

"I didn't do anything, Aidan," said Eve, folding her arms over her chest, her long red nails shining like tiny bloodied blades.

"Not yet at least. But I have your Tessa. And if you don't do what I want by midnight tonight, I will be forced to do something you are not going to appreciate."

Aidan's muscles bulged, as he pushed forward fighting against the restraints of Eve's spell. Eve snickered, leering down at his fruitless struggles, and flicked her hand. The noose on Aidan's neck tightened again and he fell back down on the bed. His every muscle tensed, his hands grasping at the rope as he strained to breathe. She held the noose on his neck tight for a few seconds, until his bloodshot eyes started to close, and his fingers unlocked.

As his vision got flooded with redness, he saw Eve waving her hand and the noose loosened up, allowing him to take in some air. Aidan inhaled sharply with his open mouth a few times, his hands pulling down on the rope that was still wrapped around his neck.

"Eve, please," he whizzed, "not Tessa. She's an innocent young girl."

"She's neither innocent, nor girl," Eve pointed out dryly. "And you must know that. Do what I asked, and she'll be just fine. I promise. But if you refuse to comply with my demands, what I will do to her would be a lot worse than death. Do I make myself clear, sonny?"

"Oh God," moaned Aidan, his trembling hands squeezing his head, his fingers buried into his hair. "Eve, no, please... I can't do what you're asking of me... I can't..."

He couldn't think, his mind on fire. He realized that under no circumstances he should do what she demanded of him, but he couldn't let anything bad happen to Tessa. He had to protect her, no matter what.

"Think hard, Aidan," seethed Eve, her eyes burning with malignant fire. "A few hundred years of curse would be nothing compared to what I would do to your sweet little lover... Think, boy, because I don't deal in empty threats. And you know that."

"Eve, please..." whispered Aidan, all color drained from his face. "Please... ask me for anything else... kill me if you wish... not Tessa. If anything happens to her—"

"You'll die?" asked Eve mockingly. "Are you pleading with me, Aidan? Begging me for the life of your lover?"

Aidan just stared at her, unable to say anything or make the tiniest move.

"If you are trying to beg for mercy, I shall teach you how to do it properly, son," said Eve, her every move breathing with arrogance and cold contempt. "Get down on your knees and kiss my feet, boy. Then I'll think if I shall grant you and your lover the mercy you are begging for."

Like a bucket of freezing water thrown into his face, her words brought him back. In a heartbeat his mind got cleared and he made an instant decision.

"I do not beg, and I kneel before no one," growled Aidan, his fingers grasping the sheet, tearing through the delicate silk. "I'll die before you see me on my knees, bitch. Yes, I do love Tessa more than my own life. And you're right – by holding her life in your filthy hands, you got me under your control. You own me. I will do what you asked me to do. But know that, once I see Tessa to safety, I will not rest until I see you dead. Do I make myself clear... Mother?"

Eve guffawed throwing her head back and got up. "My darling little son, I believe you already promised something like that to me a long time ago." She spread her arms wide and twirled around, her long red dress wrapping around her elegant legs. "And would yah look at that? I'm still alive and kicking your muscled arse. So, stop with empty promises and deliver what I asked you for, no later than by midnight. Once I get what I need, Tessa is all yours, unharmed."

Eve waved her hand and vanished from the room. As soon as she was gone, his strength returned to him. He howled in rage and flung himself off the bed. For a moment, he stood in the middle of his bedroom, looking around wildly, breathing hard. His arms went up and wrapped around his head, as he dropped to his knees and doubled down.

"I can't do it... I can't do it," he kept whispering frantically. "Oh God, how am I going to do something so awful? I can't do it... My Tessa... Oh God..."

His whole body painfully shuddered like from sobs, but he didn't cry. There were no tears in his eyes. It had been centuries since he was able to cry, and he forgot how to do it. His eyes were burning, and his throat was constricted so tight that he could hardly breathe. He lowered his hands to the floor, standing on all fours and cried out – a howl of a wounded man who had no escape, no tears to cry, and no freedom to choose his own path.

Slowly, Aidan got up to his feet and stood swaying slightly, as the room spun around him. He channeled his magic and muttered a few words, pointing down. A large circle, blazing with brilliant white light materialized on the floor in front of him. Aidan bent down and touched the circle, whispering the words of a summoning spell.

~ ZANE BURNS, A.K.A. GUNZ ~

*T*he knock on the door was loud and persistent. Gunz turned to his back and without opening his eyes, extended his Salamander senses, probing the area around the house for magical energy. Whoever was at the door was most likely human. He couldn't sense any magic around this person.

Why me? When did my house become a drive through?

Gunz sat up on the bed and rubbed his face tiredly, feeling the roughness of the stubble under his fingers. His eyes fell on the clock and he pushed himself off the bed unenthusiastically. It was only eight in the morning. So much for him getting some rest after the meeting with the Scarlet Queen. He quickly changed, putting his jeans and a shirt on, and headed downstairs.

"One moment," he yelled to whomever was trying to break his door with continuous banging. He turned the lock, pulling the door open and his jaw dropped. In the doorway, still with her hand up, was standing Missi, the cross-functional queen of *Missi's Kitchen*.

"Mr. Burns, good morning," she said casually, smiling at him like it wasn't eight in the morning and she wasn't standing on his doorsteps when no one wasn't supposed to know his address.

"Good morning, Missi," he replied, slowly getting over the shock.

"I'm sorry for the early visit," she said urgently, "but it's imperative that we talk right away."

"Yes, please come in." Gunz stepped aside, welcoming her inside. "How can I help you?"

Missi didn't move, a guilty smile on her face. "I'm sorry, Mr. Burns, but I can't just walk in. Your house is warded against a magical intrusion and it's enough that I showed up here uninvited, I didn't want to be so rude to try and break through your wards."

"But you are—," started to say Gunz, bewildered.

"Not human," interjected Missi, interrupting him. "Your wards, please, Mr. Burns."

Gunz muttered a quick spell, taking his wards down and gestured at Missi to come in. She walked inside the house and sat down on the couch, putting her small black purse on the coffee table.

"I'm sure you have questions, Mr. Burns," she started. "So, let me start by introducing myself. My name is Melissa Amber Clark and I am a Guardian mage."

"You are a witch?" asked Gunz incredulous. "Then you probably know what I am. But why can't I sense any magical energy in you?"

Missi smiled. "How about now?"

Gunz sharpened his Salamander senses, carefully scanning her and exhaled. "Oh… you're an extremely powerful witch."

"I'm a Guardian mage, which is a lot more than a mere witch, Mr. Burns. And I'm here because I need your help," continued Missi. "As a Guardian, I should never expose my true identity to anyone outside the Guardians or Wardens circles, but I have no choice and I hope I can trust you with my secret."

Gunz nodded at her. Maybe he was too tired and sleepy, but his brain still had a hard time processing it. For a full year he was visiting *Missi's Kitchen* at least a few times a week and he had no idea that Missi was a mage.

"You are a Guardian… Tessa's Guardian," said Gunz quietly as the realization dawned on him. "They sent you here after her mother died. All this time I was searching for you. You were right next to me and I had no idea."

"It means I was doing my job well, shadowing my own magic and Tessa's," said Missi with a cold breeze in her words. "But were you doing your job, Mr. Fire Salamander?"

Gunz eyes widened and he held his hand up. "Okay, hold on a second… Surely, I don't understand what you're implying, Missi," he retorted dryly. "My job is with the FBI and if you need my professional references, I can get you in touch with Agent Andrews."

"Your FBI job is not my concern, Mr. Burns," said Missi frostily. "All this time, you were next to Tessa. She trusted you. She was even a little infatuated with you—"

"And about four days ago, she told me to get lost," cut Gunz sharply. He wasn't sure why Missi's words affected him so much, but he could hardly contain his aggravation. Maybe because all this time he was trying to get hold of Tessa and she stubbornly wasn't answering her phone. Or maybe because he felt guilty for what happened that night.

"And you just went ahead and did what she said? What are you, a little boy?" exploded Missi. She got up and started pacing the living room. "I can't believe it! You knew that she was new to the world of magic and you just left her on her own? When God knows what kind of evil is brewing in the city?"

"Excuse me," said Gunz, seizing her arm and stopping her. "As far as I know, guarding Tessa is your job, not mine. I met her by pure accident."

"As inexperienced as you are, I'm sure the Great Salamander told you that every move on the Board of Destiny happens for a reason. There is no such a thing as a 'pure accident.'" Missi's dark eyebrows gathered above her light eyes and she threw her long braids to her back with a gesture that betrayed the full measure of her frustration.

Gunz let go of her arm and took a deep breath. "Okay, Missi," he said calmly, "I think we started on the wrong foot. I'm sure you didn't come here to point fingers and search for someone to blame. We both know that placing a blame never helps to resolve the issue. So, let's try it again... Tell me what happened and what I can do to help."

Missi stared at him for a moment, her expression changing from cold resentment to something slightly warmer, even a little awkward.

"I'm sorry, Mr. Burns, you're right," she said and sat back down. "I came here because my charge is missing. I can't find her, I can't sense her anywhere. It's been almost two days."

"Tessa is missing," mumbled Gunz, his chest tightened with worry. He thought of all the possible places where Tessa could be but couldn't come up with anything. "Is there anything else you know?"

"I know that two days ago, she went to visit our local Wardens. The same day, the Wardens informed us of a demonic attack on their location. When I arrived there, I saw that the building – it's an ancient church – suffered some damage and both Wardens were greatly injured. Father Collins was unconscious, but the younger Warden, Father Beaumont, said that Tessa was there when the attack happened, and Father Collins and he did everything they could to help her escape. But he couldn't say if she did."

Gunz shook his head, frowning. "I'm not going to ask you who the Wardens are. I have to assume it is some supernatural organization that works with your people. But did you check with Aidan McGrath? Tessa told him to buzz off too, but maybe she checked in with him."

"Aidan McGrath?" Missi cringed. "He's not an easy person to deal with. I didn't talk to him, but I know that she's not with him.

Whoever took her is shielding her presence better than I can. And as powerful as Aidan McGrath is, I'm sure it's not him. Aidan wouldn't be hiding Tessa from her Guardian. He may come across as an arrogant asshole, but he's one of the good guys. I hate to even think like this, but whoever attacked the Wardens, took Tessa."

"Aidan is a good guy?" Gunz shivered like from a cold wind. "I have a hard time believing it."

"Yes, he is," replied Missi, her grey eyes dead serious. "He's extremely powerful and he shadows his power so well that hardly anyone knows what he truly is. Sometimes he's a bit of a jerk and can be a little... explosive, if you know what I mean. But him and his crew are playing on our side, helping us keep our area safe. So, yeah. He's one of the good guys."

"Do you know what he is?"

Missi shook her head. "No, and even if I knew, I wouldn't tell you. Not my secret to tell."

"Fine," said Gunz, feeling a little disappointed. "Going back to the Wardens. Do they know what kind of demon attacked their location?"

"No," said Missi. "That was the first thing I asked. They had never seen such powerful evil before and they're not sure that it was a pure demon. Too much destructive power for a run-of-the-mill demon. And that's what bothers me the most – Father Collins and Father Beaumont are the initiated Wardens of Knowledge, the keepers of secret words. If anyone would know what this demonic entity was, it would be them. But they have no idea."

Gunz took his laptop from the shelf next to his TV and put it on the coffee table. He opened the laptop and clicked on a photo of the "wall of fame", turning the screen to Missi.

"It's just a guess," he said, pointing at the picture of Eve. "This woman could be the one who attacked the Wardens' Church. I hope I'm wrong, but if she's the one who has Tessa, it's a big problem." He told Missi everything he knew about Eve.

For a moment Missi stared at the screen, furrowing her brow. "Can you walk me through all that?" she asked, waving her hand at the photo.

Gunz explained to her every card and every photo on the wall, their connections and when the event took place. He told her about the involvement of the Russian mobster and his daughter's disappearance. Missi listened to him carefully and when he finished, she remained silent for a few minutes.

"I believe you're in danger, Mr. Burns," she said finally. "Whoever this Eve is, she's after you. I have no idea why she would need a Fire Salamander, you're by far not the most powerful player in this city, but there is a chance that Tessa and this Russian girl are nothing more than bait in her trap for you."

"For me?" asked Gunz, incredulous. "Are you sure Tessa is bait for me and not for Aidan McGrath? Aidan is a lot more powerful than I am and he's in love with Tessa. It would make more sense that by abducting Tessa, she was setting a trap for Aidan McGrath."

"Possibly," said Missi, but there was no assurance in her voice. "Here is what we're going to do. You're going to go and talk to Aidan. Whether we're right or wrong about Eve setting a trap for him, he must know about it." She pulled her phone out of her purse and snapped a quick picture of Eve. "I'm going to get back to the Wardens and see if they can give me any lore on this woman. Give me your phone number. I'll call you as soon as I know anything."

Gunz took her phone and entered his number into her contact list. As Missi took the phone from his hand, the room slowly started to spin around him. For a moment everything became a continuous blur. He grunted and grabbed Missi's arm to stop himself from falling. He bent forward, trying to catch his breath. The dizziness got replaced by a nagging, pulling headache and he let go off Missi, pressing his hands to his temples.

"Zane, are you okay?" asked Missi, true concern shadowing her features.

"Yes," replied Gunz, his voice strained, "but I need to go. Now."

"Go where?"

"Aidan McGrath is summoning me, and his summoning call is more demanding than any summoning spell I have ever experienced," explained Gunz.

"Zane, he may already know about Tessa's disappearance," said Missi urgently. "If you learn anything new, find me at *Missi's Kitchen*."

Gunz nodded to her and unfolded the fiery curtain of his portal.

~ ZANE BURNS, A.K.A. GUNZ ~

*G*unz walked out of his portal and found himself in the middle of a spacious bedroom. The king-size bed was in disarray and Aidan McGrath was sitting on it hiding his face in his hands, his shoulders slumped. The nagging pull of Aidan's summoning spell dissipated leaving just a light headache behind and Gunz finally was able to breathe freely.

"Master McGrath, you called?" asked Gunz.

Aidan slowly raised his face, meeting Gunz's gaze and Gunz shuddered from the haunted expression in his blue eyes. His face was bloodless and a deep wrinkle that wasn't there before was etched between his eyebrows.

"Aidan, are you okay?" asked Gunz, taking a step forward.

"Do not move," said Aidan, rising. He walked heavily and halted a step away from Gunz. For a moment, his eyes darted to the window and a torturously-wistful smile changed his face.

"What's going on, Aidan?"

Gunz took a step forward and ran into an invisible wall. A blazing white circle of light surrounded him, and a powerful shock ripped through his body, throwing him away from the wall. He hit the floor hard and his body arched as the secondary shock made his every muscle spasm. For a moment he blanked out. When he surfaced back, he saw Aidan standing over him, just outside the white circle.

"I told you not to move." He sighed, shaking his head, staring somewhere over Gunz's shoulder.

"*Listen to him, boss.*" Gunz heard Mishka's crying voice in his head. "*You can't break free. This circle on the floor is the God's Snare. Even gods can't break through it. You'll just hurt yourself. And what even worse – you'll hurt your loyal wyvern.*"

Gunz slowly pushed himself up, rising to his feet. He glanced at his watch and noticed that the second hand stopped moving. The watch seemed to be broken. He closed his eyes for a moment and pressed his jaws together as his stomach twisted. The rage slowly bottled up in him, and the fire ignited on the bottom of his eyes before he could suppress it. Aidan finally looked at him and sighed again.

"Why don't you sit down, Zane," said Aidan quietly.

"Why?"

Aidan didn't answer but walked away and sat back down on his bed, hiding his face in his hands again. Gunz followed his every move with his eyes, patiently waiting for him to get back and start talking. Finally, Aidan got up and approached the circle again.

"Because in a minute, I am going to block your magic and drain your fire energy, Zane," said Aidan, his quiet voice infused with pain. He tensed his shoulders, and the line between his eyebrows grew deeper. "You'll feel weak and dizzy, and I don't want you to fall. Sit down. Please."

"Why, Aidan?"

"I hope you weren't considering me your enemy, Zane," growled Aidan, squeezing his fists so tight that the slithering blue veins popped up on his hands. "They say that the betrayal never comes from your enemies. And I'm about to betray you in the worst possible way."

Gunz sat down on the floor and shook his head. His recent conversation with Missi flashed in his mind. Missi was right – Eve was using Tessa, but not as bait. She was using her as collateral to blackmail Aidan. She probably told him that she had Tessa and now she had him by the balls.

"So, Eve is forcing you to do her bidding, I guess," he said, a humorless smirk curving his lips.

"She has Tessa, Zane," muttered Aidan. "I'm sorry. I offered her my life in exchange for Tessa's… But it's not my life she wants. It's yours. What did you expect me to do?"

"I expected you to stand and fight, Aidan, and not roll over like a little scared puppy," barked Gunz, outraged that he had capitulated so easily. "Fight Aidan, and I will stand and fight by your side. We'll get Tessa back. Together we can beat Eve!"

"Stand and fight?" Aidan laughed, a cold, gut-wrenching sound that didn't sound like human laughter. "You have no idea what you're talking about. You don't know what she's capable of doing!"

"And you know? How—"

"Because she was my stepmother!" yelled Aidan. His eyes were blazing with a brilliant white light, his face contorted with rage and pain. "She was my stepmother and she put me and my siblings through nine hundred years of hell. Do you understand, Salamander?"

"I understand!" shouted Gunz. "You had your evil stepmother giving you a Cinderella moment. Well, nine hundred years of Cinderella moments. But it's still not a reason to give in to her now! You are not a little boy anymore."

"No, you don't understand!" growled Aidan, punching the air, his fury setting his body ablaze with the white light. "After torturing us for nine hundred years, she killed us all. I can't let her do something like this to Tessa."

"She killed you? Then how are you still alive then?" asked

Gunz, taken aback by the amount of pure torment in Aidan's voice.

Aidan turned away and walked to a small table by the window. He took a pitcher with water and poured some in a glass. Without taking his eyes off the ocean view, he downed the water and turned back to Gunz.

"It's a long story," he said, his voice hoarse.

Gunz spread his arms. "Doesn't look like I'm going anywhere – God's Snare and all. May as well tell me your story."

Aidan pulled a chair closer to the circle and sat down. "You sound so calm," he said, rubbing the back side of his hand with his thumb and Gunz noticed that his hands were slightly shaking. "If you're not afraid of what Eve may do to you, you should be."

"And how is being afraid going to help me?" asked Gunz lifting his shoulders in a half shrug. "No, Aidan, I'm not afraid of what Eve may do to me. I'm more concerned with why she wants me. Just earlier today, someone told me that I'm by far not the most powerful player here. So, why would she want me?"

"I have no idea." Aidan shook his head. "But I hope you agree that I can't leave Tessa in her hands. Tessa is... She gave me my life back, Zane, and she doesn't even know it. I love her. And I owe her."

Gunz chuckled mirthlessly. He couldn't believe that mighty Aidan McGrath, the man whom Eve herself wanted out of her way because she was afraid of him, was so broken and scared. He wasn't just scared, he was petrified. And while Gunz understood that Aidan wasn't afraid for himself, but for Tessa, he still had a hard time accepting that the fear was forcing this powerful man to act against his own beliefs, against his code of honor. He still believed that Aidan was a man of honor and his present despondent behavior was sending chills down Gunz's spine.

"Aidan, can I ask you a small favor?" asked Gunz. Aidan nodded. Gunz took his broken watch off and showed it to him. "Can you take my watch outside the circle?"

Aidan's eyes widened, but as surprised as he looked, he didn't ask any questions. Silently, he put his hand through the circle and took the watch from Gunz's hand, bringing it outside the God's Snare.

"Mishka, leave," said Gunz quietly. "Go home, save yourself."

With a light pop, the wyvern materialized in the room, hissing at Aidan angrily and spitting fireballs in his face. Gunz smirked watching Aidan wrapping his arms around his head to protect his face from the wyvern's attacks.

"Mishka, stop. It's an order," said Gunz firmly. "Please leave, my friend. I'll summon you when it's safe for you to come back. I promise."

"But, boss," objected Mishka, nervously flapping his golden wings, "Kal is not going to be pleased with me. I'm supposed to be your bodyguard."

"You can guard my body later," said Gunz, realizing that he would miss his annoying little companion, "when it safer for you. And please do not bring Kal here. I need to sort this mess out myself. Go now. I'll be all right"

"As you wish, boss," muttered Mishka and disappeared from the room, showering Aidan with a fountain of small flames and sparks on his way out.

"You carry a wyvern in your watch?" muttered Aidan, sitting back down and patting his shirt to get rid of the small flames.

"Yeah, I wanted a puppy, but my Father got me a mini-dragon instead," replied Gunz snidely. "I don't want my wyvern to get hurt when you start wielding your magic to disable me."

At the mention of Kal's name, Gunz wondered if he could summon his mentor even though he was locked inside the magic circle. He sent some fire toward his hand and a playful flame ignited in his palm. Aidan whispered something and touched the circle on the floor. The flame flickered and got extinguished.

"Don't," said Aidan quietly. "You can't summon Kal. He won't hear you through the God's Snare. No one can help you now. And if you try to fight me, I'll drain your magic to the point where you won't be able to move. I don't want to hurt you more than I have to. But I want you to know that you're no match for me, Fire Salamander."

Gunz smirked and folded his arms over his bent knees. "I figured that you were some kind of mighty power," he said, a layer of sarcasm surfacing in his voice. "Kal refused to tell me what you are. He believed that you would do it at your own volition. But you always thought that I was beneath you, I guess."

"That's not true, Zane," objected Aidan and then repeated, averting his eyes, "Not true at all. I never thought that you were beneath me. I was jealous and now I am deeply ashamed of it. I wish we could start over, and betraying you kills me inside…" His voice trailed away. He got up and walked back to the window.

"So, what are you, Aidan? Some kind of ancient Wizard or Sorcerer? Why does everyone speak of you in a whisper?"

Aidan turned around, his eyes and his whole body emitting a brilliant white light.

"Because I'm a god."

~ AIDAN ~

*A*idan was expecting some kind of reaction from Zane – astonishment, fear, even mockery, but his complete calmness was a little unnerving.

"A god," repeated Zane, his face reflecting no emotions. "Which pantheon? Irish, I assume?"

"Irish? No, not Irish," mumbled Aidan. "Welsh... What's the difference?"

"Just curious," replied Zane with a light shrug. "How is a dude with an Irish name and an Irish accent end up in Welsh pantheon?"

Aidan sat down on the chair in front of the circle, stretching his long legs in front of him. He never told his story to anyone. Even his loyal friends, Uri, Sven and Angel, never knew all the details of his life. He told them what they needed to know, but neither of them ever asked him any questions. It could be that their powers were allowing them to know certain things without asking. For the first time in his very long life, someone was asking questions about his past and he wasn't sure he was ready to answer all those questions.

"Listen, Aidan, if you don't want to tell me about yourself, you don't have to," said Zane. He lay down on the floor inside the circle and put his arms under his head. "I'm your prisoner and you're about to deliver me, powerless and weakened, to a monster that scares a god. It would be nice to know at least something about mommy dearest before you dump me there at her disposal."

His words made Aidan cringe inwardly. He turned away, unable to face this man who was thousands of years younger than him and hundred times stronger. He caught himself thinking how much he was admiring this young Fire Salamander and if the situation was different, he wouldn't mind calling him his friend. Aidan sighed, shame and remorse twisting his insides.

"I'll tell you," he said quietly, staring down at his hands. "I'll tell you anything you want to know. But please, let me do it at my own pace."

"Take your time," replied Zane lightly. "I'm not going anywhere."

"How well do you know Irish and Welsh legends?" asked Aidan.

Zane turned his head to the side, giving him an arched stare. "I know a little. Whatever I learned in school."

"Okay, if I tell you that my real name is Aodh mac Lir, would it tell you anything?"

"Aodh mac Lir," repeated Zane, furrowing his brow, like he was trying to remember something. "Aodh, the son of Lir. Son of Lir? No, really?" He sat up, staring at him in wonderment. "Are you referring to that sad Irish legend, *the Fate of the Children of Lir*?"

"Yes," replied Aidan, "I was one of four children of Lir. How well do you know this legend?"

Zane shook his head. "Not well, just a general scope. I remember that Lir had four kids and his second wife cursed them, turning them into birds, swans I think, for nine hundred years. And I recall that after the curse was broken, all of them turned back into people, but aged instantly and died. Is that what happened to you?" Aidan nodded silently. "Then how did you become a Welsh deity?"

"Well, that's a good question," said Aidan. He chuckled bitterly, the painful memories of his past life flashing in front of his eyes. "The legend is missing some important moments and even though it has three different endings, none of them tell the whole story. So, I am going to fill in the blanks and tell you the true ending of this legend. But before I start, tell me, do you know who Gwyn ap Nudd is?"

"Gwyn ap Nudd… yes, he is a Welsh deity, right? The King of Welsh Otherworld, Annwn. No wait, he is not a god though, if I recall it right. He is a fae, the Lord of the Wild Hunt or something like that," said Zane, staring at Aidan quizzically. "Normally, I would say that you can't trust any fae, but in the case of Gwyn ap Nudd, I would make an exception. I think he is one of the good guys. He helped my friends a while ago. And Kal considers him his brother, which is quite unusual for him."

"Gods, fae – you'll do well not to trust any of them. Wicked and unpredictable, going from hot to cold in a heartbeat. Anyway, you got that right. But Gwyn is different. He is one of the best people I've ever met. And you're also right about him not being a god," confirmed Aidan. "But when I saw him for the first time, he was still a god. The first time I met Gwyn ap Nudd was at the time when my stepmother placed her curse on my siblings and me. He was trying to stop her, but he was outside of his domain and he had no power over her.

"I remember what I said to my step mother that moment. But the truth is, every single word I said was meant for Gwyn up Nudd, not for her. I told him that I will pray to him every moment of my existence, begging him that one day he will help me get my vengeance. And I swore that I would not rest in this world or the Otherworld until I have it. And he heard me, Zane, and he nodded to me before he left the side of the lake.

"And here is the main hole in the legend the way it is told

today. According to my evil stepmother's curse, we were supposed to spend three hundred years at the Loch Dairbhreach, another three hundred years by the stormy Sruth na Maoile, and the last three hundred years at the Iorras Domhnann.

"And that's exactly what happened. But after the first three hundred years, when we were flying to the Sruth na Maoile, a terrible storm divided us. I got separated from my siblings and I couldn't find my way back in the midst of the raging sea. The legend states that the three swans arrived at stormy Sruth na Maoile, but the fourth swan showed up a few days later. And none of the scholars who study Irish folklore knew what happened to this one swan and how he survived the storm.

"Gwyn ap Nudd and I are the only people who know what happened. I remember the giant waves drenching me with the icy water. I remember gasping for air, drowning. And then I remember lying in a warm dry cave and Gwyn up Nudd stroking my feathers. He saved me, pulled me out of the stormy sea and brought me to that cave. He told me that unfortunately, he had no power to break my stepmother's curse and we were doomed to spend nine hundred years as swans. He also said that in nine hundred years, when the curse would be broken, we were going to become humans, but age instantly and die."

"Damn," muttered Zane, biting his lip, "what an awful thing to do to innocent children. You didn't get a chance to live, you suffered for nine hundred years and after all that she still killed you."

"That's right," said Aidan. "Anyway, Gwyn promised that when I die, he'd find a way to get my spirit into his domain. And he promised that if at that time, I still would want vengeance, he would give me everything I needed to get my revenge.

"Everything he said that day came true. According to all three alternative endings of Children of Lir, the swans turned into humans, aged instantly and died. But what the legend didn't say was that after we died, Gwyn ap Nudd took my spirit into his domain. He gave me the powers of a god of the Otherworld, trained me and raised me as his own son, and when I was ready, he set me free into this world. Gwyn wasn't happy with my all-consuming desire to seek revenge, but he was true to his promise.

"Needless to say, Gwyn ap Nudd payed dearly for breaking the rules to help me and getting involved into the affairs of another pantheon. He was put through the Destiny Council trial and they stripped some of his godly powers. But he told me many times that he didn't regret what he did and if he was presented with a second chance, he would do exactly the same thing again.

"For almost two thousand years, I could think of nothing but vengeance, searching this world and other worlds for Aoife, or Eve the way she likes to call herself nowadays. With her terrible powers of the air demon in combination with the ancient druids' knowledge, she was illusive, invisible, and dangerous. I couldn't find her anywhere. My unfulfilled desire for vengeance was killing me, burning me from the inside.

"Then about six years ago, I met Tessa. I found her in tears behind my martial arts school." Aidan fell silent for a minute, reliving that day. "She was attacked by bullies, beat up brutally. I remember that moment when I scared the bullies away and she hugged me... Just a twelve-year old child. She was the same age as I was when Aoife cursed me. I held her in my arms and from that moment, she held my heart in her hands.

"I don't know how it happened. I always had a soft spot for children. At the beginning, I just wanted to help her, you know? I wanted to teach her how to defend herself, how to be strong and confident. But she was the one who taught me. She took my life and flipped it upside down. I forgot about my thoughts of revenge. It didn't seem important any more. She was the only thing in my life that I deemed important. And I was happy, Zane... For the first time in over two millenniums, I was actually happy."

Aidan got up sharply and walked to the window. He stood

there, watching the ocean rolling its waves. He wasn't sure that Zane would understand everything, but he was hoping that he was painting a clear enough picture for him to grasp why he had to comply with Eve's demands.

"Aidan."

Aidan heard Zane calling him and turned around.

"Aidan, why didn't you tell Tessa how you felt about her?" Zane sat down inside the circle and crossed his legs. "Why did you never tell her what you were? If you didn't conceal your true nature, possibly things would be different now."

"How could I?" asked Aidan, throwing his hands in the air. "She was just a child and my feelings toward her hardly seemed appropriate. Besides, she always treated me like her brother."

"She is not a child anymore, Aidan, and you're not her brother," objected Zane, chuckling. "She's over eighteen years old. Your relationship with her would be absolutely legal and appropriate."

"Come on, Zane." Aidan smiled reproachfully. "Maybe our relationship would be legal by human standards, but how can I forget that I'm older than the Son of the God she is praying to. I'm almost twenty-five-hundred years older than her."

"So what? You don't look a day over one thousand and hopefully all your body parts are still in working order," objected Zane nonchalantly with a sly wink, but then got serious again. "And don't you think you should at least give her a chance to decide? Tell her what you are and how you feel about her. She may surprise you."

Aidan stared at Zane, doubts wrenching his soul. What if Zane was right?

"A big scary god afraid to talk to a little not-so-human girl?" Zane snickered, flicking his eyebrow at him. "Put your big girl panties on and deal with it, man. After you take Tessa home tonight, apologize to her, tell her what you are, and how you feel about her. Don't you think that over two thousand years of torment was enough? You deserve a little happiness."

Aidan bowed his head to his chest, his shoulders sagged like he was carrying a heavy load. "Knowing what I am about to do to you, you still believe that I deserve happiness?" he asked, hardly able to pronounce the words, his whole body numb and heavy. "I believe that I deserve to be flogged until no skin is left on my back."

"You medieval freaks. Why is it everything has to be about physical punishment and pain with you?" Zane tittered. "Yes, I believe that you deserve to be happy. No, I don't agree with what you are doing and probably wouldn't do it myself, but I'm not in your place. In reality, until I'm in the exact same situation as you are, I wouldn't know what I would or wouldn't do. So, I don't judge you."

Burning with shame, Aidan pivoted on his heels and walked away. He braced himself against the wall and stood there for a few seconds, guilt tormenting him. Then he grunted and slammed his hand against the wall.

"Aidan, don't do it." He heard Zane's calm voice and turned around. "Don't torture yourself, man. But if it'll make you feel a little better, there is something you can do for me."

"What is it?" asked Aidan.

"Besides Tessa, Eve kidnapped another young girl," said Zane. "Tanya Karpenko, the only daughter of Anatoly Karpenko, the head of the Russian mob. A few days ago, Anatoly made me an offer I couldn't refuse." Zane smiled sadly. "He has my friends imprisoned. And just the way Eve blackmailed you, he blackmailed me, pushing me into the corner. Now, to save my friends' lives, I must find and bring his daughter back to him."

"Why would Eve take the daughter of a Russian mobster?" asked Aidan incredulous. "I don't get it."

Zane laughed and lay down on the floor again. "Ahhh, you wouldn't believe me if I told you." He folded his arms under his head, a lopsided smile on his face. "Eve is afraid of you, Aidan. She wanted Anatoly and his ruthless gang to get you out of her way.

I'm sure she wasn't stupid enough to think that the Russian mob could fight a god, but my guess, she wanted him to keep you busy.

"Anatoly, on the other hand, was terrified of you more than he was afraid of Eve. He was so scared that he never gave me your name, calling you 'a powerful and influential person'. And here comes the funny part – he wanted to hire me to kill Eve. And when I refused to deal with him, he held my friends' lives over my head. I had no choice but to start working for him.

"So, when you take me to your darling stepmother, in exchange you must get both girls out. Once you are out of there, take Tanya to her father and make sure that Anatoly frees my friends. I don't need to tell you that you can't trust him. Get the proof of life, get something, but make sure that all three of them are alive, unharmed and free. Can you do it for me?"

"Yes, I can do it. I swear on my power, I'll get your friends to safety," replied Aidan firmly.

The shrill of the cell phone ripped through the heavy silence. Aidan flinched and pulled the vibrating device out of his pocket. He stared at the screen, not recognizing the phone number but answered the call. As soon as he heard the voice of the caller, the small hairs rose on the back of his neck and he crushed his teeth together. It was Eve. She gave him the address of the place where he was supposed to meet with her and hung up the phone.

Aidan stored the address in his phone and sat down on the floor by the circle. Zane gave him a quick once-over and smirked.

"I guess, it's time?" he asked, his eyes glowing red, and Aidan nodded silently. "Okay, go for it. It's not like I can change your mind or fight you. Just make it quick."

"I'll make it painless," said Aidan flatly.

He put his hand on the circle and the circle exploded with the blazing white light. Aidan started chanting, his enchantment sounding like a song. As he was chanting, he kept his eyes on Zane, making sure that he wasn't suffering. At first, Zane's glowing red eyes started to change, returning to their normal grey color. Then his tensed body relaxed, his lips parted slightly, and his eyes rolled back.

Aidan touched the circle and it disappeared. He gently tugged at Zane's shoulder. He didn't respond to his touch. The Salamander looked like he was asleep, but Aidan knew better. Zane wasn't sleeping. He was drained to the point where he couldn't move, couldn't even talk, but he could hear and understand everything that was going on around him.

He gently lifted Zane's body and placed him across his shoulder.

"I'm sorry, Zane," he said, heartbroken. "God knows, I'll make it up to you if we all survive this mess."

He snapped his fingers and teleported out of his apartment.

~ AIDAN ~

*A*idan materialized in his office, inside the *Elements Martial Arts* school. He placed Zane's body on top of his desk and closed his eyes, scanning the area around the school with the other sight that his magic provided. His car was parked in the back and he wanted to make sure that no one would see him walking around with an unconscious man in his arms.

Once he was sure that the parking lot was empty, and no one was watching, he took Zane to the car. Carefully, he put him in the passenger seat and strapped the seatbelt on. Since Aidan wasn't familiar with the location that Eve gave him, he decided to drive instead of trying to teleport into an unfamiliar area. Besides, after the exchange was over, teleporting back with two young girls, one of whom was human, not accustomed to the world of magic, didn't sound appealing.

The address Eve gave him was located in a rich residential area on A1A. The house, better to say an old mansion, was positioned deep in a wooded area and wasn't visible from the main gate. Aidan didn't stop and drove past the gate to see how far away the next house was. As he expected, the old mansion had a lot of acreage and the next residence on either side was a considerable distance away.

Aidan made a U-turn the first chance he got and returned to the gate. The gate was closed, and he stopped the car next to the entry intercom box. He glanced at Zane, still debating with himself if he was doing the right thing. Zane's eyelashes fluttered lightly, and Aidan thought that it was becoming too tiresome to keep the Fire Salamander under his control. Maybe Zane was right and the right thing to do was to stand and fight.

"What are ye waitin' for, lad? A special invitation?"

Eve's Irish accent sounded exaggeratedly loud and clear through the intercom system. Possibly he was too shocked to notice the accent the last time he talked to her, but most likely she was mocking him. Aidan flinched at the sound of her voice, his hands gripping the steering wheel tighter.

With a metallic screech, the gate slid to the side. Aidan drove forward, following the main road that was curving left and right between the trees. The road circled around a large fountain with a sculpture of four beautiful swans, stretching their long elegant necks toward the sky, the replica of the Children of Lir statue in Dublin. Aidan shuddered, gaping at the fountain, all the painful memories of the past crowding his mind. He made an effort, tearing his eyes off the sculpture, and directed his car toward the building.

"Figures," he mumbled parking his car in the circular driveway in front of the house. "Of course, Eve had to go and get herself a medieval castle for a home."

It was a two-story house with many narrow windows that looked like embrasures in the thick walls. Each window was surrounded by a pair of shutters. The entrance was adorned with sienna limestone, covered in slithering ivy. The large window above the entrance had an iron balcony and the dark double door looked heavy and sinister.

Aidan walked around the car, opened the passenger door and

unlocked the seatbelt. He lifted Zane and walked toward the house holding him in his arms. He wasn't surprised to see the front door opening in front of him. He stepped inside, fighting the burning desire to be as far away from this place as possible.

The house interior design was the polar opposite of its exterior style. It was as modern as it could be, with shining marble floors, tall vaulted ceilings and contemporary furniture that was chosen more for the look than for the comfort of use. Aidan spun around, wondering where to go next.

"Go straight forward, to the kitchen," commanded his stepmother's voice through the house intercom system.

Aidan crossed the spacious lobby and walked inside the kitchen. Everything here was done for the comfort and the efficiency of cooking – stainless steel refrigerator, ovens and ranges, the large middle isle table with pots and pans hanging above it. But he doubted that all this was ever used.

"Do you see a small door on the left?" asked the voice in the intercom. "Go through to this door and then downstairs into the basement."

Aidan placed Zane over his shoulder to have his hands more or less free and opened the door into the basement. The long stairway was well lit, but Aidan walked down slowly. Through all his life, he never did anything he didn't believe to be the right thing to do. Betrayal wasn't in his nature and everything inside him was protesting against it.

Every step he took down the stairs was radiating in him with the acknowledgement that for the first time in his life he was deliberately doing something wrong. He knew it and he was still walking down, one step at a time getting closer to the irreversible disaster. Aidan halted. Holding Zane with one hand, he braced himself against the wall with the other.

"Aidan, don't stop now..."

Aidan heard a soft whisper, realizing that because of his internal mayhem, Zane was slowly breaking out of his control.

"I can't... Zane, I can't do it," he whispered hoarsely, everything inside him crumbling to dust.

"You have to, Aidan," replied Zane faintly. "Maybe you were right, it is the right thing to do after all... Maybe this is the only way to find out what Eve is up to. Save the girls. Save my friends. I'll be all right. She can't kill me."

"Oh, Zane, there are things that are so much worse than death," muttered Aidan. "Trust me, I've been there. Death is just a transition into something new, unknown. Most of the people don't realize it, but it's not the actual death they're scared of. It's the unknown that terrifies them. And with Eve... God knows, she can do things that will send you into a perpetual torment where you'll beg for death and it won't come... I can't do it... I can't doom a good man to such a terrible fate."

"Why are you standing there, boy! Lost your way?" Eve was standing at the bottom of the stairs, staring at him with icy contempt. "Move it! One foot at the time."

"It's too late now," whispered Zane quietly. "Go! Save the girls."

Aidan sighed and walked all the way down. He passed Eve without giving her as much as a quick look and ended up in a tiny room without any windows. There was hardly enough space there for him to turn around.

"Give me the Salamander," demanded Eve, stretching her hand toward Zane, but Aidan shied away from her touch, pressing his back against the rough surface of the wall.

"Not so fast," he objected coldly, getting ready to fight his way out if he had to. "First, I need to see Tessa. You're getting nothing until Tessa is with me. Second, getting this Fire Salamander under my control took a lot more effort than I expected. So, I'm changing our initial agreement. Besides Tessa, there is something else I want."

"Oh, yeah?" asked Eve, putting her hands on her hips, narrowing her eyes at him. "Say one more word, boy, and you'll get nothing at all."

"Fine. Then you will get nothing either," replied Aidan, raising his hand up like he was ready to snap his fingers and teleport out of there.

"You're not going to abandon your little lover, Aidan. You're bluffing," said Eve, but there was no assurance in her voice.

Aidan didn't reply, but arched his eyebrows, staring at her without blinking. Eve squirmed under his heavy gaze and then stomped her foot, irritably.

"Okay, we'll do it your way," she grumbled, frowning. "What else do you want?"

"Tanya Karpenko is coming with me," replied Aidan frostily. "I'm giving you the Fire Salamander and I'm taking both girls home."

Aidan expected Eve to bargain with him, but she just smirked coldly and shrugged her shoulders. "Sure, you can have both of them. As long as I get what I want." She grabbed Aidan's arm, her long sharp nails digging into his skin, and teleported out of the small room.

They materialized in another room – a large concrete box with no doors or windows – lit by the blue shimmering light of florescent lights. Aidan looked around taking in his surroundings. He found Tessa right away and for a split-second, happiness expanded in his chest. She was sitting inside a large iron cage. As soon as she noticed him, she got up, his name slipping her lips.

Across the way from her, there was another cage with a teenage girl inside. Aidan didn't have to guess. It was Tanya Karpenko. Besides two cages, there were nine glass boxes inside the room. Eight boxes had people locked inside, disabled and suspended in midair. Aidan knew right away that these eight people weren't human, and he had no doubt about what they were. Their magical energy, even suppressed by Eve's magic that controlled and shadowed them, was unmistakable. All eight people were the Reapers. The ninth, smaller box was empty.

Eve opened both cages and pulled the girls out one at the time, pushing them toward Aidan. "They are yours," she said, an evil smirk stretching her blood-red lips. "Now, I need you to hold your side of the bargain."

Still holding Zane on his shoulder, Aidan approached Tessa and hugged her with his free hand, pulling her closer to his side.

"Are you all right, Tessa?" he asked quietly. His voice, overflowing with emotions, trembled. "Did she hurt you?"

"I'm fine," she replied, pulling away from him and taking Tanya's hand in hers. "We both are. What's going on here? Why is Zane unconscious?" She glanced around, noticing an empty glass box and understanding shadowed her face. "Aidan, please tell me you are not exchanging Zane for me and Tanya."

"Tessa, right now is not the time for this," hissed Aidan. He reached into his pocket and pulled out his car key. "My car is parked outside this house. I need you to take Tanya and drive straight to the Elements school. You have the key for the door. You both need to stay in my office and wait for my return. Do you understand me?"

Tessa didn't take the key. She staggered back, shaking her head. "Aidan, I know you always hated Zane, but you can't—"

"For once, listen to me, Tessa," growled Aidan, stepping closer to her. "Do what I say. I promise, I'll explain everything later!" He drew a rectangle in the air and fill it with a blinding white light, turning it into a door. "This door will take you straight to my car. Go! Both of you."

Tanya stood flabbergasted, watching Aidan with her mouth open. He grabbed her and ushered her through the door. Then he seized Tessa's hand and shoved the car key into her open palm. Tessa took the key and stepped back to the glowing doorway, her eyes filled with tears.

"If something happens to Zane, I will never forgive you, Aidan. Ever," she whispered bitterly and stepped through the door.

Aidan stilled, Tessa's words painfully cutting through his heart.

Eve cackled, staring at him, gloating over the pained expression on his face.

"Your turn, my son." She approached the empty glass box and opened it. "Get him inside this box and put these manacles on."

Aidan put Zane inside the box and shackled his wrists with the heavy iron manacles that were attached to the top of the box. Eve pulled the chains up, lifting Zane into a sitting position. After that she took an oxygen mask and placed it over his mouth and nose. The mask was attached to a medical oxygen tank.

"What are you planning to do to him, Eve?" asked Aidan. All these preparations were making his blood run cold.

"Did you knock him out? Is he unconscious?" asked Eve coldly.

"No, I'm holding him under my control by suppressing his fire," replied Aidan. "As soon as I leave, he'll regain his strength."

"You see," said Eve like it was supposed to mean something to him. "I don't want to babysit him, using my energy to keep him under control. You probably noticed by now that controlling a Fire Salamander takes a lot of magic and strength. There are modern methods that allow you to suppress the fire without using the magic. You can let go now, Aidan. I'll take it from here."

She cackled again and closed the door of the box, sealing it. Then she whispered a quick spell and another gas tank materialized inside the box. She said something, and the tank hissed, releasing some of its contents inside the box. The gas was colorless, but as soon as it came in contact with Zane's skin, he jerked in his restraints and moaned.

"What is it? What are you doing to him?" asked Aidan, stepping closer to the box.

"Bromochlorodifluoromethane, or in layman's terms, Halon 1211," explained Eve with a winning smile on her face. "You need to study modern chemistry, boy. The best agent on the market for suppressing the fire. It's a little toxic to people, but our friend here is not human, so he's not going to die. I enchanted this gas tank, to release some halon every hour to keep the Fire Salamander in him at bay.

"The halon will keep his fire restrained and weaken him physically. The oxygen will prevent him from dying a human death. Of course, this box is enchanted to control his natural state. Just in case. And yes, your friend is in a world of pain right now. But that's just an added benefit of using the chemistry as opposed to magic. Tonight, his screams will be welcome music to my ears."

No longer controlled by Aidan's magic, Zane opened his eyes. His eyes were bloodshot, and his pupils were dilated. He glanced at Aidan but couldn't say anything and closed his eyes again.

"Why do you need a Fire Salamander, Eve? This particular Salamander is in his infancy. He doesn't even know everything about his abilities," said Aidan and waved his hand around the room. "And eight Reapers. Why do you need all of them?"

"You are not seriously thinking that I'm going to reveal my plan to you, Aidan McGrath." She laughed scornfully. "How thick do you think I am? And by the way, there used to be eight and a half Reapers here just a few minutes ago."

"What do you mean, eight and a half?" asked Aidan, involuntarily stepping closer to her.

"Serious?" huffed Eve, her sinister smile getting more carnivorous by the moment. Her eyes measured him appraisingly and she clapped her hands a few times. "You really this stupid? I know that the Guardian was doing a great job shadowing her magical energy, but come on, Aidan. You're some sort of itsy-bitsy god. You should have sensed it."

"Sensed what, Eve?" growled Aidan through clenched teeth.

"Your little lover. She's a part Reaper. She's some kind of magical abomination. Part Reaper and part – even I don't know what her second part is. Not human, that's for sure. Both her parents were creatures of magic. Didn't you know that, you dimwit?" She barked laughing, throwing her head back. "I know you spent nine hundred years as a bird, but I didn't realize that you elected to keep the bird's brain after the curse was broken."

For a moment his mind went blank. *Tessa was a part Reaper?* Eve was right. How could he not feel it all this time? He sensed some kind of magical energy in her but could never recognize it. The magical energy of Reapers or any other beings associated with Death wasn't strong, but it was easily recognizable. He didn't think that Eve would lie to him about something like that. She was taking too much pleasure in his current state of bewilderment.

"Now, lad, go away. Go play with your wee friends. Mama is busy here," she said cackling, waving her hand dismissively. "Shoo, shoo!"

Aidan cringed, but not from her insulting, patronizing way of addressing him. He was looking over Eve's head at Zane's desperate situation and his legs were filled with lead. He couldn't bring himself to leave him like that. He walked around Eve toward the glass box, but before he could reach it, something struck him in the back and everything around him got blurry.

When the blurriness disappeared, he was standing outside of the main gate. He tried the gate, but it was locked. He tried to teleport inside but hit an invisible wall.

The entire territory of the property was surrounded with a giant circle of God's Snare.

No one could get in.

No one could get out.

~ AIDAN ~

$\mathcal{A}$idan teleported back to his office and searched around for Tessa and Tanya. He found them right away. Through the office window that was facing the dojang floor, he could see them both, sitting on the mats, talking. They looked relaxed and were even smiling, discussing something. He felt relieved that both girls were unharmed, but it wasn't enough to make him to feel better about everything that happened.

He gripped the edge of the desk, his fingers leaving dents in the polished hardwood surface. A wave of anger and despair slowly rose within him, threatening to spill over. He roared, flipping the desk over. The computer monitor, pens and all the documents fell on the floor, scattering before his feet. He stared down at the mess he created, breathing heavily, his gaze hollow. As the seething rage slowly started abandoning his body, he fell down to his knees and sat back on his heels, his arms dropped powerlessly by his sides.

"Aidan!"

Aidan raised his head, slowly regaining his control and focused his mind on the present. Tessa was standing in the doorway. Her arms crossed over her chest, she was scolding him with a furious gaze. Tanya was standing behind her, staring at him over Tessa's shoulder with curiosity.

"You owe me an explanation, Aidan McGrath," demanded Tessa coldly. "And it better be a good one."

"Tessa," mumbled Aidan. "Yes, of course. We need to talk. But before we talk, I have to take Tanya to her father."

"No," objected Tessa. "You are going to explain everything, and you are going to do it right now. Starting with your performance at Zane's house five days ago and finishing with you handing him over to that evil bitch."

Aidan got up heavily, adjusting his shirt and for a moment silently stared at Tessa. He approached her and put his hand on her shoulder.

"Tessa, please wait for me here," he said calmly. "I need to take Tanya home and there is something I need to do for Zane. It's important that I do it right away. I promise to explain everything as soon as I come back."

Tessa's eyes filled with tears as she silently stared at him. "Don't you dare mention his name," she said, tears now running down her flushed face. "You betrayed him. I still can't believe you were capable of doing something so... low!" She pulled her hand back and slapped Aidan across his face with all her strength.

A blinding white light exploded in Aidan's head and he pressed his hand to his prickling cheek. He looked down at Tessa, his eyes still watering from the slap and sighed.

"I'll be back as soon as I can. Please do not go anywhere," he said quietly and walked around her to Tanya. "Tanya, I'm going to take you to your father. You already know that magic is real, so I hope you won't mind if instead of driving, we teleport to your father's house."

"Thank you, sir," Tanya mumbled, hardly raising her eyes at him. "What do you need me to do?"

"Do you mind if I pick you up? It will be easier this way for both of us," he said, feeling tired and resigned.

Tanya shook her head no and he easily lifted her. Holding her in his arms, he vanished out of the office without looking back at Tessa.

* * *

AIDAN KNEW EXACTLY where Anatoly Karpenko's mansion was located. He had been monitoring Anatoly's illegal activities for years. However, lately Anatoly started to venture into a dangerous new territory – the world of magic. Mundane himself, he hired a few wizards for protection and didn't mind getting his hands dirty, dealing with vampires, werewolves, shifters and even an occasional demon who was not controlled by the supernatural rulers. Aidan still didn't figure out the nature of Anatoly's dealings with the supernatural crowd, but whatever it was, it couldn't be anything good.

They manifested on the steps of the house. Anatoly's guards rushed toward him, pulling their guns out. Aidan ignored them completely. He glanced at Tanya who was holding to him for dear life.

"Are you still a little dizzy?" he asked her.

She nodded, wrapping her arms around his neck tighter. Aidan shifted her weight to his left arm and waved his right hand, disarming the guards. The guards shouted something, trying to get in his way and stop him from entering. Maybe some other day, he would try to talk to the guards and ask them to call Anatoly, but today he had no patience for them. He waved his hand again, knocking the guards off their feet and walked through the door inside the mansion.

The main lobby was dark and empty. Aidan stopped and gently put Tanya down, still holding his hand on her shoulder for support. She wrapped her arms around his waist and pressed her cheek to his side.

"Anatoly Karpenko!" shouted Aidan, magically magnifying his voice. "This is Aidan McGrath. I'm here with your daughter."

Anatoly showed up a few minutes later accompanied by four armed bodyguards. They surrounded their boss in a protective circle, holding their guns pointed at Aidan. Anatoly's eyes fell on his daughter and for a split-second happiness lit up his face. However, he stopped a few feet away from Aidan, carefully observing him.

"Good evening, Mr. McGrath," he said cautiously. "It's not only my daughter you brought back to me tonight. You gave me back the joy of my life. Thank you." He waved his hand at Tanya to approach him, but she didn't move. "Daughter, come here, sweetheart, let me finally hug you."

"No, Papa," said Tanya, stepping in front of Aidan, attempting to shield him with her tiny body, "not until you promise that you're not going to harm Mr. McGrath. He saved my life, papa. Tell your bodyguards to lower their guns."

Aidan bent down a little and whispered into Tanya's ear, "You know that regular guns can't hurt me, right?" He smiled at her encouragingly. "Magic and all. Go to your father, Tanya. I'll be all right."

Anatoly gestured to his bodyguards to lower their weapons. Tanya gave Aidan another tight hug and ran into her father's embrace. Anatoly kissed his daughter and sent her upstairs, followed by one of his bodyguards.

"Mr. McGrath, I don't know how to thank you for saving my daughter and returning her to me," said Anatoly, taking a step forward and extending his hand to Aidan.

Aidan looked down at his hand but didn't shake it. "It's not me who you need to thank, Mr. Karpenko," he said icily. "It was Zane Burns who exchanged his life and safety for that of your daughter. And I am here to see you holding up your promise to him. I want to see his friends released, alive and well."

"I'm a man of my word, Mr. McGrath," said Anatoly dryly,

squaring his shoulders. "Rest assured, Mr. Burns' friends will be released immediately, unharmed."

Aidan chuckled and shook his head. "No offense, Mr. Karpenko, but I can't rest assured until I talk to them and see them freed with my own eyes. What is it you Russians say? *'Doveryaj, no proveryaj'* – trust, but verify. And I'm determined to do just that – trust, but verify."

Anatoly grunted, displeasure reflected on his face, and threw his hands in the air.

"Fine," he muttered grumpily and pivoted on his heel. "Follow me, Mr. McGrath. Let's conclude this business."

Aidan followed the mobster upstairs to his private office. Anatoly opened the door for him, gesturing to come in, and once inside, offered him a chair to sit down. He was polite but reserved and Aidan could sense the stench of fear lingering around this man like a Chernobyl radioactive cloud. Aidan sat down and relaxed in the chair, staring at Anatoly with narrowed eyes.

Anatoly turned around the monitor of his computer and opened a security cameras' video feed on the screen. The screen was divided into four sections. Three of them were showing semi-dark rooms that looked like jail cells. There was a person in each of the rooms. Due to the late hour, the prisoners appeared to be asleep. The last video feed was showing the street outside. The street was empty and dark, lit up by a single streetlight. Anatoly picked up the phone and dialed a number.

"Pavel," he said to the man who answered his call, "please give your phone to Mr. Shevchenko. And while I'm talking to him, please bring the other two to his accommodations."

On the screen, an armed guard opened one of the cells and walked up to the man inside. The man was asleep, but as soon as the guard shook his shoulder, he got up sharply, his body language suggesting that he was ready to fight at the first sight of danger. The guard gave him his phone, saying something, but the video feed didn't provide the sound and Aidan couldn't hear him.

"Mr. Shevchenko," said Anatoly, "your friend, Zane Burns or as you call him – Gunz, kept his word. In a minute, you'll be reunited with your friends and all three of you will be free to go on with your lives. But in the meantime, I have someone here who wishes to have a word with you."

Anatoly gave the phone to Aidan. "Go ahead."

Aidan took the phone from Anatoly and pressed it to his ear. "Hello," he said, his fingers mindlessly fidgeting with the cord. "My name is Aidan McGrath. I'm Zane's —" He couldn't bring himself to say word *friend* after what he had done to Zane and didn't know how to introduce himself. "Zane asked me to make sure that you were okay."

"Thank you, Aidan," replied Sasha, throwing a glance at the security camera. "Is Gunz okay? I'm a little surprised he's not there himself."

"I'm sorry, he couldn't be here," said Aidan, his throat dry. "This is why he sent me here. Do not hang up, stay on the phone with me so I can make sure that all of you are far away from this place and safe."

Aidan switched his attention to Anatoly.

"Mr. Karpenko, Mr. Shevchenko will keep this phone for as long as he needs it," he ordered in a no-nonsense voice. "Also, I want you to provide them with a vehicle. I will reimburse the cost of the car and the phone, of course."

Anatoly leaned forward slightly, pressing both fists into the desk, his eyes burning with scorn. He ground his teeth but nodded to Aidan.

"The reimbursement won't be necessary, Mr. McGrath," muttered Anatoly. He pulled out his personal cell phone and dialed another number, quickly giving all the instructions to the man in charge.

Aidan watched Sasha reunited with his friends and escorted out of his cell. A moment later, he saw them standing outside the building.

"Aidan, we are out," said Sasha. "We're fine. They are letting us leave and giving us a car."

"Stay on the phone with me until you're at least a few miles away from that place," said Aidan.

"Yes, sir," replied Sasha.

A black Nissan Pathfinder pulled over, shredding the darkness with bright headlights. A tall man walked out of the car, leaving the driver's door opened and threw the car key into Sasha's hands. Aidan watched Sasha getting into the driver's seat and Sergei and Lena climbing in the back. The SUV slowly took off and disappeared from the camera view.

"Aidan, I think it's finally over," said Sasha. "I'm driving fast, and it doesn't look like anyone is following us."

"I don't think they will, but stay vigilant," said Aidan with a sigh of relief. "It was nice talking to you, Sasha. Take care of yourself and your friends."

"Hold on, Aidan," Sasha said quickly before Aidan could hang up. "I know that something is wrong. I'm sorry, but Gunz would never trust anyone with our lives. If you can't tell me what's going on, I understand. But tell me if there is anything we can do to help you."

Aidan thought for a moment. He didn't think that Zane's friend could help, but he appreciated the ties of friendship these men had.

"Sasha, do you have magic?" he asked finally.

"No," replied Sasha. "Unlike Gunz, Sergei and I are not magic freaks." He chuckled softly. "No offense to present company. But it doesn't matter. Magic or not, we stand by his side if he needs us."

"The best thing you can do for now is disappear," said Aidan. "When it's all over, Gunz will find you. He'll find a way to get in touch."

"Understood," said Sasha, his voice deep with worry. "Thank

you again. And tell Gunz that we're always just a phone call away if he needs us."

Sasha hung up and Aidan gave the phone receiver back to Anatoly. He got up slowly, towering over the mobster, anger percolating inside him, and his eyes lit up with a bright white light. His heavy gaze captured Anatoly's eyes. The mobster gasped and clasped his chest with his hands like he was having shortness of breath.

"Mr. Karpenko, you would do well to stay away from me and my friends, Zane Burns included," said Aidan quietly. "Next time you do something unseemly, I may not be as nice and polite as I was today."

Aidan scanned Anatoly with his magic, and his skin crawled with disgust. He registered the swirling muddy darkness inside this man and suppressed the desire to recoil from him. After a moment, he released him. Anatoly sagged in his chair, his face glistening with perspiration.

Aidan smirked and snapped his fingers, vanishing from the room.

~ AIDAN ~

When Aidan finally made it back to his office, he found everything more or less back to normal. The desk was placed upright, and the computer monitor was sitting on top of it, amazingly still in working condition. All documents were neatly stacked in one pile. Tessa was enthroned in his chair, her feet crossed on top of the desk.

He met her eyes and his hope for a peaceful conversation disintegrated. He felt tired and dejected, but mostly he was still angry with himself. He sighed and sat down in a chair across from her.

"Start talking," ordered Tessa. She took her feet off the table and folded her arms on top of the desk, slightly leaning forward. Despite the fact that she was a full foot shorter than Aidan, somehow she managed to stare down at him.

"What do you want me to tell you?" asked Aidan, getting ready for a long and painful conversation.

"Let's start with a simple question. What are you?" asked Tessa. "And please, Aidan, for once in the last six years, tell me the truth."

"I never lied to you, Tessa," he objected quietly, feeling hollow inside. "I just didn't think that it was important for you to know that I had magic and what kind of—"

"What are you?" Tessa repeated the question louder, interrupting him.

"I'm a god," said Aidan, bracing himself for her reaction. And the reaction followed like a category five hurricane.

"What the hell, Aidan!" she yelled. "I'm done with your lies, you asshole. And I'm done with you!"

Rising, she grabbed the computer mouse from the table and threw it forcefully at his head. Aidan didn't flinch. He raised his hand up, freezing the mouse in midair, a few inches away from his face. Carefully, he grabbed the mouse and put it back on the desk. Tessa stilled, staring at him flabbergasted.

"Like I said," he noted with a sigh, "I am a god, Tessa. I didn't lie to you. I'm more than two thousand years old and I'm a god of the Otherworld." He channeled his power and his body lit up with the bright white light. "Look at me, Tessa, do I look like I'm lying to you now? I swear on my power that every word I'm saying to you right now is the truth. Sit down, let's talk."

"More than two thousand years old," whispered Tessa sitting down. "The God? Like Jesus?"

"I'm not Jesus," said Aidan with a smirk. "And I'm not *the* God. I'm one of the old ones. Before Christianity."

"Oh, that really helped," muttered Tessa. "You're an ancient god. And what the heck is the Otherworld? Are you like... Hades?"

"Did I say I was a Greek God? I'm not Hades, but Otherworld is the world of spirits, kind of like the Greek Underworld, but not quite the same."

Tessa shook her head stubbornly, her eyebrows gathering above her eyes. "You know, Aidan, it doesn't really matter what kind of god you are. How could you do it to Zane? Why do you hate him so much?"

"I don't hate him. I never did—"

But Tessa didn't listen to him. Her eyes swam with tears and she slammed her hands on the desk. "You are a god, for Christ's sake! Why didn't you smite this ugly bitch? You're a traitorous coward, that's what you are!"

"I couldn't smite her! She's an immortal air demon, Tessa. I don't have the power to kill her. No one does!" He covered his face with his hands, throwing his head back. "Please, please... ahh... give me the benefit of the doubt—"

"Hell no! I can never forgive you for what you did!"

"It was either you or him!" yelled Aidan, exploding out of his chair. "And for me, it wasn't a choice. I will always choose to protect you!"

"Why?" Tessa yelled back, rising. "Zane was a fighter! He could help you beat this woman... demon... whatever she is! I'm useless when it comes to magic. All I can do is talk to the spirits of the dead! Totally useless! What makes me so special? Why, Aidan?"

"Because I love you!" shouted Aidan and fell silent, stunned by the realization of what he just said. He rubbed his forehead tiredly and fell back in the chair. The words slipped out and there was no way of taking them back. All he could do was stand by what he said.

"Wow," she said. Her temper slowly cooled down, but unfortunately for him, sarcasm took the place of anger. "A two-thousand-year-old grandpa is in love with me. I'm thrilled! I had to be born under some crazy friggin' star."

"Tessa, before you annihilate me with your undying sarcasm, let me tell you something you must know," said Aidan, swallowing the bitter disappointment. He didn't expect that she would return his feelings, but he was hoping that she would be at least be kind about it. "It's important—"

"Something that is more important than your everlasting love?" she asked, a crooked smirk on her lips.

"Tessa, please, let me finish," said Aidan. More than anything he wanted to leave and be as far away from her as he could. He wanted to find a quiet place where he could think in peace. "It's not easy for me either—"

"And do you think it's easier for Zane right now? Being imprisoned by that evil creepy bitch?"

"Tessa, what I need to tell you has nothing to do with me or Zane. It's about you and the magic you have," said Aidan. Tessa fell silent, her mouth opened, and he used this opportunity to keep talking. "If you remember, Eve was holding eight more people in her basement."

"Yes, I remember," said Tessa quietly. "They were unconscious or dead, I think. Who were these people? Do you know why Eve was holding them?"

"All of them were Reapers. They weren't dead, but Eve was keeping them under her control."

"Reapers?" parroted Tessa. "Grim Reapers? The Death? How is it possible? I always thought that the Death was a singular entity. There were eight of them."

"There is such a thing as Death and he is a singular entity, the way you put it," explained Aidan patiently. "But there are also many Reapers. When people die, Reapers help them cross behind the veil."

"Oh, no..."

The blood drained off Tessa's face and she stretched her hand back, blindly searching for the chair behind her. She looked disoriented and confused. Aidan walked around the desk and helped her to sit down. She pushed his hands away, refusing his help, expression of disgust on her face. Her icy gaze raked him across his face and it was more painful than when she slapped him with her hand. He shrank back, away from her and halted by the wall.

"Are you saying, I am a Reaper?" she asked, almost whispering.

"Only a part of you," said Aidan. "One of your parents was a Reaper. But I don't know what your other parent was. From what I understand, both of your parents weren't human."

She nodded, but he could see that her mind was elsewhere. "So, why did that demon want Reapers and a Fire Salamander?"

"I don't know."

"Another good move, Aidan," said Tessa, pursing her lips. "You delivered her what she needed and took back a half-Reaper and a little human girl. Great job, Ancient One. Now she has the Fire Salamander and eight real Reapers. Anything else you can assist her with?"

Aidan didn't answer, too exhausted to continue this conversation. "Tessa, it's very late," he managed to say, hardly moving his lips. "May I drive you home?"

"No, you may not," she said, rising. "I don't think I can stand your presence long enough to make it all the way home."

She walked out of the office, pushing him with her shoulder on the way out. Without paying any attention to him, she headed toward the exit and a moment later he heard the door closing behind her.

"Tessa, wait," he called and rushed toward the door.

By the time Aidan ran out of the school, he saw Tessa getting into a yellow Volkswagen Beatle which he had never seen before. The car took off, quickly picking up speed.

~ ZANE BURNS, A.K.A. GUNZ ~

*G*unz wasn't in pain. The pain had become him. It surrounded him, caressed and embraced him like a tender lover; it turned him inside out, took him apart cell by cell and put him back together like a bunch of Legos, recreating him in its own image. He didn't know if he was screaming. He couldn't hear anything and the pain in his tormented voice cords was melting into the misery of the rest of his body, or whatever was left of it.

He didn't know how long he was like this. Time lost its meaning. It could have been a minute or a year – to him it made no difference. The only thing he knew was the pain. The only thing he saw was the darkness. And the only thing he could hear was the shouting of nothingness.

When the pain finally released him, pulling its hideous claws out of his shredded body, he didn't realize what happened. He felt someone touching him but was afraid to open his eyes or make a move. The fear coiled in him filling the empty space that was left by pain, and he remained motionless and unresponsive.

"Child of Fire."

He heard a pleasant female voice calling him but didn't react.

His ability to think slowly returned to him, obediently supplying the information to his awakened brain. Child of Fire. That's right. He was the Child of Fire. He was the immortal Fire Salamander. He just needed to revert into his natural state and he would be whole again. He reached for his power and found none. His fire, his magic, everything that was making him what he used to be was gone. A silvery laughter responded to his hectic attempts. Gunz felt someone touching him again, gently wiping his face, drenched in sweat.

"Open your eyes, Child of Fire," the woman said. "Try to remember."

Terrified of what he may find, Gunz cracked his eyelids half-open and looked at the world around him through his eyelashes. He was sitting on the floor inside a glass box, his body stretched up by his chained wrists. A woman was squatting in front of the box, observing him with carnivorous curiosity.

Eve.

His memories came back, restoring his sense of reality and bringing back something new, something he didn't experience since he had become the Fire Salamander – the cold. He shivered violently, clenching his chattering teeth.

"Aw, baby," said the woman. Her voice sounded almost kind, but Gunz knew better than believing her. "I think I got carried away yesterday. You lost too much of your fire. That's okay, sweetie, I can fix it. I can make it all better." She was talking to him like he was a sick toddler, caressing his face with her fingers and he had no strength left in him to recoil from her touch. "Now, don't be afraid, my child. After all, tonight is a glorious night, and I'm going to need you performing at your full strength.

"Tonight, I will rip the veil and I will have my revenge on this world and the Otherworld. They all will pay for everything they put me through over the centuries. I will see the fear in the Hunter's eyes and I'll rejoice, basking in his screams."

Gunz stared at her with his half-closed eyes, just now noticing that the oxygen mask was gone, and he was breathing normal air. The tank with Halon was also gone. But he couldn't understand why he was so cold. While Eve looked comfortable, dressed in a sleeveless shirt and tight pants, he felt like he was thrown in the middle of the Siberian tundra, clothed in nothing but speedos. He couldn't stop shivering and all his body felt numb, frozen, bordering with hypothermia.

"That sounds... a bit dark," he managed to say through his chattering teeth.

"Dark? Are you kidding me?" She laughed, sitting down in front of his glass prison. "No, Child of Fire, it's not dark. The mere thought of this moment makes me feel elated, jubilant, ecstatic. There are no words to describe how it makes me feel. But you are way too young to understand it.

"For centuries I sought revenge. I was craving it with every fiber of my being. My whole existence was driven by the thought of seeing the Hunter pay for everything he did to me, for destroying my life, and for aiding my useless stepson. But to get my retribution, I had to find a way to break through the veil. After centuries of endless search, the solution finally is in my grasp. I can do it. I know how. And it's so much easier than I thought."

"What... do you mean... easier?" asked Gunz. Her bloodcurdling excitement and eerie happiness were making him colder than he already was.

Eve gaped at him voraciously, a slow sneering smile stretching her lips. She patted his cheek and he took in a sharp breath through his teeth.

"The process of breaking the veil is fraught with danger. It's a tricky business, you know," she began her explanation. "When I was turned into a demon, I swore that I would do anything it takes to get my revenge. Even the mighty Bodb Derg, the King of the Tuatha Dé Danann, didn't realize that by turning me into an air demon, he provided me with the powers, some of which were scarier and mightier than his own."

Eve cackled, rubbing her hands together, obviously pleased with herself. Gunz swallowed with an effort and closed his eyes, lowering his head to his chest. Either the effects of the hypothermia or his general disgust with everything Eve was saying and the way she looked while saying all these obscenities, was making his stomach churn.

"No, Child of Fire, open your beautiful grey eyes," said Eve. She seized his chin, lifting his face up. "I need to know that you are listening. I know, you're freezing, and I promise to help you with that, as soon as I explain everything to you. I need you to know how you fit into my ingenious plan. After all, without you, my revenge will be impossible."

"Why?" muttered Gunz hardly moving his frozen lips, his body quivering. He cracked his eyelids open just a little, but he had a hard time keeping them open. "Why is it… so important to you… that I know your plan…"

"Why?"

She cackled and ran her sharp fingernail over his nose and down to his chin, cutting his lips. He felt the metallic taste of his own blood on his lips and jerked weakly in her hands. She stared down at him, enjoying his reaction and then brought her finger up to her slightly open lips, wiping a drop of blood off her nail with a quick touch of her tongue.

"I want to see your eyes when you realize that it's you who are going to rip the veil for me, making my revenge possible. I want to see your despair and helplessness. Open. Your. Eyes…" The last three words she said quietly, pronouncing them one at the time, but he had no doubt that it was an order.

Gunz fully opened his eyes and looked at her. "Fine… I don't have a choice but listen to your revolting stories, Eve. Although, I think I would rather die than to hear another word coming out of your venomous mouth."

"Oh, you may just have your wish granted, boy," seethed Eve and continued, "Nevertheless, let's move on. Besides all the magic and power that I had as an air demon, I was also immortal, indestructible, and invisible. I was incorporeal and had nothing but time on my hands. Through the centuries, I learned a few things and I acquired some new powers. I also learned how to restore my physical body."

She got up and twirled around in front of him. As she was twirling, her pants and shirt got replaced by a long red dress, that looked like something one would wear for a Renaissance Fair.

"Am I not beautiful, Child of Fire?" she asked smirking at him.

"Yeah," he muttered, "you're irresistible. A Miss Universe. Please give me your photo, so I can look at it if I ever need to vomit."

"Aw, sweet little Salamander, don't tempt your fate." She laughed sitting back down on the floor. "When I was finally able to walk this world, I started searching for my good-for-nothing stepson. I heard some whispers, that Lord Hunter restored him in this world. And I thought that if I find Aodh – you know him as Aidan, the Hunter would be somewhere nearby. It took me a while, but I found him.

"As soon as I found him, I knew that the time had come, and I needed to start working on my plan. At that time, I thought that the only way to get through the veil was by forcing the Reapers to open it for me. As you probably know, the Reapers are the only creatures of magic who can walk freely through the veil. So, I killed a few people in different areas, and captured a few Reapers. But by holding the Reapers captive, I soon realized that neither of them would comply with my demands willingly. They would rather die than help me.

"So, I started to experiment. I was killing people and infusing their souls with demonic energy. Every time when an infected spirit was moving through the veil, it was damaging it slightly. But the problem was, the Reapers could cleanse the soul before sending it through the veil.

"This is when I understood, that the only way my plan would

work was, if I had hundreds of infected spirits moving through the veil at the same time. There was not enough Reapers left in this whole area to clean so many infected spirits. But I didn't know how I could kill hundreds of people instantaneously. Using the modern mundane weapons was messy and acquiring them would surely attract unwanted attention. I didn't have the power I needed.

"Still not sure how I would make my plan work, I kept following Aidan. I knew that the Hunter endowed him with the power of a god and I didn't want him to stand in my way. Thinking about how to get rid of him, I found out that the boy was in love. So, without further a due, I sent a few demons after his little lover. I didn't want to kill her, but I wanted to get Aidan's attention. And this is when I met you – a wonderful Child of Fire. A Fire Salamander. Who knew? I thought your kind was extinct centuries ago. I watched you dealing with those worthless demons and my heart was singing.

"So, the next day, I enchanted an upir and sent him after Tessa, hoping that you'd be there to protect her. Lo and behold, I was lucky again and you were there. Irish luck, wouldn't you say? As expected, you killed the upir, but you still didn't use your full power. Instead you used your magic. Don't get me wrong, your magic is impressive, but it's not what I needed. I needed to see your full might, the Fire Salamander in action. Not the young and inexperienced wizard."

"You were the one who sent two packs of volkolaks after me," whispered Gunz, feeling sicker by the moment.

"Yes, I did," confirmed Eve, a maniacal gleam in her eyes. "I watched you reverting into your natural state. And you were magnificent, child." Eve sighed wistfully. "I wish you were on my side."

"When hell freezes over…" mumbled Gunz, shuddering.

"Well, I'm watching a Fire Salamander suffering hypothermia. Who knows? One day hell may freeze over too." She smirked at him and continued, "Anyway, once I saw you for the first time, I knew what I needed to do to make my plan work. I needed to capture you and get Aidan's attention away from what I was doing. I approached this Russian mobster, ordering him to get rid of Aidan. But this idiot did a better service to me – he hired you to kill me."

She laughed, throwing her mass of blond hair to her back. By this time Gunz was on the border with unconsciousness. His body was shaking uncontrollably, and his mind was swimming on and off, hardly registering what Eve was saying. The only thing that was clear to him was that Eve wanted to rip the veil and he was the main weapon in her plan for revenge.

As little as he knew about the world of magic and its rules, he knew that the veil was well protected for a reason. Ripping the veil could create a devastating effect, by colliding the world of the living with the world of spirits and demons. If Eve would succeed in her plan, the world as he knew it would cease to exist.

"Eve," whispered Gunz, stuttering, "you can't do it... you'll... destroy this world..."

"That's the idea," she replied with a light shrug. "The rest of the story you know. I abducted Tanya Karpenko, hoping that Anatoly would send you after his daughter. And when you didn't come, I lost my patience and decided to use my dimwitted stepson. I took his lover and demanded your life in exchange for Tessa's. Anyway, enough talking. Let's take care of my frozen Fire Salamander here."

Eve extended her hand and muttered a short spell. A large fireball manifested in the palm of her hand. She leaned forward, draping her free arm around Gunz's shoulders and forcefully thrusted the fireball through his chest. An overpowering wave of searing fire surged through his body. As his element spread through him, warming him from the inside, he cried out in joy, pulling against the chains that were binding him within his glass prison, slowly rising to his knees. His grey eyes got filled with flames and the wave of the fire energy expanded around him.

"Oh God," exhaled Eve, pressing her hand to her chest. Her lips parted, her breath quickened and for a quick moment her eyes darkened with lust. "You are a magnificent creature, Zane Burns. Almost as impressive as your legendary master, the Great Salamander."

Gunz sat down on his heels, breathing heavily and scrutinized Eve with his burning eyes. "I will never do anything for you," he said quietly. "You can torture me for as long as you wish, I will never give in to you."

Chuckling, Eve leaned forward and fixed his face between her hands. She leaned closer and planted a gentle kiss on his bleeding lips.

"Who said anything about any torture? I don't need you to give in to me, Child of Fire," she said, raking him with a scornful stare. "All I need you to do is die. A human death, that is. And for that, I don't need neither your obedience nor your consent. Now you understand why you are so important to my plan?" Eve observed him, and he caught something resembling sympathy in her eyes. "Well, it's almost time. Now, go to sleep."

She whispered a spell, softly touching his forehead with two fingers. His eyes closed, and the darkness softly embraced him. A last painful thought lingered in his mind a moment longer, the words that Jim said to him a while ago.

You are a supernatural weapon of mass destruction.

~ ZANE BURNS, A.K.A. GUNZ ~

"**W**ake up!"

Gunz felt someone shaking him roughly. An even noise filled his ears and he forced himself to crack his eyes open. His vision was still a little blurry and the dizziness made everything around him dance. As his eyes started to focus, he lifted his head and saw a large crowd of people, standing in front of him. The mass of people seemed to be extending to his sides and farther, outside his area of visibility. Some people were dressed in regular modern clothes, but some were wearing the strangest set of garments. He couldn't help but wonder if he was on a set of some crazy mix of historical and fantasy movies. The people were chatting and laughing, pointing at him.

Gunz moved to get up, just to realize that he couldn't. He could hardly turn his head from left to right as his neck was secured by wooden stocks. He couldn't see his body, but he was sure that he was lying on a horizontal platform and his body was bound to it with heavy chains. His arms were twisted behind his back at a most uncomfortable angle and shackled together. With his every move, the iron cuffs were painfully biting into the skin of his wrists.

He looked from left to right and saw a wooden poll on either side of him. With an effort he turned his head as far to the side as he could and glanced up. Chills went through him and his heart thundered in his chest. He was lying down at the bottom of a tall wooden frame. At the top of the frame, he saw a large, angled blade. The edge of the blade was either bloody or rusty, but it still looked dangerously sharp.

Holy shit! It's a guillotine, he thought, struggling against his restraints, just to realize that he was bound in a way that was leaving him completely immobilized. He wanted to scream, but his jaw was sealed shut by some kind of leather straps, most likely a mouth harness. A cool evening breeze touched his skin and with aggravation, he noticed that on top of everything else he had no shirt on. *A goddamn dominatrix nightmare!*

Gunz stopped struggling and took a few deep breaths through his nose, trying to calm down. Eve had him strapped to a guillotine and he was surrounded by a huge crowd of humans. If this blade fell, decapitating him, all these people were as good as dead. Hundreds of people. Where was he? Why was he surrounded by so many people? And, come to think of it, why were they dressed so strange?

"Aw, look who is awake and back with us."

He heard Eve's voice somewhere above him and the crowd responded to her words with a loud laughter and cheers. She strolled around the guillotine and squatted next to Gunz.

"Welcome back, Child of Fire," she said quietly, so except for him, no one could hear her. "How do you like the settings?" Gunz stared at her, breathing heavy as anger swept through him, but couldn't say a word. "Aw, I'm sorry, I forgot you're a little inarticulate at the moment. Blink once for yes, blink twice for no. Do you understand me?"

Gunz blinked one time, his chest locked with fury.

"Hush, little one." Eve chuckled, patting his cheek. "I can't even imagine how angry you must be. But I'm sure by now you already appraised your situation and you know that you have no way to escape. My magic keeps the Fire Salamander in you under control and these wonderful iron chains are keeping the human in you immobilized. Do you agree that you can't escape your destiny?"

Gunz blinked once and a low growl escaped his tightly shut mouth.

Eve laughed quietly, a carnivorous fire burning in the bottom of her eyes and waved her hand at the crowd. "Do you see all these people? I would say, there are at least a few hundred humans here surrounding you." She tugged at the rope that was holding the blade suspended at the top of the frame. "As soon as I release this rope, the blade will fall. You'll die a human death. Your wonderful fire energy will rush through this place like an atomic blast, in a heartbeat obliterating hundreds of humans. All I need to do is infect all these newly dead spirits with my demonic energy. With no Reapers to get in my way, it'll be a piece of cake."

Gunz grunted, straining to break his restraints. Eve got up, her eyes sliding up and down his unobstructed torso.

"I think I already told you how magnificent you are as the Fire Salamander." She stroked his shoulders, brushing her fingers over the strained muscles of his arms and back. "I would love to tell you to stop struggling, but you have no idea how delectable your unclothed back and arms look when you're straining to break these chains. So, keep fighting, boy. You are eye candy for this hungry mob. The more people you attract, the easier I'll break the veil. So, please, don't feel shy to show off your breathtaking physique to your adoring fans."

Gunz grunted and turned away from her. His stomach heaved, and the leather harness that was keeping his mouth shut didn't help with the nausea. Eve was telling him the truth. As soon as the guillotine did its bloody job, all these people would be burnt to ashes. He wasn't afraid to die. It wouldn't be the first time for him. Back in Kendral, during his swordsmanship training, Kal decapitated him a couple of times, just to demonstrate what happens when he dies a human death. The agony of the sword slicing through his neck was something he could never forget. But as soon as his heart stopped beating, his magical fire energy exploded, immediately restoring his physical body and bringing him back to life.

It wasn't the prospect of his own death that terrified him. The idea that he would kill every single person around him was making his blood run cold. The understanding that there was nothing he could do to stop this massacre was sending him into an abyss of despair. He moaned softly, his hopeless situation making his eyes sting with angry tears.

Eve walked around him and leaned down, wiping his eyes with a white handkerchief. "Aw, my sweet lad, is that a tear I see in your gorgeous eyes?" she said softly, but her face lit up with ravenous anticipation. "Don't cry, Salamander. It'll hurt just for a second. You know that guillotine was considered a more humane form of execution?"

Gunz blinked once and then moved his eyes down, staring at the leather straps that kept his mouth sealed. Eve followed the movement of his eyes and snickered.

"Are you trying to show me that you want to talk?"

Gunz blinked once, staring at her pleadingly.

"No, Salamander," she objected icily, rising. "I'm one step away from getting my retribution. There is nothing you can say that would make me stop what I'm doing."

She glanced at her wristwatch and a monstrous smile stretched her lips, distorting her features, displaying a set of long sharp fangs that could rival the fangs of any vampire. For a moment, her eyes flooded with a yellow light and the true face of the air demon gaped at Gunz. He held his breath, shocked by the grotesque, repulsive sight. Finally, Eve's horrid face was truly representing her vile insides. A split-second later, Eve's human appearance was restored, and she smiled at him sweetly.

"It's time, Child of Fire," she said, straightening and fixing the folds of her long medieval dress. "Let's give these people a spectacle they would take with them to the other side."

Eve raised her arms up, requesting the attention of the crowd.

"Welcome to the first day of the Florida Renaissance Festival!" she announced, going down in a deep elegant curtsy. The crowd cheered loudly.

Oh, no, thought Gunz, feeling numb on the inside, *I'm in the Quiet Waters Park. God damn it all! There are thousands of people here, not hundreds.*

The Florida Renaissance Festival had grown into one of the biggest in the country, with the attendance record of nearly a hundred thousand people. As far as he could see, the first day of the Festival drew a hefty crowd.

"For the opening of our beloved Festival, we prepared an unusual spectacle for you," continued Eve. She walked toward the guillotine and waved her hand up and down in a fluid gesture, like a model demonstrating the latest prototype of an iron. "Even though this particular guillotine was built after the Renaissance era, during the Reign of Terror in France, and it still remembers the taste of the blood of its famous victims – King Louis XVI and Marie Antoinette, the true reign of this spectacular machine began a lot earlier.

"The proud ancestors of this guillotine were the Italian 'mannaia' that was popular during the Renaissance era, and the 'Scottish Maiden'. Both of them claimed hundreds of lives way ahead of the French Revolution."

I wonder if she witnessed "the proud ancestors" at work, thought Gunz, attempting to reach his fire. It was unavailable, and he switched his attention back to Eve's historical lecture.

"Let me introduce my wonderful assistant, Zane," said Eve to the crowd, ruffling Gunz's hair with her hand. "Normally, he is extremely obedient, but yesterday he decided to be a bit nutty. Well, I thought that he needed to learn his lesson and today I volunteered him for this demo."

She slapped Gunz playfully on his shoulder and the audience responded with giggles and laughter. Sick of her cheesy jokes and humiliation, he growled and jerked in his restrains, earning the next wave of titters and chuckles.

"So, Kings and Queens, noble Knights and beautiful Ladies, and other creatures of the unknown realms, are you ready to see this terrifying device in action?" Eve raised her arms up and the crowd exploded with applause, cheers, and laughter. "And don't you worry, after all said and done, Zane will still have his head firmly attached to his shoulders."

She squatted in front of his face and whispered into his ear, "As I release the blade, I will also free the Fire Salamander in you. Brace yourself, Child of Fire, for death is eminent and it's coming for you now."

At a funeral pace, Eve rose and sauntered toward the place where the raising rope that was supporting the blade was tied up. Gunz watched her, his heart beating slower with her every move. She untied the knot and held the rope with her both hands, keeping the blade at the top of the frame. Her cold eyes found his and he silently pleaded with her for the life of all these innocent people.

In response to his desperate plea, her eyes gleamed yellow and the revolting face of the air demon emerged again. Her blood-stained thin lips separated, flashing the terrifying set of fangs.

There was no reasoning with her.

No one was coming to help.

There was no hope.

Gunz moaned and turned his head to the opposite side, staring up at the blade. Like through a thick wall, he heard the crowd shouting something and then a collective gasp flew through the field as Eve released the rope.

The time slowed down, all sounds disappeared, and the blade started to descend.

~ ZANE BURNS, A.K.A. GUNZ ~

The time was almost at a standstill and Gunz had no idea why he was counting as the blade was slowly progressing down. Once it passed the half way mark, he closed his eyes and braced himself for the excruciating pain. The pain never came. Instead he heard a light popping sound and a powerful impact crushed the stocks into dust and slivers of wood.

Time resumed its full speed. The noise of the crowd, shouting and applauding, hit him like a sledgehammer. He turned his head to the side and raised his eyes to see the sharp edge of the blade lingering within an inch off his neck. Eve was shrilling and chanting somewhere behind his back. He was still bound to the platform and couldn't move a muscle. Gunz growled and pushed with all his strength against the chains.

Slowly the blade was pulled all the way up to the top of the frame and Aidan stepped forward where Gunz could see him. He snapped his fingers and all the restraints were gone, including the leather mouth harness. Gunz inhaled a deep breath through his mouth and tried to sit up, fighting the dizziness. Aidan helped him up and tapped him on his shoulder.

"Zane, you wanted me to stand and fight?" he asked, a ferocious smile on his lips. "So, here I am."

"About time," mumbled Gunz, "I wonder what woke you up."

"Your friend, Sasha Shevchenko. They're all alive and free, by the way. But let's kill first, tell tales later." Aidan laughed, his eyes burning with excitement and the brilliant glow of his magic. "I hope you will honor me by fighting by my side, Fire Salamander."

"Hell, yeah," said Gunz jumping off the platform.

Finally in a vertical position, standing on firm ground, Gunz could see that the machine was positioned in the middle of a wide field that was supposed to be used for the knights' tournaments. The crowd was still surrounding them in a wide circle, standing around the perimeter of the field. They cheered and applauded, thinking that everything that was happening on the field was a part of a play.

Eve was levitating a few feet above the ground inside a semi-transparent bubble, furiously chanting something. Her voice was fluctuating, going lower and higher, switching to wild shrills once in a while. Her arms were raised, and a rotating dark mass was gathering between her hands. Gunz had no doubt that the bubble was some kind of protective shield, conjured by Eve's magic.

"I tried to break through her shield alone and couldn't," said Aidan. "Let's try together. Maybe by combining the powers of Fire and Water, we could burst her bubble."

He gave a dark chuckle, pulling the long sword out. The weapon glistened in his hands like it was made out of ice. A collective gasp swept through the mass of people as they watch Aidan in awe.

"Aidan," whispered Gunz, "with all these humans around, I can't use my full power to fight. Too dangerous." He reached into his pocket and pulled his Swiss army knife out, turning it into a long sword and ignited it with the fire. "We need to guard the people from my fire energy but also from Eve's magic. Have you ever seen anything like this before?"

Aidan glanced in Eve's direction and cursed quietly. As Eve kept chanting, the dark mass between her arms was growing bigger, long slithering tentacles spewed out, moving through her shield toward the crowd. A few of them already reached people. They wrapped around their necks, entering their bodies through their eyes, nostrils and mouths. The people didn't scream and didn't struggle, hanging limply sprawled in the air. No one in the excited crowd noticed that and Gunz wondered if their oblivion was inflicted by Eve's magic.

"Uri!" yelled Aidan over the noise. "We need a protective dome! NOW!"

"On it! Almost there!"

Gunz heard Uri's raspy voice coming somewhere from above and looked up. The creature that he saw above the field was Uri, but it wasn't him. The man was levitating a few yards above the ground supported by giant flaming wings. The only creature of magic that Gunz knew of, that had fiery wings was the Phoenix. Gunz saw him flying enough times to recognize that Uri wasn't a Phoenix.

His body was glowing with fierce flames, but he wasn't emitting any heat. His fire was shining with golden shades and was completely cold. Besides that, Gunz didn't sense the presence of the elemental power in Uri's magical energy signature. Yet Uri's whole appearance was breathing with dangerous power the likes of which Gunz never sensed before.

Uri outstretched his arm forward and shouted something. However, no matter how much Gunz strained his hearing he couldn't make out his words over the noise of the crowd. A wall of flames surrounded them, leaving all the humans outside the circle, isolating Eve inside. The fire was rising high in the air creating a large dome, but there was neither heat nor smoke.

As soon as the golden fire touched the black tendrils of Eve's magic, they hissed and dissipated. Eve noticed the fire and shrieked, the air demon's true face manifesting through her human face, her yellow eyes blazing with fury. Shouting curses, she pointed her hand at Aidan and hissed something. A wave of dark energy emerged from her hand and impacted Aidan in his chest.

Aidan cried out and fell to his knees, wrapping his head with his arms. He was whispering something incoherent, bending forward like he was trying to conceal his face. Gunz grabbed him, shaking his shoulder, but Aidan didn't respond. Gunz scanned him with his magic, noticing that Aidan was surrounded by a powerful illusion. Uri realized the same thing and swooped down, kneeling next to Aidan.

"Zane," said Uri urgently. "I can take care of this illusion. Can you keep Eve busy? We need to wait for Angel to arrive. He has what we need to send Eve where she belongs."

Gunz spun around. The wall of fire was separating them from the humans, but he wasn't sure if that was enough to contain his power. Uri noticed his hesitation and gave him a heavy stare, infused with a golden glow.

"Don't hesitate to unleash your full power, Salamander," he ordered. "My purifying fire can contain your natural state. We need to keep Eve busy just a while longer."

This momentary distraction gave Eve time to regroup. She reverted to her demonic state, tapping into her full power of the air demon. Rising at least ten feet tall, her look was bloodcurdling. Her vile face resembled a scull with parchment-like skin stretched over it. Deep in the eye sockets of the scull, a venomous yellow fire was burning with abhorrence and malice. Her hair got longer, and its dirty strands were slithering in the air around her head like a bunch of entangled snakes. Her spine twisted, forming a large hump on her back and a bony spike protruded on each of her vertebra. Her hands morphed into giant talons and she struck Uri's protective wall with her raiser-sharp claws.

Her strike made a tiny opening in the fire shield and she cackled, sending a small wave of her dark magic through the opening.

The hole closed up almost immediately, but her magic escaped into the outside world. Gunz heard cries of fear outside the protective circle. He carefully touched the wall of cold flames and found that just like a regular fire, it obeyed his command.

Gunz commanded the fire to let him through, walked outside of Uri's fire dome and halted, staring at the mayhem and devastation that unfolded before his eyes. The whole Festival was in a state of mass panic. The people were running, screaming and crying, chased by a pack of volkolaks. Enormous vicious animals were attacking people, slashing them with their claws, ripping their flesh with their monstrous fangs. He heard a few gunshots, but he knew that regular bullets would do no damage to the volkolaks.

Dammit, I'm sure someone already called 9-1-1... and probably animal control too. More people for volkolaks to have fun with, Gunz thought, swinging his flaming sword at a nearby monster.

He killed a few volkolaks and stopped, realizing that without reverting into his natural state, he couldn't get rid of the pack of monsters of this size.

"Hey, Fire Gecko." Gunz heard a familiar voice and snapped around. Sven was standing next to him, his oversized eyes glowing with a bright phosphoric light. "Go back behind the fire circle, little lizard. Angel should be here in a moment. Aidan and Uri need you there. I'll take care of these mutts. After all, I am a god of nature."

"Svyatobor," said Gunz, "I hope you noticed that these are not wolves. These are demons. There is nothing natural about these monsters."

"I know," said Svyatobor, snickering. "If I die, I'll ask you for help." He laughed and pushed Gunz through the fire back inside the circle. In the last second, Gunz saw that Svyatobor started to change his appearance, shifting into a large brown bear that was holding an enormous axe in his paws.

Here is something you don't see every day. And I thought all those

Russian legends and myths were nothing but children's bedtime stories, thought Gunz, switching his attention to what was going on inside the dome.

Aidan was back in action, but both Uri and Aidan seemed to have a problem dealing with Eve's demonic powers. Eve kept disappearing, morphing into her incorporeal state. Using their confusion, she was popping in and out, attacking them from behind when they couldn't see her.

"Aidan, why aren't you using your other sight," yelled Gunz. He wasn't a hundred percent sure, but he thought that Aidan as a god would have the magical sight.

Gunz roared, reverting into his natural state, rising to the same height as Aidan. The energy of fire spread around him, filling every inch within the protective dome. Eve yelped in pain materializing right in front of Aidan. As soon as Aidan saw her, he struck her with his icy sword, but before the blade could reach her, she already shifted into her incorporeal state and his sword did no damage.

Gunz closed his eyes and observed the area using his Salamander's sense. Eve was playing a game of cat and mouse with them. With her bodiless presence, they had no real weapon against her. Both Uri and Aidan were attacking her with their magic and their swords, wielding the fire and the ice, but nothing was working. Gunz joined their attack striking Eve with the undiluted energy of the elemental fire. She was avoiding all their strikes easily, appearing once in a while, either to assault them from behind or to mock them acidly.

"Hey, guys!" Sven's desperate voice sounded in his head. Gunz flinched, not expecting that the Russian deity could communicate telepathically. *"What's wrong with you? Three young god-like men can't handle one ancient demonic hag. I need help, guys. People are dying. There are too many of these furry monsters here and I can't be in every corner of this park at the same time. They seem to multiply faster than I can kill them..."*

Police sirens sounded somewhere in the distance. It meant more humans were coming to the park. They would charge the wolf-looking demons with their mundane weapons that would do no damage to them except making them angrier and more vicious. More people to kill, more possible deaths, more spirits for Eve to infect with her demonic energy and throw at the veil.

I wish Mishka was here, thought Gunz with regret. Last time the wyvern got rid of volkolaks like it was nothing for him.

"Yeeha!" Mishka's joyful battle cry rang through the air, right outside the fire dome. "You called, boss?"

I wish I had a million dollars, thought Gunz, chuckling. "Mishka, I am so happy to hear your voice, buddy!" yelled Gunz, stabbing the air demon as she popped right in front of his face. "Sven is dealing with a little volkolaks infestation in the park. Can you assist him?"

"You want me to help that cruel trickster, boss?" asked Mishka carefully.

"Yes!" yelled Gunz, twirling in place to avoid a stream of Eve's foul magic.

"Okay, boss, I'll get rid of these assorted mutts, but can I also dispose of the mean trickster at the same time?" asked Mishka.

"No, Mishka. Sven is on our side."

"Aw, too bad," mumbled the wyvern with a sigh, sounding crestfallen. "But after I'm done with the mutts, can I at least fry the mean trickster a little?"

"Ugh, Mishka, no!" roared Gunz, expending his fire energy to draw Eve out of the shadows. "Help Sven! Save humans! Kill volkolaks!"

A moment later, he heard Mishka's happy battle cry carried through the circle of fire, joined by Sven's wild laughter. The wind sped up outside the fire dome. Something clapped and knocked loudly, and a wild cacophony of sounds accompanied whatever Svyatobor was doing. But as long as Gunz could hear the howling and yelping of dying volkolaks, he didn't really care what it was.

In the meantime, the situation inside the fire dome hadn't changed. Gunz had to keep his fire energy flowing all the time to stop Eve from keeping her incorporeal state for too long and give a fighting chance to Uri and Aidan.

It wasn't news that neither of them could kill Eve and keeping her inside the dome forever wasn't an option either. While Uri seemed to be unphased by all the use of his magic and fighting, Aidan was starting to slow down. With dread, Gunz realized that if Angel wasn't going to show up any time soon, Eve would break through. She managed to damage the protective wall of fire once, she probably could do it again on a bigger scale.

A light wind brushed through the area, penetrating the fire dome. The evening light started to dim down and gradually got replaced by an impenetrable darkness. The ground trembled slightly. The only light that illuminated the area isolated by the dome was the burning fire and white light emitted by Aidan's body and his sword.

"Finally," exhaled Aidan, breathing laboriously. "Angel is here."

The fire dome opened up at its apex and a figure of a man, supported by enormous black wings, started to slowly descent to the ground. Gunz stared at him in awe, hardly recognizing the cheerful young Spaniard he met in Aidan's school. Angel was dressed in black pants and shirt with a long black trench coat over it. His long dark hair was flowing down his back, falling below his shoulders. His obsidian eyes were sparkling with danger below his thick black eyebrows, as he was whispering an enchantment in a language that sounded either like Latin or the Dragon tongue.

"Aidan, I'm ready to open the void," said Angel. His voice filled all the space, surrounding them with the magical energy Gunz finally recognized. It was the energy of Death itself.

Angel folded his wings behind his back and twirled in place. As he was spinning, absolute darkness surrounded him. Aidan seized Gunz's arm and pulled him to the opposite side of the fire circle. Uri flew all the way to the top of the dome. In complete silence, Eve's shrills of horror were deafening. She attempted to disappear, but Gunz hit her with the fire energy, bringing her back to visibility.

Angel stopped spinning and opened his magnificent wings to their full extent. Behind him there was an absolute nothingness, a dark shapeless void. The winds were howling inside the void and only the bright zig-zags of lightnings were splitting the pureness of its blackness.

"It's ready," said Angel, approaching Aidan and standing by his side. "We need to do it fast as it takes a lot of my strength to sustain the void open."

Eve hooted laughing, the yellow light of her demonic eyes becoming brighter. She flew higher up and folded her bony arms over her deformed chest. Her scornful gaze darted from Angel to Gunz and then stopped on Aidan.

"You never had what it takes to kill me, stepson," she hissed, venom dripping from her lipless mouth. "What makes you think that you can do it now? Two thousand years later, you're still the same scared twelve-year-old boy."

"You're right, I couldn't fight you then," said Aidan calmly. "Almost twenty-five hundred years ago, I was a little child, helpless and scared, begging you for the life of my beloved siblings and you showed us no mercy. But I don't know if you noticed, I'm not that little boy anymore and I'm not facing you alone."

"Good luck to you and your flock." Eve guffawed, throwing her ugly head back and the entangled strands of her hair moved around her head, shaking with her sinister laughter. Eve waved her talons goodbye and melted into thin air.

The ground shook again, and green leafy vines broke the surface. They were growing quick, stretching up into the air, their stems becoming thicker and stronger. The vines wrapped around Eve's arms and legs, pulling her back down and suspending her in the air, as she struggled fruitlessly.

"Where do you need her, boys?"

Gunz turned to see Sven standing a few steps back, Mishka nestled on his shoulder. Sven swung his arm and the vines obeyed him, moving Eve and positioning her in front of the void. Eve shrieked curses and spells, but nothing was working against Sven's power over nature.

Realizing that she couldn't break free, Eve changed her tactics. She stopped threatening Aidan and started pleading with him, calling him her favorite son and promising him all the riches of this world and any other world. At her words, color drained off of Aidan's face and if he could look any paler, he would probably be green. As he pressed his hand to his stomach, Gunz started to worry that he was about to throw up.

"Let's get it over with, Aidan," said Gunz, squeezing his shoulder.

Aidan channeled his full power and his appearance started to change. For a moment his whole body shone with an unbearable white light and when the light subsided, Gunz saw not the Aidan McGrath, but Aodh, a god of the Otherworld, in the way he had never seen him before. He was dressed in clothes of an ancient hunter-warrior – leather pants and jacket, trimmed with furs and feathers. He stood tall with his icy sword in his hand and a bow with a quiver was strapped to his back. A heavy gaze of his blazing white eyes stopped on Eve and his lips curved in a glacial smile.

"I've been waiting for this moment forever," he whispered.

He pointed his sword at Eve and a powerful stream of his power walloped her in her chest. Eve cried out as Aidan's power surrounded her, immobilizing her. Gunz channeled all his fire and his whole body got engulfed with smoldering flames. He halted next to Aidan, rising to the same height as him and directed the flow of the fire at Eve, joining his attack.

As Sven released his vines, Eve got pushed a few feet closer to the void. A dangerous growl rumbled in her chest as she started to weave her rancorous magic again. The dark mist rose from beneath and she started accumulating it between her arms. Dark tentacles were sprouting from the mist, wrapping around her arms and her body like an indestructible body armor. Seemed like this spell was giving her back some of her strength, as she started to fight their powerful assault, inching her farther away from the void.

"Aidan, I don't know how much longer I can hold the void opened," said Angel quietly. "It sucks my power like a vacuum."

Gunz threw a quick glance at Angel and frowned. His face was tensed, his outstretched arms were shaking, his black wings opened fully, and it was obvious that a few minutes later he would be out of power and out of strength.

"We need help, Aidan," said Gunz, "do you want me to summon Kal?"

Aidan eyes darted to Gunz for a brief second and he shook his head no. He shouted a spell and a dense bubble of his power shield surrounded Eve, cutting off her connection with the dark mist. Eve swiped her talons across his shield, ripping it to shreds. The mist got thicker and now she looked like she was wearing a long shimmering robe that was wrapping, moving and slithering all over her oversized grotesque body. Its movement was sickening and entrancing at the same time.

Uri extended both his arms forward and sent two rays of his power toward Eve. He wasn't trying to strike Eve. He was aiming his power at the dark mist of her spell. As soon as the golden flames touched the mist, it hissed, shuddered violently and started to dissipate. Eve howled in rage, but her connection with the darkness she was wielding got severed. Slowly, the joined offense of Aidan and Gunz started to push her back toward the void.

"Aidan!" growled Angel. "I can't hold the void any more... do something! And do it quick!"

The help came unexpected. The wall of the fire dome came widely apart in the middle and two women walked inside. One was tall and slim, her body clad in medieval armor, completed with chainmail and a long travel cape. She had dark skin and piercing grey eyes and Gunz recognized Missi. The second woman was none other than Tessa, but she looked strong and self-assured, even a little taller.

Neither Tessa nor Missi asked anything and seemed that they knew exactly what was going on here. Missi quickly assessed the situation and walked to Angel, stopping by his side.

"My lord, may I assist you?" she asked, bowing to him.

"Yes, please," moaned Angel, "I would deeply appreciate your assistance."

She placed her hands on Angel's shoulders and whispered something, channeling her magic through him. He took in a ragged breath, but his tensed face relaxed a little, his hands stopped shaking and he was able to fold his wings behind his back.

Tessa approached Aidan but didn't say anything to him and looked at Gunz. Her eyes filled with warmth. Gunz smiled at her tentatively but couldn't talk to her as Eve was starting to break through again.

"Tessa, I know you're new to all this," yelled Missi, "but you need to try, girl. Let your power flow!"

Tessa stepped closer to the void. It seemed that the void didn't affect her in the way it was affecting all of them. She reached up and lightning struck from the clear evening sky connecting with her hand, and the thunder rolled over, rattling the fire dome. Tessa's eyes twinkled as she enjoyed her own strength and power.

"I can do it," she said mostly to herself.

She gathered the electricity in her body and redirected its flow toward Eve. After that, she kept reaching for the lightning bolts, propelling them forcefully at Eve one after another. Eve cried out, shouting curses and spells, but nothing could help her against the joined assault. Little by little, she was pushed to the edge of the void. She stood there, swaying, scolding Aidan with her glowing yellow eyes.

Gunz stopped the flow of his fire and approached Tessa. "Tessa, let Aidan finish it," he whispered in her ear. Tessa lowered her arm and gave him a surprised stare but didn't argue.

"Aidan," said Gunz, turning to him, "she's all yours."

Aidan glanced at him, his face frozen in cold determination. With a last effort, he channeled more power and the whole dome got flooded with the brilliant light of his magic. He cried out, like someone was tearing him apart and slammed Eve with all he had.

She moaned and waved her talons at Aidan. For a moment, her demonic face got replaced with her beautiful human features, her blue eyes filled with tears and she stretched her hand to Aidan. He ignored her silent pleas, increasing the flow of his power. As she got pushed farther back, the shadows of the void swallowed her.

Angel closed the void and let go of his magic. With a sigh, he eased himself down to the ground and rested his arms atop his bent knees. His dark wings disappeared completely, and he morphed back into the normal young man Gunz used to see at *Elements Martial Arts.*

With agonizing slowness, Aidan walked unsteadily toward the place where the dark nothingness of the void was just a second ago. He moved his hand from left to right, like he wasn't sure that it was all over – the void was closed, and his evil stepmother was no more.

"She's gone... she's truly gone," he whispered, his voice painfully hoarse. "Oh, God..." He dropped to his knees, hiding his face in his hands, and his whole body shuddered. "After almost twenty-five hundred years, I'm finally free of her curse."

Gunz let go of his power and looked down at him. Tears of relief was running down Aidan's face as he raised his eyes and met Gunz's steady gaze.

~ ZANE BURNS, A.K.A. GUNZ ~

*A*s soon as the void was closed, Mishka moved from Sven's shoulder to Gunz's. He embraced him with his golden wings and whispered into his ear that as much as he regrets it, he had to go. The wyvern promised to come back tomorrow and vanished, leaving a warm trail of fire behind. Sven walked up to Missi and they conversed about something in hushed voices. After that, he put his hand on her shoulder and they both disappeared. The situation Eve created in the park needed to be taken care of and between Missi's magic and Sven's godly powers, they could take care of it easily.

When Eve started her show, she sealed all exits from the Quiet Waters Park with her magic. The spell Eve used wasn't anything special – a basic blocking spell. But since it was supposed to hold only unsuspecting humans, it was working perfectly well. Technically, Eve wasn't dead, so her spell was still holding, and no one could exit the park.

Besides that, they couldn't let humans leave the park with all the memories of the supernatural stuff, magic and monsters. Usually, people who didn't know anything about the existence of the world of magic, didn't believe in the supernatural. Whenever they came across something out of the ordinary, they managed to find some rational explanation that didn't involve magic, monsters and powers. But with everything that happened today at the Quiet Waters Park, even the best scientific minds wouldn't be able to find a rational explanation.

Uri extinguished the fire dome and told Aidan that he would take care of the guillotine. It didn't sound like a good idea to leave the blood-thirsty device in the middle of the park. Before Uri vanished with the guillotine, Gunz threw a last glance at the spine-chilling machine, thinking how close he came to experience the horrors of the Reign of Terror on his own neck.

Tessa was standing, staring down at her hands, expression of surprise still on her face. Gunz was familiar with this expression just too well. The same kind of expression he saw on his own face reflected in the mirror of his car after he pulled his friends out of the burning house. The house he set on fire, using his elemental power for the first time in his life. He remembered the chaos in his mind and the emotional turmoil he went through when the Fire Salamander in him reared its flaming head for the first time. He took a step closer to her, but Aidan beat him to the punch.

"Tessa," called Aidan, approaching her, "thank you—"

"What are *you* thanking me for?" asked Tessa dryly, holding her hand up to stop him. "I'm not here for you, Ancient One. I'm here because I didn't believe that you would do the right thing. Because I couldn't trust you with Zane's life."

"Tessa, please, let me explain," pleaded Aidan, the unconcealed pain in his voice making Gunz cringe inwardly.

But Tessa just gave him a dismissive wave of her hand, unwilling to listen to him. Turning away from Aidan, she walked up to Gunz and looked at him, like she was expecting him to say something. He remained silent, not quite comfortable with this whole situation.

"Are you okay, Zane?" she asked finally.

"Yes," he replied, tense, "Aidan arrived on time. Tessa, you should at least hear him out. He's a good man. Give him a chance."

Tessa smirked, shaking her hand. "What is it? Did you develop Stockholm syndrome while he held you captive? This man betrayed you, Zane! What's wrong with you? How can you just forgive something like this?"

"I understand why Aidan did what he did," replied Gunz. "Understanding makes forgiveness a lot easier. You should try it sometime. Think back, Tessa. Since you were just a child, Aidan was always there for you. He trained you and protected you. You told me that yourself. After your mother passed away, he was the only person who was there when you needed help and support. Don't you think that he deserves a second chance?"

"And for all these years, he lied to me," said Tessa, her lips pressed in a resentful straight line.

Gunz sighed. She was a stubborn teenage girl and she behaved the part. It was driving him crazy. There was no way of reasoning with her, but he decided to give it another try.

"Now that you have power and magic of your own, you'll see how hard it is to tell anyone about it," said Gunz. "It's hard to open up to people not knowing how they would react to what you're saying. You'll see. Maybe at that time you would find it in your heart to forgive him. Aidan loves you, Tessa. Did you know that he offered his life to Eve in exchange for yours? I think you're making a huge mistake."

It was all good for nothing. Tessa stared at him with slight interest in her dark eyes and then shrugged her shoulders. "I doubt that. But speaking of powers," she said switching the subject away from Aidan. "I know that one of my parents was a Reaper, but controlling the lightening is not one of the Reaper's powers. I need to find out who my other parent was. Missi thinks that knowing my background would allow me to understand and control my power better."

"Maybe your father is Thor," suggested Angel, flashing his bright smile at her. "The god of Thunder, you know."

"And the mighty crow has spoken," parried Tessa, rolling her eyes. "Do you even know who your parents were? Wait! Don't tell me. I don't think I what to know what you are, Angel."

"Well, one thing for sure – I'm no angel." He chuckled, lying down on the ground and folding his arms under his head.

"How did Missi find you?" asked Gunz as soon as she turned back to him.

"She said it was easy. As soon as Eve stopped shadowing me, Missi sensed my presence," explained Tessa. "After all, she is my Guardian. She came to the *Elements Martial Arts* at the perfect time. Anyway, Zane, I wanted to say goodbye. Missi and I are leaving."

"Leaving?" asked Aidan, his voice slightly above a whisper. "When? Where?"

Tessa gave him a freezing once-over but answered his question. "We're leaving immediately. I need to learn the truth about my origin. And Missi is going to help me. We'll be going together. She wanted us to leave earlier, but I couldn't leave Zane's life in your *capable* hands." She placed so much sarcasm in the word 'capable' that Aidan flinched and recoiled from her. Tessa ignored his reaction and continued, "So, when Missi sensed a powerful magical energy spike, we assumed that it had something to do with Eve. We came here as soon as we could."

Aidan was about to say something, but Tessa turned away from him, making it obvious that her conversation with him was over. Gunz had a feeling that Tessa was not only avoiding Aidan, she was even avoiding saying his name.

With a light pop, Sven and Missi materialized next to her. Tessa approached Gunz and embraced him, softly kissing him on his cheek. Gunz seized her arms and gently pulled away from her.

"Tessa," he said quietly, almost whispering, "I'm going to miss you. I wish I could help you in your search, but the truth is, Missi knows a lot more than I do. You have my phone number. If you ever need me, I'm just one fire portal away."

"Thank you, Zane. But you have your hands full here."

She gently caressed his cheek and he uncomfortably shied away from her touch. He glanced at Aidan over Tessa's shoulder and frowned. Aidan looked like he was dying a slow and torturous death, his hands dangling powerlessly at his sides, his head bowed down.

Gunz sighed again. "Tessa, can you do something for me before you leave?"

"Sure, what is it?"

"Please, go to Aidan, talk to him," said Gunz. Tessa's cocked her head and crossed her arms over her chest resentfully. "Say goodbye. Give him some hope that maybe one day you will forgive him—"

"Zane, every time I close my eyes, I see you, unconscious and helpless, thrown over his shoulder as he delivered you to this monster," hissed Tessa. "You could have died, and it would be him killing you, not Eve."

"First of all, I can't die. I'm immortal," objected Gunz calmly. "Second, I wasn't unconscious. I heard and knew everything that was happening. And Aidan had my consent. Tessa, please, don't leave Aidan like this. He didn't deserve it. If not for him, do it for me."

Tessa chuckled, gazing at him with warmth. Her eyes glistened, and she looked like she was about to say something else but changed her mind. Instead she waved her hand goodbye. "See yah, Lizard-boy." She winked at him and added softer, "Take care of the Ancient One. I have a feeling, he'll need you."

Here you go – no name again, thought Gunz as he nodded to Tessa.

She walked past Aidan and gave a quick hug to Sven and Angel, saying her goodbyes. Then she approached Aidan and halted in front of him. He didn't move, his face blank. Tessa gently took his hand and gave it a little squeeze.

"Bye, old man," she said to him awkwardly, staring down at his hand in hers.

"Will I ever see you again?" he asked, speaking slowly and evenly like he was afraid that if he would show any kind of emotions, she would vanish into thin air or run away.

"I'm not coming back until I know who I am," she replied, dropping his hand. "But I will come back eventually. And since you're an immortal god, I'm sure our paths will cross at some point."

"Tessa, I'm sorry—," he started to say, but she smirked, holding both her hands up and he cut himself in mid-sentence.

"Don't apologize to me, Almighty, apologize to him," she said, jerking her chin toward Gunz and flicked her fingers in a light wave. "Catch you on the flip side, Oldie."

She nodded to Missi and they both walked away from the field.

~ ZANE BURNS, A.K.A. GUNZ ~

he night fell over the empty silent park, concealing the last traces of the magical battle. The cool evening breeze touched Gunz's hot skin and he sucked in a deep breath, enjoying his newly acquired freedom and the fact that another dangerous demon was gone from this world. Angel and Sven vanished from the field and Uri was still gone.

Aidan glanced at him and a lighthearted grin split his face. The haunted expression was gone from him eyes and he seemed to be finally calm. Possibly he was just wearing a well-manufactured poker face, but Gunz didn't think so. He smirked back, completely understanding the way Aidan probably felt now. He didn't want to see Aidan demolished and down, and he definitely didn't want to hear him apologizing again. When he told Tessa that he forgave Aidan, he truly meant it.

"You're probably ready to drop," said Aidan, "but do you mind giving me a few more minutes of your time?"

Gunz nodded, wondering what this was all about. Aidan put his hand on his shoulder and snapped his fingers, teleporting them into his martial arts school. They materialized in the middle of the dojang floor. With interest, Gunz noticed that Uri, Angel and Sven were already there. They were sitting on the mats but got up as soon as they appeared.

"Uri, any problems?" Aidan asked, lowering himself down to the mats tiredly and gesturing for all of them to sit down.

"No, no problems," replied Uri with a dismissive wave of his hand. "Your stepmother decided to get creative. It took me a while to figure out where she borrowed that guillotine from. Anyway, I returned it back to the Musée D'Orsay in Paris. Luckily no one noticed that it was gone. Tell me, she couldn't just take a modern 9 mm and shoot him between his eyes in the middle of the crowd?" He winked at Gunz.

"Well, where is the fun in doing that, Uri?" asked Aidan, shivering like from a cold wind. "Eve always had a thing for theatrics. But today, for the first time in the last couple millennials, I was glad she did. If Eve did what you said, Uri, we would end up with hundreds of dead humans and a torn veil on our hands. And an extremely pissed Fire Salamander on top of all that."

Gunz knew that Aidan was joking about the extremely pissed Salamander, but the fact about hundreds of dead humans and a torn veil wasn't a joking matter.

"Yeah, I already know," he said, bowing his head to his chest, "I'm a weapon of mass destruction. And you were probably right, Aidan. I shouldn't be anywhere next to humans. I thought it would be enough if I learned how to suppress my fire energy, but now I can see that it's not. It's not about me controlling my power. It's about others using it against my will to murder innocent people. I don't think I can live with that. So, I thought, I'd go back to Kendral. Kal told me that there was always a place for me in his domain."

When Gunz finished speaking, he was expecting to see relief on Aidan's face and hear that he agreed with his decision. But Aidan didn't say anything. No one did. Complete silence hung in the dojang, lingering over his head like the blade of that guillotine.

"I was wrong," said Aidan finally. His voice reverberated from the tall ceiling in the silence of the school. "I was wrong and I'm not afraid to admit it. This is the reason why I asked you stay a few more minutes. So I could to do something I should have done from the very beginning." He turned to his friends and they all nodded. "Let's start with Uri."

Uri got up and unfolded his fierce wings, his whole body glowing with his strange golden fire. He nodded to Gunz and extended his hand. Gunz got up and shook his hand, still wondering what Uri was and once more confirming his suspicion that the fire Uri was wielding wasn't an elemental Fire.

"Allow me to introduce myself," said Uri losing his rolling Russian accent, a soft smile playing on his glowing face. "I'm Archangel Uriel."

Gunz stilled in shock, gaping at Uri with his mouth open. One thing was to know that the world of magic was real with its powers, demons, ancient gods and fair folks. But the realization that the angels and archangels were real was a revelation on a completely different level. *So, if angels were the real thing, does it mean that God with the capital letter G was real too? And Lucifer, come to think of it...*

A light snickering from the rest of Aidan's crew brought him out of his state of shock. He blushed and smiled uncomfortably. "I'm sorry. I didn't mean to stare, it's just you don't meet a real angel every day, you know." Gunz chuckled, scratching the back of his head. "So, you are the angel of Wisdom, eh?"

"Yes, I am," confirmed Uriel. He dimmed down his fierce glow and his mighty wings disappeared. "You probably noticed that my fire wasn't elemental by nature and I thought that you'd figure it out. The meaning of my name – Uriel – is *Fire of God*."

"I would have probably figured it out sooner or later," said Gunz. "It's just the thought that angels are walking among us, never crossed my mind."

"Everything is real. Anything your mind can hardly fathom is real. Just get used to that idea and your life in the world of magic will be a lot easier and safer." Uri laughed and sat down, waving at Angel. "Your turn."

Angel got up slowly and as he was rising, his appearance began to change. His black hair got longer, falling over his shoulders, down to the back of his black trench coat and giant obsidian wings sprung behind his back. The eerie magical energy of Death washed over Gunz and he involuntarily took a step away from him.

"Are you the angel of Death?" asked Gunz.

Angel chuckled and shook his head no. "I know my wings promote the name," he replied, expending his black wings, "but I'm no angel. Just the Death."

"Just the Death," echoed Gunz flabbergasted. "One of the four horsemen?"

"No, that was my evil twin," said Angel snidely, with a wide grin on his face. "Just kidding. Yeah, that would be me, but to tell you the truth – I don't enjoy horseback riding that much. Nowadays I prefer my Ferrari. Over six hundred horses in one beautifully-streamlined body and no saddle sores."

"I wondered how a modest martial arts instructor could afford driving a Ferrari," asked Gunz with a touch of sarcasm. "Doesn't the IRS come knocking on your door?"

"I pay my taxes," said Angel, laughing. "Me and taxes are like this." He crossed his fingers tightly, showing his hand to Gunz. "We're the only sure thing in life, don't you know? So, once in a while, I knock on their doors. And it's a lot scarier... well... at least I hope it is."

Angel morphed back into his everyday appearance and sat down. Gunz gaped at him, wondering what the Death and Archangel were doing working at a small martial arts school in Parkland, Florida.

"Wow, Aidan. You have the Death, the angel of Wisdom and a Russian deity on your payroll," said Gunz, raking his fingers through his hair.

Aidan cracked a guilty grin. "I guess you met Svyatobor already," he said. Sven's eyes lit up with phosphoric light as he tittered. "Sorry, I shouldn't have sent this trickster after you." He scratched the back of his head. "I wasn't thinking clearly at the time. I should have expected that after a few tours of duty, you would have some messed up memories."

"Yeah, he made quite a mess for me... and out of me," admitted Gunz, cringing inwardly as he recalled all the painful visions that Svyatobor brought forth with his magic.

"Anyway, Zane, I believe, I'm speaking for everyone here," said Aidan, waving his hand at his divine motley crew, "when I say, don't leave. Work with us."

This night is full of surprises, thought Gunz. He remembered the first time he crossed the threshold of Elements Martial Arts and the icy welcome Aidan threw in his face.

"You want me to work for you?" he asked, doing his best not to let any sarcasm through.

"Not *for* me," objected Aidan, putting an accent on the word 'for'. "I believe you already have a job, working for the FBI. I'm offering you to work with us. After all, what we do is in line with what Agent Andrews is trying to accomplish anyway. He's been on my ass for years, trying to figure out what I am and what my goals are. I'll come clean to Agent Andrews and our alliance would be beneficial to both sides."

"Thank you, Aidan... guys," said Gunz, feeling a little uncomfortable. "I'm grateful for your offer and it would be my honor to work with you all."

"Why do I feel like a giant but coming up?" muttered Sven, grinning.

"But the last few weeks taught me a humbling lesson," continued Gunz. "Kal was right. I'm not ready to walk this world. I need to go back to Kendral and learn more about my power, and I definitely need to know more about magic. All this time I was trying to fit in, be a human in the world of humans. Instead I need to learn how to be the Fire Salamander, living surrounded by humans."

"There are quite a few things we can teach you here, too," said Uri. "You're so young, Zane, and so new to the world of magic, that any of us here easily can be your mentor. You know that out of the four of us, Aidan is the youngest."

Holy shit! They all have more than two thousand years behind their backs, thought Gunz. He swallowed hard, for the first time in his adult life feeling like an insignificant little boy. For some reason neither Kal nor the Ancient Master of Power made him feel like this, even though they were a lot older than him.

"We also can teach you the kind of martial arts that no mundane can practice," offered Angel. He got up to his feet and made a few spin kicks, twisting his body in the air one time too many to look natural, obviously using his magic to achieve the desired effect. "The divine school of martial arts. Interested?"

"A lively bunch for a geriatric ward, aren't yah?" said Gunz snickering and had to jump to the side to avoid Angel's round-house. He raised his hands up laughing, asking Angel to stop. "You all are making me feel like I'm a newborn. And I would love to learn anything you can teach me, but first, I need to talk to my mentor. Only Kal can teach me how to be the Fire Salamander. I'll be back as soon as I can, if that's okay with all of you."

"That's fine," said Aidan. "Come back whenever you're ready."

Uri got up and tapped him on the shoulder. "Trust me, we all are still going to be here, no matter how much time you spend in Kendral." His Russian accent was back, and his hazel eyes lost their golden gleam, shining with humor instead.

Gunz waved his hand unfolding the fire curtain of his portal.

"Don't forget to learn how to teleport, Fire Gecko," said Sven, snickering.

Gunz gave them a light nod and walked through the portal.

~ ZANE BURNS, A.K.A. GUNZ ~

*J*t was nice to be home and not have to worry that someone was after you. Gunz checked all his protection spells and wards. Everything was functioning perfectly. With his eyes half-closed, he headed upstairs to his bedroom with one desire only – to fall on his bed and to sleep for as long as he wanted.

No more Eve, and whatever else supernatural was brewing in the area could wait until tomorrow. Anatoly Karpenko got his daughter back and he should be out of his life too. At least for now. Not for a minute did he believe that Anatoly would keep his word and leave him be. But this night, if he valued his life, he better stay away.

Gunz walked into his bedroom and looked in the mirror, observing his state of undress and his dirty demeanor with horror. *Shower?* He glanced at the bathroom door unable to take a step toward it and then flung himself on top of the bed. *Screw it... it can wait until morning... No one better wake me up in the morning—*

His thought slipped away as he fell asleep on top of the bedcover, without changing or even taking his pants and shoes off.

* * *

HE WAS WARM AND CONTENT. His body wasn't aching with tiredness, he wasn't bleeding or freezing, and no one was threatening
his friends. Gunz sighed, enjoying this feeling of peace. *Fire...
yeah... I needed it.* Gunz turned on his back and stretched luxuri-
ating in the loving embrace of his element. *A little too warm?*
Slowly, he opened his eyes and jolted upright, hitting the back of
his head on the backboard of the bed. A wave of laughter that
accompanied his move added to his aggravation and general
discomfort.

Right above him he saw Mishka. The wyvern was hovering
over him, gently sending one wave of fire energy after another
through his body. Kal and the Ancient Master of Power, Mrak
Delar, were standing next to his bed, laughing. Master Mrak
Delar was the first person who told him that he had the Fire
Power in him. And he was the one who told him not to be afraid
of it and do what came naturally. His advice saved him and his
friends lives, but it also brought the Fire Salamander to life.

Kal pushed Mrak Delar on his shoulder, pointing at Gunz.
"Mrak," he said stifling the laughter, "you're younger. Is that
something the new generation does nowadays – sleeping half-
dressed and in shoes?"

"It's a new fad, Kal," muttered Gunz, rubbing the back of his
head. "Try it sometime, quite enjoyable."

Mrak Delar and Kal exchanged a quick look and burst out
laughing again. Mishka decided to come to his rescue.

"I think all this dressing-undressing is overrated. What's the
point in taking all the clothes off, if in the morning you have to
put them back on?" he asked, landing on top of Gunz's head and
spreading his golden wings protectively.

Gunz moved the wyvern from his head to his shoulder and got
off the bed, just now realizing how inexcusably filthy he was. His
torso was covered in dirt and dust. Brown streams and stains of

dried out blood were covering his arms and wrists where the iron manacles used to be. He raked his fingers through his matted hair, shifting uncomfortably from one foot to another.

"Ahhh, this is not the kind of morning I wanted to have," he mumbled.

"Feeling a bit uncomfortable?" asked Kal, his thin lips stretching into a snide smirk.

"A little. I'm sorry, I was dead beat yesterday. I hardly made it to bed," said Gunz apologetically. "I didn't expect early morning visitors." He made a pause staring at his mentor and the Ancient Master. "Come to think of it... What are you two doing here so early in the morning."

"Don't worry, it'll get more uncomfortable soon," promised Kal joyfully.

"How much more uncomfortable can it get?" muttered Gunz, staring at his mentor, wary.

Mrak Delar gave him a light tap on his shoulder and smiled, a humorous twinkle playing in his black eyes.

"Why don't you take care of yourself first, young Salamander," he said. "Your mentor and I will go down to the kitchen and make some coffee in the meantime."

"Thank you," replied Gunz and rushed into the bathroom.

Twenty minutes later, Gunz walked into the kitchen. Kal and Mrak Delar were sitting around the kitchen table with steaming coffee cups in their hands. Mishka had his head down a coffee cup, slurping the burning-hot beverage and purring over it. Gunz walked up to the table and sat down next to Mrak Delar.

"Coffee?" asked the Ancient Master, moving another cup of coffee toward him. "My wife turned me into a coffee addict. Now I need to have it every morning or I feel partially crippled. It's becoming problematic, considering that Kendral doesn't have coffee and I need to bring it from this world."

Gunz thanked the Master of Power and took a large gulp of

coffee. "Kal," he started the conversation, "there is something I wanted to ask you."

"What is it, my child?" asked Kal, suddenly serious.

"You were right, Father," said Gunz, lowering his eyes. "I'm not ready to live in this realm. My presence here is endangering humans. I think I should go back to Kendral with you."

For a moment silence enveloped the kitchen. Even Mishka stopped slurping his coffee, staring at Gunz over the rim of his coffee cup.

"Why would you say that?" asked Kal, his eyebrows rising.

Gunz told him everything that happened in the last couple weeks. He gave him a detailed recount of his conversation with Aidan and the fight with Eve. He also told him about his meetings with the two demonic queens and how unprepared he was.

"As far as I can see, you didn't do anything wrong," said Mrak Delar, shrugging his shoulders. "Both the Scarlet Queen and the Demonic Queen are a lot older and more experienced than you. Something like that is expected. And Eve and the likes of her will always try to get the best of you."

"Exactly," agreed Gunz. "Eve and the likes of her will try to use my power against my will and I can't allow that to happen." He turned to Kal, his chest tightened with guilt. "Father, I need to go back to Kendral with you. I must learn more about my power and how to use my magic. Without that, I am a danger to all humans. I can't let evil use me ever again."

"I agree with Mrak," said Kal, shaking his head. "You handled everything the best you could, my child."

"Gunz," said Mrak Delar and Gunz turned to him a little surprised. He never heard the Ancient Master using his nickname before. "I've known the Scarlet Queen for years and this is the first time I heard that she offered someone lessons in swordsmanship. I think you should take her up on this offer. Just be careful, don't get yourself into her servitude. She's an ancient vampire and she knows how to manipulate an inexperienced youngster like yourself."

"Agreed, take lessons with the queen. Not only in swordsmanship. Open your eyes and learn. Vampires and upirs are dangerous creatures, smart and insidious. The more you know and understand how their species work, the better you'll be able to protect your people," said Kal. "But I also agree with you – there is a lot that you still don't know. So, here is my offer. Come back with me to Kendral for six months. I'll teach you everything you need to know about your power and Master Mrak Delar can give you extra lessons in magic and Dragon tongue."

Kal stopped talking, taking in Gunz's appearance. Then he sighed and picked up his coffee cup off the table, taking a sip of his drink. Neither Gunz nor Mrak Delar said anything, allowing him to continue.

"It's been centuries since the last Fire Salamander left this world," said Kal slowly. "And you, my child, are unique in more ways than one. You are a Fire Salamander with magic. Do you know how rare this gift is?"

"It's rare?" mumbled Gunz. "I thought all Fire Salamanders had magic."

Kal exchanged a heavy look with Mrak Delar and shook his head no. "My son," said Kal, "between all the worlds, through the thousands of years, there was only one more Fire Salamander that could wield not only the elemental Fire power but also magic. The rest of Fire Salamanders were only commanding the Fire."

"It's you, Father, isn't it?" asked Gunz staring at his mentor in awe. "You are the only Fire Salamander who has magic?"

"That's right," confirmed Kal. He put his large callused hand on Gunz's shoulder and smiled warmly at him. "Do you realize what it means for you? You are the only Great Fire Salamander besides me who ever walked these worlds. I'll be happy to have you by my side for eternity, my son. But the truth is, right now your heart is in this world. And you're needed here. So, stay in Kendral and learn all you need to know. But once you feel ready, you should come back here."

"And as far as your failure with the Demonic Queen, it wasn't only your lack of knowledge that made you fail," said Mrak Delar, his black eyes crinkling with a smile. "It was your physical body that responded to the succubus' magic. Mishka told us what happened at the *Temptress of the Night*. There is a way to control your body just like there is a way to control your mind."

"Oh shit," mumbled Gunz, feeling close to a heart attack. "I can just imagine what Mishka told you."

Mrak Delar pressed his hand to his mouth fighting to suppress his laughter but then threw one look at Kal and both of them barked laughing.

"Anyway," he said after he was able to calm himself, "after we heard the story of your encounter with the Demonic Queen, your Father and I agreed that you require my assistance with this delicate matter. At least until you learn enough to know how to control the magic of succubi and similar creatures."

"A delicate matter?" parroted Gunz, throwing a quick glance at Kal. "Sorry, Mrak, but I have no idea what you are referring to."

Mrak Delar rubbed his forehead, and then ran his fingers over his eyes and down his cheeks, like a person who didn't feel comfortable with what he was about to say.

"The kind of matter that Kal can't help you with, but as a Master of Power, I can." He reached in his pocket and pulled a bracelet with a single red stone embedded in it. He offered the bracelet to Gunz. "Put it on. Tell me what you feel."

Gunz took the bracelet and put it on his wrist. As soon as the metal touched his skin, he felt dizzy and a little weaker. "Mrak, what is this thing?" he asked, swaying a little, fighting the dizziness. "It makes me weak and dizzy. Why?"

"Don't worry, the side effects will go away in a moment," said Mrak Delar. "But try to conjure the fire. Tell me if you can."

Gunz connected with the Fire within him and he felt its presence right away, but when he tried to conjure a flame, he couldn't. The Fire couldn't go past his skin. His magic was functioning just fine, but the fire power was caged within his body.

"I can't," mumbled Gunz. "But why are you giving me a bracelet that suppresses my Fire power?"

Mrak Delar glanced down at him and shook his head. "You're not too fast on the uptake, are you?" He laughed, his dark eyes filled with good-natured humor. "I'm sure, when the time comes, you'll figure it out. Just keep in mind, every time you put this bracelet on, it's good for one hour and after that your Fire will break through."

Gunz took the bracelet off, staring at the red stone, as the understanding flashed over him. "Holy shit," he whispered, razing his eyes at Kal, flush creeping up his cheeks.

The Great Salamander tilted his head a little, giving him an arched stare. "My child, I'll give you thirty-six hours to settle everything at work and with your friends here," said Kal, rising. "Visit the Scarlet Queen and tell her that you'll be starting on the training with her in six months. She will appreciate this courtesy. In thirty-six hours, I'll summon you to Kendral."

"Thank you," replied Gunz, bowing to the Great Salamander and Master Mrak Delar. "See you soon in Kendral."

Kal waved his hand, unfolding his fiery portal and both the Ancient Master and the Fire Elemental disappeared behind the swirling flames.

EPILOGUE

* * *

~ Zane Burns, a.k.a. Gunz ~
Modern days, South Florida

THREE-THIRTEEN.

Gunz was standing in the long hallway of a South Florida high-rise condominium building, staring at the number on the door. Three hundred thirteen. Angelique's apartment.

A few lightbulbs burnt out a while ago and the condominium association wasn't in a rush to replace them. The hallway was dark and empty. He was standing in front of the door, asking himself what brought him here. Out of thirty-six hours that Kal gave him, he spent thirty-four hours elsewhere, but now he was here, feeling lost, unsure if he should be knocking on this door.

He spent most of the day yesterday finalizing all the work he was doing for the FBI. Agent Andrews wasn't happy with Gunz's decision to leave this world for six months. He needed him here more than ever. Even though Eve was gone from this world, weird cases kept popping up all over South Florida. Some of them

383

probably weren't supernatural, but nowadays anything that sounded even slightly off was sent to Jim and his team to investigate. Jim's department was overloaded and losing his main asset for such a long time was troubling him.

Gunz decided to take Aidan up on his promise and called him, asking him to meet with Agent Andrews in person. To Gunz's surprise, Aidan agreed right away and a few minutes later, he called from the lobby of the FBI building, asking for a visitor's pass.

The conversation between Jim and Aidan wasn't easy as both parties didn't feel comfortable with each other. Aidan was right when he said that Jim was on his case for years. Jim had a lot of questions and since it was never easy for Aidan to be open with anyone, he had a hard time answering some of the questions that Jim had. However, when Jim asked him what kind of magical entity he was, Aidan smirked and told him straight that he was a god.

Gunz expected that Jim wouldn't believe him and would get upset. But Jim just cocked his head and arched his eyebrow at Aidan, accepting what he said without any further questions. Aidan explained to Jim what kind of work he and his team were doing and offered his help. He said that for the six months when Gunz would be in Kendral, he could take over his responsibilities, working closely with Jim's team.

Aidan didn't expose the identity of his supernatural crew members but told Jim that he and his team would be at his service any time he needed them. Agent Andrews didn't try to get into any details about Aidan's team and Gunz was wondering if Jim had enough shock for one day after Aidan dropped the "god-bomb" on his head. One thing was to know that the supernatural existed, another thing was to realize that the ancient gods still existed, and they lived and functioned, well-blended into the midst of modern society.

It was late evening when Aidan and Jim finally dotted all the i's and crossed all the t's. Gunz and Aidan left the FBI building together. As they were standing outside the building, Gunz had a feeling that Aidan wanted to say something but for whatever reason, he didn't feel comfortable. To alleviate this general atmosphere of discomfort between them, Gunz offered him to get a bite to eat. Since Aidan teleported here, they used Gunz's car to drive to *Missi's Kitchen*.

The restaurant hadn't changed a bit, even though the cross-functional queen of *Missi's Kitchen* was gone. It had the same laid-back atmosphere that Gunz loved so much and a quiet, semi-dark room. He walked toward the bar and sat down, offering the stool next to him to Aidan.

A young woman, in her early twenties walked out of the kitchen and stopped in front of them. She was nothing like Missi. Short and slender, she had a pleasant round face and her marble-white skin was covered with bright freckles. Her sky-blue eyes were sparkling from under her copper eyelashes and an uncontrollable mop of red hair was pulled into two ponytails on either side of her head. She looked warm and cheerful like a summer day.

However, one thing about this young lady was unmistakable – she was a witch. Gunz wondered if she was one of the Guardians or just some witch Missi asked to take care of her precious restaurant while she was gone. After a moment of consideration, he decided that the girl wasn't a Guardian. The Guardians were famous for concealing their magical energy, making it invisible to other creatures of magic. Her magical energy was loud and clear.

The young woman smiled at Gunz and Aidan, and he felt a touch of her magic as she carefully scanned them with her magical sight. She placed the menu in front of Aidan and then asked Gunz, "Your usual, Mr. Burns?"

Gunz raised his eyes at her taken aback by her question but nodded. She quickly wiped the bar counter in front of them and placed three empty shot glasses. In one fluid motion, she filled all three with vodka and turned to Aidan.

"What can I get you, Mr. McGrath?"

If Aidan was surprised, he didn't show it. He smiled back at the girl and waved his hand at Gunz. "I'll take the same. On everything."

She placed three more shot glasses on the counter and filled them with vodka. After that, she wrote the order in her little notepad and disappeared behind the kitchen door. Aidan picked up one shot glass, raising it.

"To the future," he said quietly, clinking his glass with Gunz's.

They drunk in complete silence. It had been a while since Gunz had a drink or a peaceful moment for that matter. The harsh liquid rushed down his throat and he closed his eyes, enjoying the feeling.

"Akhh," exhaled Aidan, grimacing, "it truly tastes like gasoline."

Gunz chuckled. "I know," he agreed. "No one ever said that drinking was a pleasure. It's a bad habit of mine. I drink…"

"With the kind of lifestyle that you have, I can't imagine why," replied Aidan, all serious.

"Yeah, and after over two thousand years, you are still drinking for the future?"

Aidan bowed his head, averting his eyes, his fingers mindlessly playing with the empty shot glass. After a moment, he put the glass on the table and raised his eyes, a sad smile playing on his lips.

"Maybe after over two thousand years, for the first time I feel like I have a future?"

Gunz raised the second shot glass and clinked it with Aidan's. "For our friends."

"For Tessa," added Aidan, downing the contents of the second shot glass in one gulp.

"She'll come around," said Gunz putting the empty shot glass next to the first one. "You need to give her some space and a little time."

"I know," replied Aidan calmly. "Missi was right. She needs to learn about her true origins. As she'll rub shoulders with the world of magic, she'll understand why I had to conceal my true identity." He fell silent and then added after a short pause. "At least, I hope she will... I can wait."

"What surprised me the most about Tessa's situation was that Angel never felt that she was part Reaper," said Gunz. "You would think that being the Death, he would sense one of his own."

"Oh yeah, he sensed it alright," muttered Aidan. "But because of the Guardians shadowing her power, he couldn't sense it clearly. So, he never voiced his suspicions until yesterday. I wish he said something to me earlier."

Gunz picked up the third shot glass, wrapping his fingers tightly around it and Aidan repeated his gesture.

"The silent one. For the fallen," said Aidan rising.

Gunz got up and carefully bumped Aidan's fist with his. They drank the last shot of vodka and put their empty shot glasses on the counter. They both sat down and Gunz glanced at Aidan with curiosity.

"I'm surprised that you know this tradition," he said, running his finger over the rims of the empty shot glasses. "Not too many people in Russia know about it."

"Old Russian military tradition," said Aidan. "I knew a Russian man who fought in Afghanistan in late eighties. He taught me that a long time ago. And I thought that since you were from the same region and you were in the military, you would probably want to observe it."

"Thank you," said Gunz, thinking that the last time when he drank the silent one with his friends was more than two years ago.

Missi's replacement showed up, sporting a tray with their orders. She took away the empty shot glasses and placed the plates with burgers and steaming fries on the counter. They ate quickly, without talking. When they finished their meals, Gunz gestured at the hostess, asking for the check. She smiled brightly at him and shook her head no, making her thick orange ponytails swipe across her face.

"No, Mr. Burns," she objected. "When Missi was leaving, she said that you probably would be coming here a few nights a week and she made it very clear that no matter what you order, everything is on the house. Always."

"Thank you—," he started to say just now realizing that he never asked the new girl's name.

"Peyton," she introduced herself. "Nice to meet you both. After everything that Missi told me about you two, I couldn't wait to meet you in person."

"I'm leaving for six months, Peyton," said Gunz and waved in Aidan's direction, "but he might be coming once in a while."

"You are both welcome at any time," replied Peyton nodding to them and walked back into the kitchen.

After they left the restaurant, Aidan bid his farewell and vanished. Gunz drove home, thinking about his meeting with the Scarlet Queen that was scheduled for the late afternoon the next day.

The next day passed quickly. Gunz was busy taking care of the house and the bills to make sure that everything was in order for his prolonged absence. At five o'clock in the afternoon, he opened his portal into the lobby of *EverSafe Security* office. The secretary, the same vampire girl whom he met before, greeted him with a tense duty smile and announced that the queen was expecting him.

The queen was a little surprised that he requested a meeting on such a short notice. Gunz had to explain that tonight he was leaving this world for six month and since they had an agreement about the swordsmanship lessons, he felt that it was necessary to make her aware of his plans. The queen nodded, appreciating his courtesy and promised him that she was ready to start with his training as soon as he was back home.

She already heard about the battle at the Quiet Waters Park and knew that Eve was vanquished from this world. She asked him to give her all the details of the fight and listened to him with undivided attention, her cold unblinking eyes fixed on his face.

After he was done, she smiled with her usual tiny smile where the corners of her lips moved up ever so slightly, but the eyes remained untouched by it.

"Well, Eve is gone," she said softly, "but your troubles are far from over, young Salamander."

Gunz stiffened at her words, expecting bad news. "What do you mean, Akira?"

She shrugged her shoulders, pinning him with her icy gaze. "A great evil like this, even after it's vanquished, doesn't disappear without leaving a scar on the world," she explained, twisting the diamond ring on her middle finger with her thumb. "I understand why you need to go back to Kendral. You have a lot to learn and your master, the Great Fire Elemental, is the only one who can teach you everything you need to know. But the timing may not be the best..." Her voice trailed away, and she looked back at the wall where her katanas were mounted.

"I'm leaving this world in good hands," replied Gunz. "And I'll be back in six months. I'm not staying in Kendral forever."

Akira got up and walked him toward the door. As she put her hand on the door handle, she glanced up at him and smiled, this time a real smile showing her sharp white teeth.

"I'm looking forward to having you back, Zane," she said a humorous twinkle playing in her angled eyes, "and to kicking your lizard's tail in training."

* * *

GUNZ WASN'T sure why he did it, but after the audience with the

Scarlet Queen, he opened his portal to the back of Angelique's condominium building. He did it without thinking about what he was going to tell her. He didn't doubt that Jim told her about his decision to leave. And now he was standing in front of her door, his eyes reading the numbers three-one-three over and over again.

I shouldn't be here, he thought, biting his lip. *Angelique deserved a man who can commit to her fully. Someone who is always going to be there for her. Not a man who doesn't know when he is going to be summoned at any moment. I'm not free to have any kind of real relationship.* He rubbed his forehead tiredly. *With my job, she will always be in danger. I can't do it to her.*

"What was I thinking," he mumbled, stepping away from the door.

The door opened, and a bright electric light cut through his eyes that already got accustomed to the darkness of the hallway. He raised his arm, shielding his eyes. In the shining yellow rectangle of the doorway, he saw Angelique's silhouette.

"I thought you were a lizard, but you're really just a chicken," she huffed, shaking her head.

Before he could say anything, she seized his shirt and yanked him inside her apartment. He stood silently, gazing down at her as she locked the door and put her hands on her hips, tapping her foot.

"Zane Burns, I could feel your magical energy as soon as you stopped in front of my door," said Angelique with reproach. "You stood there doing nothing for twenty minutes. Did you know that?"

"Angie—"

"Don't Angie me, Zane," said Angelique, angry tears gathering in her eyes. "Were you going to leave for six months without saying goodbye to me?"

"Of course not, Angie. I was going—"

"You were going to what? Text me that you are going to be

gone for half a year, you asshole?" Hot tears were running down her face, leaving glistening traces on her flushed cheeks. "You showed up, you said your goodbyes. Woohoo! Now get the hell out!"

Her words deeply cut through him, but he silently turned around and put his hand on the door handle, ready to leave. Before he opened the door, Angelique grabbed his shoulder and pulled him around. He stood with his arms down, staring at her, hurt and confused, not sure what to do next.

"You're such an idiot," whispered Angelique, tears still shimmering in her eyes. She cupped his face with her hands and kissed him, stretching up to her tiptoes.

Carefully, like he was afraid that she would reject him, he encircled her waist, pulling her closer. The salty taste of her tears on his lips and the delicate scent of her skin made his head spin. He groaned softly as the warmth spread through him, reigniting the fire within. With effort, he pulled away from her, taking her hands into his and noticed that his hands were trembling slightly.

"Angie..." He swallowed, his throat dry.

"I know what you are going to say," muttered Angelique, "and I don't care to hear it. You're afraid to hurt me. Your fire. Blah blah blah."

Gunz chuckled. He let go of her hands and wiped the tears off her face with his fingers. "Fire Salamanders don't say, blah blah blah, Angie," he said imitating the voice of Dracula from the cartoon *Hotel Transylvania*. Then he sighed, switching back to his serious mode. "I can do it, I just don't think we should."

"Okay, let me hear your next lame excuse, Zane," muttered Angelique, throwing her hands in the air.

"I don't have excuses," replied Gunz. "My lifestyle is complicated and dangerous, and I don't want to drag you into the mess I'm living in. You deserve someone who will give everything to you – his love, his attention, full commitment. With my job, I can't."

Angelique stared at him for a moment and then sighed, looking heavenward. "Did I mention that you're an idiot?"

He nodded, smiling at her. More than anything he wanted to reach into his pocket and put on the bracelet that Mrak Delar gave him, but something was stopping him. He looked at his watch – less than an hour left before Kal would summon him.

"Angie, we have about thirty minutes before Kal will open the portal to Kendral for me," said Gunz.

"I don't care. Then these thirty minutes are mine. For these thirty minutes, you belong to me," she whispered, gently pressing him against the wall. She put her hand on the back of his head, pushing his face down and kissed him, a short and passionate kiss. "No more excuses…"

She wrapped her arms around his neck and kissed him again. As he returned her kiss, he found the bracelet in his pocket and locked it around his wrist. For a few seconds, the world around him spun in one continuous blur. Gunz held his breath, feeling her demanding lips crushing his, and he wasn't sure if it was the magic of the bracelet that was making him dizzy or the desire that was permeating between them. Effortlessly, he lifted her, gently holding her to his chest and carried her to the couch.

* * *

GUNZ FELT the persistent pull of Kal's summoning spell in his head, but he didn't want to move. It wasn't as bad as the summoning spell that Aidan used, but it still wasn't pleasant. He gazed down at Angelique. She laid her head on his shoulder and her long dark hair spilled all over his chest. He wished he could stay like this forever. He sighed and tenderly kissed the top of her head. Her lips quirked up in a blissful smile.

"Is it time?" she whispered, sitting up, caressing his unclothed chest with her eyes.

Gunz nodded and got up. He got dress quickly and kneeled in

front of the couch where Angelique was sitting. Holding her hands in his, he turned her hands palms up and kissed them one at the time.

"I have to go, Angie," he said rising. "Kal is summoning me. It's not a good idea to make him wait."

"You come back to me." It wasn't a question. Her statement sounded like an order.

"Yes, ma'am," he replied, lifting his hand in a military style salute. "Six months from now and you'll be the first person to know. And when I come to see you, I promise, I'm not going to stay twenty minutes in front of your door."

"I know how to wait…"

Gunz leaned forward and gently kissed her goodbye. As he pulled away, he forcefully switched his mind back to the less pleasant reality. For six months he will be going through Kal's rigorous boot camp. When it came to learning magic, neither Kal nor Mrak Delar were taking it easy. He realized perfectly well what kind of torture it would be, but he had to do it. He had to understand the full extent of his Great Fire Salamander power. To fight what was coming, he had to be ready. Hence, he needed to know his power and his magic and have experience wielding them.

From what the Scarlet Queen was saying, Eve left a supernatural turmoil in her wake by infecting other supernatural creatures with her twisted demonic energy. He was sure that Jim and Aidan would deal with some of it, but there would be enough left to go around. Akira wasn't an easily scared type and if she was concerned with the situation, it had to be as bad as it could get.

Besides that, there was Tessa on her quest to find her birth parents. He was sure that at some point she would need his help. The way she left, she wouldn't be calling Aidan. She would be contacting him.

Gunz sighed and conjured a small flame, a doubt tearing at his soul. He was leaving in the middle of this mess, dumping everything on Aidan and his crew. Even though they all agreed that he needed to go back to Kendral and even after Aidan promised to summon him if things would get out of hand, he still had his doubts.

He leaned over the flame and whispered his mentor's name, replying to the Great Salamander's summons. Immediately, the fire curtain of Kal's portal unfolded in the middle of Angelique's living room. Gunz gave Angelique a quick hug and walked through the portal without looking back. As the fire surrounded him, her quiet words, filled with sadness and love, reached his ears.

"Fire Salamander – go..."

BOOK 2 EXCERPT

READ ON FOR AN EXCERPT FROM

N.M. Thorn's new book
The Burns War
The Fire Salamander Chronicles. Book 2

* * *

~ Zane Burns, a.k.a. Gunz ~

MODERN DAYS. KEY WEST, FLORIDA

The evening was warm and humid. The street lights and neon gleam of the storefronts were promoting a festive and slightly mysterious atmosphere. The street was overflowing with people. The unsuspecting crowd of tourists was promenading along Duval Street, completely unaware of everything that was going on right before their noses. Carefree, they were chatting, eating, and gaping at the colorful windows of shops.

Gunz quickly crossed Duval and walked into a shadowy alley between two stores. As soon as he escaped the crowded street and dove into the muggy darkness of a small narrow alley, he reached into his pocket and pulled his Swiss army knife out. Holding the knife in his hand, he switched to a light run. His Salamander senses were heightened to the maximum revealing the presence of dark vampiric energy all around him. The vampires realized that he wasn't human, and they didn't like it. They were in front of him and behind him, surrounding him, creeping up closer and closer, following his every step.

A light breeze brought a much-needed freshness infused with the light scent of the ocean. Gunz smirked. He was almost there.

Not too far from the oceanside, there was an old semi-demolished house. This house was his final destination, marked by the Scarlet Queen.

A few months ago, a large group of rogue vampires settled there, using it as their nest. The vampire queen, Akira Ida, approached them, but they refused to accept her as their queen and comply with her rules. The Scarlet Queen wasn't the type to accept the rejection easily. And since Gunz needed some practice using his newly improved sword skills in the real-life situations, she decided that sending the young Fire Salamander to deal with the rebels was the right thing to do. Gunz had no doubt that it was a win-win situation for the queen – her student would get some practice and the rebellious fraction of vampires would be vanquished, serving as a lesson to others who dared to disobey her.

Akira had been giving Gunz the swordsmanship lessons since he got back from Kendral and she was happy with his general progress. She expressed her complete confidence in his skills, stating that he would be able to deal with the situation at hand without any problems.

Before Gunz opened his fire portal to Key West, Akira didn't forget to remind him that the point of this exercise was to destroy all the rogue vampires without using his magic or the Salamander fire power, only his sword. What she neglected to mention was how many vampires were in this nest. Right now, he could count at least ten vampires around him, if not more. And he had no idea how many of them were inside that house.

"Come out to Key West, get yourself a little vampire action, have a few laughs…" muttered Gunz, channeling John McClain as he kept running toward the ocean.

Two vampires materialized in front of him and he skidded to a screeching halt. Teleporting wasn't one of the vampires' powers, but they moved so fast and soundless that it looked like they just popped up out of nowhere. The first vampire threw a punch. As a Fire Salamander, Gunz wasn't as fast as the vampires, but he was fast enough to see it coming. He took a tiny step back, turning his head to the side and watched the vampire's fist sailing less than an inch away from his face, missing him.

The force with which the punch was thrown, pulled the vampire forward and all Gunz had to do was use his opponent's momentum to send him rolling onto the ground. As the infuriated vampire scrambled to his knees growling, Gunz whispered a short spell, turning his knife into a long medieval sword. Before the dumbfounded vamp could get back to his feet, he swung his sword, decapitating the kneeling monster in one swift motion.

The dead body disintegrated in a matter of a few seconds, leaving nothing but a pile of dirty ashes behind. The second vampire roared as he launched at Gunz, his lips curled in a wolfish snarl. Gunz caught him in the air, his fingers firmly wrapping around the vampire's neck and threw him down. Before the vampire could get up, Gunz's sword whistled through the air and cleanly cut his head off.

He didn't wait for the beheaded corps to turn into ashes and continued on his path to the vampires' nest. As he approached the house, at least ten vampires who were guarding the entrance separated from the shadows and leisurely paced toward him, the cold grins on their faces exposing their dangerous fangs. All of them were tall and looked strong enough to stop a rhino with their bare hands even without the use of their vampire's strength. Gunz didn't slow down, a grim uneven smirk playing on his lips.

The vamps didn't wait for him to reach them. Baring their sharp fangs, all of them attacked at the same time. Gunz rolled on his shoulder, avoiding their grabby hands with long hooked claws. As he came out of the roll with one knee down, his sword hissed through the air, cutting through the muscles and ligaments of their legs.

Cursing furiously, they pulled back for a moment. The vampires were healing fast, but the damage Gunz inflicted gave him the opportunity he needed to regroup. He hopped to his feet just in time to see the growling mass of monsters closing up on him again. He spun around, his sword finding its victims as he moved in a circle with the unexpected speed that could rival the velocity of any vampire.

A few minutes later, only ten piles of grey ashes remained on the ground. It seemed that all the vampires were gone. At least on the outside. Gunz looked down at his bloodied sword, breathing hard. His clothes were torn in a few places and hot streams of blood were running down his arms, chest and back, where the vampires managed to catch him with their claws. One of them was quick enough to sink his teeth into his shoulder leaving behind a gaping hole filled with dark blood. He touched his wounded shoulder and winced in pain.

Gunz probed the house with his Salamander senses and grunted, frustrated. The house was filled with the undead, their dark energy fused into a heavy venomous cloud. He couldn't even count how many of them were there. The house was dark, and nothing was moving inside. But it didn't mean that the vamps inside weren't alert and ready to spring into action as soon as he opened the door.

Gunz carefully moved his left arm, checking the mobility of his damaged shoulder. *No good, I have no strength in my left arm. It's useless,* thought Gunz, but slowly moved toward the door of the dark house.

"If I survive this, I swear, I'm going to give a piece of my mind to Akira," he mumbled, walking up the steps, ready to kick the door open.

"Why don't you give it to me now."

Akira's soft voice filled with authority sounded behind his back. Gunz lowered his sword and turned around. He bowed to her awkwardly as his torn shoulder responded with sharp twinges of agony to his every move. She approached him and unceremoniously pulled his shredded shirt off his shoulder, wiping a few drops of his blood off the edge of his ripped flesh with her finger. For a moment her eyes lit up with a hungry scarlet glow, but she pulled his shirt back up and took a deep breath, wiping the blood off her fingers on her pants.

"Do you want me to heal you?" asked the Scarlet Queen, her voice calm and even, like she wasn't ready to sink her fangs into his neck just a moment ago. "You know that vampire's blood has some healing properties."

"Thank you, Akira, but no," replied Gunz. "I don't want your blood circulating through my system, giving you some kind of control over me."

She shrugged her narrow shoulders indifferently. "I don't know if this so-called control would work on a Fire Salamander," she said, raising her eyebrows at him. "Zane, are you seriously considering fighting a giant vampire nest one-handed?"

Gunz shrugged and cringed, clasping his shoulder. "Unless you have a better idea, I'm going in," he said dryly. "I can't leave so many rogue vampires running around a tourist destination."

Akira shook her head. "I do have a better idea," she said with a sigh. "I was watching you fighting... How many vampires did you vanquish alone?"

"Twelve, I think. Why?"

"Because, it's enough for one day of training. We're going to go in together and you're going to use your magic, not your sword."

He nodded, a tiny lopsided smile making an appearance as he kicked the door with his leg. The door flew open hitting the wall with a loud bang but remained on its hinges. A couple of vampires that were standing closer to the entrance staggered backward, stumbling into the dark mass of other vamps. The house was so dark inside that Gunz still couldn't count how many monsters he was dealing with. It seemed like the chain of glowing red eyes was endless.

"*Ventius,*" he whispered extending his right hand forward. A powerful blast of wind rushed toward the vampires, blowing them off their feet and throwing their bodies against the wall.

Akira slipped inside, touching his arm on the way in. "Give me a second," she whispered.

She approached the squirming mass of vampires who were still struggling to untangle their limbs and get up, staring down at them from her formidable height of five feet. The undead shuffled around and a few of them got up to their feet, silently glowering at the Scarlet Queen, gnashing their fangs.

"This is your last chance. I will not ask again," said the queen calmly. "Bend your knee and pledge your fealty to me and I will let you live."

A large vampire that looked like a biker with his leather jacket and long greasy hair, stepped forward. He tongued his cheek and spit on the floor aiming at her feet. "Never," he hissed, fury making his eyes glow bright red. "You work with a hunter. Against your own kind. You are not fit to be our queen."

"A hunter?" asked Akira. "Hardly. He is so much more than that. And he's not my employee. He is my student."

"Whatever he is, he's killing our kind!" yelled the vampire, scowling at the queen with freezing contempt. "We will never accept your rule."

"As you wish," said Akira indifferently and turned around. As she passed Gunz, she touched his arm again and whispered into his ear, "Fire Salamander, make this house burn hotter than hell. Kill them all." She walked out of the house and closed the door, leaving Gunz alone.

As quiet as the Scarlet Queen spoke, the vampires heard her. They all screamed at the same time, some hurdled toward Gunz, some tried to break out through the boarded windows of the house.

"Ignius Amplio," hissed Gunz, entwining his magic with his elemental power.

The fiery inferno unfolded before him, swallowing the house and its inhabitants within a few seconds. Guns walked out of the house when the roof caved in and the last screams of the burning monsters died out. He found Akira standing a few feet away from the burning house, her sharply angled eyes squinting at the brightness of the flames. All around her, the ground was covered in ashes. That was everything that remained of the vampires who somehow escaped from the smoldering trap that Gunz created.

Her eyes shifted to Gunz and the corners of her small mouth quirked up. For a moment she looked like a cat who was watching a canary. He glanced down and grunted. His shirt that was already shredded before the fire, completely fell apart and his pants were torn in few places, too.

"Well, my student, you presented yourself nicely," she said attempting to sound serious. "I'm talking about your fighting skills, of course."

"But of course you are," muttered Gunz, shaking his head.

Akira giggled pressing her hand to her mouth. Gunz rolled his eyes, wondering how an ancient vampire, who killed more people than anyone cared to count, could still have the laugher of a little girl.

"I'll see you next week, Zane." Akira waved her hand and was gone before he could say anything else to her.

Gunz sighed and turned back to the house. It was still burning, smoldering flames rising high, the dark clouds of smoke disappearing into the night sky. He waved, silently commanding the fire to cease. He was positive that by now all the vampires were dead and leaving the fire burning would just attract the attention of humans. It wasn't necessary.

As he was watching the fire gradually die down, he felt a light vibration in his pocket and reached for his phone. Good news – his phone survived the massive fight with the vampires. Bad news

– his boss, Agent Andrews, was calling him at one o'clock in the morning.

"Hello," Gunz answered the phone, expecting problems.

"Gunz, did I wake you up?" Jim didn't sound sleepy. Most likely he was still in his office.

"No. What's going on, Jim?"

"I need you to come in," said Jim calmly. "There is something we need to discuss as soon as possible."

"I'll come in first thing in the morning. 8 AM sharp," replied Gunz, knowing ahead of time what would follow.

"No, I need you to come in immediately," objected Jim, notes of aggravation breaking through his calm front. "It can't wait until morning."

"Jim, it's going to have to wait until tomorrow," said Gunz with a sigh. "I'm in Key West. Just finished cleaning a giant vampires' nest. One of the vamps managed to bite a chunk off my shoulder. I'm bleeding, and my clothes are half-gone. I have to go home and heal myself, Jim. I'm in the world of pain. Sorry."

Jim grunted and Gunz heard him slamming his fist on his desk. "Bad timing, Gunz. Very bad timing. I'm sure it was the Scarlet Queen who sent you to clean up her mess."

"Yes, sir," confirmed Gunz. "But what did you want me to do? Leave a huge population of rogue vampires hunting the tourists around the Keys? It's been over a month since I came back from Kendral and I'm swimming up to my eyeballs in supernatural bullshit! It's worse than it's ever been here. I don't understand what's going on."

"I don't know," replied Jim dryly. "Your buddy Aidan is saying the same thing. Him and his team don't have a minute of peace. Anyway, I need you in my office stat. Just open your portal into my office as soon as you are ready."

"Jim —," started Gunz, but Jim interrupted him.

"Go home, heal yourself and come to my office right away. Not in the morning. Right away! Do you understand me?"

"Yes, sir. I'll see you in an hour."

Gunz hung up the phone, putting it back in his jean back pocket. Then he turned his sword back into the Swiss army knife and put it away.

"Fire Salamander – go," he muttered to himself and waved his hand, opening the fire curtain of his portal.

DEAR READER!

*T*hank you so much for reading The Burns Fire. I hope you enjoyed the book and will join Zane Burns' next adventure in the second book of the series, The Burns War.

IF YOU WOULD LIKE to stay up-to-date on the latest information about new releases, special offers, and more, sign up for my mailing list. Click here to join.

FOR MORE INFORMATION follow me on
    Facebook
    Instagram
    Or visit my website www.nmthorn.com.

BEFORE YOU GO...

*Y*our reviews mean the world to me and are greatly appreciated. If you enjoyed the Burns Fire, please take a few minutes to leave a review. It doesn't have to be long. It can be just a few words or stars rating.

PLEASE HELP SPREAD the word by taking this small extra step and leave your review on one of the following links:

Amazon US

Amazon UK

Goodreads

ABOUT THE AUTHOR

N.M. Thorn currently lives in South Florida with her husband and son. Owner of a digital marketing agency by day and a writer by night, she loves spending her times creating new worlds, paranormal planes of existence and anything that could be described as supernatural.

When she is not busy working with everything digital or exploring fantasy worlds, she enjoys spending time with her family, reading, painting and martial arts.

If you would like to share your thoughts, ideas or just send N.M. Thorn a message about the Fire Salamander world, feel free to contact her at: nmthornauthor@gmail.com